Turn the page for more praise...

RULES OF PREY

Sandford's smash bestselling debut—introducing Lucas Davenport...

"Sleek and nasty . . . it's a big, scary, suspenseful read, and I loved every minute of it." —Stephen King

"A haunting, unforgettable, ice-blooded thriller." —Carl Hiaasen

SHADOW PREY

Lieutenant Davenport goes on a city-to-city search for a bizarre ritualistic killer...

"When it comes to portraying twisted minds, Sandford has no peers." —Associated Press

"Ice-pick chills . . . excruciatingly tense . . . a double-pumped roundhouse of a thriller." —*Kirkus Reviews*

EYES OF PREY

Davenport risks his sanity to stalk the most brilliant and dangerous man he has ever known, a doctor named Michael Bekker...

"Relentlessly swift. Genuinely suspenseful . . . excellent." —*Los Angeles Times*

"Engrossing . . . one of the most horrible villains this side of Hannibal the Cannibal." —*Richmond Times-Dispatch*

SILENT PREY

Michael Bekker, the psychopath Davenport captured in Eyes of Prey, escapes...

"Superb!" —*St. Paul Pioneer Press*

"*Silent Prey* terrifies . . . just right for fans of *The Silence of the Lambs*." —*Booklist*

WINTER PREY

In the icy woods of rural Wisconsin, Davenport searches for a brutal killer known as the Iceman...

"Vastly entertaining . . . a furious climactic chase . . . one of the best *Preys* yet." —*Kirkus Reviews*

"An intense thriller with an unlikely killer." —*Playboy*

NIGHT PREY

Davenport faces a master thief who becomes obsessed with a beautiful woman—then carves her initials into his victims...

"One of the most engaging characters in contemporary fiction." —*Detroit News*

"*Night Prey* sizzles . . . positively chilling." —*St. Petersburg Times*

MIND PREY

Lucas Davenport tracks a vicious kidnapper who knows more about mind games than Lucas himself...

"His seventh, and best, outing in the acclaimed *Prey* series." —*People*

"Grip-you-by-the-throat thrills . . . impossible to put down." —*Houston Chronicle*

SUDDEN PREY

Davenport falls prey to the purest, simplest criminal motivation: revenge...

"The story will clamp down like a bear trap on all who open its covers." —*Publishers Weekly*

"Unquestionably the best [*Prey*] yet, a tale of perverse revenge that strikes very close to home." —*Cleveland Plain Dealer*

Continued...

Also by John Sandford

the night crew

john sandford

BERKLEY BOOKS, NEW YORK

THE NIGHT CREW

A Berkley Book / published by arrangement with
the author

PRINTING HISTORY
G. P. Putnam's Sons edition / April 1997
Berkley edition / June 1998

ISBN: 0-425-16338-5

BERKLEY®
Berkley Books are published by
The Berkley Publishing Group, a member of Penguin Putnam Inc.,
200 Madison Avenue, New York, New York 10016.
BERKLEY and the "B" design are trademarks
belonging to Berkley Publishing Corporation.

PRINTED IN THE UNITED STATES OF AMERICA

10 9 8 7 6 5 4 3 2 1

For Susan, Again

one

The corner of Gayley and Le Conte, at the edge of the campus:

Frat boys cruised in their impeccably clean racing-green Miatas and cherry-red Camaro ragtops, with their impeccably blonde dates, all square shoulders, frothy dresses and big white teeth.

Two skinny kids, one of each sex, smelling of three-day sweat and dressed all in black, unwrapped Ding-Dongs and talked loud about Jesus and the Joy to Come; celebrating Him—and vanilla-creme filling.

At the Shell station, a tanker truck pumped Premium down a hole in the concrete pad, under the eye of a big-bellied driver.

And above them all, a quarter-million miles out, a buttery new moon smiled down as it slid toward the Pacific.

The Bee was impatient, checking her watch, bouncing on her toes. She was waiting at the corner, a JanSport backpack at her feet. Her face was a pale crescent in the headlights of passing cars, in the Los Angeles never-dark.

The Shell tanker driver stood in a puddle of gasoline fumes, chewed a toothpick and watched her in a casual, looking-at-women way. The Bee was dressed by Banana Republic, in khaki wash pants, a t-shirt with a queen bee on the chest, a photographer's vest with fifteen pockets, hiking boots and a preppy black-silk ski mask rolled up and worn as a watch cap.

When she saw the truck with the dish on the roof, she pulled the mask down over her face, picked up the backpack, and stepped out to the curb. The Bee had small opaque-green eyes, like turquoise thumbtacks on the black mask.

Anna Batory, riding without her seatbelt, her feet braced on the truck's plastic dashboard, saw the Bee step out to the curb and pointed: "There she is."

Creek grunted and eased the truck to the curb. Anna rolled down the passenger-side window and spoke to the mask: "You're the Bee?"

"You're late," the Bee snapped.

Anna glanced at the dashboard clock, then back out the window: "Jason said ten-thirty."

Jason was sitting in the back of the truck on a gray metal folding chair, next to Louis. He looked up from his Sony chip-cam and said, "That's what they told me. Ten-thirty."

"It's *now* ten-thirty-*three*," the Bee said. She turned her wrist to show the blue face on a stainless-steel Rolex.

"Sorry," Anna said.

"I don't think that's good enough," the Bee said. "We might be too late, and it's all wasted."

Behind the Bee, the Shell gas-delivery man was taking an interest: a lot of people in a TV truck and a blonde in a ski mask, arguing.

"You better get in," Anna said. She could smell the fumes from the gas as she turned and pushed back the truck's side door. Louis caught it and pulled it the rest of the way. The Bee looked at the two men in the back, nodded and said, "Jason," to Jason, said nothing to Louis and climbed aboard.

"Around the corner to Westwood, then Westwood to Circle," the Bee said. "You know where Circle is?"

"Yeah, we know where everything is," Creek said. They'd been everywhere. "Hold on."

Creek took the truck around the corner, humming to himself, which he did when he was tightening up. Anna turned back to the Bee, found the other woman gaping at Creek, and grinned.

Creek looked vaguely like the Wookiee in *Star Wars*: six-seven, overmuscled and hairy. He was wearing a USMC sweatshirt with the sleeves and neck torn out. Tattoos covered his arms: just visible through the reddish-blond hair on his biceps was an American flag in red, blue and Appalachia-white skin, deeply tanned, with the scrolled sentiment, "These colors don't run."

"Hello?" Anna lifted a hand to break the stare. The Bee tore her eyes away from Creek. "We need some facts and figures," Anna said. "How many people on the raid, where you're based, what specifically you object to—like that."

"We've got it all here, but we've got to hurry," the Bee said. She dug into the backpack, came up with a plastic portfolio, and took out a sheet of crisp white paper. Anna flicked on the overhead reading light.

The press release was tight, professional, laser-printed. A two-color pre-printed logo of a running mustang set off the words "Free Hearts" at the top of the page.

"Are these quotes from you or from the collective?" Anna asked, ticking the paper with a fingernail.

"Anything that's in quotes, you can attribute to either me or the Rat. We wrote the statement jointly."

"Will we meet the Rat?" Anna asked. She passed the press release to Louis, who slipped it in a spring clip on the side of the fax.

"He's in the building now," the Bee said, leaning left to peer past Anna out the windshield. "Turn left here," she said. Creek slowed for the turn.

"We'd like to get an action quote when they come out, as they release the animals," Anna said.

"No problem. We can accommodate that." The Bee looked at her Rolex, then back out the window. They were right in the middle of the UCLA medical complex. "I'm sorry I'm so . . . snappy . . . but when Jason agreed to ten-thirty, we specified *exactly* ten-thirty. The raid is already under way."

Anna nodded and turned to Louis. "How're the radios?"

Louis Martinez sat in an office swivel chair that was bolted to the floor of the truck. From the chair, he could reach the scanners and transmitters, the dual editing stations, the fax and phones, any of the screens in the steel racks.

He fiddled with the gear incessantly, trying to capture a mental picture of after-dark Los Angeles, in terms of accidents, shootings, car chases, fires, riots.

"All clear," he said. "We've got that shooting down in Inglewood, but that ain't much. There's a chase down south, Long Beach, but it's heading the other way."

"Track it," Anna said. Cop chases had produced at least two famous video clips in the past couple of years. If you could get out in front of one, and catch it coming by, it was a sure sale.

"I got it," Louis said. He pushed his glasses up his nose and grinned at the Bee with his screwy nerd-charm. "Why'd you choose Bee?" he asked.

"I didn't want a warm and fuzzy animal. That's not the point of animal rescue," the Bee said. Her response was remote, canned, and Louis' grin slipped a fraction of an inch.

"And that's why Steve picked Rat," Jason suggested.

The Bee frowned at the use of Rat's real name, but nodded. "Yes. And because we feel a spiritual affinity with our choices."

In the driver's seat, Creek grunted again, shook his head once, quick. Anna was watching him, taking his temperature: He didn't like these people and he didn't like the professional PR points—the press release, the theatrical ski mask. Too much like a setup, and Creek was pure.

A smile curled one corner of Anna's mouth. She could read Creek's mind if she could see his eyes. Creek knew that. He glanced at her, then deliberately pulled his eyes away. And said, quickly: "There's a guy on the corner."

Ahead and to the right, a woman in a ski mask was standing on the corner, making a *hurry-up* windmilling motion with one arm.

"That's Otter," she said. "And that's the corner of Circle. They must be out—turn right."

Creek took the corner, past the waving woman. The street tilted uphill, and a hundred yards up, a cluster of women spilled down a driveway to the street, two of them struggling with a blue plastic municipal garbage can. A security guard was running down from the top of the hill, another one trailing behind.

"Got them coming out," Anna said, over her shoulder. A quick pulse ran through her: not quite excitement, but some combination of pleasure and apprehension.

Nobody ever knew for sure what would happen at these things. Nothing much, probably, but any time you had guards with guns. . . . Did the guards have guns? She took a half-second to look, but couldn't tell.

As she looked, she reached behind her, lifted the lid on the steel box bolted on the back of her seat, pulled the Nagra tape recorder from its foam nest. Jason was looking past her, through the windshield at the action, and she snapped: "Get ready."

"Yes, Mom," he said. He fitted a headset over the crown of his head, plugged in the earphone. Creek was driving with one hand, pulling on his own headset.

"Everybody hear me?" Anna asked, speaking into her face mike. The radios were one-way: Anna talked, everyone else listened.

Creek said, "Yeah," and took the truck over the curb, one big bounce and a nose-down, squealing, full stop. Jason had braced himself, and Louis had swiveled to let the chair take the jolt. The Bee toppled over and yelped, "Shit."

Ahead of them, the women carrying the garbage can were jerking and twisting down the driveway, doing the media polka—looking for the cameras, running for the lights, trying to stay away from the guards.

The raiders had gone into the back of the building, over a loading dock; the dock was contained inside a fence, with a concrete patio big enough for fifteen or twenty cars. At least a dozen women, all masked, milled around the patio; then a man ran out of the medical building, carrying a small, squealing, black-and-white pig. Then another woman, carrying boxes, or maybe cages.

As the truck settled, as Bee yelped, Anna was out and running, the Nagra banging against her leg. Jason was two steps behind her with the backup Sony, and Creek was out the driver's door, his camera up on his shoulder, off to Anna's left. Bee, a little out of shape, sputtered in their wake.

Then Creek lit up and Anna yelled at the man with the pig, "Bring the pig. Bring the pig this way ... Bring the pig." The man saw them coming and walked toward them, and she had the Nagra's mike pointed at the squealing pig and Jason lit up.

The security guards saw the camera lights and the first one turned to the man trailing, yelled something to the other, who ran back up the hill. The first one continued down, and shouted at Creek, "Hey, no cameras here, no cameras."

A group of masked women headed toward him, walled him off from the rest of the milling crowd, pushed him toward the ramp. Frustrated, he climbed up the loading dock and hurried to the open door. Just as he was about to go through the door, he jumped back, and a young man in a blue oxford cloth shirt and jeans ran out of the building and headed toward the lights.

Anna said to the microphone, her voice calm, even, "Creek, there's a kid coming in, watch him. Jason, stay with the pig."

Creek backpedaled. When Anna spoke into his ear, he'd looked up from his eyepiece and spotted the kid in the blue shirt: trouble, maybe. Trouble made good movies. The kid was striding toward them, a dark smear under his nose, one hand cupping his jaw. He seemed to be crying.

"They were gonna kill this pig, for nothing—for soap tests or something, shampoo," the masked pig-man shouted at Jason's camera. The pig was freaking out, long shrieking bleats, like a woman being stabbed. "She's gonna live now," pig-man shouted, as the pig struggled against him. "She's gonna live."

The patio was chaos, with the cameras and the pig-man, the women with cages, all swirling around: Blue shirt arrived and Anna saw that he *was* crying, tears running down his cheeks as Creek tracked him with the lens. The dark smear was blood, which streamed from his nose and across his lips and chin.

"Give me that pig," he screamed, and he ran at the pig-man. "Gimme that." The animal women blocked him out, not hitting him, just body blocking. Both Creek and Jason tracked the twirling scrum while Anna tried to stay out of their line; she kept the Nagra pointed, picking up the overall noise, which could be laid back into the tape later, if needed.

The Bee caught Anna's arm: "He's just a flunky, forget him," she shouted, over the screams and grunting of the struggle. "But we're gonna do the mice now. Get the mice, in the garbage cans."

The women with the blue garbage can were waiting their turn with the lights, and Anna spoke into the mike again: "Jason, get out of there. Go over to that blue garbage can, it's full of mice, they're gonna turn them loose." Jason took a step back, lifted his head, spotted the garbage can. "Creek, stay with the kid," Anna said. "Stay with the kid."

As Jason came up, the women with the garbage can, who'd been waiting, popped the lid and tipped it, and two hundred or three hundred mice, some black, some white, some tan, scurried down the sides and ran out onto the patio, looked around and headed for the nearest piece of cover.

Jason hung close and then the kid in the blue shirt went that way, screaming, "Gimme those," and, sobbing, tried to corral the mice. They were everywhere, running over his feet, over his hands, avoiding him, making the break. He finally gave up and slumped on the ground, his head in his hands, the mice all around.

Jeez: this is almost too good, Anna thought.

As Creek tracked him, the Bee came back with her nagging voice: "Do you want an on-camera statement?"

And Anna thought, *Who's running this thing?* But she had to smile at the other woman's effective management: "Yeah, but we'd better hurry," Anna said. "The cops'll be coming."

Anna said into the mike, "Jason, get on the Bee, she'll make a statement." She pushed the mike up, raised her voice, shouted, "Rat, where are you?"

The man with the pig turned toward her: "I'm the Rat," he said. His teeth were bared, his face spotted with what looked like mud, but could be pig shit.

"We're gonna need you over here: we need a comment," Anna said.

"No problem," he said. He handed the struggling pig to a woman. "What exactly do you want?" The Rat had a deep, smooth voice, a singer's baritone. His eyes were pale blue behind the black mask.

"Just tell us why you did it," Anna said, nodding at Jason's camera.

He leaned forward and stage-whispered, "For the publicity."

Anna grinned back and said, "Tell that to the camera."

Jason yelled, "Hey, Rat: You wanna do this, or what?"

As the Rat and the Bee talked to Jason's camera, Anna pulled the mike down in front of her face and said, "Creek, let's talk to the kid. Let me in there first."

Creek hung back a couple of steps, so the camera wouldn't be right in the kid's face. Anna squatted next to him, and patted him on the shoulder. "Are you okay?"

The kid looked up, dazed, a pale teenage child with brown eyes behind his gold-rimmed glasses. "What?"

"Are you okay?" Anna asked again.

"They're gonna fire me," he said. He looked back at the building. "I was supposed to watch them. They were my responsibility, the animals. I was supposed to keep everybody out, but they came in so fast . . ."

"How'd you get the bloody nose?" Anna asked.

"I tried to hold the door, but they kicked through. Then about four of them held me and I couldn't get to the phone, and they tipped everything over in the lab, all the animal cages, everything." He touched his face. "I think the door hit me . . ."

"Look, there's gonna be two sides to this," Anna said. She looked back at Creek, and said, "Creek."

Creek stepped away, spotted a mouse looking at him from the top of the loading dock and closed in on it. Behind him, the Bee and the Rat were still talking to Jason's camera; the pig was still struggling with the woman who'd taken it, but the squealing had stopped, and the scene was almost quiet.

Anna turned back to the kid and continued, "The animal rights guys will be heroes to some people. And some people will be heroes to the scientific community."

She patted his thigh. "Now, go like this. From your nose."

She made an upward rubbing gesture with her hand, on her own face.

The kid gulped. "Why?"

"Want to keep your job?" Anna grinned at him. She was a small woman, dark-haired, with an oval face and corn-flower-blue eyes behind gold-rimmed glasses: she had an effect on young males. "Be a hero. Smear a little blood around your face and we'll put you on camera, telling your side. Believe me, they won't fire you."

"I need the job," the kid said tentatively.

"Smear a little blood and stand up . . . what's your name?"

The kid was no dummy: He'd been born in front of a TV set. He wiped blood up his cheek and said, "Charles McKinley . . . How do I look?" His cheek looked like a raw sirloin.

"Great. That's McKinley, M-c-K-i-n-l-e-y, Charles, regular spelling."

"Yeah." He touched his face again: the blood was brilliant red.

"What's your job up there, Charles?" Anna got a few more details about the job, his age, where he lived.

"That's really great," she said. "Now what . . ."

The pig screamed, and Anna turned.

The woman who'd been holding it had carried it toward Jason's camera, where Jason was interviewing the Rat. As it screamed, the animal kicked free, and ran.

The Rat stooped and tried to scoop it up, like a bouncing football; but the pig went through, smacked into his ankle, and the Rat fell squarely on his butt: "Shit," he shouted. "Get the pig . . ."

Jason was still on him, lights in his face: He rolled and the pig, now panicked, ran behind the woman who'd originally held him, did another quick turn, and as the Rat tried to get to his feet, ran squarely into the Rat's chest, knocking him flat on his butt again.

Jason stayed with it as the Rat scrambled to his feet.

Anna grinned and turned back to the kid: ". . . Tell us what happened, talk to this camera," Anna said, pointing at Creek. "Creek, come on back."

Creek lit up and the kid told his story, breaking into tears again as he got caught up with it.

Anna stepped away to watch Jason, and when the Rat got tangled in a long complicated explanation of animal rights, she broke in: "How come all the women in the group?"

"There are some guys—they just didn't make it tonight," Rat said. He started to say more, when Anna's cell phone rang.

She unclipped it and stepped away, glanced at Creek, who was still with the kid. "Yeah."

Louis, calling from the truck seventy-five feet away, excited: "Jesus, Anna, we got a jumper on Wilshire, he's on a ledge."

"Where?" A basic rule: everything happened at once. Anna looked back at the two interviews, calculating.

"I don't know, somewhere on Wilshire, close, I think. I'm getting the address up."

"Get it now," Anna rapped. Very tense: a jumper would make everything. The networks, CNN, everything—if they got the jump. She could hear Louis tapping on the laptop keys, where he kept the address database. "C'mon, c'mon."

"I'm getting it . . ."

"How're we doing on the cops here?"

"You got a couple-three minutes, I just heard the call."

"Get the address, Louis."

"I'm hurrying."

Anna turned to Creek: "Get ready to wrap it up."

And to the kid, "Cops'll be here to help, minute or two."

Louis came back on the phone: "Jesus, Anna, it's just down the street, we're a half-mile out. And he's still up there."

Anna spoke into the mike, her voice urgent: "Jason, Creek. Back in the truck. Now! Kill the lights. Move it!"

"Hey, what, what?" Jason kept shooting.

"Close down! Get in the truck. Now."

Creek's light went down and he was moving, no questions, but the Rat shouted at her, "Wait a minute, wait, what're . . . Hey, Anna, we didn't talk." And the Bee started toward her.

Anna, the phone pressed to her ear, walking back toward the truck, fumbled a card out of her shirt pocket and thrust it back at the Rat: "Call me. We gotta go."

Creek yelled at her: "What?"

"We got a jumper," she shouted back. "Let's go, Jason . . ."

They ran toward the truck: Louis had climbed into the driver's seat and was backing off the sidewalk.

As Anna and Creek came up, he jammed it into park and climbed over the seat into the back, as Jason came through the side. Creek slipped into the driver's seat and Louis shouted, "Down Westwood, then left on Wilshire, it's three blocks, it's a place called the Shamrock."

Creek: "I know the place: Jesus, it's two minutes from here."

"Gotta hustle," Anna said. "Gotta hustle, gotta hustle."

Creek spun the truck in a U-turn, paused at Le Conte long enough to make sure he wouldn't hit anything, then swept through.

"Louis, whatever happens with the jumper, this animal thing is an A-tape," Anna said over her shoulder. "We want the bloody-nose kid to be a hero . . ."

Jason said, "That pig really pissed off the Rat, I think it's heading for a barbeque."

"I got a great shot of this little mouse, Louis, really cute," Creek shouted over his shoulder.

"Shut up, shut up," Louis said to them all. He had an earphone clamped over one ear. Then, "The guy's still out there. On a ledge. There's hotel people talking to him. He's from a party, high-school kids."

Creek had the gas pedal on the floor and they just caught the light at Wilshire. As they swept through the intersection, Anna said to Jason, "Give yourself some space on your tape. You gotta be ready, but the first tape is good, too."

"I'm ready," Jason said.

"Creek?"

Creek nodded. Creek was always ready.

"Louis, talk to me," Anna said.

Louis' eyes were closed, and he was leaning away from them, listening hard. "There're cars on the way, we got maybe a minute by ourselves. Maybe two minutes."

Anna said, "Where's that Three truck? Weren't they still out?"

"They were drifting down south after that chase," Louis

said. "They're way the hell down by Huntington Beach. They're out of it."

Anna said, "Jason, I want you tight on the guy. Creek will pull back a bit, get the full jump, if he goes. But I wanna see his face . . ."

"You got it, sugarbun," Jason said.

Creek showed his teeth: "Sugarbun?"

Jason grinned at him: "Me'n Anna getting intimate."

"Yeah?" Creek glanced at Anna, who rolled her eyes.

"Me'n Anna doing the thing," Jason said. He was almost talking to himself, looked as though he might giggle. He was wound, his eyes big: He liked the movement, maybe too much. He was talented: might go big in Hollywood someday, Anna thought, if he didn't blow his brains out through his nose. "Doin' the thing," he muttered.

"Shamrock," Anna said, and pointed. Ahead, a twenty-story green-glass-and-steel building showed a bright green neon shamrock at the top. And Jason, who'd crawled between the seats, spotted the jumper: "There he is! He's toward the bottom, like five or six stories up, you can see him . . ."

He pointed, and Anna noticed that his hand had a tremor: not the trembling of excitement, but the jerk of a nerve breakdown. She glanced at his stark, underfed face: Christ, she thought, he's back on the crank.

She turned away from his straining face, and looked where he was looking. Five stories, Anna counted: And there he was. The would-be jumper wore dark pants and a white shirt. From a block away, in the lights that bathed the outside of the building, he looked like a fly stuck to a sheet of glass. "Get us there, Creek," Anna said, breathlessly.

They were doing seventy-five, the wheels screaming, right up to the hotel, then Creek hammered the brake and cut sideways and they went over the curb again and Jason spilled out, running toward the hotel with his camera.

The man on the ledge had his back to a sheet of plate glass, his arms spread. The ledge, Anna thought, wasn't more than a foot wide—she could see the tips of his shoes.

"Guys, I'm gonna try to get up there," Anna said into her mike as she dropped from the truck. "You're gonna be on your own for a minute: Jason, I want *face*." She sprinted toward the hotel's front entrance, the Nagra flapping under her arm.

Hotels didn't want to know about media. As far as hotels were concerned, no media was good media. Anna had two options. She could try to sneak in, but that took time. Or she could run. She ran forty miles a week on the beach and if the stairs were placed right, no hotel security man in California could catch her.

She hit the glass doors and went through the lobby like she was on a motorcycle. Two bellmen huddled at the reception desk with a couple of clerks, and one of the bellmen saw her and just had time to turn, to open his mouth and shout, "Hey," when she was past him. The elevators were straight ahead, and a brass plaque with an arrow pointing to the right said *Stairs*.

She took the stairs. Ran up one flight, two, then a man shouting again, from the bottom, "Hey . . ." Third floor, not even breathing hard. Anna got off at the fourth: There'd be security on the fifth floor, and the desk people might have called them. She ran into the hall on the fourth floor, looked right and left, decided that the right end would be the far end of the hotel. There should be another flight of stairs that way.

She ran down the hall, now aware of her heart pounding in her chest, turned a corner past a niche with Coke, ice and candy machines, to another stairway. She pulled open the door, looked up and down, heard nothing and ran up to Five. She took three seconds, two long breaths, pulled off her headset, shoved it with the Nagra up under her jacket in back, held it with one hand and sauntered into the hallway. Halfway down, three older men—security, probably—stood outside an open doorway. A dozen kids were scattered up and down the hall, a few of them talking, most just looking down at the open door. All the kids were dressed up, the boys in suits and ties, the girls in pink-and-blue party dresses, all with the stark white look of fear on their faces.

One of the security men looked toward Anna, and even leaned her way—but as he did, a woman shrieked, and the men in suits turned and ran through the open door.

My God, Anna thought, *he jumped.*

The girls in pastel dresses were looking at the door, the boys were looking at each other, all were frozen. Anna knew that this was one of the moments she'd remember: they were like sculpture in some modern wise-cracking installation called *California Kids.*

Then Anna moved, and when she did, a couple of the girls began sobbing, and one of the boys yelled, "Oh no. No, Jacob . . ."

Anna ran lightly down the hall, found another open door a few rooms closer than the one where the security men had been. She looked inside: a man and woman, both gray-haired, horrified, were standing at their window, looking out. Anna stepped inside:

"Did he jump?"

The woman, white-faced, looked at her, her mouth working, nothing coming out, then: "Oh my God."

Anna stepped around an open suitcase, walked across the room and looked out the window. The jumper was facedown, a black-and-white silhouette on the yellow stone, six feet from the pool. Ten feet from the body, Jason was moving in with his camera. From across the pool, Creek also focused on the body.

Anna took out the recorder, hit the record switch, held it by her side: didn't hide it, just held it like a purse.

"What happened?" she asked.

"I don't know . . . I think it was just kids, having a party. They were making noise, we could hear them running in the hallway. The next thing we know people were screaming and the hotel people came."

Anna could feel the recorder taking up tape: "Did you see him go?" she asked the gray-haired man.

"I think he was coming in," the man said. "He turned and it was like he lost his balance and all of a sudden he jumped, like he was trying to make the pool . . ."

The woman turned to her husband. "Jim, let's get out of here."

Anna stepped back, looked at the luggage tag on the suitcase: James Madson, Tilly, OK. "Are you Mr. and Mrs. Madson?"

The woman turned toward her. "Yes, yes . . . Are you with the hotel? We'd like to check out."

"You'd have to talk with the people downstairs. Are you all right, ma'am? What is your name?"

"Lucille . . . I'm all right, but the man, the boy, he . . . Jim, I think I'm going to throw up."

She started toward the bathroom with her husband behind her, one hand in the middle of her back, patting her, and Anna stepped to the door and looked out.

Hotel security was there in force, along with four or five uniformed cops. She stepped back, said, "Madson, M-A-D-S-O-N, Tilly, Oklahoma, T-I-L-L-Y," to the Nagra, then popped the recording tape and slipped it inside the waistband of her pants. She had two spare tapes in a black pouch on the carrying strap: she took out a spare, slipped it into the recorder. Hotel security usually didn't ask if they could have the tape, they simply took it, destroyed it, and apologized later.

Anna stepped into the hall. Two of the men who'd been in the room were just coming back out. Hotel security and a manager-type. Before either could say anything, Anna said, "Could somebody help my mother? I think she's gonna be sick."

The manager-type asked, "What's wrong?"

"She saw the man jump, she's in the bathroom . . ."

The manager went by, into the Madsons' room, while the security man ran down the hall toward the elevators. Anna turned the other way and walked back down the hall to the steps.

Into the stairwell, down and around, and around, to the first floor. Pause, listen. Nothing. She stepped into the hall-way, saw a sign that said *Parking Ramp,* and went that way.

Creek was standing fifty feet from the body. No blood, no movement, nothing but a hotel clerk and three cops walking reluctantly toward it. Creek saw her coming and made his open-handed "Got anything?" gesture.

She'd pulled the headset back on. "Quick quotes from a witness," she said into the mike. "They said there was some kind of party before he jumped, or fell, or whatever." Anna spotted Jason, headed toward them. "Creek, look up there, fifth floor, about one, two, three, four, five windows to the right of the jumper's window . . . See where the curtain comes through?"

Creek nodded.

"I'm gonna see if I can get the Madsons to come over there."

Jason came up and Anna asked, "How'd you do?"

"I got his face all the way to the ground," Jason said, with trembling satisfaction. "He hit twenty feet away."

"That's great," Anna said. "Look up there, to the left of where he was. I want you to yell, 'Jim and Lucille Madson, come to the window.' "

"What?"

" 'Jim and Lucille'—I don't have the lungs for it."

"You got nice lungs," Jason said; and his eyes seemed to loop. Stoned, or coming down. Too much of this lately; the last time she'd gone to pick him up, he'd been wrecked.

"Just yell the names, huh?" she said.

"Yes, Mom."

Jason yelled, and after a minute, the Madsons came to the window and peered out.

"Get them?" Anna asked.

Creek had the camera on the window. "Yes."

The Madsons went inside and Jason dropped the camera off his shoulder, his face suddenly somber.

"You know what?"

"What? Look, we gotta get . . ."

"I think I'm gonna hurl . . ."

Anna leaned closer to him: "What the heck are you doing, Jase? Are you stoned?"

"No, no, no . . . I'm just having a little trouble dealing with this," Jason said. He looked at the body.

"At what?" Anna cocked her head, puzzled.

"I'm just . . . my head's fucked up," he said. Then: "Anna, I'm sorry, but I gotta go," he said. He pulled off the headset and handed it to her, shamefaced. "I'm sorry, but I've never seen this before. I've seen bodies, but this was . . . He was smiling at me."

He turned his knees in, so he was standing on the edges of his tennis shoes, head down, like an embarrassed little boy. "I gotta go. You gotta couple of bucks I could borrow until we sell this shit? Take it out of my cut?"

Anna stared at him for a second. Concerned, not angry. "Jase, how bad is it?"

"It's nothing," Jason insisted. "You're probably done for tonight, anyway. You gotta couple of bucks?"

"Yeah, sure," Anna said. She dug in her pants pocket, came up with a short roll of twenties, gave him two.

"Thanks."

And he went, hurrying away across the stone patio, Creek peering after him. In the background, they could hear sirens: fire rescue, too late.

"What was that all about?" Anna asked, watching as Jason went out to the street.

Creek shook his head. "I don't know."

"Well . . ." Anna hoisted the camera, looked through the eyepiece, focused on the group of cops around the body and ran off fifteen seconds of tape. Then she ran it back, forty-five seconds, and replayed.

The jump was there, in and out of focus, but undeniably real, taking her breath away: and at the last second, the man's arms flailing, his face passing through the rectangle of the lens display, then the unyielding stone patio.

"Jeez," she said. She looked at Creek. "This is . . ." She groped for a concept, and found one: "This is *Hollywood*."

Creek muttered, "Better go. The pigs are about to fly." She nodded and they headed for the truck, walking fast, but not too fast. The cops were disorganized at the moment, but five minutes from now they wouldn't be. This would not be a good time to be noticed.

Louis had backed the truck into the street, jockeyed it into a no-parking zone.

"Where's Jason?" he asked, as Anna and Creek unloaded the cameras.

"Took off," Anna shrugged.

"How come? Did he shoot it?"

"Yeah, he got some great stuff," Anna said. "I don't know what his problem is: he freaked."

"Don't sound like the Jason we know and love," Louis said, puzzled.

An ambulance went by, and Creek turned the truck in another U and they headed through light traffic back west down Wilshire.

"We get it all?" Louis asked.

"We got it all," Anna said. "The jump is an A-plus-plus. Probably the best thing we've ever had, exclusive. I'm gonna sell it with the pig as a package."

"As a poke," Louis said.

"Yeah. Let's find a spot where we can see the mountain." Anna pushed a speed-dial button on the cell phone, waited a moment, then said, "Let me speak to Jack Hatton. Anna Batory. Tell him I'm on Wilshire at the Shamrock Hotel."

Creek looked at her curiously, and Louis said, "Hatton? Why're you calling Hatton?"

"Revenge," Anna said, and grinned at him . . .

Jack Hatton came on ten seconds later, his voice the perfect pitch of good cheer: "Anna, how you doing?"

"Don't 'how you doing' me," Anna shouted into the phone. "Remember the swimming cats? I hope you got lots more cat tape, you jerk, because we got the jumper coming off the ledge, all the way down. Two cameras, in focus, twenty feet, and there was nobody else here. So go watch channel Five, Seven, Nine, Eleven, Thirteen, Seventeen and Nineteen and then tell the Witch why you don't have it, you cheap piece of cheese."

"Anna . . ."

"Don't *Anna* me, pal. And I'll tell you something else. We got there quick 'cause we'd just been up to UCLA for the animal raid, which you probably heard about by now, too late, as usual. We got a mile of tape on that, too, we got animals screaming, we got a riot. We got a kid beat up and bleeding. And when you see it on Five, Seven, Nine, Eleven, Thirteen, Seventeen and Nineteen tomorrow, you can explain that, too, dickweed.''

"Anna . . ." A pleading note now.

"Go away." And she clicked off.

Beside her, Creek grinned. "I'm proud a ya," he said.

From the back, Louis said, "Such language . . . we really gonna blow off Three?"

"No," Anna said. "But they'll be sweating blood. I'm gonna jack them up for every nickel in their freelance budget."

"Most excellent," Louis said, with great satisfaction. "Get me to a place where I can see the mountain and I will crank this puppy out."

Anna punched the next speed-dial button: "I'll start selling."

two

All done.

Anna sat in comfort and quiet at her kitchen table, a cup of steaming chicken-noodle soup in front of her, pricking up her nose with its oily saltiness. She yawned, rubbed the back of her neck. Her eyes were scratchy from the long night.

At moments like this, coming down in the pre-dawn cool, Creek and Louis already headed home, she thought of cigarettes; and of younger days, sitting in all-night joints—a Denny's, maybe—eating blueberry pie with a cardboard crust, drinking coffee, talking, smoking. Chesterfields. Some old name. Luckies. Gauloises or Players, when you were posing. She didn't do that any more. Now she went home. Sometimes she cried: a little weep didn't make her feel much better, but did help her sleep.

Anna Batory was a small woman, going on five-three, with black hair cut close, skater-style, or fencer-style. And she might have been a fencer, with her thin, rail-hard body. The toughness was camouflaged by her oval face and white California smile—but she ran six miles every afternoon, on the sand along the ocean, and spent three hours a week working with weights at a serious gym.

Anna wasn't pretty, but she wasn't plain. She was handsome, or striking, a woman who'd wear well into old age, if that ever came. She thought her nose should have been shorter and her shoulders just a bit narrower. Her hands were as large as a man's—she could span a ninth on the Steinway upright in the hall, and fake a tenth. She had pale blue killer eyes. One of her ancestors had ruled Poland and had fought the Russians.

Anna pushed herself away from the table and, carrying her cup of soup, prowled her house, making sure that everything was right. Looking out windows. Touching her stuff. Talking to it: "Now what happened to you, old pot? Has Creek been messing with you? You're over here by the picture, not way out at the edge."

Sometimes she thought she was going crazy, but it was a happy kind of craziness.

Anna lived on the Linnie Canal in the heart of Venice, a half-mile from the Pacific, in an old-fashioned white clapboard house with a blue-shingled roof. The house made a sideways "L." The right half of the house, including the tiny front porch, was set back from the street. The single-car garage, on the left side, went right out to the street. The small yard created by the L was wrapped in a white picket fence, and inside the fence, Anna grew a jungle.

Venice was coming back—was even fashionable—but she'd lived on Linnie since the bad old days. Anyone vaulting the fence would find himself knee deep in dagger-like Spanish bayonet, combat-ready cactus and the thorniest desert brush. If he made it through, he'd fall facedown, bloody and bruised, in a soft bed of perennials and aromatic herbs.

The interior of Anna's house was as carefully cultivated as the yard.

The walls were of real plaster, would hold a nail, and were layered with a half-century's worth of paint. Hardwood floors glistened where the sun broke through the windows, polished by feet and beach sand. They squeaked when she walked on them, and were cool on the soles of her feet.

The lower floor included a comfortable living room and spare bedroom, both filled with craftsman furniture. A bathroom, a small den that she used as an office and the kitchen took up the rest of the floor. The kitchen was barely functional: Anna had no interest in cooking.

"The fact is," Creek told her once, "your main cooking appliance is a toaster." Creek liked to cook. He considered himself an expert on stews.

On the second floor of Anna's house, under the steep roof, were her bedroom and an oversized bathroom. Creek and four of his larger friends had helped her bring in the tub, hoisting it from outside with an illegal assist from a power company cherry-picker.

The tub was a rectangular monstrosity in which she could float freely, touching neither bottom nor sides nor the ends; in which she could get her *wa* as smooth and round as a river pebble.

In the adjoining bedroom, the queen-sized bed was covered with a quilt made by her mother, the material taken from clothes her parents had worn out when they were young. Under the canal-side window, the quilt looked like rags of pure light.

•   •   •

Creek and Louis had dropped her at the corner of Dell and Linnie just after dawn. The truck couldn't conveniently turn around on Linnie, a dead-end street no wider than most city alleys.

"Sorry about the Witch," Louis said. The Witch would be calling her. Anna hated to bring work back to her house.

"That's okay," Anna said. "For this one time, anyway." She waved good-bye with the cell phone, and walked down the narrow street to her house. A neighbor in his pajamas, out to pick up the paper, said, "Hey, Anna. Anything interesting?"

"Guy jumped off a building," Anna said.

"Nasty." He smiled, though, as he shook his head, and said, "I'll watch for it," and padded back inside.

Anna had sold thirteen packages of the jumper wrapped with the animal rights raid. At fifteen hundred dollars for local transmission, she'd sold to nine stations, and at three thousand for the networks—Southern California stations out—she'd sold four. Hatton at Channel Three had called back twice, pushing. They wanted it, had to have it. Finally said the Witch would call.

She did, five minutes after Anna got home. The cell phone buzzed, and Anna went to the kitchen table and picked it up.

"Screw us on this, we'll never use your stuff again." The Witch opened as she usually did, with a direct threat.

"We can live with that," Anna said. She looked out the kitchen window, at the dark line of the canal. In a couple of hours, the reflected ball of the morning sun would start crawling down its length, steaming the water, bringing up the rich smell of algae soup. She'd be asleep in bed, this whole conversation no more than a pleasant memory. "We already told Hatton that. I only agreed to talk to you as a courtesy."

"Courtesy my large white Lithuanian butt," the Witch

snapped. Anna could hear the pause as she hit on a cigarette. "If we don't buy, you lose a big source of your income. Gone," she said. Exhaling. "Outa here. I promise you, we won't buy again."

"You take a bigger hit than we do," Anna said. "You never know when we're gonna come up with something like this jumper . . ."

"You're not *that* good . . ."

"Yeah, we are: we're the best crew on the street. And your career life at Three is what? Four or five years? And you've been there three? You'll be gone in a year or two, and we'll sell to your replacement. And we'll make our point: You don't steal from us. Even if it's swimming cats."

"I apologized for that," the Witch shrilled.

"What?" Anna shouted. She banged the cell phone three times on the table top, then yelled into the mouthpiece. "Did I hear that right? You *laughed* at us."

"So I'm sorry now," the Witch shouted back. "Name the price."

"Network price," Anna said. She sipped at the soup. "Three thousand for the package. Plus two grand for the cats."

"Fuck that," the Witch said. "Network for the package, okay, but the cats we did, we did with our own crew."

"C'mon, c'mon," Anna shouted. "I'm making a point here."

"So'm I . . . Five hundred for the cats."

"I'm serious, we don't need you. Network plus a thousand for the cats."

"Deal," the Witch said. "I want to see the fuckin' pictures in ten fuckin' minutes." She slammed down the receiver.

• • •

Anna called the truck, and spoke to Louis. "Send it to Three."

"How much you get?"

"Four thousand—I got a thousand for the cats."

Louis said, "Examonte, dude," and repeated the price to Creek, whose laughter filled the background. Anna grinned and said, "We're dropping thirty-five thousand bucks in the pot—that's three times the record."

Creek shouted at the phone, "We might as well quit, we'll never do this again."

"How're the radios, Louis?" Anna asked.

"Good. Nothing happening."

"Call me."

Anna hung up with Creek still laughing about the money. She'd wait until Creek had dropped Louis, and there was no chance of recovering for a quick run. Good stuff sometimes broke just at dawn, although the regular station trucks would be out prowling around fairly soon.

Waiting for bed, Anna trailed by the Steinway, touched a few keys, yawned, flipped through the sheets for Liszt's Sonata in B Minor. She'd been trying to clarify the fingerwork in the fast passages.

She didn't sit down—her head wasn't quite right yet. She put the music on the piano, said hello to a couple of plants, enjoyed the quiet. Went into the utility room and got a plastic watering can and filled it.

Barefoot, humming to herself—something stupid from *Les Misérables* that she couldn't get out of her mind—Anna took the watering can out to the porch, and started watering the potted plants. Geraniums, and some daisies: plants with an old-fashioned feel, bright touches in the shade of the jungle.

Back inside, she refilled the can and walked through the house, checking with two fingers the soil in a hundred more plants: some of them were named after movie stars or singers, like Paul, Robert, Faye, Susan, Julia, Jack. Most were small, from a desert somewhere.

On a broken-down Salvation Army table, the first piece of furniture she'd bought in California, she kept a piece of Wisconsin: a clump of birdsfoot violets, dug from the banks of the Whitewater River, and a flat of lilies-of-the-valley. Just now, the lilies-of-the-valley were blooming, their tiny white bell flowers producing a delicate perfume that reminded her of the smell of dooryard lilacs in the Midwestern spring.

Behind the California tan, Anna was a Midwestern farm kid, born and raised on a corn farm in Wisconsin.

The farm was part of her toughness: She had a farm kid's lack of fear when it came to physical confrontation. She'd even been in a couple of fights, in her twenties, in the good old days of music school and late-night prowls down Sunset. As she climbed into her thirties, the adrenaline charge diminished, though her reputation hadn't: The big guys still waved to her from the muscle pen on the beach, and told people, "You don't fuck with Anna, if you wanna keep your face on straight."

The toughness extended to the psychological. Farm kids knew how the world worked, right from the start. She'd taken the fuzzy-coated big-eyed lambs to the locker, and brought them back in little white packages.

That's the way it was.

Anna finished watering the plants, yawned again, and stopped at the piano. Liszt was hard. Deliberately hard. Her home phone rang, and she turned away from the piano and stepped into the small kitchen and picked it up. This would be the sign-off from Louis and Creek: "Hello?"

"Anna: Louis."

"All done?"

"Yeah, but I was talking to a guy at Seventeen about the animal rescue tape. I don't know what they did, but it sounds a little weird."

"Like how, weird?" Anna asked.

"Like they're making some kind of cartoon out of it."

"What?" She was annoyed, but only mildly. Strange things happened in the world of broadcast television.

"He said they'll be running it on the Worm," Louis said. Channel Seventeen called it the Early Bird News; everybody else called it the Worm.

Anna glanced at the kitchen clock: the broadcast was just a few minutes away. "I'll take a look at it," she said.

She went back to the piano and worked on the Liszt until five o'clock in the morning, then pointed the remote at the TV and punched in Seventeen. A carefully-coiffed blonde, dressed like it was midafternoon on Rodeo, looked out and said, "If you have any small children watching this show, the film we are about to show you . . ."

And there was the jumper, up on the wall like a fly.

Anna held her breath, fearing for him, though she'd been there, and knew what was about to happen. But seeing it this way, with the TV, was like looking out a window and seeing it all over again. The man seemed unsure of where he was, of what to do; he might have been trying, at the last moment, to get inside.

Then he lost it: Anna felt her own fingers tightening, looking for purchase, felt her own muscles involuntarily trying to balance. He hung there, but with nothing to hold on to, out over the air, until with a convulsive effort, he jumped.

And he screamed—Anna hadn't seen the scream, hadn't picked it up. Maybe he *had* been trying for the pool.

Anna and the night crew had been there for the pictures, not as reporters: Anna had gotten only enough basic information to identify the main characters. She left it to the TV news staffs to pull it together. At Channel Seventeen, the job went to an intense young woman in a spiffy green suit that precisely matched her spiffy green eyes:

". . . identified as Jacob Harper, Junior, a high-school senior from San Dimas who was attending a spring dance at the Shamrock, and who'd rented the room with a half-dozen other seniors. Police are investigating the possibility of a drug involvement."

As she spoke, the tape ran again, in slow motion, then again, freezing on the boy's face—not a man, Anna thought, just a child. He hung there in midair, screaming forever on Jason's tape. The Madsons, from Tilly, Oklahoma, were also shown, but their faces at the window were cut into the jump, so it appeared that the Madsons were watching—as they had been, though not when the tape was shot.

At the end of the report, the tape was run again, and Anna recognized the symptoms: They had a hit on their hands.

Too bad about the kid, but . . . she'd learned to separate herself from the things she covered. If she didn't, she'd go crazy. And she hadn't seen the jump, only the aftermath, the heap of crumpled clothing near the pool. Less than she would have seen sitting at her TV, eating her breakfast, like a few million Angelenos were about to do.

Anna drifted away from the television, sat at the piano and started running scales. Scales were a form of meditation, demanding, but also a way to free herself from the tension of the night.

And she could keep an eye on the television while she worked through them. Five minutes after the report on the jump, the blonde anchor, now idiotically cheerful, said something about animal commmandos, and a version of the animal rights tape came up.

The tape had been cut up and given a jittery, silent-movie jerkiness, a Laurel-and-Hardy quality, as the masked animal rights raiders apparently danced with the squealing pig, and dumped the garbage can full of mice. Then the Rat was bowled over by the pig—they ran him falling, crawling, knocked down again; and falling, crawling and knocked down *again:* they had him going up and down like a yo-yo.

The guards, who'd come and gone so quickly, had been caught briefly by both Creek and Jason. Now they were repeatedly shown across the concrete ramp and up the loading dock; and then the tape was run backward, so they seemed to run backward . . . Keystone Kops.

The tape was funny, and Anna grinned as she watched. No sign of the bloodied kid, though. No matter: he'd get his fifteen seconds on another channel.

"Good night," Anna said, pointed the remote at the television and killed it.

She worked on scales for another ten minutes, then closed the lid of the piano, quickly checked on the back to see that the yellow dehumidifier light wasn't blinking and headed up to the bedroom.

In the world of the night crew, roaming Los Angeles from ten o'clock until dawn, Anna was tough.

In more subtle relationships, in friendly talk from men she didn't know, at parties, she felt awkward, uneasy, and walked away alone. This shyness had come late: she hadn't always been like that.

The one big affair of her life—almost four years long, now seven years past—had taken her heart, and she hadn't yet gotten it back.

She was asleep within minutes of her head touching her pillow. She didn't dream of anyone: no old lovers, no old times.

But she did feel the space around herself, in her dreams. Full of friends, and still, somehow . . . empty.

three

The two-faced man hurried down the darkened pier, saw the light in the side window, in the back. He carried an eighteen-inch Craftsman box-end wrench, the kind used in changing trailer-hitch balls. The heft was right: just the thing. No noise.

He stopped briefly at the store window, looked in past the *Closed* sign. All dark in the sales area—but he could see light coming from under a closed door that led to the back.

He beat on the door, a rough, frantic *bam-bam-bam-bam-bam.*

"Hey, take an aspirin." The two-faced man nearly jumped out of his shoes. A black man was walking by, carrying a bait bucket, a tackle box and a long spinning rod.

"What?" Was this trouble? But the fisherman was walking on, out toward the end of the pier, shaking his head. "Oh, okay."

He must've been beating on the door too hard. That's what it was. The man forced a smile, nodded his head. Had to be careful. He balled his hand into a fist and bit hard on the knuckles, bit until he bled, the pain clearing his mind.

Back to business; he couldn't allow himself to blow up like this. If there were a mistake, a chance encounter, a random cop—he shuddered at the thought. They'd lock him in a cage like a rat. He'd driven over here at ninety miles an hour: if he'd been stopped, it all would have ended before he had her.

Couldn't allow that.

He tried again with the door, knocking sedately, as though he were sane.

Light flooded into the interior of the store, through the door at the back. The man knocked again. Noticed the blood trickling down the back of his hand. When did that happen? How did he . . . ?

The door opened. "Yeah?"

The boy's eyes were dulled with dope. But not so dulled, not so far gone that they didn't drop to his shirt, to the deep red patina that crusted the shirt from neckline to navel, not so far gone that the doper couldn't say, "Jesus Christ, what happened to you?"

The two-faced man didn't answer. He was already swinging the wrench: the box end caught the boy on the bridge of the nose, and he went down as though he'd been struck by lightning.

The two-faced man turned and looked up the pier toward the street, then down toward the ocean end. Nobody around. Good. He stepped inside, closed the door. The boy had rolled to his knees, was trying to get up. The man grabbed him by the hair and dragged him into the back.

Jason was wrecked. As in train wreck. As in broken. As in dying.

Even through the layers of acid and speed, he could feel the pain. But he wasn't sure about it. He might wake up. He might still say, "Fuck me; what a trip." He had done that in the past.

This stuff he'd peeled off the slick white paper, this was some *bad shit*. A bad batch of chemicals, must've got some glue in there, or something.

He wasn't sure if the pain was the real thing, or just another artifact of his own imagination, an imagination that had grown up behind the counter in a video store, renting horror stories. The horror stories had planted snakes in his mind, dream-memories of bitten-off heads, chainsaw massacres, cut throats, women bricked into walls.

So Jason suffered and groaned and tried to cover himself, and frothed, and somewhere in the remnant of his working brain he wondered: *Is this real?*

It was real, all right.

The two-faced man kicked him in the chest, and ribs broke away from Jason's breastbone. Jason choked on a scream, made bubbles instead. The man was sweating and unbelieving: Jason sat on the floor of the shack, his eyes open, blood running from his mouth and ears, and still he said nothing but, "Aw, man."

The man had been hoping for more: he'd hoped that the doper would plead with him, beg, whimper. That would excite him, would give him the taste of victory. That hadn't happened, and the heavy work—kicking the boy to death— had grown boring. The boy didn't plead, didn't argue: he just groaned and said, "Aw, man," or sometimes, "Dude."

"Tell me what it's like when you fuck her," the man crooned. "Tell me about her tits again. C'mon, tell me. Tell me again what it's like when you *do the thing*." He kicked him again, and Jason groaned, rocked with the blow, and one arm jerked spasmodically. "Tell me what it's like to fuck her . . ."

No response: maybe a moan.

"Tell me about Creek: he looks like a monster. He looks like Bigfoot. Tell me about Creek. Was he with you two? Were all three of you fucking her? All three at once?"

But the doper wasn't talking. He was in never-never land.

"Fuck you," the two-faced man said, finally. He was tired of this. He could hear the ocean pounding against the pilings below them, a rhythmic roar. He took a long-barreled Smith & Wesson .22 revolver from his coat pocket and showed it to the bubbling wreck on the floor.

"See this? I'm gonna shoot you, man."

"Dude." Jason was long past recognizing anything, even his own imminent death, the killer realized.

He squatted: "Gonna shoot you."

He pointed the pistol at the boy's forehead, and when the roar of the surf started to build again, fired it once. The boy's head bumped back. That was all.

The two-faced man waited for some sensation: nothing came.

"Well, shit," he said. He'd been having more fun when the doper was alive. Had he really fucked her? Anna? He had all the details. So maybe he had.

He stood up, pulled open the window on the ocean-side wall, and looked down. Deep water. Everything dark, but he could hear the water hissing and boiling.

Just like it should be, he thought, looking out, for this kind of scene.

four

At a little after one o'clock, Anna stirred, then woke all at once, aware first of her pillow, then the room, then the faint whine of a jumbo jet blowing out of LAX. She lay in bed for a few minutes, rolled over, looked at the clock, yawned, sat up and stretched.

Showered, washed her hair.

Anna liked dresses, a little on the hippie side, small flowers and low necklines, when she wasn't working, or working out.

For work, she had a carefully thought-out uniform, designed to make her fit in as many social slots as possible. The uniform consisted of cream-colored silk or white cotton blouses with black slacks, expensive black boots, and one of several linen or light woolen jackets, depending on the season. She had three Hermès silk scarves, and always carried one or another in a buttoned inside pocket, along with a pair of gold earrings. If she dumped the jacket in the truck and rolled the sleeves on the blouse, she was hanging out. If she wore the coat, she was all business, still casual, but working. If she added the scarf and earrings, she could get by at anything short of a formal affair. Even at a formal affair, she could pass as a caterer.

Any of the looks might be necessary in a night's work, doing reconnaissance before the cameras lit up, especially if the work scene involved cops or security people allergic to publicity.

She also needed a more formal look if she'd be on-camera herself. She didn't like going on-camera—anonymity made everything easier—but sometimes an interviewer was necessary. When there was no choice, she needed the right look.

For the camera guys, appearance didn't matter: there was no way to camouflage the video lights.

Now, out of the shower, she dried her hair, pulled on a pair of shorts and a t-shirt, and laced her running shoes. Stopped in the kitchen for a glass of orange juice, bracing against the wall to loosen her calves as she drank it.

The day was fine, cool, with blue skies and a light breeze from the ocean. The beach was a half-mile away, and she loosened up as she walked over on Venice Boulevard, then took a finger street down to the beach.

A very large black man, who'd once been a second-string linebacker for the L.A. Raiders, was doing pull-ups on a rack set into the sand. He lifted a hand to Anna, continuing the pull-up with only one hand. Anna waved back and continued on to the water's edge, turned right and started running. Six miles: three miles up, three back. She ran along the surf, through the shore birds, a quarter mile behind another runner, feeling the sun.

When she started running, her brain was empty. The further along the beach she got, the more it filled up: Maybe go south tonight, haven't been south for a while. Wonder what happened to that burned kid, at that house fire, the last time we went south? Kid was trying to save a cat, wasn't he? Could be a feature on his recovery? It'd have to be the first item on the run. Louis could get a phone number . . . On the other hand, it might be a bone to throw to Channel Seventeen . . .

Six miles, a little over forty-two minutes. When she got back, the linebacker was sitting on the bottom bench of the basketball bleachers, putting braces on his knees.

"Hey, Dick," Anna said. "How're the knees?"

"Snap-crackle-pop, just like cornflakes," he said.

"Rice Krispies," Anna said.

"Yeah, whatever; ain't been gettin' nothing but worse."

"Gonna have to decide," Anna said.

"I know." He pushed himself up, hobbled around the edge of the court. "So stiff I couldn't walk down to the water."

"Take the knife, man," Anna said. "Anything's better than this."

"Scared of the knife. They put me to sleep, I don't think I'll wake up. I'll die in there."

"Oh, come on, Dick . . ."

They talked for another five minutes, then Anna headed home. As she left, the sad linebacker said, "If I could run half as good as you, I'd still be playing."

The cell phone was chirping when she got home. Louis again, ready to set up for the new night? A little early for that. "Hello?"

Not Louis.

"This is Sergeant Hardesty with the Santa Monica police." He sounded a little surprised to be talking with someone. "Is this Anna Batory?" He pronounced her name "battery."

"Ba-Tory," she said. She spread her business cards around, and often got tips on the cell phone. "What's happening?"

"Ma'am, I'm sorry, but there's been an accident. One of the persons involved carried a card in his billfold that said you should be contacted in case of trouble."

She didn't track for a second, and then the smile died on her face: "Oh my God, Creek," Anna said. "Is his name Creek?"

"I don't know, ma'am," the voice said, shading toward professional sorrow. "I don't have an identification on the person. Could you go down there?"

The body was on the beach, just at the waterline. If she'd run another five or six miles that morning, she would have tripped over it.

A line of three cop cars, two with light bars and a plain white institutional Chevy, marked the spot; a medical examiner's van sat ten feet above the water, the longest fingers of surf running up between its tires. At the back of the van, a cluster of civil servants gathered around what looked like a pile of seaweed: a body covered with a wet green blanket. Two uniformed cops kept a semicircle of gawkers on the far side of the cop cars.

Out on the ocean, two Jet Skis chased each other in endless wave-hopping circles, their motors like distant chain saws; beyond them, a badly handled sloop pushed south toward Marina Del Rey, its jib flogging in the stiffening breeze.

Anna trudged across the sand toward the cop cars with a growing dread. She'd tried to call Creek at home, but there'd been no answer. Creek was always out on the water. She'd thought, any number of times, that he would someday die there.

One of the uniformed cops sidled along the line of cars, cutting off her line: "They called me," she said, pointing toward the group on the waterline. "They think that's a friend of mine."

"If you could just wait here . . ."

She waited by the cars while the cop walked down to the group by the water and said something to a plainclothesman, who looked briefly at Anna and nodded. The cop waved her over, and passed her on his way back to the car. "Hot," he said as he passed. And he added, "Hope it's not your friend."

Anna jerked her head in a nod, but the kind words did nothing to help the growing sourness in the back of her throat.

At the water, a balding man in jeans and a t-shirt squatted beside the body, probing it. Two more men sat on the bumper of a medical examiner's truck, chatting, one with a set of Walkman headphones around his neck. Two plain-clothes cops, one male, one female, were watching the man at the body. As Anna came up, they both turned to her.

The woman cop wore designer jeans with a crisp white blouse, and carried a blue blazer folded over one arm. Her round retro-chic sunglasses might have been stolen from one of the three blind mice. She was dark-haired and dark-complected, a little taller than Anna, with a square chin and square white teeth. She carried an automatic pistol in a shoulder rig.

Her partner was a large man, balding, gray-haired, a little too heavy, with deep crowsfeet at the corners of his eyes. His clothes were straight from JCPenney, and his black wingtips and pant cuffs would be filled with sand.

Like the woman, he'd taken his jacket off, and carried

what appeared to be an antique Smith & Wesson revolver on his belt. There was an odd body language between them, Anna noticed. When they moved, even a foot or two, the guy tracked her, but the woman was unaware of it.

The man smiled, and the woman wrinkled her nose, as though Anna were a smudge on an antique table.

"I'm Jim Wyatt," the cop said. "This is my partner, Pam Glass." The woman nodded, cool behind her glasses. Wyatt frowned, then said, "Do I know you? I've met you . . ."

"I do TV news, cop stuff," Anna said. "You've probably seen me around."

Wyatt nodded, grinned again, the openness of a good interrogator: "That's it. You were at that raid on the burglary ring, God, couple years ago. They thought the guys had killed that woman on Marguerita . . ."

Anna pointed a finger at him, felt as though she was babbling. She didn't want to look at the body; she'd do anything to delay it. "You were the guy who kicked the door."

A good piece of tape: the cops filtering across a yard to the target house while a neighbor's dog went crazy, barking; Wyatt drawing his gun, waiting for others to get in position, but not waiting too long, because of the dog. Then he turned the corner of the house with two guys in body armor and they took down the door.

Creek had gotten the good shots and the cops'd taken three men, a woman, and two hundred pieces of stolen electronic equipment out of the place, everything from home blood pressure kits to cell phones and bread machines. There really hadn't been much danger, but the tape was nice.

Stalling: *Don't be Creek, don't be Creek . . .*

"That was me," Wyatt said, flattered that she remembered, pleased to meet her again. He'd been a hero for several hours. "Are you still doing the TV stuff?"

Anna nodded: "Yeah, same stuff, cops, fires, fights, accidents, movie stars."

"A lot of police officers don't like to be called cops," Glass said, breaking in.

"I know," Anna said. She glanced toward the blanket—an army blanket, olive drab. The man squatting next to it was doing something to an exposed paper-white ankle. Looked too small to be Creek, and too white. No shoe or sock. The skin wrinkled by the water. The victim's face was still covered by the blanket. To Wyatt, she said, "I hope to God this isn't my friend."

"His ID said Jason O'Brien . . ."

She almost fell down. Jason? She'd never thought of Jason. A sense of relief flooded through her, followed instantly by a sense of shame, that she should be so relieved.

Wyatt said, "Are you all right?"

She caught herself. "Aw, jeez . . . Jason?"

"He had a card that said to call you," Glass said.

Wyatt, looking down at the blanket, said, "So you're pretty close?"

"Not close, but he's a friend. He was our backup camera, our second camera when we needed one. He used to call me Mom," Anna said. "He's a kid—was a kid."

"Did you see him yesterday?"

"Yeah. He was shooting with us last night. He split around eleven."

"You didn't see him after that?" Glass asked.

"No." Anna explained about the animal rights protest and the jumper, and Glass and Wyatt nodded. They'd seen the stories. "So what do you think?" Anna asked. "Drugs?"

Wyatt shook his head: "Wasn't drugs: why'd you think it was?"

Anna shrugged. "Jason did a lot of dope, I think. He got weird."

"All your friends do dope?" Glass asked.

"A couple," Anna said. She wasn't intimidated: there was no crime in knowing dopers. "Jason did some crank, a little crack when he could get it. He liked cocaine, but he couldn't afford it most of the time. Some weed."

"Why'd he leave last night?" Wyatt asked.

Anna shook her head. "I don't know. He said he was gonna ride all night, but then, after the jumper . . . I don't know." She thought about it for a second: now that he was dead—if he was dead, she thought, if that was Jason under the blanket—his hasty departure seemed even odder. "He said the jumper made him feel bad and he was gonna take off. We all figured that was bullshit—the rest of the crew and me. Maybe something was going on."

"Why was it bullshit?" Glass asked.

" 'Cause I've seen him crawl inside a car with a decapitated woman to get a better shot, and the head was laying on the front seat with the eyes still open and a smile on the face," Anna said. "How's a jumper gonna bother him? There wasn't even any blood."

"Huh." Wyatt nodded, and stared north up the beach, toward the mountains hanging over Malibu, like the hills might have the answer. When it didn't come, he sighed and said, "Will you take a look? Just to make sure we've got the right guy?"

Anna nodded, swallowed, found she had no saliva in her mouth. She saw dead bodies all the time, but not dead friends.

Wyatt said, "Frank, lift the corner of the blanket, huh?"

Frank stopped whatever he was doing with the leg and picked up the corner of the blanket—Wyatt was watching her face—and there was Jason.

No drugs, this one.

He was lying on his stomach, his head slightly downhill

toward the water, his face turned toward her. He didn't look like he was asleep: he looked like he'd been changed to wax. The visible eye was cracked open, and his tongue hung out, like the limp end of a too-long suede belt.

His head looked wrong, misshapen, and something had happened to his cheeks. There was no blood, so the outlines weren't clear, but he seemed to have been slashed by a knife or razor. But that hadn't killed him: a bullet had. In his forehead, just above the visible eye, was a clean dark bullet hole.

"Aw, God," Anna said, turning away. She felt like she ought to spit. "That's him."

"All right," Wyatt said. Frank dropped the blanket.

"When did you find him?"

"He washed up about, mmm, two hours ago. People saw his body in the surf, thought he was drowning. One of the lifeguards went in after him, pulled him out."

As he spoke, a tear rolled down Anna's cheek, and she frowned, and brushed it away. No tears. She didn't cry. Then another one started.

"He involved with any gangs? Buying dope, causing them trouble?"

"No ... I don't think so. But I don't know him well enough to say for sure. Why?"

Wyatt shrugged: "Those cuts on his face. They looked like they might be gang signs. They look the same on both sides, both cheeks."

"I don't know," Anna said.

"Okay. Listen, we're gonna need a complete statement from you," Wyatt said. "When you last saw him, where he lives, who he knows, any troubles he might have had. Family. That kind of stuff. The address on his ID isn't any good."

Anna nodded. "He moved around a lot—he was living down in Inglewood, I think, an apartment. I've never been to his place, but I've got a phone number. We'd usually pick him up at the pier, he worked at the ShotShop photo place.''

Glass looked down at the pier, a mile south. ''Right here?''

''Yeah.'' They all turned to look down at the Santa Monica pier, a gray line of buildings thrusting into the water a mile to the south.

''Has he been having trouble with anyone? Buying the crank or anything?'' Wyatt asked.

''He was pretty cheerful last night: he was riding with us because he heard about the raid, and set up our contact—he only rides with us once or twice a month, when we've got something complicated going on. He just seemed like . . . Jason. Nothing special.''

''And you don't know about the crank. Who his supplier might have been.''

''No. I don't,'' Anna said.

''You don't know much about anything, do you?'' Glass said.

''Get off my case,'' Anna snapped. ''I got a goddamned friend dead on the beach and I don't need any bullshit from cops.''

Glass took a step toward her, Anna stood her ground, but Wyatt took a half-step himself, between them. ''Pam, take it easy.'' And to Anna: ''You too.''

Anna spent another ten minutes with them, picking up their weird body-dance again, and agreed to drive herself back to the station to make a statement. Wyatt walked part of the way back to her car with her.

''Sorry about Pam,'' he said. ''She hasn't been doing homicide all that long. She's still kind of *street*.''

''She like to fight?'' Anna asked.

''She's not afraid of it,'' Wyatt said, glancing back at the woman, who was peering down at the body.

"Listen, last night," Anna said. "Jason might have been high. I don't know, I can't always tell, because he was so hyper. But when we got up to the hotel, for the jumper, he was shaking like a leaf. He was okay when he was shooting, but when we were riding up, he was . . . shaking. Jerking, almost, like spasms in his arms."

"All right, we'll tell the doc. You're gonna be around, right?"

"Yeah. Wait." Anna dug in a pocket, took out a business card, borrowed a pen from Wyatt and said, "Turn around, let me use your back." Using his back as a writing surface—he seemed to like it—she scribbled two phone numbers on her card, and handed it to him. "The first number is my home phone, it's unlisted with an answering machine. The next one is the cell phone I carry around with me. And on the front is the phone in the truck. I'm always around one or two of them."

"Thanks. Make the statement." He looked back at his partner, sighed and started that way.

"Makes your teeth hurt, doesn't it?" Anna said after him.

He stopped and half-turned. "What does?"

"Wanting to sleep with her so bad."

Wyatt regarded her gloomily, then broke down in a self-conscious grin. "I don't think a woman could ever know how bad it gets," he said. He started walking back, then turned, and in a tone that said *this is important*, he added: "And it's not just that I want to sleep with her, you know. That's only . . . the start of it."

five

Anna made the statement, and headed south. Creek lived in a town house in Marina Del Rey with two Egyptian Mau cats, seven hundred sailing books and a billiards table he claimed had been stolen from the set of a James Cagney movie. He still wasn't answering the phone, and Anna suspected that he'd be on his boat.

Lost Dog was a centerboard S-2/7.9 with a little Honda outboard hanging off the stern, and Creek had sailed it to Honolulu and back. On his return, Anna had presented him with a Certificate of Stupidity, which hung proudly in the main cabin, over the only berth big enough for Creek to sleep on.

Anna dumped her car in a parking lot, walked across the tarmac to the basin, down the long white ramp, through the clutching, pleasant odors of algae and gasoline. She spotted the *Lost Dog*'s kelly-green sail covers, so at least he wasn't out sailing.

He was, in fact, down below, installing a marine head where he'd once carried a Porta Potti.

"Creek," she called, "come out of there."

Creek poked his head up the companionway. He was shirt-less, had a hacksaw in his hand, and his hair was sodden with sweat. He read Anna's face and said, "What happened?"

"Jason's dead," Anna said bluntly.

Creek stared at her for a moment, then shook his head wearily, said, "Aw, shit." He ducked down the companionway and the hacksaw clanged into a toolbox. A moment later, he emerged again, wearing gym shorts, his body as hairy as a seventies shag carpet. "Fuckin' crank, I bet," he said.

"He was shot," Anna said.

"Shot?" Creek thought about it for a moment, then shrugged, an Italian shrug with hands. "Still, probably dope."

"Yeah, maybe," Anna said.

"What else would it be?"

"I don't know," Anna said. She filled him in on the details: where the body was found, how. "I was afraid it was you."

"Naw; I won't float."

She let some of it out, now: "His face looked like note-book paper: it was white, it was like . . ." She happened to look into the harbor water, where a small dead fish floated belly-up. ". . . Like that fish. He didn't look like he'd ever been alive."

"You know who he hung out with," Creek said. "You give those kids enough time, they'll kill you. Fuckin' crazy Hollywood junkie crackheads."

Anna looked up at him, nibbled her lip. She didn't want to tell him that she'd given his name to the cops, but she had to. He had to be ready. "Listen, I had to make a state-ment to the cops. We might have been the last people who saw Jason alive, except for the killer. I told them about Jason using the crank and the other stuff, 'cause it might be relevant.''

Creek exhaled, threw his head back and looked at the Windex at the top of the mast. "Wind is shit today," he said. And: "They'll be coming to see me."

Anna nodded. "That's why I stopped by. They wanted the names of everybody on the crew with Jason," she said. "I think we ought to bag it tonight, maybe for a couple of days."

"Fine with me. I've got work to do on the boat," Creek said. He flopped his arms, a gesture of resignation. In the bad old days, Creek had run boatloads of grass up from Mexico. He'd never been caught with a load, but at the end, the cops had known all about him, and when he'd been tripped up with a dime bag, they'd used it to put him in Chino for three hard years. He considered himself lucky.

"If this was Alabama, I'd still be inside," he said. He hadn't smuggled or used drugs in a decade, but if the cops ran his name as a member of the night crew, they'd get a hit when his name came up: and they'd be around. "You better get in touch with Louis."

"Already did, on the phone," Anna said. "But I wanted you to know they'll probably be coming around. I woulda lied to them . . ."

"Nah, they would of caught you, and then they woulda wondered why you were lying." He grinned at her: "You want to go out and sit in the sun?"

On the afternoons when Creek wasn't working, he'd crank up the Honda outboard, motor out of the marina into the Pacific, raise just enough sail to carry him out a bit further, then back the jib, ease the main, lash the tiller to leeward and drift, sometimes all night, listening to the ocean.

Anna shook her head at the invitation: "I don't think so,"

she said. "I want to get back home, take a bath. I smell like a . . . dead guy. I've got it in my nose."

Jason had worked with them on and off for two years—they'd probably been out with him once a month, perhaps a little more often. Say, thirty times, Anna thought, a few hours each time. He was good at it: he had an artistic eye, knew how to frame a shot and wasn't afraid to stick his face into trouble.

His main shortcoming was a lack of focus: he would get caught by something that interested him—might be a face, or visually tricky shot, and lose track of the story.

Anna cleaned up the house for a half-hour, bored, on edge and depressed all at once, and finally dragged two old Mission chairs into the back and began sanding the paint off. She'd found them in a yard sale, in reasonable condition, and figured she'd make about nine million percent profit on them, if she could ever get the turquoise paint off them.

The work was fiddly, dull, but let her think about Jason: not puzzling out the murder, not looking for connections, just remembering the nights he'd spent in the back of the truck— the decapitated woman on Olympic; the crazy Navajo with the baseball bat in the sex-toy joint, the pink plastic penis-shaped dildos hurtling through the videotape like Babylonian arrows coming down on Jerusalem.

She grinned at that memory: stopped grinning when she remembered the fight at the Black Tulip, when the horse-players had gone after the TV lights. Or the time they taped the two young runaways, sisters, looking for protection on Sunset, the fifty-year-old wolves already closing in . . .

At seven o'clock, with the daylight fading, she quit on the sanding, went inside, made a gin and tonic. The TV was running in the background, as it always was, and as she turned to go back outdoors, she saw the tape of the guy being hit by the pig. He was getting more than his money's worth, she thought, and grinned at the sight. Then: *Jason got that shot.* She stopped smiling and, still smelling of the paint-stripper, carried the drink out to the canal-side deck and dropped into a canvas chair.

"Anna." Her name came out of the sky.

She looked up, and saw Hobart Page looking down from his second-story sundeck next door. "We're having margaritas. Come on up."

"Thanks, Hobie, but, uh, I had a friend die. I just want to sit and think for a while."

Another voice: Jim McMillan, Hobie's live-in. She could see his outline against the eastern sky. "Jeez. You okay?"

"Yeah, yeah. Bums me out, though," she said.

"Well, come over if you need company."

She'd just finished the drink when the phone rang—the home phone, the unlisted number. Creek or Louis, maybe her father, or one of a half-dozen other people, she thought.

But it was the cops: "Ms. Batory . . . Lieutenant Wyatt."

"You're working late," Anna said.

"We're just wrapping up here," he said.

"Wrapping up? Did you find out who did it?"

"Afraid not. We did locate his apartment, not much there. Unless we get a break, we're not gonna be able to do much with it . . . it looks like dope, or just random."

"So you're giving up?"

"No—but right now, we've got nothing," Wyatt said. "We checked out the ShotShop and I think he might have been killed there. He could've been dropped right out the back window into the water, and the window was unlocked, which it wasn't supposed to be."

"Was there any blood? He was pretty beat up . . ."

"Not visible blood, but there was a roll of photo paper in the back—you know, one of those printed scene things?"

"Yeah . . ."

"Anyway, the owner said it was back there, half unrolled, and now it's gone. Maybe he was killed on the paper, and the paper was thrown out the window. It would've sunk . . . So we've got crime scene guys looking for blood, and checking around to see if the paper's under the pier, but even if we find it, it won't be much. We're looking for anyone who saw anything, but we haven't found anyone so far."

"Did you talk to the fishermen out there? There are always a few . . ."

"Yeah, yeah, and we'll talk to more of them tonight. But listen—I didn't call to update you. We found O'Brien's next of kin, an aunt and uncle out in Peru, Indiana. I don't think they're too well off, but, uh . . . They'd like to talk to you."

"Me? What for?"

"I think they'd like you to make the arrangements for a funeral and so on . . ."

She rubbed the back of her neck: "Aw, jeez . . ."

"Well, you're the only friend we can find," Wyatt said. "There was nothing of value in his apartment—some electronic gear and an old bike, clothes. Anyway, I didn't want to give them your unlisted phone number, but told them I'd ask you to call back."

"All right, give me the number."

Nancy Odum answered the phone in Peru and passed it off to her husband, Martin. Martin Odum said, "We don't fly, and it's a long way to come to get a stereo set. If you could handle the arrangements, we'd be happy to pay you somethin' for your time."

"No, that's okay," Anna said, thinking, *No it's not.* She'd never arranged a funeral, and hoped she'd never have to.

Martin Odum continued in the same glum tone: "His mother and father are buried here in Peru, we thought maybe . . . cremation? We could sprinkle the ashes on their graves. If that'd be okay with you."

"I'll take care of it," Anna said. "He had a few hundred dollars coming from my company, I'll use that for the cremation and to ship the remains. Uh, his stuff, do you want me to sell it? I don't know how much I'd get, but I could send you whatever it is."

"That'd be nice of you, ma'am."

They worked out the rest of the melancholy details, the phones making funny satellite sounds; and the Odums sounded as morose as Anna felt. When they were done, she hung up, mixed another drink, thought about making it a double and did.

Back outside, sitting in the canvas chair, she let her mind drift: and it drifted, under the influence of the alcohol, to the last funeral she'd been to, so long ago . . .

Anna had grown up on a farm in south-central Wisconsin, a 480-acre corn operation that lay in the crook of the White-water River, not far from Madison.

Her mother was a piano teacher, and she'd died in an automobile accident when Anna was six. She could still remember the melancholy, almost gothic circumstances of the funeral at the small Baptist church, and the slow procession to the tiny graveyard down the dusty gravel road: how bright and warm the day had been, the red-winged blackbirds just beginning to flock, one particular bird perched on a cattail, looking her in the eye as the procession passed . . .

Death and music . . .

Anna was the best pianist at the University of Wisconsin–Milwaukee, the year she graduated. She moved to UCLA, and the year she took her MFA, she was one of the best two or three in the graduate school. Not good enough. To make it as a concert pianist, she would have had to have been the best in the world, in her year and a year or two before and after. As it was—one of the best at UCLA—she got session gigs; movie music.

She still played the hard stuff, out of habit, and, really, out of a kind of trained-in love. But in her one last semi-regular gig, Sunday nights at the Kingsborough Hotel, she played a dusty, romantic, out-of-date jazz.

Her mother's music: they'd played a piece of it at her funeral, and all those Wisconsin farm folks had thought it was a wonderful thing.

Too early, half-drunk, Anna went to bed.

Alcohol never brought sleep.

Instead, it released unhappy images from some mental cage, and they prowled through her dreams, kicking old memories back to life. From time to time, half-awake, she'd imagine that she'd just groaned or moaned. At three in the morning, she woke up, looked at the clock, felt herself sweating into the sheets.

At three-fifteen, she heard a noise, and was instantly awake. The noise had a solid reality to it.

Not a dream noise.

Anna slept in a pair of Jockey underpants. She slipped out of bed, groped around for a t-shirt that she'd tossed at a chair, but hadn't found it when she heard the noise again. She moved silently to the head of the stairs, listened.

Tik-tik . . . scrape.

Back door, she thought. Definitely real. She was getting oriented now, stepped to the nightstand, found the phone. When she picked up the receiver, the dial lighted and she pushed a speed-dial button. Two rings and a man answered on the other end: Jim McMillan, from next door, groggy with sleep. "What?"

"Jim, this is Anna. We got one: he's right outside my back door."

"Holy cow." Then she heard him speak to Hobie: "It's Anna, she's got one outside her back door," and Hobie: "Okay."

Jim said to Anna, "We'll call the cops and start the web. You lay low." A little excitement in his voice now.

"Yeah. Be careful."

Life in Venice was getting better, but there'd been some tough times; still were. Their version of the Neighborhood Watch was a little heavier-duty than most, knowing that the cops would always take a while to get there. Jim would start a calling tree, which would branch out over the surrounding two blocks, and in five minutes there'd be people all over the street.

But she had to get through the five minutes.

Anna had both a handgun and a fish-whacker in the bedroom. There'd be people around, so she went for the whacker, which she kept against the back side of the chest of drawers. On the way, in the dark, she stepped on the t-shirt, picked it up, pulled it over her head. She found the whacker . . . and heard a windowpane break.

Quietly. Like somebody had put pressure against it to crack it, and then tried to pick out the pieces—but at least one piece had fallen onto the kitchen floor.

Damn them. They'd hurt her house.

Anna went to the stairs, began to creep down. The whacker was made of hickory, looked like a dwarf baseball bat, and was meant to put ocean game fish out of their misery. Creek had drilled out the business end, melted a few ounces of lead sinker on his barbeque grill and poured the lead into the bat. If anyone was hit hard with it, surgery would follow.

At the bottom of the stairs, Anna heard another piece of glass crack. She moved to the open arch between the living room and the kitchen, risked a quick peek. The obscure figure of a man hovered outside the back window, three feet to the right of the door. He'd done something to the window, and had then broken out a piece. As she watched, a hand came through the broken pane, and a needle-thin ray of light played across the inside of the door. He was trying to see the lock.

Even if the posse arrived in the next couple of minutes, she didn't want to be trapped inside the house with some crack-smoked goof. She bunched herself in the arch, eight feet from the door. The hand with the light disappeared, and then, in the near darkness, she saw another movement. He was reaching far inside, trying to get to the deadbolt. She waited until the hand was at the door, then launched herself across the room, one big step with the whacker already swinging, and

Whack!

Hit too high, and caught the window frame and the arm at the same time. And as she swung, she screamed, "Get out!" and raised the whacker again, but the man outside groaned and jerked his arm back through the window, tearing out more glass.

She heard him step once heavily on the porch, a running step, and then a heavy-duty spotlight caught him from a neighbor's yard across the canal, and someone yelled, "There he is."

Anna stepped to the door and flipped on the porch light, and at the same time, someone yelled, "He's going west," and someone, from the front of the house, "There he is, Larry, there he is."

Anna ran through the house to the front door and out, down the short sidewalk to the street—ten yards away, a man in jeans and a black jacket was running away from her, along the edge of the street. He was hurt, she thought: something funny in the jerky way he held his left arm.

Pak Hee Chung, the Korean businessman from across the street, ran out of the front of his house carrying a shotgun, saw Anna and shouted, "Get back inside," and then fired the shotgun in the air, a three-foot flame erupting from the gun as the muzzle blast shook the street.

The man in black, now thirty yards away, spun, crouched. Anna shouted, "Pak, he's got a gun," just as the man fired, four quick *pok-pok-pok-pok* shots, and Pak fumbled the shotgun and went down on his stomach.

"Gun," Anna screamed. "He's got a gun."

Hobie ran out of the house behind her and shouted, "Get out of the way."

Anna ran back a few steps and turned to look at the man in black, now running again, forty yards, and Hobie opened up with a handgun, five fast shots into the night. The man kept going, turned the corner. There was a flash of lights, another searchlight, somebody screamed, "Stop or I'll shoot," and again she heard the *pok-pok-pok* and a louder *bang-bang*.

Pak was on his feet again, running down the narrow street, apparently unhurt, and for no apparent reason, fired the shotgun into the air again. Again the lightning flash and the muzzle blast rattling the neighborhood.

Like her dad's twelve-gauge, Anna thought in an instant of abstraction. She found herself on her knees, looking up the street.

Then Hobie was there, next to her in his pajamas, fumbling shells into a revolver. "Goddamn," he said excitedly, "I just shot the shit out of Logan's garage. Don't tell them it was me, huh? Let them think it was the asshole, Logan'd like that anyway."

"Yeah . . ."

Pak ran back, still carrying the shotgun: "Everybody okay?"

"What happened to the guy?" Anna asked.

"I don't know. Everybody was shooting, nobody got hit. Bet we scared the shit out of him, huh?" He looked back up the street and suddenly laughed wildly, a long scary cackle, and Hobie and Anna looked at each other. This was something new . . .

Then three more men came running around the corner at the end of the street, one of them carrying a rifle; they stopped when they saw Pak, Hobie and Anna.

"Who's that?" the rifleman shouted.

"Pak and Hobie and Anna," Hobie yelled back.

"Everybody okay?"

"Yeah . . ."

"He came back that way—you see him? He's stuck down Linnie."

"Didn't see him this way."

"Get the guys up here, get the guys up here . . ."

"Better get off the street," Pak said. "Anna, lock yourself inside. We'll get a line set up and dig him out of here."

"Be careful," Anna said. She looked down at her bare legs. "I better go put some pants on."

Pak said, "You're okay with me," and jacked another shell into the shotgun and grinned.

Hobie was standing behind Pak and he winked at Anna, while Anna blushed and said, "I'll be back in a second," and Pak yelled, "Get those guys going . . . we need a skirmish line . . ."

By the time Anna was dressed, fifteen neighborhood men, a half-dozen women and two cops had walked the street, and found nothing at all. Anna walked with them as they checked again, knocking at every door.

"Like smoke," Pak said. "Must've swum the canal."

When the last house was checked, they gathered at Pak's, wallowing in the scent of testosterone. Pak started a stream of instant coffee coming out of the microwave, and Pop-Tarts from the toaster; Logan, the old Vietnam vet, was saying, "Like this night in fuckin' Dong Ha, man, pop-pop-pop a fuckin' firefight in the front yard, my garage is all shot to shit . . ."

He *did* seem pleased, Anna thought.

The debriefing—party—at Pak's lasted an hour, and everybody went to look at the broken glass on Anna's back porch. The intruder had used masking tape to tape off one pane in the multi-pane window, then used pressure to punch out a hole. Anna made a brief report to the two cops, who seemed more interested in Pak's coffee and Pop-Tarts. Larry Staberg brought his jigsaw and a piece of plywood over, cut out a shape to fill the small broken windowpane, and nailed it in place.

"Pretty much good as new," he said, as his wife rolled her eyes at Anna.

"Good until I get it fixed," Anna said. "Thanks, everyone."

As the party broke up, Logan said to someone else, as he walked away from Anna, "When I heard him firing, it sounded like a twenty-two, but the holes in my garage are bigger than that, maybe thirty-eights . . ." When she heard "twenty-two," a small bell dinged in the back of Anna's mind, but she forgot about it on the way upstairs. She wouldn't sleep much during the rest of the night, but as much as she turned the whole episode over in her head, she never put the .22 used by the dark man together with the .22 used on Jason.

Not then.

six

Late afternoon.

The day felt like it had gone on forever. Anna was a night person. A full day in the sun left her feeling burned, dried out, and the midday traffic magnified the feeling. At night, Los Angeles traffic was manageable. If she had to drive during the day all the time, she'd move to Oregon. Or Nevada. Or anywhere else. In the small red Corolla, half a car length ahead of a cannibalistic Chevy Suburban, walled in by a daredevil in a brown UPS truck, she felt like she was trapped in a clamshell, and she was the clam.

After the excitement of the prowler, she'd tried to go back to bed; not because she was sleepy, but because she felt she ought to. She never got up until noon, at the earliest.

But she hadn't been able to sleep. She'd gone to bed too early, under the influence of the booze, and the chase had gotten her cranked up.

So after lying awake for an hour, she got up, showered, went downstairs, ate breakfast—and got sleepy. She fought it for a while, and finally, at eight o'clock, crashed on the couch. When she got up, three hours later, she felt like her mouth was full of fungus. Off to a cranky start: and trying to figure out the funeral made her even more cranky.

Since the case involved murder, and was believed to involve drugs, the medical examiner wanted to get tissue tests back before releasing the body for cremation. She should call back, she was told, every day or two.

For how long?

"Well, you know . . . whatever it takes," the clerk said.

The cops had no similar problems with Jason's apartment. They had taken out two cardboard cartons of paper, and that was it. A sleepy Inglewood police sergeant, a fax from the Odums in his hand, gave her the keys.

"We're all done with it," he said.

"Are you really working hard on this?"

He yawned and rubbed his eyes, causing her to yawn in sympathy. "Yeah, yeah," he said. "We are, but it's basically a Santa Monica case. Nothing happened down here."

She borrowed the cop's phone to call Wyatt, at Santa Monica, and as she waited for the transfer, frowned at the fax from the Odums. They had a fax? Did everybody have a fax?

"Yeah, Wyatt . . ."

"I'm down in Inglewood. Are you doing anything up there?"

Wyatt talked for a couple of minutes, and Anna decided that he wasn't doing much.

"There's nothing to go on," Wyatt said. "Nobody saw anything, nobody heard anything—we had a guy out on the pier all last night, talking to the fishermen, and he came up with exactly zero. We don't have anything back from the lab yet, so we're not even sure that's where he was killed. And the most likely motive involves the worst anonymous ratshit dopers in the whole goddamn country. So I don't know what more to do. Keep talking to his friends. Like your pal, Creek.''

"Creek's okay," Anna said.

"He did time for dope," Wyatt said. "He was dealing big-time, is the word."

"He was smuggling, not dealing. And he quit cold. He hasn't had anything stronger than Jack Daniel's since he got out." She could hear him yawn, and it irritated her: "Maybe you need a nap," she suggested.

Wyatt ignored the sarcasm. "Yeah, I could. And Pam backs you up on Creek, by the way. She went out to talk to him."

"Pam? Your partner?"

"Yeah." Anna half-smiled, and even on the phone, Wyatt picked up the vibration.

"Why? He's a Romeo or something?"

"Not exactly. He does have an effect on . . . a certain kind of woman."

"What kind?"

"The anal, blazer-wearing, Hermès-scarf owning, power-sunglasses type, with no kids."

"Huh. Like you."

Anna almost started, then grinned into the phone: she'd deserved it. Wyatt continued, "Pam's got a collection of Hermès, but no kids."

"Big surprise," Anna said. "Good-bye."

"Hey, wait . . ."

He wanted to talk more about Pamela Glass; Anna wasn't in the mood.

• • •

From the Inglewood police station, Anna headed over to Jason's apartment. The apartment was a neat, four-building complex surrounded by an eight-foot chain-link fence. She took the car through a narrow access gate, which a sign said would be locked at midnight; the sign had been over-painted with gang graffiti. She glanced at her watch: already three o'clock. She had to move. Creek and Louis would be at her house in two hours, ready to roll.

She left the car in a guest parking slot, and headed into the complex. A dozen people sat in lawn chairs around a swimming pool, drinking beer, talking in the fading sunlight. Old Paul Simon tinkled from a boom box, "Still Crazy After All These Years."

Get it over.

Jason's apartment was routine California stucco, tan, concrete steps going up to external walkways, rust stains running down from roof-edge gutters. The weather had been dry, but the walkways smelled like rain. Green, red, yellow and blue doors alternated down the walkways, an uninterested attempt at decor. Anna looked at the keys—237—found the door, a red one, looked around, waiting for somebody to object. Nobody did; she was alone on the walk. She had a little trouble with the key, finally got it to go and pushed inside.

Smelled carpet cleaner. He hadn't been here long.

The apartment was nearly dark, the only illumination coming through the open door and a back window. The room she was in, the front room, was littered with empty pizza cartons, comic books, Big Gulp plastic cups. A *Playboy* and a *Penthouse* lay in the middle of the carpet. The cops had dumped everything, and left the litter where they dumped it. She left the door open, groped for the light switch, found it, flicked it. Nothing happened. Lights out.

"Jeez," she said. Her voice didn't quite fill the room, and she paused, and thought, *What?* She stepped back and looked out along the walkway, heard voices, a woman's, then the deeper rumbling from a man.

Coming up the stairs. Still worried about being taken for an intruder, she pushed the door shut, stood for a moment in the gloom, waiting for her eyes to adjust. There'd be a circuit breaker somewhere, she thought. Probably in a closet or back in the kitchen.

The apartment was almost *too* quiet: like the ghost of Jason had muted all the little normal sounds, the creeping subliminal pitter-patter of cockroaches, warping of wood, flaking of paint. She pushed the feeling away and headed toward the small kitchen nook: *Find the light.*

He got her as she stepped into the kitchen.

He was off to the right, next to a small dinette table.

Anna was looking the other way, sensed him a fraction of a second before he was on her, started to turn, started to say something, to cry out . . .

He threw a large hand over her mouth, wrapped a heavy arm around her chest, tripped her with a sweeping leg, and they lurched back into the living room and hit the floor, Anna on the bottom. The impact took her breath away for a second, and she thrashed frantically, trying to get an arm loose, trying to get her feet working, trying to kick, but he was very strong, very professional: he'd done this before.

The arm around her chest tightened and he pulled her head back and said, close by her ear, "If you scream, I'll punch your lights out. If you stop kicking I'll let you breathe. C'mon . . ." They thrashed for another moment, but he'd wrapped a leg around her legs and she felt as though she were fighting an anaconda.

And he said, "C'mon, goddammit, I don't want to hurt you, I just want you to shut up. If you'll shut up, nod."

Exhausted, sweating, scared, she relaxed, involuntarily,

and nodded and he said, "I swear to God, if you scream, I'm gonna bust you in the mouth."

And he took his hand away from her mouth.

She drew a breath to scream, reconsidered: "Let me go," she said, trying to look at him. She started thrashing again, trying to turn, but he held her. All she could see was his chin.

"We're gonna go like this over to the couch, and I'm gonna sit you down. I'll be right in front of you and if you yell I'll hit you. I want to be clear about that."

"All right, all right." Not hurt yet.

"Here we go." He rolled, and pried one arm around behind her, caught her fingers in a hold, and she thought, *Cop,* and said, aloud, "That hurts."

"Not much," he said. "Not yet, but it will if you put a move on me."

"Are you a cop? You sound like a cop."

"No." He'd released her legs, got his knees under himself, and slowly pushed up to his feet, pulling Anna along, past a cable reel that Jason was using as a coffee table. Then he pushed her and twirled her at the same time, she found herself staggering uncontrollably backward, until the couch hit her calves and she fell back onto it. He was right there, his face obscured in the gloom, a fist an inch from her chest.

"What's your name?" he asked.

"Let me out of here."

"What's your fuckin' name?"

"Fuck you." He didn't seem frightening, somehow. "Let me out of here."

"In a minute. Gimme your arms."

"What?"

"Gimme . . ." He grabbed one hand, and she tried to jerk free, but he put a hand on her forehead and said, "Sit still, goddammit."

"What do you want?"

"Needle tracks."

What? She stopped fighting, and a penlight clicked on. He turned her arm wrist up, and played the beam down her forearm.

"Other arm."

She turned her other arm up, and he looked it over, then shined the light into her eyes, dazzling her.

"What's your name?" he asked again.

"Fuck you. Who are you? What the hell are you doing here?"

"You oughta watch your mouth," he said. "And it's none of your business. You sit right there. If you start to get up . . ."

"Yeah, I know, you'll beat me up."

He sounded embarrassed: "Yeah."

He was groping around on the floor, keeping his eyes on her, but not until he moved back to her did she see that he'd picked up her purse. He popped it open and dumped it on the wire-reel table, shined the penlight on it and stirred through it.

Anna's purse was small, and there wasn't much: a billfold, a comb, a lipstick, a roll of Clorets, a handful of change, a couple of ripped-in-half movie tickets. He opened the billfold and looked at her driver's license. She still couldn't see his face, and the light, held chest high, made it more difficult.

"Anna Batory," he said. He looked up from the license. "You were with the TV crew."

She wasn't going to be raped, she decided; probably not beaten up. The guy had a hard force about him, but not the hyped energy that produced an attack. And he knew about her: "Yeah, I'm with a video crew."

"You shot the video on Jacob Harper."

"Who?" Now she was confused.

"Jacob Harper—the kid who tried to fly off the Shamrock."

"Oh. Yeah, we were there." What did the jumper have to do with Jason's apartment?

"Where'd Jason O'Brien get his dope?"

"I don't know . . ."

"C'mon, he worked for you, you've got a key to his apartment."

"He didn't work for me; he was a part-time guy, like once a month. And the cops gave me the key."

"The cops." After a moment's silence, he asked, "Why would they do that?"

"Because nobody wants his body. I'm supposed to take care of funeral arrangements and there's nothing more here that the cops want."

"Huh." He stood up, looked around in the gloom and said, "Damn it."

"You hurt me," Anna said. She was getting a feel for him. He hadn't wanted to hurt her. "You could have broken my arm."

"Ah, shut up," he said. "You're not hurt and we both know it." Then: "Your boyfriend's a doper."

"What?"

"This guy Creek."

"He's not my boyfriend, he's my partner. He hasn't done any dope for ten years."

"Bullshit. He's got no job, he lives in a nice apartment at the Marina and he's got a yacht."

"No job? I'll tell you what, pal, we're out there two hundred and fifty nights a year . . ."

"Yeah, some Tinkertoy fuckin' movie wannabees with cameras, for Christ's sake."

Now she was getting hot: "Yeah? We grossed better than three hundred and fifty thousand last year. Me'n Creek and

Louis took home better than ninety apiece, after expenses. How much'd you make?''

"That much? Ninety?" Surprise.

"Yeah." She would have sulked, if she thought she could have afforded to. But she had to stay on top of him.

Another moment of silence, then he was moving away from her. Over his shoulder he said, "Fuckin' L.A., you goddamn people are a bunch of ghouls, you know that? Making a buck off of snuff films.''

She kept her mouth shut: she was about to get out of this, and didn't want to argue. A step or two later, he added, "Don't scream after me. It'd just piss me off and I'd have to run and I'm probably gonna come back and see you again.''

Anna was on her feet: "About what?"

"I need to know about O'Brien. I'm not done with him yet, and you're the only connection I've got.''

"Listen, if you think Jason had anything to do with the jumper, you're wrong.''

"No. You're wrong," he said. He hesitated, then said, "I came down on you a little hard, when we went to the floor. You oughta take a couple ibuprofen. Hot bath, or something. You could have pulled something.''

"You're so thoughtful.''

"I bit my lip when we hit.''

"Well, that's just too bad." She couldn't believe the gall: he seemed to be looking for sympathy. She crossed her arms over her chest.

"Well, it stings like hell," he said. Then he was out the door, slamming it behind him. As he went through, she got a better look at him in the late afternoon: an impression of sandy-brown hair, very white teeth. Probably blue eyes, she thought. Athletic, but not stripped down to muscle and bone: maybe a few extra pounds, in fact. Big shoulders. And gone.

She went to the door after him, thought about screaming, jerked the door open and stepped outside . . . and saw the top of his head disappearing down the stairwell. Opened her mouth, shut it again. She was safe enough, unhurt and still alone—maybe she *didn't* want to piss him off.

The circuit-breaker box was in the kitchen, the door open. She threw the switch and two lights came up. She went back through the living room, shut the door, and then took out the cell phone, found Wyatt's card in the pile of purse litter and dialed him. A clerk answered the phone, and she asked that Wyatt be called at home and that he call her back; he called back two minutes later.

"What?" he asked without preamble, when Anna picked up the phone.

"I just got to Jason's apartment and there was somebody here. He jumped me."

"You hurt?" He sounded cautious, nervous. Why?

"No, he just tripped me and held me down and then he pushed me on the couch and then he left. I thought he might be a cop, but he said he wasn't."

"White guy?" The odd tone still in his voice.

"Yeah . . . Hey, you know him?"

"Probably another doper." But he was lying; and he wasn't good at it. "As long as you're not hurt . . ."

"The door was locked and he was inside. How'd he do that?"

"He's probably a friend of O'Brien," Wyatt said. "Look, do you want a car to come around? I can call Inglewood."

She thought about it for a moment. "No, I guess not. I mean, unless you wanted to look for fingerprints. You know, detect something."

Wyatt sighed and said, "We got thirty sets of fingerprints

out of the ShotShop, and we could probably get thirty more.''

Anna said, ''Tell me the truth about something. You know, instead of lying.''

''Sure.''

''Do you think Jason might be connected to the jumper we filmed?''

Wyatt hesitated before he answered, and Anna read it: ''You do!'' she said. ''So'd the guy here. Tell me why.''

''Look, Miss—Anna—goddammit, you're not a police officer, okay? Just clean up the apartment, pack up his stuff and get out of there.''

''Maybe you better call Inglewood,'' she said. ''I better file a complaint: the guy was trying to rape me.''

Silence.

''Okay, I'll do the call,'' Anna said. ''I know where his prints are, too. They're all over my purse and billfold. I'll mention to the Inglewood cops that you might have some idea about who it is.''

''Jesus, you're a hardass. You're just like Pam, bustin' my balls all day, now I gotta deal with you. I'm tired of it.''

''Life sucks and then you die,'' Anna said.

More silence. Then: ''The kid who jumped off the building was tripping on wizards.''

''I don't know that brand,'' Anna said, breaking in.

''Acid and speed. Maybe a lick of PCP.''

''Okay. Like rattlers.''

''Rattlers were last year,'' he said. ''But yeah—like that. A little heavier on the acid. Anyway, he popped a couple and decided the ledge was a runway and that he could fly.''

''So . . .''

''So the wizards are little pink extruded dots on strips of wax paper.''

''I've seen them,'' Anna said.

"When you buy them, the dealer just rips off however many dots you can pay for," Wyatt explained. "So the kid had a strip of dots in his jacket pocket. When we rolled your friend over, so did he; what was left of them, anyway, coming out of the water."

"Huh. That's weird."

"*That's* not weird," Wyatt said. "That's just a coincidence: these fuckin' wizards are all over the place. But I get this wild idea, and put the two strips together, and guess what? The two papers matched up. Your friend's strip had been ripped off the jumper's."

"What?"

"Yeah. Now *that's* weird."

Anna made a quick connection: "So how'd the guy here know about it?"

Wyatt sighed again, and said, "Look, you seem like an okay . . . person. Huh?"

"Yeah, I'm an okay person." *Okay* meant that a cop could trust her—*person* expressed a belief that she was some kind of wacko feminist to be doing what she was doing, and he didn't want to argue about it.

"He's an ex-cop," Wyatt said. "He's a decent guy."

"He's a jerk, he scared my brains out," Anna said, angry at Wyatt's defense. "What'd he want?"

"He's interested in the case," Wyatt said.

"Interested? Is that all it takes?"

Wyatt cut her off: "His name is Jake Harper," he said. "The jumper was Jacob Harper, Junior. His son. His only kid."

"Ah." What had Harper said? *Ghouls making a buck off of snuff films?*

She let it go. *I'm okay,* she thought, when Wyatt hung up.

• • •

Jason's apartment was a sad clutter of heavily used clothing, cheap film gear, books on directing and movie-making, portfolio tapes, cans of Campbell's soup: all the hopes a kid might have in Hollywood, California. Bundled up and sent back to Peru, Indiana, it wouldn't mean a thing.

Anna did a quick survey, separating the potentially salable stuff from the useless, stacked the salable stuff, and then found the apartment rental office and talked to the sleepy manager.

"... not worth much, but we'll be taking it out in the next few days. Until then, it's under police seal," Anna said. "They still need to process some fingerprints, so if you could keep your eye on the place, we'd all appreciate it."

"If it ain't too torn up, he's got some deposit money coming back," the manager said.

"Nice of you to mention it," Anna said.

The manager was a chunky square-faced Iranian with a black beard and an accent that combined Detroit and Esfahan: "Ain't my building. And the owner's an asshole. Why should he get the kid's cash?"

"Right on, brother," Anna said.

seven

A long bad day, and still not over.

On the way home, Anna stopped at a traffic light on Santa Monica, and her eyes drifted to a Mobil station on the corner.

A man was washing the windshield on a Volvo station wagon, at a self-serve pump. He was wearing jeans and a loose, wide-sleeved white cotton shirt, like might be advertised in *The New Yorker*—Sea Island cotton, like that.

The instant she saw him—his hair thinner, maybe lighter, maybe speckled with white, a few pounds heavier, but the way his hands connected to his body, something almost indefinable—the very instant she saw him, she thought:

Clark.

She slid down in her seat, but couldn't tear her eyes from him. He finished with the squeegee, turned and deftly flipped the squeegee stick back toward a water can hung on the side of the gas pump. The sponge end of the stick hit and slipped perfectly through the hole in the water can: exactly as she'd seen him do it fifty times before.

"Oh my God," she said aloud.

A car behind her honked, and her eyes snapped up to the

rearview mirror, then down to the traffic light. Green. She automatically sent the car through the intersection, then pulled over and turned.

The Volvo was still there, but Clark had gone inside. A moment later, he came back out, slipping his wallet into his pocket, climbed in the car, turned on the lights, eased into the cross street, then zipped across Santa Monica and headed the other way.

She thought about following him.

Thought too long, and he was gone.

Clark.

She drove home on autopilot, random thoughts, images and memories scrambling over each other like rats. She stuck the car in the narrow garage, slipped sideways past the front fender into the house and, without turning on the lights, went to the phone.

She had messages waiting on the answering service: she ignored them, and dialed Cheryl Burns in Eugene, Oregon. She mumbled the number to herself as she poked it into the handset, praying that Cheryl would be in her shop. She was: she answered on the first ring. "Hello, Pacifica Pottery . . ."

"Cheryl? This is Anna."

"Anna!" Pleasure at the other end. They got together every year or so, when Cheryl and her husband brought a load of their wood-fired pots from Oregon down to the L.A. basin. In between visits, they talked on the phone, once every two or three months. Anna and Cheryl shared one of the close connections that time and distance didn't seem to affect. "How are you? How is everything?"

"Sort of messy right now," Anna said, thinking about Clark. "A guy I work with . . . was murdered."

"Not Creek!"

"No. A guy named Jason, he was a college kid we used

part-time, you don't know him." Awkward segue: "Listen, what do you hear from Clark?"

There was an empty heartbeat there, then an almost masculine chuckle: "Uh-oh. Are you seeing him again?"

"Not seeing him, but I just saw him," Anna said. "At a gas station. He's here in L.A. I saw him on Santa Monica."

"I know. He called and asked for your phone number, last month sometime. I didn't give it to him."

"He called! Why didn't you tell me?"

"Because you messed each other up so bad the first two times. I didn't want the responsibility."

"Cheryl," Anna said, pushing hair up her forehead in exasperation, "I can take care of myself."

"No, you can't." In her mind's eye, Anna could see her shaking her head. "Not with Clark . . ."

"Damn it, Cheryl . . ."

". . . But I saved his L.A. address and phone number in case you called and wanted it," Cheryl said, with a teasing tone. "I had the feeling you might hook up. Cosmic vibrations, I guess."

A little jolt, there. Pleasure? "What's he doing here?"

"He's got an artist-in-residence gig with UCLA. Composition. Two years, he said, so . . . he'll be around." Another dead space, then Cheryl again. "Well? You want his number?"

"I don't know."

"I better go get it . . . then you can tell me about the murder."

Cheryl read Clark's phone number; Anna noted it, doodled around it as they talked. At six-thirty, still chatting, Anna casually picked up the TV remote, aimed it at the set in the corner, hit the power and mute buttons and flicked through the channels.

At CNN, the Harper kid was flying off the ledge, followed by ten seconds of talking head, then a shot of the pig taking out the Rat. They'd picked the Keystone Kops version.

"Cheryl, have you seen the TV news thing about the guy who jumped off the ledge here in L.A.?"

"Well, sure, everybody's seen it. You can't get away from it." Then, excitedly, "Was that you guys?"

"Yeah. It's getting around. Have you seen the animal rights thing, at the medical center?"

"Oh, the guy with the pig. Cracked me up. Was that you, too?"

"About two minutes apart, story to story. And you're getting them way up there in Oregon?"

"Hey, it's not like we're in Tibet . . ."

As they talked, the Blue Shirt kid came up—Anna had forgotten his name—but he'd been interviewed again, probably the day after the animal rights fight. The interviewer was not familiar. The kid was wearing a lab coat, had a fat lip, and a couple of grinning professor-types hung in the background of the interview. Louis had made him into the hero of the piece, and that had influenced the stations who'd picked it up: and it was still building.

What was his name? Like the mountain, right? Not Everest. McKinley. Charles McKinley. He was playing the role just right, Anna thought, watching the muted TV as Cheryl chattered in her ear, a sort of charming, little-boy bashfulness.

Anna and Cheryl were still on the phone when Creek arrived, doing his shave-and-a-haircut knock. Anna walked out to the end of the phone cord to let him in, said, "Cheryl," to him, and he called out, "Hi, Cheryl," and stuck his head in the refrigerator.

"Cheryl says she wants your body," Anna said, as he emerged with a bottle of Leinenkugel Light.

"She can have it, as long as she gives it a good cleaning once in a while," Creek said. As Anna repeated his answer, Creek popped the top on the beer and wandered down the hall. A moment later, Anna heard him tinkling on the piano.

When she got off the phone, she ripped Clark's number off the scratch pad where she'd written it, looked at it for a moment, then folded it in two and stuck it under a magnet on the refrigerator.

Clark. She got a Coke from the refrigerator and sat on the piano bench with Creek, facing away from the piano. Creek smelled pleasantly of sun-sweat and turpentine.

"You're early," she said.

"Thought you might want to talk, running around after Jason like that." He was chording his way through a fake-book rendition of "Autumn Leaves."

"Yeah." She'd told him that morning about the prowler, now she told him about the man in the apartment.

"Maybe I ought to look him up," Creek growled, when she finished.

"I don't think so," she said, reaching over to pat his back. His back felt like a boulder. "He's got connections with the cops and the cops are talking drugs. You better stay low."

"I don't want him fuckin' with you," Creek said.

"I don't think he will," Anna said. "I talked to Wyatt about him—I was scared, and called Wyatt, and he knew who he was . . . Oh, and Wyatt told me that his partner was over to interview you."

"Yeah, I . . . guess."

She felt the sudden evasiveness in his voice: "Look at me, Creek," she said.

He shook his head. "I ain't looking at you."

"Oh my God, you jumped her," Anna said, half-amused, half-horrified.

"Did not. Jump her," Creek said. "And that's a nasty phrase anyway. High school." He segued to a couple of bars of "Ain't Misbehavin'." "But she is a *tasty* little thing."

"Pretty hard edges for a cheesecake," Anna said. Creek's adventures with women sometimes grew complex.

"Hey, you know, nobody really appreciates what a woman cop goes through every day," Creek said tartly. "Especially one with some decent looks."

"Just how much of her did you look at?"

"None of your business."

"Ah. And would I be right to suspect that this somehow leads to your getting the cabin painted on the boat? You smell like paint."

"She wants to learn to race and she's gonna help me with the maintenance," Creek said defensively. "So shut up."

"Help like Teri did."

Creek shuddered: "I asked you never to mention that name."

"Sorry."

"Now I have to find a priest," Creek said. "To cleanse me."

She smiled now. "Sorry again."

"Easy to be sorry," Creek said. "You don't have to live with the pain."

Anna snickered and Creek laughed and went to the "Jelly Roll Blues," running down the chords.

And after a little while, Anna said, "Clark is in town."

The music stopped. Creek turned to her, suddenly pale, as though the tan had run out of his face, like blood. "Aw, shit," he said.

• • •

They left Anna's at nine-thirty, the long, brutal day dragging on. Creek was brooding, silent. Anna was annoyed by the silence, the annoyance layered atop her already general grumpiness. She'd wanted to talk about Clark, but Creek didn't want to hear it. "That's *too* personal," he said. "I can't tell you what to do and I don't want to think about it. Go find a girlfriend to talk to."

Louis was waiting outside his apartment, standing on the curb in his white shirt and plaid jacket, carrying the laptop. He'd updated the address database with GPS numbers, and claimed that with his new GPS receiver he should be able to put them within a few feet of their actual position, anywhere in L.A. County, southern Ventura or Santa Barbara.

"What's happening with Jason?" he asked, as he ducked his head and climbed aboard.

"I'm trying to figure out a funeral," Anna said, as he sat down. Creek pulled away from the curb and Louis brought up the electronics. Anna asked, "What's going on?"

Louis started monitoring the cops from his apartment, an hour or so before they went out. He had a scanner on an old trunk at the foot of his bed, and Creek claimed to have seen him adjust the volume dial with his toes, without opening his eyes. "Nothing really heavy, but something's going on with the hookers up on Sunset," he said, twiddling a dial. "Hard to tell what's going on, but I think it might make a movie."

"Boys or girls?" Anna asked.

"Girls. There was a call about ten minutes ago. The cops hit a club up there, cocaine thing, and I guess dumped a bunch of girls out on the street, lined them up, and a fight started. Somebody said it looked like a riot . . ."

"Everybody'll be there," Creek said. He sounded as grumpy as Anna felt.

"I don't think so," Louis said, not yet catching the crankiness in the front seat. "There hasn't been much on the air. You sorta had to be following it."

"So let's go," Anna said.

The riot was a bust.

A few cop cars still lingered, a few girls strolled along the street, mostly looking at reflections in the store windows. There was the familiar air of trouble immediately past, but no action—like arriving ten minutes after a thunderstorm, with nothing but puddles to show for the violence.

They headed toward the valley, Anna thinking about cruising Ventura. Louis got some movement on the radio, but it was small stuff, and too far south. By the time they'd arrive, there wouldn't be anything to see, or other crews would already be working it.

"Wish the bitches had been doing something," Louis said. "Would've made the night simple."

"Don't call them that," Anna snapped.

"Why not?" Louis asked. "That's what . . ."

"Shut the fuck up, Louis," Anna said.

"Ooo, what's your problem?" He was smiling, trying for a bantering attitude, but he didn't understand.

"Best be quiet, Louis," Creek said, and Louis shut up. A minute later, Anna, now in a sulk, said, "Sorry, Louis. You can talk now."

"Is there a problem I don't know about?" he asked tentatively.

"Yeah, but it's mine," Anna said.

"Fatburger coming up," Creek said. Creek knew every Fatburger in L.A. County.

"Stop, I need some caffeine," Anna said. "Louis?"

"Diet Coke."

"Fatburger and a Coke," Creek said.

•   •   •

Anna got the food, waited, paid, carried it out to the parking lot. Two valley guys, in their late teens or early twenties, both with buzz cuts, three-day-artist-hangout stubble and black jackets, were leaning against the hood of a beat-up Buick, and one of them said, "Hey, mama."

Anna put the Fatburger sack and three cups of coffee on the hood of the truck and turned back to them: "Hey, mama, what? Huh? What?"

One of the guys straightened up and said, "Hey, mama, what'cha doing tonight?"

"I'll tell you what I'm doing. I'm working instead of leaning my lazy fat ass on a piece-of-shit junker outside a Fatburger."

"Hey. . . ." The second guy pushed away from the Buick. Then Creek got out of the driver's side of the truck and the second guy leaned back against the Buick again, while the first one hitched up his jeans. Creek said, "Anna, get in the truck."

"This guy wanted to talk to me," Anna said.

"Anna!" Creek wasn't taking bullshit. "Get in the fuckin' truck."

Anna, still fuming, picked up the food and got in the truck and Creek said, "Sorry, guys." Back in the truck, as they pulled out, Creek said, "What was that all about, huh? You want to get in a fight outside a Fatburger and spend some more time talking to cops? Huh?"

"Bad day."

"Bad day, my ass," Creek said. "Take your fuckin' bad day someplace else."

"Jesus, you guys, go easy," Louis said, nervous. Creek and Anna didn't fight.

"Yeah, yeah, gimme a Fatburger," Creek snarled.

They rode in silence until Anna's cell phone rang.

"Anna Batory?" Male voice. Familiar. *Heavy stress,* she thought.

"Yeah."

"This is the guy you met in O'Brien's apartment this afternoon."

"Yeah, Harper," Anna said. "What do you want—where'd you get this number?"

He ignored the use of his name and the demand for an explanation of the number. "I need to see you," he said. "Like *right now*. Actually, I need you to come to where I am."

"Why should I?"

"Because it has something to do with you," Harper said. "I gotta call the cops pretty soon, but I need you over here first."

"What has to do with me?"

"Look, you might be in serious trouble. If you want to know about it before the cops come banging on your door, come see me now. Otherwise . . . and hey, you might even make a few bucks."

She thought for a second, then said, "I'm bringing a friend."

"It'll cause them trouble," Harper said.

"I'm not gonna be alone with you. Not after you jumped me, like that, you . . . abuser."

Creek looked at her oddly, and Harper, after a second, said, "Whatever you want to do."

Harper was waiting under a streetlight on Cumpston, a couple of blocks south of Burbank Boulevard, a neighborhood of stucco ranch homes. The yard behind him was bordered with an evergreen hedge, long untrimmed, and pierced by a picket gate that had curls of white paint peeling off.

Creek got out with Anna.

"I understand you had a problem with Anna," Creek said, and Anna suddenly realized that she might have a problem with the two men.

Harper had turned toward Creek with a small crouching movement that suggested he'd just set his feet; and he wasn't backing up.

He was good-looking in a mildly beat-up way, Anna thought, a big man with broad shoulders, big hands, a nose that had been broken a couple of times. He carried a heavy tan, with sun-touched hair, like a beach bum, but he was too old for that: late thirties, she thought. He wore an expensive black sport coat, silk, she thought, over a pair of jeans.

And way down in the lizard part of her brain, something went, "Hmm . . ."

Creek was gliding sideways and Harper was pivoting to cover him, and Anna said, "I swear to God, the first one of you guys who throws a punch, I'll kick him in the balls."

Creek stopped moving and Harper relaxed, spread his hands. He glanced quickly at Anna but spoke to Creek: "If you had the same problem, you would've done the same thing, pal."

Creek stared for another moment, then nodded abruptly: "So what do you want?"

"I want you to come in here," he said. He tipped his head back toward the house. "But don't touch anything."

"Whadda we got?" Creek asked, interested now.

"We got a dead dope dealer," Harper said.

Anna stopped: "Have you called the cops?"

"No. I will, soon as you've gone through."

"The cops could put you in jail for not calling in right away," Anna said.

"Yeah, maybe, but I've got bigger problems than that. Come on. Maybe you want to bring a camera?"

He said it in a cheap way, and Anna said, "Shove it."

While Louis waited with the radios, Harper led them up the walk. The door was just ajar, a light on inside, and Harper took a ballpoint pen out of his pocket and pushed the door open with the butt end of it. "Don't touch the door, don't touch anything."

"Was the door open when you got here?"

"Yeah, and the light was on," he said as they stepped across the threshold. "As soon as I got in, I knew . . ."

"Aw, jeez," Anna said. The smell hit her, and she flinched away from it. Old blood and human waste, mixed up and curdling.

"Flies," Harper said absently, tilting his head back. Anna looked up, saw hundreds of bluebottle flies clustering around the light. "Back here."

He led the way to a bedroom with mustard-colored walls and *Rolling Stone* covers thumbtacked to the walls. But the main attraction was a man who, at first glance, looked like a grotesque German Expressionist painting, muscles and blood exposed, everything gone black. He'd been handcuffed to the bed, his feet tied with ripped sheets. He was nude except for a pair of briefs, face up, and gagged. He'd been cut to pieces with a knife.

And not quickly, Anna thought. The face looked as though the skin had been peeled off. A halo of blood surrounded the head, as if it had been violently shaken back and forth. So he'd been alive for the peeling . . .

"Christ, what is this, what're we here for?" Creek asked. "We've seen this shit . . ."

"Yeah, so've I," Harper said. He looked at Anna. "You know him?"

"Even if I did, I'm not sure I'd recognize him," she said. "But I don't think so."

"Name is Sean MacAllister," Harper said. "Been busted

three times on minor drug stuff, once with O'Brien in the car . . ."

Anna was nodding: "Jesus, we do know him. Sean, oh my God . . ."

Harper was going on: ". . . The bust never got to trial because there was some problem with the stop. O'Brien lived here for a couple of weeks, between apartments."

"I don't know—we never picked up Jason here. Are you sure that's him?" As she said it, she had to turn away.

"Pretty sure," Harper said. "His billfold was still in his pocket."

"So what do you want from us? Why don't you just call the cops?" Creek asked.

"I wanted you to look at this," Harper said. He was standing next to the bed, and he pointed to the man's bare chest. A knife rip crossed it from armpit to armpit.

"What?" Anna asked.

"Read it," Harper said.

"Read it?"

She and Creek edged closer. She couldn't see it, but Creek could: he looked at her suddenly and she said again, "What?"

"Says 'Anna,' " Creek said, almost to himself.

And then she saw it: her name in carved flesh. "My God." She stood in shock for a moment, then turned to Harper: "Why?"

"I don't know." He was watching her closely. "He was a small-time dealer, that's about all I know."

"Your son's dealer?"

"I don't know. I hope not. I tracked him through your pal O'Brien." He looked around the room. "All I found was a little grass. Nothing else."

"No dots," Anna said, and he nodded. She looked at the

grotesquerie again, the muscle mass that had once been human, the *Anna,* and she turned away from the bed, suddenly felt as though a hand had been clapped over her mouth, suffocating her: "I gotta get out of here."

eight

Harper and Creek followed her outside, and Anna held her head over the picket fence and gagged. Nothing came up but a stream of saliva. After a moment, she turned back to the two men: "Sorry."

"So you didn't know the guy," Harper said, a statement, not a question.

"Not except to nod to. I never met Jason's friends, except on the job."

Harper was looking at her skeptically, and Anna said, "Look, Jason was a part-timer. He worked maybe once or twice a month, when he came up with something."

"Dope stuff?"

"No. Usually UCLA stuff. The night your son died, that was the last time we saw him. He had the inside track on a college animal rights group that raided the medical labs at UCLA . . ."

"I saw it on TV, the pig thing," Harper said. "How'd that connect with my kid?"

Creek said, "It didn't. The raid was college kids, and your son was at a high-school party. The only connection was that they were a few blocks apart about the same time, and we happened to catch them both."

Harper rubbed his chin, looking at Creek: "You're sure?"

"Work it out yourself."

Harper looked away, into the middle distance, then back, and nodded. "All right. But my kid's dead, your friend's dead, they shared a dealer, and now a dealer's dead—and Anna's name is carved on his chest. *Something*'s going on."

"Did you see any of those dot things in there—the wizards?" Anna asked.

"How'd you know about the wizards?" Harper asked sharply.

"Wyatt told me. He told me about you so I wouldn't report that I was mugged."

"Okay." He looked at his shoes. "Sorry about the thing at the apartment. I didn't know who it was, I was in there illegally, sort of. Not a good place to be caught messing with an apartment . . ."

"So how'd you track this guy down?" Anna asked, looking at the house.

"Got Wyatt to check Jason on the computer, found the arrest, got MacAllister's name, checked with the phone company and got an address. No problem."

"You keep stepping into shit like this, it's gonna be a problem," Creek said. "Leave it to the cops."

"I can't." Harper shook his head: "I've got a slightly different agenda than the cops."

"What? Revenge?" Anna asked.

"Nah," Harper said. He looked back at the house, as Anna had. "But I'd like a little justice."

"Leave it to the cops," Creek said again.

"You don't get justice from cops," Harper said. "You get

procedure. Sometimes you get arrests. Occasionally you get convictions. You never get justice."

"So what do we do here?" Creek asked.

Anna took out her phone. "Make a call."

They called Wyatt at home, hoping for a charitable referral to the local Burbank cops.

"What?" Wyatt grumbled into the mouthpiece. His voice was thickened by sleep.

Anna identified herself and told him about the man on the bed.

"Stay out of the house, don't touch anything," Wyatt said. He was awake now, and unhappy. "I'm gonna call L.A."

"I think we're in Burbank," she said.

"All right, I'll call Burbank. You wait."

"We're in the street right outside the house," Anna said, glancing at Harper. "It's a little complicated. I'd better let you talk to your friend Jake."

"Jake? What's he doing there?" Wyatt asked, even more unhappy.

"I'll let him tell you," Anna said, and she handed the phone to Harper.

Louis stuck his head out of the truck: "We've got a fire in Hollywood Hills, the girlfriend of somebody big, the way the fire guys are talking."

"Forget it," Anna said, cutting him off. "We've got problems."

The first cop car arrived five minutes after Harper got off the phone: not Burbank, but North Hollywood. Burbank was two blocks away. The cops talked to Harper, briefly, a little chilly, and started the murder routine: cops around the house, neighbors on lawns, yellow crime scene tape, medical examiners, L.A. homicide detectives and, eventually, Wyatt. He nodded wordlessly as he passed them, flashed a badge at a cop outside the door and went in. Five minutes later, he was back out.

"What a mess," he said.

"Yeah," Anna said. "And we had a prowler at my house this morning. He had a gun . . ."

"I hope you called someone," Wyatt said.

"I live in Venice. The neighbors chased him off, the cops came over and had a Coke."

"Might not be you," Wyatt said. "I mean, on the guy's chest."

She got a quick mental flash of the body, and felt herself tighten up: whoever had done that was far gone. But she wouldn't fool herself, either: "C'mon, how many Annas do you know?"

Wyatt said, "All right. I don't want to scare you any more than you are, but—remember the cuts on O'Brien's face? I thought they looked like gang marks?"

"Yes?"

"They were like this, remember?" He made a quick slashing triangle design on the palm of his hand with the opposite index finger.

"Triangles," Anna said.

"Or A's," Wyatt said quietly. "Upside-down A's."

"Oh, no." She put her hands to her cheeks. "Can't be A's."

"Could be," Wyatt said. "We gotta have a serious talk with the L.A. guys."

"Are they upset?" She looked toward the house. "About us going inside?"

Wyatt glanced toward Harper: "Not as much as you might think."

"Wasn't her fault anyway," Harper said, stepping into the conversation. "She didn't know what she was gonna see. I took her in. I thought she might say something—might know the guy."

"Did she?"

Harper glanced at her, then suddenly grinned, the first time she'd seen him smile. *Nice smile,* she thought. "No. She went outside and barfed."

"Did not," Anna said.

Creek, looking past them, said apprehensively, "Uh-oh, here we go."

An L.A. detective was headed their way, the languid, dangerous stroll affected by cops when they were being cool. He was carrying a rolled pamphlet. He glanced at Anna, nodded at Creek and said to Harper, "How are you, Jake?"

A movie line: one that should have been followed by a cigarette flicked into the street. Harper shrugged: "You heard about my kid."

"Yeah. Brutal." The detective looked back at the house, and then said, "Listen, I know this is a really horseshit time to ask you this, but I got a problem . . . I gotta come see you. About Lucy."

"Gonna do it this time?"

"I gotta. She's crazier than a shithouse mouse. If I don't get out of there . . . but I can't leave the kids."

"Call me," Harper said.

"I'm hurtin' for cash . . ." The cop was embarrassed.

"We'll put it on your Sears card," Harper said. He poked the cop in the ribs, and the cop nodded and said, "I'll call you—thanks." He nodded at Anna, glanced at Wyatt and strolled away.

"What was all that about?" Anna asked Wyatt.

"Jake's a lawyer," Wyatt said. "He has about half the cop business in the county."

"I thought you said he was a cop."

"*Was.* Ten years ago."

• • •

The lead detective's name was Carrol Trippen, a tall, impatient, prematurely white-haired Anglo. He split them up, talked to each of them for a moment, compared their stories and finally sent them downtown to make statements.

"Are we in trouble? Should I get a lawyer?" Anna asked, as Trippen started back toward the house.

"Harper pisses me off, calling you guys," Trippen said sourly. "But it wasn't your fault, and I know where he's coming from. I got bigger things to worry about than hassling people who looked at a dead guy."

The cops kept Anna, Harper, Creek and Louis apart until the statements were done. Anna was interviewed by a sleepy cop with bad breath and a yellow shirt with a new coffee stain.

When they finished, he peered at her over his coffee cup and said, "Tell you what: You know this guy. The killer."

"If it's me." She'd been having second thoughts.

"C'mon. Even *you* think it's you."

"So what do I do?"

"First thing is, with this prowler you had, I'd move out of your house. Stay at a motel for a few days, don't tell anybody where you are. When you've got to work, meet your friends somewhere. You got a cellular, anybody can get in touch if they need to."

"I'll think about it," Anna said, but she wouldn't leave her house.

"Do that. And I need you back this afternoon, if you can make it—we got a shrink and a serial killer profiler, they're gonna want to talk to you."

"You're sure he did both Jason and Sean?"

"Trippen talked to Wyatt, and they think so. He says there's a level of violence there. You don't see it in the

"So...you going to show me around?"

Sophie stared at Cade. "Why?"

"So I can figure out what kind of shots you could use."

"Look, I don't want anything from you. I am no one's charity case." She wanted to say more but thought a retreat was smarter. "Besides, I hear my guys coming in, and I have a lot of work to do. Today's not a good day. You should go."

With one hand on her jumpy stomach and the other in a fist, she rapidly made her way out of the room.

It was a full hour before she realized that Cade hadn't left. Instead he'd somehow acquired a pair of work gloves and was busy cleaning out underbrush.

With his shirt off.

Dear Reader,

Ever since the last of the five Deep in the Heart books was published in 2004, I've been hearing from many of you who fell in love with the Montalvo/MacAllister clan and wanted me to write Cade's and Jenna's stories. It wasn't that I didn't want to, but Jenna was too young and Cade was too mysterious. He was still a mystery when I started this book, but I'm happy to report that I fell hard for him, too, though I thought my heart belonged to Diego (okay, and Jesse and Zane and Vince and...). Actually, I think that, just like Sophie in this book, what I really fell in love with was this wonderful, loving family.

This April, in the second book of this trilogy, you'll again encounter J. D. Cameron, the playboy detective from *Most Wanted* (Jesse and Delilah's book), and then in June, Jenna will, at last, get her own story.

It's always lovely to hear from you. You can reach me via my website, www.jeanbrashear.com, or through Harlequin's website, www.Harlequin.com.

Very best wishes,

Jean Brashear

ABOUT THE AUTHOR

Three RITA® Award nominations, an *RT Book Reviews* Series Storyteller of the Year award and numerous other awards have all been huge thrills for Jean, but hearing from readers is a special joy. She would not lay claim to being a true gardener, but her houseplants are thriving. She does play guitar, though, knows exactly how it feels to have the man you love craft a beautiful piece of furniture with his own hands...and has a special fondness for the scent of wood shavings.

Jean loves to hear from readers, via email at her website, www.jeanbrashear.com, via Harlequin's website, www.Harlequin.com, or by postal mail at P.O. Box 3000 #79, Georgetown, TX 78627-3000.

Books by Jean Brashear

HARLEQUIN SUPERROMANCE

SIGNATURE SELECT SAGA

Other titles by this author available in ebook format

For all the lovely readers who kept asking me where Cade's story was...better late than never, right? And, as always, to Ercel, my own white knight

Acknowledgments

Many thanks to Amber Pearce for chatting about the lives of the thirtysomethings in Austin.
Thanks also to everyone at Rachel and Co., especially Emily Clear and Beth Ontiveros for her genius suggestion about Cade's unattainable trip.
Thanks also to the wonderful staff at Koy Animal Clinic, especially Ted Koy, who's cared so well for years' worth of our pets, and Christina Knape, who helped me figure out what Finn—er, Skeeter's injury was.

PROLOGUE

CADE MACALLISTER STOOD braced on the rock ledge right beneath the summit of the Andean peak. He knew the perfect shot would come once the cloud bank drifted a little more. The way the wind had suddenly gusted, it wouldn't be long.

He leaned out, camera still tight against his eye, his core muscles locked, his weight balanced on a razor's edge. Pebbles showered down the steep grade, and he shifted quickly to regain his equilibrium.

He was cold and tired and hungry.

But he was happy as hell.

It was shots like this that had made his career soar, the ones that required guts, steel nerves and a keen eye that saw beyond the expected to capture images that transported the viewer into the unimagined.

"Cade."

"Yeah?" he said, never looking away from the view-finder.

"I've got to climb to the east or my shadow will fall on your shot in a minute."

"Thanks, man." His friend and guide, Jaime, was the best for many reasons, but his ability to understand the needs of the shot was what made him indispensible. They'd first worked together nearly ten years ago, and

Cade relied not only on Jaime's climbing skills—which exceeded Cade's own quite competent ones—but his ability to be present, always waiting to help without spoiling the mood Cade was caught in. Jaime understood Cade and his passion as few ever had.

If Jaime weren't happily married and a father of three, Cade would never accept an assignment without him. But a life of constant travel, while perfectly suited to Cade, wasn't for everyone, and definitely not for a man with a family.

"I've played out the rope a little," Jaime said quietly. "Brace yourself, and I'll be done in two minutes."

He nodded, but Cade didn't—couldn't—let go of the camera or take his eye off the scene. He was close, so close.... He braced his legs. "Go," he said to Jaime, only focused on the small rectangle of the viewfinder. *Now...now...*

There. He had it. One, two, four more shots in rapid succession, though he knew in his gut the first one was perfect—

Abruptly the wind roared, whipped him around, jerked him off balance.

The mountain rained stones down on him.

"Jaime—" But he knew what was happening—above him, Jaime must also be scrambling for balance. If he couldn't hold on and hadn't properly secured himself when he moved, he could fall—and take Cade with him.

By instinct, Cade shoved his camera inside his jacket even as he grappled for a handhold. He didn't need anyone to tell him the situation was bad. "Jaime!" His eyes teared against the bitter wind, and he blinked furiously, trying to make out his friend.

A muffled shout to his left. The thunder of rattling stones roaring louder and louder…then Cade watched in horror as Jaime tumbled like a slow-motion puppet, out of his reach. Cade stretched toward him, too late, too late—

Cade cursed as a savage gust knocked him off his feet, yet he fought to cross the distance even as Jaime vanished over the edge. "No!" he screamed as his world turned on end.

Pain exploded in his head.

Then…nothing.

A HAND LAY QUIETLY ON his arm. Voices murmured. Machines beeped.

Cade struggled upward through the thick tar of darkness. Cold trapped him, no light, no…

"Look," a deep male voice said. "Did he just frown?"

Where was he? Who… "Uh…"

A gasp. "Sweetheart? Cade? Talk to us." The hand stroked his skin. "You're fine, honey. Just open your eyes."

His lids were so heavy… His body weighted by concrete…

"Son, you're safe. You've been hurt, but you'll be okay." The man's voice was familiar in his bones, but worry crackled beneath the words.

He turned his head toward the voices until needle-sharp pain seized him.

"Don't move, sweetheart. You're all right. Just

don't... Please lie still." The woman again, only now he could see her in his mind's eye, the face of love.

"M..." His throat was dust-dry. He tried again. "Mom?" he croaked.

A cheer rose, several voices. "Yes, oh, sweetheart, yes—" His mother's voice was thick with tears. "You're in a hospital. You've been hurt, but you're going to be all right." Determination laced through her fear, and he tried to remember, but his thoughts darted away like silvery minnows.

"Rest easy, son," said the man he realized was his father. A large hand on his shoulder, squeezing. "We've sent for the doctor to tell him you're awake at last." Gruff with emotion, his father's voice pulled Cade through the unrelenting agony that threatened to suck him back down.

Cade forced his eyes open, blinked once...twice... Figures swam in and out of focus. Other men—his brothers, he realized, Zane, Diego and Jesse—and the fierce angel face of his sister, Jenna, crowded around the bed.

"What...happened?"

His mother put a straw to his lips, and the cool grace of water slid down his parched throat.

Then he realized that both his always-composed mother and his dad, the bulwark of a whole family, were crying.

"How bad is it?"

His mother's lips pressed into a tight line, and his father's eyes spoke of worry. "You'll be fine. You had a climbing accident, but you're going to make it, I swear. Thank God you've come back to us."

But in that way of souls who've skimmed the edge of death, Cade knew it had been close.

And he wasn't done yet.

"Tired…" He couldn't keep his eyes from closing. Then he stirred. "Jaime—"

Oh, God. Grasping…searching…losing…failure. His fingers flexed weakly at the memory of watching his friend fall. "I have to…"

"Sleep, son," his dad ordered. "We're here. We won't leave you." Strong, reassuring fingers squeezed his shoulder.

Cade gave up the struggle and let sleep take him.

CHAPTER ONE

Davis Mountains, West Texas
Seven months later

CADE SLOUCHED IN A ROCKING chair on the porch of his brother's log cabin as the sun crawled its way below the horizon. Beside him, Diego's old dog, Lobo, shifted and groaned.

"I don't know which of us is more pathetic, fella. You at least have old age to blame." Cade's head sank back against the rocker, and he pushed it into motion with an impatient shove of his heel. *A rocking chair,* he thought in disgust, fingers drumming. *I'm thirty-nine years old, and I've been in this spot for two hours.* He wanted to run, but he could barely walk. Wanted to race halfway across the world...but had no reason to leave and nowhere to go.

Even if anyone in his family would let him move an inch without hovering.

"Cade, honey?" called his mother from inside. "Do you need something?" Grace MacAllister appeared at the screen door.

Cade glanced up at the woman who never seemed to age. At sixty-six, Grace's hair was still more blond than silver, her back straight, her figure slender. At six foot four, he towered over her—as did all her four sons and her husband—but pure steel ran through her spine.

He adored her. They all did. She was their queen, gracious and every inch the lady, strong and loving and cherished.

But if she didn't stop treating him like an invalid… His hand clenched on the rocker's arm.

"I'm fine, Mom."

She meant well, he reminded himself. He hadn't come home often as an adult, not because he didn't miss and love his family—he did. But he'd needed solitude since he was small, and he was accustomed to that life now. He'd spent the past twenty years as an adventure photographer, roaming the globe with a camera in his hand, never settling, never resting. He'd been a wanderer since he'd first learned to walk, to the dismay of his parents. He'd always needed to see what was over there. Whatever *there* meant at the time.

But nearly dying in the Andes had a way of changing things.

And watching his friend and guide die…

He still hadn't figured out how to handle that.

So when his mother placed a hand on his forehead, testing him for fever as she had when he was little, Cade forced himself not to tense. Instead, he clasped her hand and squeezed it in his. "Thanks, Mom. You've taken good care of me."

Grace was no fool, however, and her smile was wry when she responded. "You're restless." Not a question; she knew him well. "Itchy for a camera in your hands?"

God, no. He couldn't even look at his cameras,

hadn't been able to touch one without seeing his friend's broken body. He couldn't speak to anyone of the panic that kept him awake at night, how his fingers shook when he simply picked up a camera, knowing that his obsession with the perfect shot, the one that required risk and nerves to obtain, had cost a good man his life. He'd lain there on the mountain after he'd crawled toward Jaime, waiting for death to take him, too, and somewhere during that endless night he'd lost his eye for the story behind the frame, the gift of making an image tell far more than a thousand words.

Even if he recovered fully from the injuries he'd suffered in the fall, the one thing that had made his life matter was gone. He'd lost the thirst that had driven his life.

Besides, what did his career matter in the face of three children left fatherless?

But he couldn't tell his mother any of that. "Soon," he said instead, mustering a smile for her even as he saw worry shimmer in her eyes.

She, in turn, stroked his hair as if he were still small, then bent and pressed a kiss to his forehead. "It'll get better," she murmured. "Just be patient. You'll be back on the road before you know it."

He wished he still had that small boy's faith in his mother's reassurance. He'd like to believe that he'd have another spread in *National Geographic* or *Smithsonian* soon.

But something essential inside him remained broken after his bones had healed, and he didn't know what to do or where to go. Solitude had always been his refuge, yet right now he couldn't stand being with himself. He was dodging his agent's calls because he had no idea how he was supposed to organize the photo collection his publisher had paid him a sizable advance on.

It'll get better. He hoped with all his heart his mother was right.

He could never settle for taking average photos, and if he wasn't able to spend his life wandering the planet and documenting nature's beauty and heartache for those not free to roam, what on earth would he do? He was nothing without a camera in his hands and frame after frame blooming in his mind.

Cade shoved to his feet and started down the steps. He'd taken to sneaking out at night and walking to build up the strength his family didn't want him to tax yet. Sitting still only made him crazier.

"Hal," called his mother to Cade's dad. "Come walk with Cade."

"No." Cade turned. "I'm going alone, Mom."

"Honey, I only…" She pressed her lips together and nodded just as his father came through the door. She placed a hand on his dad's arm to restrain him. "All right, just…be careful, sweetheart."

Cade looked from one concerned parent to the other. They'd never understood his need to be alone, but they'd been supportive all these years, despite the many important family occasions he'd missed.

He owed them better than this.

But he was going out of his freaking mind. "I won't go far, I promise," he said, trying not to feel he was five.

"You go ahead, son," boomed the man who'd first

put a camera in his hand and given him a way to relate to the world. "We'll be here when you return."

They would be, he knew. They always had been. Emotion crowded his throat when he nodded back. "Thank you."

He wasn't good with words, only with photographs. He'd spent years attempting to show his parents what they meant to him by giving them the gift of places they'd never travel to because they were so rooted in home. And now…

Cade made his way slowly down the slope to the cabin he'd moved to last week, one Diego kept for family and friends to use on visits.

And with every step he tried not to think about how something inside of him had gone still and cold after that fall, and how empty his life would be if his gift never came back.

Austin, Texas

SOPHIE CARLISLE COLLAPSED on the widow's walk of the house where she'd just spent fourteen hours refinishing the wood floors. She was so tired she wasn't even hungry, yet morning—and still another long day—would come all too soon and she needed her strength.

Despite four months of backbreaking work, the remodeling to make the wreckage of an old mansion into Hotel Serenity was behind schedule; she was out of money and the bank was withholding funds.

And she had guests booked to arrive in only four weeks.

But she'd picked herself up and beaten the odds before, hadn't she?

With this unique jewel of a hotel, she'd found the courage to dream again, to try again…to start over for the third time in her life. She'd lost much in her thirty-six years—parents, husband, child, then the career and reputation she'd spent fifteen years building.

She was not going to lose this dream. Hotel Serenity would open on time, and it would sparkle. Those who believed her washed-up after the scandal would be put on notice. Sophie Carlisle would not be defeated. Not by loneliness, not by her unscrupulous rival Kurt Barnstone, not by disgrace staining a spotless career. Not by anything.

Besides wanting—needing—to prove herself, she also owed a debt. Maura Halloran had spotted promise in her when Sophie was first starting out as a night clerk at the hotel Maura managed. Maura had brought Sophie along with her as she rose in the corporate structure, grooming Sophie to one day succeed her.

More importantly, Maura had been, at times, the closest thing to a mother Sophie had.

When Sophie's career had been cut short by the scandal, one of the worst parts had been Maura's disappointment in her for resigning instead of fighting the charges. But Maura didn't know everything—and Sophie couldn't tell her without breaking her heart.

Despite Maura's dismay, when Sophie had bought this place, the older woman had insisted on investing a huge chunk of her life savings in the venture. Savings that Sophie would flush down the toilet if she failed.

Sophie owed Maura more than she'd ever be able to repay—on so many levels. She had to do this one thing right for the woman who meant so much to her. She had to open, and on time.

"You missed yoga," said a familiar voice from behind her. "And I need to ask you a favor— Whoa!" Her dear friend Jenna MacAllister appeared through the attic window. "You look terrible."

"Thanks."

"No, I mean worse than usual. You can't keep this up, Soph. This place is going to kill you." Earnest blue eyes shone from a gamine face surrounded by strawberry blond hair. "I'm going to call my brother Jesse and brother-in-law Vince to help. Both of them have done lots of renovation work on their own homes, and they could bring some of their cop buddies."

"No!" She was horrified. "I mean, that's a lovely offer, but this is my problem, and I'll handle it."

"Look, I get that you're a private person and very independent. I understand that the hotel is your baby, but don't be silly. I can round up some help, and face it—you need it."

"I'll be fine." Sophie had had to depend on herself for a long time. Jenna, with her warm and loving family and fairy-tale childhood, couldn't possibly understand. Sophie had been orphaned at fifteen and been a runaway from foster care. Then she'd lost her second chance at family. But she'd adapted. On her own.

"But that's just it," Jenna protested. "You don't have to. You have me, and I'm going to help you. That's what friends do."

"Jen, no. I really appreciate the offer, but I'm the one who decided to gamble on being ready for September and advertised to all those Texas Longhorns season ticket holders and Austin City Limits Festival goers. I could have opened slowly and let the clientele build." But she so badly wanted to prove herself, to show those who'd written her off just what she was worth. To make Maura proud of her again.

She noted the stubborn set of Jenna's chin, and she knew enough about Jenna to understand that her friend wouldn't rest until she could do something. "Okay, how about this? Do you have anyone working on your affordable housing project who wants extra work? I can't pay a lot, but…"

Jenna headed a local East Austin nonprofit focusing on inner-city issues, and she had a network anyone would envy. "Actually, I know several people who need work."

"Great. Send them to me, and I'll be forever grateful—but leave your family alone. Promise me? I'm not comfortable taking charity."

"It's not charity, it's friendship," Jenna insisted. "But okay. I get it, even if I don't like it. I promise you I will have someone here to help with the work tomorrow, but there's a condition. Take the night off, you hear me? You're exhausted, and you can't open this hotel if you're in the hospital."

If she didn't open on time, the hotel's reputation—and hers—would never recover. Her dream would die stillborn. "I'll be fine." She rose and hugged her friend. "Thanks, Jenna, truly."

Jenna hugged her back but lingered. "Sophie, I, uh…" Jenna's reticence was completely unlike her.

"You okay?"

"I'm fine, but…"

"Something's worrying you."

Jenna looked as serious as Sophie had ever seen her. "It's Cade."

The famous photographer brother who'd nearly died in a fall. "I thought he was doing a lot better."

"Physically, yes. Not completely recovered, but improving every day." Jenna worried at her lower lip then glanced up. "Did you ever find the photographs you wanted for the rooms?"

"Not yet." Sophie's shoulders sagged at the reminder of another looming failure. She'd had this vision for the artwork on the walls that would be unique—unusual photographs that would function as windows onto another world, images that were not strictly realistic but would capture the viewer's imagination without destroying the sense of peace Sophie wanted the entire hotel to exude.

But she hadn't found anything suitable, and she was running out of time to keep looking. "I'm beginning to believe the types of images that are in my head don't exist." She worried her lower lip. "But I just don't want something…ordinary." Then she connected the dots, and her mouth dropped open. "You can't think… Jenna, Cade's work is way out of my price range. His photos are hanging in museums."

"Normally I'd say you're right, though that wouldn't stop me from nagging him into helping you out, but nothing's normal right now. I need your help. He needs your help."

"How can that possibly be?"

"From my earliest memories, Cade always had a camera in his hand or nearby. It's more than a career for him, it's his life. It's how he communicates with the world." Her eyes filled. "He hasn't even picked one up since the accident. He doesn't talk about it—not that he ever talks about anything—but something's wrong, and we're all so worried about him. My folks won't push the issue—they're afraid he'll just take off one of these days because he's not used to being idle, but it's too soon for him to resume his career." She glanced at Sophie. "Maybe he can't go climbing mountains or hiking the wilderness yet, but that doesn't mean he couldn't have a project. Why not you?"

"You can't be serious."

"Wouldn't it be great, though?" Jenna clapped her hands. "A win-win for both of you."

Sophie didn't know Cade except from Jenna's stories, but the picture she painted was of a man who wouldn't appreciate meddling. "Of course it would be great. I mean, his work is incredible. But there's no way I can afford him." Yet even as she denied the possibility, the mere notion sent her imagination soaring.

"I'll take care of his prices, don't you worry. Anyway, there's a bonus in it for him—a place to stay where no one will hover over him."

Sophie grinned. "*You* won't hover…right?" Jenna was a force of nature, and woe betide anyone who got between her and whatever notion she was set on.

"Well, not much, anyway. Less than my mom. So what do you think? You get amazing art and Cade has a project, with the bonus that he can come stay with me. He'll fall down on his knees in gratitude to me for springing him. He's got cabin fever, bad."

Sophie wondered if Jenna's brother would truly be so grateful. Regardless, she had to nip this notion in the bud. "I know you want to help me out, but I refuse to take a handout."

"It's not about you, though," Jenna said, and seemed serious. "I mean, yes, I want to help you, too, but I'm more worried about Cade. You can't tell him, of course—he's snarly and unbearable now, though he'd be a lot worse if he thought he was being coerced. But I just *know* that a change of scenery and work that's not too taxing will help him, without sending him back up a mountain. None of us are ready to see him do that, so you'd be doing all of us a favor. He has millions of images in his files, and if he doesn't have anything that would work for you, maybe this would at least get him taking photographs again."

"Jenna, he can't possibly like that you are promising his work to strangers." She shook her head. "And I'm uncomfortable with it myself."

"But wouldn't it be fantastic?"

Fantastic was an understatement. She'd seen Cade's work, knew he had a real gift.

"Look," Jenna continued, "if he doesn't want to do it, you're no worse off than now, right?"

"Maybe I could work out a payment plan...."

"I said don't worry about his prices."

Jenna was such an optimist. Sophie loved her for that. "You know you're insane, right? This will never work." Jenna opened her mouth to speak, but Sophie charged ahead. "But if by some miracle you can pull this off, I'll take you up on it. Cade MacAllister photographs in my hotel? Do I look stupid enough to turn down that possibility?" Already her head was whirling with images she'd seen and ideas of what she could do with this bonanza.

"You most certainly do not." Jenna all but skipped over to hug her. "Yes! I'm going to call him now." She was already punching numbers into her phone as she left.

Sophie watched her go. She meant what she'd said. She wouldn't count on Jenna succeeding, but...wow. To be able to advertise that she had *Cade MacAllister* photos in each room? A venture like hers, catering to the elite, thrived only if it was different. Unique. Offering what couldn't be found elsewhere. Cade's pictures would give her a distinct edge.

But as she headed for the carriage house where she did most of her furniture restoration, she spared a few seconds to pity the brother who'd survived a near-fatal fall only to be run over by his sister the steamroller.

Then she tucked away that far-out notion. Jenna's idea would never work, and Sophie couldn't spare the time to worry about it—she had too many more pressing items to worry over. She had artwork she could use, even if it wasn't ideal, and in a month she would open— had to open. She'd called in chips all over the industry and had rooms already booked into November.

The cell phone in her back pocket rang. This late at night, it could only be one person. She glanced at her display and nearly didn't answer. Her worries were too close to the surface.

In the end she relented. "Hello, Maura."

"Hi, doll," said the older woman. "Why aren't you out on a hot date?" A throaty chuckle. "I know, I know… You're working, probably too hard."

"Isn't that a bit of the pot calling the kettle black? Tell me you're not sitting at your desk right now."

Maura snickered. "You know me too well. But I'm sick of looking at these piles of paper on my desk. Talk to me about your day."

Well, my blisters have blisters and I'm behind schedule and I'm scared half to death that I'm going to fail. "Nothing very exciting, I'm afraid. Oh! Wait—" This was honestly good news. "Remember that Mission bureau I found in Santa Monica?"

"Vaguely." Maura had spotted it first but would never admit it.

"Fraud. You let me have it, Maura." *Just as you've done a thousand other kind things for me.*

"Don't let that get around. Bad for my reputation. So what about it?"

As Sophie talked about the antique, she lost herself in their shared love of restoring old furniture to gleaming new life, a pleasure which Sophie had learned from Maura. They discussed staining versus oiling wood, how to choose among varying grits of sandpaper and the merits of sanding by hand. For a few precious moments she let herself pretend she wasn't scared half to death of letting this woman down.

"Okay," Maura said at last. "You've erased my day's aggravations. I'm shutting down my computer. Promise me you're not going to keep working, that you'll get a good night's sleep. It will all be there for you in the morning, you know, Sophie."

Sophie didn't want to lie to her, but hesitated too long.

"You're not reassuring me, kiddo. Do you have all the help you need? I could take some time off and come down there."

"No!" Sophie fought to keep the panic from her voice. "I'm fine, Maura, I promise. Of course I'd love to see you, but I'd rather surprise you with the final result." She bit her lip. "And it's not like it's easy for you to get away."

"It was when you were around." A pause. "Sophie..." Next, Sophie knew, would come yet another plea to return, to fight for her job.

"This is what I want, Maura." That much was true— at least it was now that she'd accepted her new reality. "And yes, I'm working hard, but when did you ever see me lounging around?"

"Never, but still, you shouldn't be overdoing it."

"Again, pot, meet kettle."

"All right, all right," Maura grumbled good-naturedly. "Good night, sweetie."

"Good night, Maura. And thanks."

"For what?"

"For believing in me." When no one else had.

"Easiest thing I ever did, kiddo. You'll call if you need me?"

"I'm doing fine, Maura." She wouldn't make promises she couldn't keep. Maura had done too much for her already. She'd do whatever it took to protect the woman from hurt. "Bye now."

After Maura disconnected, Sophie stood in the darkness for a long time.

She was scared, yes, but she could still make this dream live, and she would, just as she'd beaten so many other odds. She hadn't bet her heart in a very long time, but the die was cast now. She could still lose big, and she knew there were some who were betting against her, most notably her former-lover-turned-foe Kurt, who'd set her up for a fall and been extremely clever in his deceptions.

But if she went down, it wouldn't be without the fight of her life.

One more piece of furniture tonight, then a sandwich, a very long hot shower and five hours' sleep.

Then she'd be up with the sun to start all over again.

CHAPTER TWO

CADE WATCHED THE YOUNGEST MacAllister brother, Zane, as he landed the plane at the private airport in Georgetown, north of Austin. He'd wanted to drive himself—alone—from West Texas to Austin, even though the trip was long and exhausting, but in the end, it had been easier just to go along with this plan. No commercial flights for him, though, not with a movie-star brother who'd learned to fly his own jet and loved showing off.

"Amazing," Cade drawled. "This from the skinny kid with the Coke-bottle glasses."

"Up yours," *People* magazine's *Sexiest Man Alive* for the second time shot back. "I grew up. No thanks to you, I might add. How many times you figure you pounded my butt into the dirt?"

Cade grinned. "Not as many as I should have. You needed toughening up." They both knew that the only person the family felt more protective of than Jenna was the youngest brother who was now the world's heart-throb. All Zane's brothers had conspired to keep that skinny little geek safe until he eventually, if quite late, reached the height and muscle of the others.

But brothers seldom use genteel means to protect one another. Making sure the little kid whose nose was always in a book learned to fight had been Cade's way of showing the love he'd never had the words to express.

"Yeah, well, I can take you now," Zane said, then winced as he remembered Cade's current physical state. "Sorry."

"Not you, too." Cade glared back at him as they descended from the plane to see his artist brother Jesse waiting for them. "He and Jenna better not hover," he muttered.

"You know Jesse," Zane responded. "He'll be cool. Jenna, though..." He snorted. "Good luck on that, bro."

Cade asked himself yet again why he'd said yes to Jenna. And yet the more appropriate question might be who in the world had *ever* managed to say no to that small package of dynamite every one of her brothers would die to protect.

Though she'd hardly thank them and was more likely to spit in their eyes for suggesting she was not perfectly capable of managing her life on her own. She was a frightening mix of cute and sweet and charming all mingled up with enough moxie and guts to take on the world bare-handed.

Which was one of the main reasons he'd accepted her invitation to come stay with her for a while. Her latest cause, housing for the disadvantaged, had her spending most of her time in the worst areas of Austin.

Cade would have the perfect vantage point, living right there with her, to make sure she wasn't being reckless. Plus, it wasn't as if he had anything better to do. Even if he had the sneaking suspicion that Jenna, too, had a hidden agenda. She generally did.

Just then they reached Jesse. "Hey, bro," said Zane. "Glad you're taking over guard duty on The Silent One." He shot Cade a glance filled with mischief.

Jesse gave Cade a quick one-armed guy hug, then caught Zane in a headlock. When Zane socked him in the ribs, Jesse merely sidestepped while exchanging grins with Cade. "Sure thing, little brother. Better me than you."

Cade couldn't agree more. Jesse understood his need for solitude in a way no other family member could. Cade was trusting his brother to respect his privacy.

"Amen to that," Zane said. "Now let's go devil our little sister." He tried to take Cade's duffel from him, but Cade stubbornly refused to yield, though the weight of his cameras was sizable and he was still getting back to full strength. He'd wanted to leave them behind, but that would have attracted more of his family's attention when he needed less.

He couldn't talk about any of it, not how he woke up sweating in the night, how he couldn't forget the image of his friend's body, crumpled and bloody, how the gift that had defined him had vanished and he didn't know who the hell he was without it.

It would come back. It had to. In the meantime he needed to occupy his mind with *anything* else. "Anybody know what Jenna's got up her sleeve?"

His brothers glanced over and both shrugged. "No idea," said Jesse.

"Me, either," responded Zane. "But sure as shooting, there's something."

Jesse grunted acknowledgment as they made their

way to his car. "On second thought, maybe you'd better hang around," he said to Zane.

"Not happening, dude. I'm sure you two can handle her." Zane snorted rudely then started laughing.

Even Cade found himself smiling.

"WANT A BEER, CADE?" Jenna called from the kitchen the next night.

"Sounds great." He rubbed his hair with a towel then slung it around his neck. "So who's coming to this party and why do I have to be here for it?"

Jenna rolled her eyes. "You don't have to act like you're being sent to the slammer. It's just some of my friends from work and stuff." She frowned and pointed at his belly. "That's an old scar. Not from the fall."

"Nope. I was shooting tigers in Kenya. Crossed paths with a cub whose mama didn't think much of that idea."

"You never told us."

He shrugged. "I don't like to worry Mom and Dad."

Her eyes rose to meet his. "We worry, anyway. It's hard never knowing where you really are or if you're safe." She popped the cap off the beer and handed it to him. "Are you itching to get out there again?"

"I'm not finished with physical therapy," he said, dodging. He took a sip. "But I couldn't stay with the folks anymore. I love them, but…"

"I understand, and they do, too. You need something to do to make the time pass. I can put you to work."

"Doing what? Swinging a hammer on your housing project?" That actually sounded good, and it wasn't as though he'd never done manual labor. His dad was a firm believer in everybody pitching in and kids not being idle. By the time he'd left home after high school, he'd performed every job available on a cattle ranch, everything from riding herd to construction to dosing cattle.

"I could definitely use you, though Diego would kill me if you tore anything loose, but I had another idea."

Cade grinned. "Zane owes Jesse and me steak dinners. We knew you had something up your sleeve."

Jenna sniffed and set her pageboy-cut hair swinging. "That's a rude thing to say."

"But…?" He chuckled. "Come on, Jen, this is me, your big brother."

"I have entirely too many big brothers."

"Tough break. So what's your game plan?"

"Well, I have this friend…"

"You have about a zillion, always have."

"Sophie's special."

"Oh, crap, you're not trying to fix me up, are you? Jen…"

"You should be so lucky." She glared at him. "For your information, I'm asking for your *help,* not matchmaking."

"Not that you wouldn't try."

She stuck out her tongue at him. "This is serious. She's in a bit of a bind and I want you to sell Sophie some of your photographs."

"I can do that."

"Cheap."

He cocked his head. "And I would want to…why?"

"Because you love me?"

"Maybe not that much." He grinned. "How cheap?"

"Very. Though…since you're not doing anything… I was actually thinking maybe you could take new photographs just for her."

His chest felt tight at the thought of picking up a camera. "Not happening."

"Look, this could be good for you, too. You're not ready to go back on the road, but you're tired of sitting around. Your skills are wasted swinging a hammer. Sophie's such a nice person and she's had a hard life and she's in a real spot and I want to help her but she won't let me and she's about to kill herself doing too much of the work but she has this great idea for the decor and I know you could—"

"Whoa, kid. Take a breath."

The doorbell rang. "Drat. Well, we'll discuss this later. Go put your shirt on." Jenna raced from the kitchen, leaving Cade staring after her.

His little sister had always been a sucker for a sob story. From the time she learned to walk, she'd been trying to fix things for other people. Her heart was as big as North America, but her common sense left much to be desired.

And now this Sophie chick had played the sympathy card, and Jenna was donating his hard work—forget new shots, which he was not taking for anyone—for peanuts. It wasn't that he couldn't afford to do so or wouldn't for a good cause, but he knew better than to trust Jenna's judgment. His little sister always had a scheme and had absolutely no qualms about dragging her family into her latest enthusiasm.

If this Sophie was on tonight's guest list, he'd scope her out, see what her game was.

Nobody was going to take advantage of his little sister.

SOPHIE SLIPPED THE EARRING with its delicate fall of citrine drops through her earlobe and reached to close the antique jewelry box she'd found abandoned in a corner of the attic.

As she lowered the lid, the cheap locket tucked into a corner of the box caught her eye, and for a moment, her hand lingered on the carved gold trinket.

She brushed her fingers over the surface before prying open the clasp. Inside she traced the features of the lost boy who'd loved her and the child she'd buried with him.

So young. So long ago. In the sixteen years since, she'd made a life utterly unlike anything she and Kenny had dreamed of. There was little left of the runaway girl who'd been so scared when she'd met him. So alone.

Luck had dropped Kenny in her path, a boy with countless strikes against him and precious few reasons to hope.

But in spite of everything, they'd loved and they'd hoped, anyway, two babies having a baby. They'd lived in what others might call squalor, but the efficiency apartment had felt like a castle to her back then, the close-knit, loving little family they'd built exactly what she'd longed for ever since her parents had drowned.

Then she lost everything again, this time to a careless driver who stole the people she loved and left her with nothing but a pile of twisted metal.

Sophie stared sadly at the images of the dark-haired boy and the grinning baby. With a quiet click she closed the locket's clasp, then the box. The past should stay where it belonged, locked away. She was not that girl anymore, would never be again. Home and family were not her future.

Instead she'd create a place of peace for others, a temporary home, a refuge.

So she went down the stairs and headed off to meet Jenna's brother, who would probably never agree to Jenna's crazy plan. He'd likely turn up his nose and consider Sophie's hotel a lousy venue for the art of a world-renowned photographer, but Sophie wasn't going to let his fame intimidate her.

If Cade balked, fine. She'd survived far worse.

JUST AS CADE WAS ABOUT to join Jenna's party, the cell phone in his pocket vibrated. Grateful for the escape, he answered without looking first. "MacAllister."

"Cade," a very familiar voice said. "It's Karen."

His agent. Whom he'd been dodging.

"Hey."

"How are you?"

"Coming along," he said more lightly than he felt.

"I'm glad." She hesitated, and he knew what was coming next. "How's the book?"

"Fine."

She wouldn't settle for that, but she was too blasted perceptive for him to offer some flimsy excuse. "Any idea when you can finish? The first deadline is long past—not that everyone doesn't understand, of course."

She didn't have to remind him he'd been paid a princely advance on a book the publishing house had already put a lot of support behind. It was supposed to be a collection of his favorites, aptly billed *Eyes on the World*. Preorders were sizable, even in this day of declining coffee-table book sales.

"I'm working on it, Karen." Or at least he'd tried. But he couldn't look at his portfolio without thinking of what it had cost. Every glimpse into his files only made him want to throw something against the wall.

"That's good." Even if she suspected otherwise, she had always been quietly encouraging. "They have another idea they want to run past you."

"What is it?"

"They want to change the focus of the book, frame it as a view through the eyes of someone who nearly died for his work."

"What the hell does that mean?"

"They were thinking it would be a journey through your life, beginning with your first efforts, leading up to your accident and ending with what it feels like to look back on your career and measure it in terms of what you nearly lost."

"Bullshit. I'm not baring my soul in print. It's no one's damn business."

"But it's a tremendous marketing angle. Sort of like Sebastian Junger's work, only better because you're not just writing about someone else who nearly died, you're relating firsthand experiences. They'll give you a ghost-writer if you want one."

What Cade wanted was to crush the phone in his hands. "No."

"Don't say no yet. They'll make it worth your while."

"Not possible."

"Cade, you're under contract. You've missed a deadline. If they decide you've reneged on the contract terms, they could make you pay the advance back, and it's a sizable chunk of change."

"I don't care. Tell them to go to hell." He was not reliving the last several months or using his friend's death to make more money, not for anything. "They have no right."

"Not to your story, maybe, but to what you promised them when you signed the contract? Absolutely."

"Then I'll pay them back."

"And then what? They've been financing your expeditions for ten years now. You torpedo your relationship with the publisher and your career will be over."

I can't do the work. And I'm nothing without it.

"Just think it over, Cade. Not while you're mad, but later." She hesitated. "I'll need your answer within two weeks. I can hold them off that long, but no longer."

How could two weeks, hell, two years make any difference? He'd been physically well enough to work on the original concept for a while now, but that wasn't the problem.

Maybe if he believed the shots he'd have to weed through wouldn't turn out to be the last good ones he'd ever take, or if he didn't have to stumble over memory after memory of Jaime… "I gotta go, Karen," he said.

"Cade…"

"Not now. I'm…I'm sorry."

"You can call me anytime to talk," she responded. "You know that. I care about you, Cade, and not just as your agent."

He ended the call as politely as he could, only too aware that she'd been a friend as much as a business partner and that she deserved better than for him to behave so unprofessionally. He'd never done anything like this before.

Then again he'd never been trapped in a cage of his own fear before. He'd been in countless hairy situations all over the world and never blinked an eye. But he'd never nearly died before, either, or been haunted by the death of someone whose only crime was being a friend to Cade. Nor had he ever faced losing the most essential element of his existence.

Sick to death of stumbling around in the labyrinth his mind had become, Cade jammed his phone in the top drawer and clenched his jaw. Dodging and doubting…who the hell had he become?

CHAPTER THREE

A FEW FRIENDS...RIGHT. Cade should have remembered that Jenna did nothing by halves and had never met a stranger in her entire life. He hung around the edges of the crowd for as long as he could stand it, letting himself be introduced to a whole bunch of people whose names he would never remember, and didn't care to.

But none of them had been called Sophie, he was positive. So where was she, his sister's latest charity case? Not that most of the people present couldn't qualify for that same status. She'd invited several families for whom her nonprofit organization was building homes, as well as unemployed workers she thought needed a good meal or a chance to find jobs, the old lady next door, a waitress she liked...

He had to hand it to her, though. Everyone brought something, even if it was only a bag of chips, so all got fed but no one felt like a beggar. Every one of them thought the world of Jenna, that much was clear, and he couldn't fault their taste. His baby sister had a heart of pure gold, one she took no care to guard. In the world of the downtrodden, Jenna was a rock star.

Good-natured as the gathering was, however, there were too many people for him, and their first question was always "what do you do?" After an hour or so, he slipped out the back door and decided to take a walk.

Instantly he was reminded that he was in a city. Jenna's little street was not much traveled, but South Congress was only a handful of blocks away. Sirens and traffic, music escaping from some club, all within hearing distance.

Why had he said yes to coming here? If he was going to be grounded somewhere, West Texas suited him far better. There you could go a whole night and only hear the occasional coyote and the sound of the wind.

In West Texas, however, his family would watch his every move, alert to any sign he was pushing himself too hard—or worse, doing nothing at all—and worrying over how long it would be until they saw him again once he left. They loved him, of course, or they'd never have put up with the life he'd chosen. But acknowledging that love meant he'd have to acknowledge the guilt that came with it. He was a lousy son and brother, he saw now, and wondered why he'd been so blind to that before.

Maybe he should return and offer to work on his dad's ranch. Hang around for a while.

And wasn't that just a dandy way to dodge the fact that he didn't know if he could ever resume the career that had been all he'd ever wanted since the day his dad had placed a camera in his ten-year-old hands?

Damn, but he was sick of himself. He'd never in his life felt lost or uncertain and now he was swamped by both feelings. To top it all off, he'd skipped out on Jenna's party when all she'd asked was for him to help out a friend.

He'd go back inside and make nice soon, but for now, he just had to move. He let himself out through the front gate and onto the sidewalk.

SOPHIE DECIDED TO WALK to Jenna's party. The hotel was only eight blocks away, and she knew Jenna's street didn't have many parking spaces. Plus, the pickup she'd traded her snappy convertible for had proven invaluable, but it wasn't good in crowded parking conditions.

The day had cooled a little, thank goodness, though summer nights remained very warm in Austin. She crossed South Congress Avenue, went down a block and turned west onto the street that would intersect with Jenna's. The trees in this part of town were old, their branches creating canopies that cast shadows on the streets. The homes were small in the neighborhood, most of them frame and surrounded by abundant foliage. Roses scented the air, and once she caught a whiff of honeysuckle, which made her smile. She'd uncovered a patch of it on the grounds near the carriage house, and that had decided her to go with her instinct and make the apartment above it into the honeymoon suite.

Just then her heel twisted on the cracked, uneven sidewalk and she grabbed the nearby picket fence, silently cursing the high heels of her sandals. She was clearly out of practice at walking in anything but work boots or sneakers. The thought brought a grin. Who from her former corporate life would have imagined such from Sophie of the trim suits and killer heels?

"You okay, child?" called out a voice from the porch of the frame dwelling.

So much for thinking no one had witnessed her gracelessness. "I'm fine, thank you."

"Nice night for a walk, but you be careful, hear? World's got some meanness in it nowadays."

"I'm always careful, but thank you for your concern. I'm just headed over to a friend's house."

"Don't you walk yourself home late, child. You get a cab or have some nice young fella walk you back."

Sophie grinned to herself. She'd been in all the major cities of this country as well as several abroad and, as a single woman, caution was ingrained. The faceless woman was right, but she felt safe in this neighborhood. The more she walked through the area, the more she fell in love with it. SoCo might be trendy now, but the neighborhoods surrounding it still held their original charm, their hometown feel. Here and there the original modest dwelling had been replaced by new construction that took up almost the entire lot, but for the most part, the neighborhood remained a mix of young families drawn to the center of the city and old people who'd been around a long time. Not to mention neighbors who made sure perfect strangers were all right when they fell.

"You have a nice night now," she called to the woman.

"Next time you're by, you come visit. Name's Mrs. Ransom."

"I'm Sophie Carlisle, and I'd like that. Thank you."

She sincerely hoped that once the hotel was up and fully staffed, she'd have time for such luxuries.

Visit with neighbors. Imagine that.

The worry that dogged her lifted a little with this pleasant glimpse of a possible future. She wouldn't be making social calls anytime soon, but somewhere down the road...

Maybe she'd invite her new acquaintance, Mrs. Ransom, to a preview party, along with other neighbors. She'd already been planning an event for important figures in Austin who had contacts with those in the income brackets to afford her prices. Why not mix the two? It was such an Austin way to do things, mingling the glamorous with the down-home. That was her vision for the hotel, as well, to create the cachet of an exclusive hotel with the ambience of take-off-your-shoes-and-relax comfort. Everything she was doing was intended to make her guests feel that they'd entered a refuge, your grandmother's home with five-star service and absolute privacy...and the option to mingle for those who wanted it.

She had hammocks ready to hang between trees for a lazy afternoon, bent willow furniture that was ideal for sitting on the porch with a glass of cold tea, and a variety of overstuffed chairs and sofas perfect for napping or settling in with a good book.

Lost in dreams of how her hotel would look, she nearly tripped over a lump at the edge of the sidewalk before realizing it was a dog. Her foot connected with his side before she could catch herself, but the animal only whimpered and didn't move. She glanced around for signs of an owner, but the street was empty. She crouched, though not too close, as she scanned the long-haired form of what appeared to be an Irish setter. The dappled moonlight obscured her vision, and she dug in her purse for the little flashlight attached to her key chain.

"Hey, fella," she said, hesitating before touching him. This dog couldn't be in less knowledgeable hands. She'd never had a pet, though as a child she'd wanted one badly.

She couldn't see any foaming at the mouth or any-thing—wasn't that what dogs with rabies did? As she scanned the dog's face, the eyes were sad and lost. The tail wagged faintly and he looked up, then his head collapsed back to the sidewalk.

"What's wrong, buddy?" Gingerly she ran her hands over matted fur. When she reached the dog's hindquar-ters, he yelped. What had happened? Was he injured?

What should she do? Clearly she couldn't pick up the dog, for fear of injuring him further, to say nothing of potential harm to herself, but she couldn't just walk away.

In her hotel management days, she'd always made certain she and every one of her staff was trained in first aid and CPR, but none of that applied here.

Except one thing might. *Keep the patient calm.* "You're okay, boy," she said, and stroked his head.

The animal trembled, but as she continued to stroke and talk, he settled and closed his eyes.

Don't die. Please don't die. Sophie shivered. She'd lost too many people in her life. She'd lain awake

nights, wondering about their last moments and imagining what she could have done to prevent their deaths.
This was not a human, or a dog she knew, but somehow every bit of *I wish I could have* thinking that had
haunted her for years pressed in on her now. She could
not let this animal die—or if he couldn't be saved, she
wasn't going to let him die alone.

But if she called Animal Services, even if they were
available at night, there was no telling if she'd be allowed to stay with the dog—likely not. She didn't know
a vet, didn't have clue who might…except Jenna. She
didn't want to interrupt Jenna's party, but she didn't see
an alternative.

Just as she pulled out her phone, she spotted a man
approaching on the sidewalk.

"You okay?" he asked.

"I'm fine. Do you live around here?"

"Not really. I'm visiting."

"Oh, dear. I need a veterinarian."

He looked past her. "What happened to your dog?"

"It's not mine. I found him like this."

He sank to his knees a little stiffly, though his frame
was tall and powerful. "Hey, boy." He extended a hand
and let the dog sniff it. The dog's tail thumped again,
but only once.

"Here." She handed him the flashlight. "I don't
know anything about dogs, but he won't move. When
I touched his back legs, he cried out."

The man ran his hands over the animal, and he felt
his way down the front legs. When he reached the back

ones, the dog trembled and whined piteously. "I don't think we should try to move him yet."

"I considered calling nine-one-one, but I doubt they'd appreciate it, and anyway, I don't want him to get taken to a shelter."

"But he's not yours, you said."

"He's hurt and scared. He needs me."

"He doesn't know you."

She frowned. "That doesn't matter. He's alone." She gave him a look that had always sent her employees scurrying. "Never mind. I'll handle this. There's no need for you to hang around," she said in her frostiest voice. "Don't let me inconvenience you further."

He scowled. "Give me your phone."

"Why?"

"Do you want to help this dog or not?"

She seethed at his peremptory tone, but he was right. This was about the dog. She shoved the phone at him.

He punched in a set of numbers. "Delilah, who's your vet?"

Delilah. Figures.

"Will he take night calls?" He listened. "I came upon an injured dog on the street, an Irish setter that doesn't want to move and is sensitive about his hindquarters. I'd like to talk to someone before moving him." He waited for her to speak, then glanced over at Sophie. "What's your cell number?"

She told him and he relayed it to the woman on the other end.

"Great. Thanks, Delilah. I'll wait for his call." He clicked off and handed her the phone.

She took it. "I'll stay here and deal with it. You go on."

"Well, now, like it up on that high horse, Queenie?"

Her eyes went to slits. "Don't call me that."

"Then don't dismiss me like some peon."

"Look, I'm not sure what your problem is, but I've told you I don't need you. Just return to your...Delilah. I'm sure she misses you, heaven knows why."

He stared at her, his hand on the dog's head. "All this tension you're producing isn't good for the dog."

"*I'm* producing?" She barely resisted the urge to scream.

He grinned, and the sight of his smile silenced her. He might be a jerk, but he had a bone-melting smile, blast him. "I'm not the one doing all the yelling, Queenie."

She seethed but didn't speak.

He exhaled. "Sorry. I'm not in the greatest mood, but it's not right to take that out on you."

Their hands bumped on the dog's head, and she yanked hers back as if burned. "I couldn't agree more."

"Don't give an inch, do you?" But he smiled, and there was a dangerous level of charm in that smile.

An awkward silence fell. Somehow, though, his presence was a comfort. He seemed to know something about dogs, and she was terrified that her inexperience would kill this poor creature.

Finally, Sophie unbent. "I'm sorry, too. Do you want to talk about it? Why you're in a bad mood, that is?" After all, they were stuck here until the vet called.

"Huh?" He dragged himself from his reverie. "Oh— just family stuff. I have a kid sis who's a sucker for a sob story, and she's trying to guilt me into helping her latest charity case." He shook his head. "And she plans to empty my wallet along the way."

"Your sister? Is that where you're visiting?"

"Yeah." He gestured with his thumb over his shoulder. "Heart as big as the planet but the common sense of a gnat. At the moment, she's throwing a party for a houseful of her projects. Shoot, she'd take this dog, too, if I brought him to her—which is why I won't."

Sophie froze. His sister sounded entirely too much like Jenna, whose house was only a block away. And the charity case sounded way too much like her.

Sophie tilted her head to get a better view of him in the light of the streetlamp. His hair was a darker shade than Jenna's strawberry blond, but still blond. Two of Jenna's brothers had blond hair and two dark when she'd seen photos of Jenna's family. Was he one of the faces?

Please. No. "There's no reason for your sister to be bothered," she said, reeling. Was that all she was to Jenna, a charity case? She was no one's project. No one's sob story. Certainly not this ill-tempered jerk's. "You should go. I'll take the vet's call whenever it comes, and I'll deal with the dog."

"Listen, lady..." She wasn't sure *lady* was much better than Queenie, but at least he wasn't mocking her. "I said I'd stay and that's that." He frowned. "If nothing else, I was raised better than to leave a woman on a street alone at night."

"I can take care of myself."

His brows snapped together. "Maybe so, but the dog can't. How about you be the one to leave instead?"

He was insufferable. Gorgeous, maybe, in a rough-hewn way, but a total jerk. Surely he couldn't be related to the kindhearted Jenna. She opened her mouth to argue just as her phone rang.

He snatched it from her hand. "Cade MacAllister."

Crap.

"Got it. I'll be there in a few minutes. Thanks, Doc." He snapped her phone shut and handed it back. "Where's your car?"

"I didn't drive. I was walking."

"Then I'll get the one I'm renting. Be right back." He rose a little gingerly and walked off without waiting for a response.

Sophie realized her mouth was hanging open and shut it. She shook her head and texted Jenna to say she wouldn't be making it to her party. Then she cleared her mind of anything but the dog. "I'll get you fixed up, sweetie, don't you worry."

Even though doing so meant more time spent in the presence of the arrogant Cade MacAllister, who thought of her as nothing more than a failure begging for a handout.

CADE SLID DOWN IN A chair in the vet's reception area and watched the woman pacing across the linoleum. She was a looker, that was for sure, tall and graceful, with nice curves and an impressive set of long legs beneath the filmy blue sundress she wore. Whiskey-colored hair more red than brown escaped from the clip in which she'd tried to corral it. He thought her eyes might be green if they weren't alternately trying to freeze him or make him burst into flames with a look.

Queenie was a knockout, though in a quiet way. Too bad her personality was atrocious. It wasn't that he wasn't used to strong-willed women—his mother and sister were prime examples while Diego's cardiac surgeon wife Caroline gave them a run for their money. But even Caroline at her iciest, way back in the beginning, didn't hold a candle to Queenie.

And yet he was intrigued, in spite of himself. He'd rejected the notion of a permanent relationship with a woman long ago. His nomadic lifestyle would doom a marriage from the get-go. He preferred his women fun, warm and temporary.

But if he'd ever toyed with the idea of permanence, he thought he'd want someone sweet and kind, a real homebody, not an iceberg like the woman pacing in front of him.

He frowned. "What's your name, anyway?"

Her head whipped around. "Why?"

He drew back. "Whoa. I'm not asking for your ATM password or your dress size, just a name. Most people have them, you know." When she hesitated, he held up both palms. "Fine by me. Queenie, it is, then."

She glared at him and started to speak, but the vet appeared in the doorway. He glanced between them and settled on Cade.

"Your dog has suffered a fracture at the top of the femur where it joins the hip socket, likely caused from being hit by a car. I'll have to perform surgery on him in the morning when I have staff to assist, a femoral head ostectomy, which will smooth off the ragged edge. He's stabilized for now and resting comfortably. Which one of you is the owner?"

Queenie stepped forward. "I am. Well, I will be. I only found him tonight. He didn't have a tag."

The vet nodded. "No microchip, either, and the state of his neglect inclines me to believe he's been abandoned for some time. I can call the shelter, if you prefer."

"That won't be necessary. I want him. I'll—" She pressed her lips together and twisted her hands. "Do you have any idea what this will cost?"

"I can take care of the bill," Cade heard himself saying. Heaven knew he didn't spend much of his income.

She turned, and he spotted a conflict in her gaze right before she straightened her shoulders. "I don't need your help."

You keep saying that. Cade shrugged. "Whatever."

She faced the vet. "How long will he have to stay here?"

"He'll require cage rest for at least a week, then his activities will need to be restricted for another week or so until the sutures are removed. If you're not in a position to provide that, we can take care of him here. I'll know more about the time frame after the operation."

"When can I call to find out how the surgery went?"

"I have a full day of appointments, but you can speak to my assistant, Christina." He handed her a business card. "Here's the number. Probably after lunch is best."

She handed him a card in return. "Thank you so much. I'm sorry for the late-night call."

"No problem. Delilah is a favorite of mine."

"I'll be in touch tomorrow." She left quickly.

Cade lingered and spoke quietly to the vet. "Delilah's my sister-in-law. If there's any problem with the bill, please let me know. I'm good for it."

"Are you and the lady friends?"

"Never met her before. Thanks, Doc. I'll be calling tomorrow, too." He waved good-night and left.

Outside he looked for Queenie, only to spot her quickstepping toward the corner and away from—not toward—his SUV. "Hey! I'm parked back that way."

"I'll get a cab."

"Don't be an idiot. I'll take you."

She didn't respond, only hastened her steps and rounded the corner.

Cade raced after her faster than his still-healing body appreciated.

But when he reached the corner, she was gone.

CHAPTER FOUR

SOPHIE WAS UP AND ATTACKING weeds well before dawn to make up for work not done the night before. The landscaping contractor wouldn't be here for two more days. She'd been forced to cut back on the scope of his work due to both time and money constraints, but she was determined that the grounds would be a source of beauty and peace for those who stayed there.

As she yanked at vines trying to choke what she'd identified as snowball bushes next to the foundation, she thought about the dog she'd rescued the night before.

Well, *they'd* rescued. She had to give Cade Mac-Allister that much. He'd been quick and efficient at getting the animal help, so he couldn't be heartless, even if he rubbed her the wrong way.

Queenie. She snorted. Jerk.

Like it up there on your high horse?

He had no idea what she'd been through in her life, he who'd been blessed from birth with parents and siblings who adored him. His family was still alive and together, and his biggest problem was that perhaps they loved him too much.

Some problem.

Not that she needed love in her life, she thought

as she tugged at a stubborn vine. She didn't want it, didn't have time for it. Sure, maybe occasionally she was lonely and thought about how nice it would be to have someone waiting up for her, someone who cared about whether her day had been wonderful or not.

But after she'd rebuilt her life and started climbing the corporate ladder, she'd never met anyone she'd considered important enough to divert her from her career. Maybe she was simply meant to be alone. She did have friends, after all, even if most of them were scattered across the globe. Such was the nature of her business. Still there were emails and phone calls and occasional visits. And she had Jenna close by.

A thorn slashed her skin. She grabbed a clean rag out of her back jeans pocket and wrapped it until she could go inside and wash it off. It didn't hurt that much.

Not as much as knowing that Jenna considered her pathetic and in need of charity. That was no kind of friendship, and she wouldn't allow it to continue.

But she *liked* Jenna. Her friend was one of the reasons she'd come back to Austin after her career had gone down in flames. They'd met in a yoga class when she'd been posted to an Austin hotel two years ago, and Jenna's warm, giving nature—obvious even in a yoga class—had appealed to Sophie. As Sophie got to know her, she admired Jenna's drive to make the world a better place and her willingness to help anyone in need. During the scandal, Jenna had been her lifeline and had urged her to start over here in Austin.

It was a treat to be in one place, to have a girlfriend right in town to see chick flicks with, to call about a lousy date story—not that she had time for dates, but Jenna had plenty. Sure, Jenna was always dragging her away from work to listen to live music or walk the hike-and-bike trail, but she had to admit it was fun. And in fact it had been on a walk with Jenna that she'd first spotted this former eyesore.

Having a girlfriend wasn't too much to ask, was it?

Her pride was hurt, that was all. *Don't throw out the baby with the bathwater.* She and Jenna could still be friends, she just had to make it clear that Hotel Serenity would be just fine without Cade's art. *Leave your brother out of this,* she would tell Jenna. *I don't think his work is right for my hotel,* she would say. *I have a different plan now.* She would never reveal that she knew just how much Cade resented Jenna making free with what were, after all, his photographs. And how much he resented Sophie for taking her charity. Well, he wouldn't have to worry about that. She would be in no one's debt, not even a friend's.

Besides, Cade was a wanderer. As soon as he was well enough, he'd be on his way. She and Jenna could still be friends in spite of her brother.

In the meantime, she'd reclaim her new dog, dodge Cade and focus on getting the hotel open, on showing everyone in the hotel business that she was a force to be reckoned with, that she could make it on her own. That no scandal would break her.

Nor would losing out on Cade's photographs. She hadn't planned on having them and wouldn't lose sleep over the loss. Moving forward was all that mattered.

As she loaded yet more vines into her wheelbarrow,

she paused to use the tail of her shirt to wipe sweat off her face. After she dumped these, she'd go inside and perform a little first aid on her arm, then call the vet's office to get an update. Too soon for the surgery to be over, maybe, but she wanted to know how the dog had passed the night.

Poor guy. He needed a name.

Well, it wasn't like she didn't have plenty of time to think of one while performing mindless manual labor.

"I'LL JUST BE A LITTLE late to the office," Jenna said as she drove. "But I have to find out why Sophie didn't come to the party last night. She texted to say something had come up, but not what it was. I hope she didn't work all night. I mean, she's worried sick about getting the hotel ready to open, but we agreed she needed that break. She's been working really long hours."

When Jenna remained silent for a full minute— amazing—Cade tipped up the bill of his ball cap. "And you're bringing me along...why?"

"So you can meet her and see which of your photos will fit."

"Jen, I don't know..."

She huffed. "Look, Mr. Cranky, you said you were bored back home. And my friend needs help— not that you're allowed to say that, remember?" Her knee bounced as they waited for the stoplight to turn. "Where did you disappear to last night, anyway?"

"Went for a walk."

"I'm sorry." She heaved a sigh. "I know you don't

like large gatherings. I didn't really think so many would show up." She glared at him. "But what if Sophie had made it? You'd have missed her."

He could explain everything that had happened, but what was the point? Next thing he knew, after stopping at this Sophie person's place, Jenna would be detouring to check on the dog and making arrangements for him to come live with her.

By end of day, she'd probably have everything neatly tied up in a bow, but that wasn't what he wanted. He would deal with the situation himself.

Queenie didn't really want that dog, did she? She probably lived in a condo, and the poor guy would be trapped inside all day and half the night. A lousy fate for an animal that had already seen more than his share of hard times.

So what do you plan to do about it? Take a dog on your next shoot?

He wouldn't have a next shoot, though, would he, if he couldn't even pick up a camera? Go back to West Texas and ranch? Swing a hammer for Jenna?

Cade sat up straight and stared out the passenger window, seeing only the black hole where his constant curiosity had lived for so long. He couldn't live like this, so…okay, scared. Bone-deep scared in a way no cliff had ever been able to make him feel.

"Here we are," Jenna said.

With relief he dragged his attention to an amazing old house painted a soft yellow with dark green shutters. "This is a hotel?"

"Not yet, but it will be. It was originally a mansion

that was turned into a boarding house long ago. It had been empty for fifteen years when Sophie spotted it." Jenna smiled. "It's going to be unique—the quaintness of a bed-and-breakfast with full, five-star hotel service. She has a refuge in mind, a place where even the most famous guests can stay and not be bothered, luxury and the feeling of home all in one. I'm not doing her vision justice, but she'll describe it better. Come with me."

Cade followed his sister slowly, taking in everything around him. The grounds were badly overgrown with weeds and vines, but parts of the front had already been cleaned up to reveal mature bushes and trees, and flowers spilled from the wide covered porch like frothy skirts. The trees were enormous, and for a second, he thought he caught a glimpse of water behind the house.

"Amazing, right? That's why we have to help her."

"We?"

"Sophie is very closemouthed about her past, but from what I can tell, she's got no one. And something bad happened on her job—she won't say what exactly, but I know it had to be bad for her to leave when she was on target for a big promotion. She's very independent, and she hates asking anyone for help or a favor." Jenna halted. "She's put everything she has into this place, and it's set to open in a month, with rooms already booked. This isn't just a business, it's very personal to her, and her reputation is on the line. If she can't open on time, well…she'll lose everything. I can tell she's really worried. And working way too hard."

Maybe there was more to this Sophie than he'd assumed. "But what do my photos have to do with anything?"

Jenna rolled her eyes. "You may be merely an irritating older brother to me, but you're as famous as Zane in your field, only it's your photos that get plastered on the covers of magazines, not your face. Having Cade MacAllister originals hanging on her walls would be a big drawing card for this unique refuge Sophie is trying to create."

"Originals? Jen, I told you…"

Jenna flushed. "Why not take new ones? What else have you got to do while you're here?"

"She put you up to this?"

"No!" Jenna hissed. "I thought of it, okay? And she'd be thrilled with third-rate rejects from you if that's all you would sell to her, but the more I think about it, why shouldn't you create new work so she'd have something truly unique?"

Because I lost my eye at the bottom of an Andean mountain beside the broken body of my friend. Because I can't even touch a camera without having a panic attack. "Jenna…"

But his sister had moved forward already to greet someone. "Hey, Sophie!" she hailed.

Ahead, a figure clad in threadbare blue jeans and a ratty T-shirt had pulled up the shirttail to wipe her face, leaving a sweet glimpse of smooth, taut belly that snagged Cade's full attention.

"Jenna," she said, smiling widely. "What are you…" Her voice trailed off as her gaze traveled to him.

He couldn't quite make out her face beneath the

bill of the ball cap she wore with a ponytail sticking through the opening in the back, but he could see that she'd gone very still.

She whirled and grabbed the overloaded wheelbarrow. "Let me just empty this." She began striding away too quickly and her load tilted, about to topple.

Cade loped ahead and bent to restack it. "Here, let me help."

"I'm fine," she said, her head turned away, her shoulders stiff.

She was tall but slender. "This load is too much for you. Where do you want it?" he asked as they resettled all the vegetation inside the wheelbarrow.

Her head remained ducked down, and her voice went cold. "I don't need your help."

Something in that tone grabbed his attention. His brows snapped together.

She started to pick up the handles, and he caught a glimpse of her profile at the same instant her hair color registered. He gripped her shoulder and turned her to him.

"Let go of me." The ice was unmistakable. She tensed to push the load again, but he wouldn't release her.

"Well, well. Hello, Queenie."

Her head whipped around, and wary green eyes locked on his. "Let me go," she whispered fiercely. "Do not make a scene in front of Jenna. Better yet, just go away." She shrugged him off and quickly put distance between them.

Cade stood there, staring after her.

"What was that about?" Jenna asked as she approached.

"Nothing."

"Didn't look like nothing. What did you say to her?" Jenna demanded.

Which time? he wanted to ask as he recalled their conversations the night before. *My sister's trying to guilt me into helping her latest charity case and plans to empty my wallet along the way.*

He removed his cap and raked fingers through his shaggy hair, staring in the direction Sophie had disappeared. Then he looked at the sister who was glaring at him. He sighed. "It's a long story."

"I'm going after her," Jenna insisted.

"No," he said. "I will."

"You? Why?"

"Go on to work, Jen. This is mine to fix."

"But…"

He turned her gently toward her car. "You'll be late."

"You don't have a car here."

"Walking is part of my physical therapy. It's not that far. I'll see you later."

"Cade, what on earth…?"

"Go to work. Please."

Jenna's hands rested on her hips. "You'd better not upset her, and I expect a full accounting when I get home."

"Scram, little sister. I've got this. Trust me."

"How can I? You have no people skills. Cade, she's a good person and her life has been really hard."

"Kid gloves, I promise."

"If not, I'm taking a skillet to your thick head."

"Yeah, yeah, yeah. Beat it." He squeezed her hand and smiled. "Seriously, trust me."

"This better not be a mistake." But reluctantly she complied.

Cade watched her leave, then turned to attempt to melt the ice queen.

PLEASE. NOT NOW. NOT HIM. Sophie rounded the corner too fast, and the loaded wheelbarrow hobbled again. She'd been working on her argument to Jenna about why she'd changed her mind about buying Cade's photographs, but she needed more time. She could not work with this man, even if he didn't hold her in contempt as one of Jenna's unfortunates.

She was no one to pity. So maybe she'd gotten her hopes up a little about the stunning images of his she'd seen and the extra cachet having them in her rooms would have given her, but no way was it worth it now. She should have known. It had been too good to be true. Nothing in life ever came without working for it.

She yanked another handful of vines and tossed them on the holding pile for her compost. She wanted to make this place as self-sustaining as possible, and with all the pruning and weeding she was doing, she'd have materials galore to compost. The compost would then fertilize the flower beds and shrubs. She even had her eye on an area near the carriage house that she could turn into an herb garden. She'd make old-fashioned tussie-mussies and potpourri to perfume the quarters....

"I've got this," a deep voice said from behind her. Cade elbowed her out of the way and finished emptying the wheelbarrow.

She shoved right in and used her hip to bump him aside and wrest back the handles. "I can do it myself, and I thought I told you to go away."

"You need help. Jenna says—"

She whirled on him. "Jenna says what? That I'm in trouble? That I'm pathetic? Did you two laugh over me? Did you tell her you wouldn't even consider letting her empty your pockets for her *charity case?*"

"Don't drag my sister into this."

She shoved him in the chest. "Get off my property."

"Slow down, Queenie."

"Don't call me that!"

But his attention had gone to her arm. He grabbed it. "You're hurt. And there's *dirt* in this cut. What do you think you're doing?"

Next thing she knew, he was towing her across the lawn.

In the side yard, she heard workers arriving. "Let go of me or I'll…"

Strong fingers maintained their grip, and soon she found herself in the kitchen. He turned on the water in the sink then dragged her forearm under it. "Wash that out. I'll be back." He halted. "Where's your first-aid kit?"

"I'm not telling. You can't make me." *Wow,* she thought, falling silent. *How junior high is that?*

He threw up his hands. "You know, I don't like people much…"

"No kidding."

His eyes narrowed. "But I'm usually slow to anger." He approached her again. "You get all snotty and frigid with me, though, and it just pushes my buttons."

"Frigid? *Snotty?*" She wanted to hit him.

Then he smiled. *Smiled.* All the way into those thick-lashed, dark blue eyes. Up close in daylight, he was even more gorgeous than he'd been last night. Which completely infuriated her. "What are you grinning at?"

"Steamed looks better on you than frigid, Queenie."

She refused to react to that name again. "I have work to do." She pushed away from the sink.

He caught her arm. "Look, I can tell you're swamped. Do you really have time to be arguing with me over what you know is sensible?"

He was right. And she was too tired to fight. "The kit is over there." She nodded toward the cabinet to the right of the sink.

He followed her directions then proceeded to dry the wound and put antibiotic ointment on it. He covered it with a waterproof gauze pad and tape, sealing the ends to keep dirt out. "You need a long-sleeved shirt. Your skin will burn."

"It's too hot. Sunblock works just as well."

"Are you always so argumentative?"

"I'm easy to get along with. The problem is you."

He shrugged. "I don't have to talk much in my line of work."

"You could use some practice."

"So my family tells me." That smile again, no less killer hot. "How's our dog?"

Her gaze flew to his. "*My* dog."

"I think we should call him Rusty. Or Skeeter."

She rolled her eyes. "Please."

"You got a better idea?"

"He's my dog. His name is an important decision. I'm still thinking."

"We'll see." At last he stepped away, and she could breathe. "So…you going to show me around?"

She stared. "Why?"

"So I can figure out what kind of shots you could use."

She stiffened. "I don't want anything from you."

One tawny eyebrow cocked. "Oh, really?"

"Really," she said, and tried not to mourn the loss. "I am no one's charity case. Your pockets will stay nice and full." She gave him her back. "Besides, I don't have time for a tour. I hear my guys coming in, and I have a lot of work to do. Today's not a good day. You should go."

With one hand on her jumpy stomach and the other in a fist, she rapidly made her way out of the room.

It was a full hour before she realized that he hadn't left. Instead he'd somehow acquired a pair of work gloves and was busy cleaning out underbrush.

With his shirt off.

Revealing acres of golden skin.

And all kinds of muscles.

Sophie closed her eyes for a second and prayed for

patience. Also for convenient blindness. Dear heaven, was there no justice?

She snapped off her lurid thoughts at the stem, then fisted her hands and stalked in Cade's direction.

CHAPTER FIVE

"WHAT EXACTLY DO YOU think you're doing?"

Cade was hot, tired and more than a little worried he couldn't push his body much longer without embarrassing himself, but for the first time in months he felt content and *useful*. But that didn't mean Queenie was going to order him around. "What does it look like I'm doing?" He removed his cap and the T-shirt he'd wrapped over his head and left to trail down his back as he'd learned to do years before on his first desert sojourn. "This place must have been a real dump when you first saw it." He glanced past her to the house. "She's coming back to life, though," he murmured. "Wonder who built her?"

Sophie's gaze followed his. "A lumberyard owner. The woodwork inside and out is amazing. Not that you could see it at first—there were vines obscuring the entire front porch and growing up to the second story."

"But you have the eye, don't you?"

She looked at him. "The eye?"

The one I used to have, he thought. He shrugged. "I always knew the shot that would tell the story." In his mind, he could still picture the images that had made his career, even if he could no longer grasp the feeling that used to sweep over him as he peered through the viewfinder. "Rarely was it the dominant feature of a given landscape or the moments when everyone else had shutters clicking at a lion standing majestically. Those were the expected shots, the clichés. Those were never the ones I wanted to take. You've done the same thing here, taking a property that others would have believed ready for the bulldozer and making it into something magnificent."

"I appreciate you saying that. Clearly your gift for seeing beyond the expected isn't restricted to exotic locations and wild animals."

"I don't know about that…."

"That picture," she said, "of the gazelle stumbling… do you remember it?"

He gazed down at her. "I remember all of them."

"The writers who do the text for your photos must be in heaven when they're assigned to your work. You always give them something fresh to write about, something powerful. Unforgettable." Her green eyes were warm with admiration.

He had to look away. He might not ever give them a story again, and it was on the tip of his tongue to blurt out that he'd lost that inner knowing. "The writers would say that my photos were the accompaniment to their stories."

"They'd be wrong. I don't see their work hanging in galleries or museums."

He grinned past the ache in his chest. She made that ache ease a little, at least as long as he was willing to live in the past. The coward's way.

Abruptly he wasn't eager to talk about photography anymore. "So after I get this cleared, what's next?"

She frowned. "I told you I didn't need your help. I have a landscaper coming soon."

"Then why are you doing his work?"

"I had to trim the budget, so I offered to do some of his prep work. If Jenna insisted that you help—"

"Jenna doesn't know I'm still here. She did tell me, though, that if I made you unhappy, I could expect a skillet upside the head when she got home."

They shared a moment of amusement.

"She doesn't mean it," Sophie said.

"Bet me. That girl can be meaner than a snake."

Sophie laughed, and the happy sound stopped him in his tracks.

"Call any of my brothers if you doubt my word." He shrugged. "Though to be fair, we usually deserve it." He watched the smile as it lingered on that beautiful mouth of hers. He didn't like that she tugged at him, that he was powerfully tempted to grab a taste of her.

Besides, they were actually getting along for a few minutes, and yielding to that particular impulse would wreck that. "I called about our dog," he said.

"*My* dog." Her eyes snapped.

"We'll see. Anyway, the surgery was over, and he came through fine. Still out for the count, though. Wanna go visit him later?"

The line between her brows deepened as she looked around. "There's so much to do." She shook her head. "I can't."

"Everyone needs a break—even you, Queenie."

"I've decided to ignore that horrid name. You'll get tired of using it at some point."

"Doubt it. It's growing on me."

Her eyes went to slits. "I have to get back to work." She touched his forearm. "You really should stop. Or take a break yourself."

"Last time I looked, my mother was six hundred miles away. I know my limits."

"Are you just doing this because you know I don't want you to be here?"

"Nope, that's a bonus." He studied the dark circles beneath her eyes that hadn't been so visible in the moonlight last night. "Look, you need help. I'm restless. It's been years since I took time off, and I'm no good at it. I have to be active. And believe it or not, Jenna's not the only one in the family who cares about lending a helping hand to a friend."

"We're not friends."

"You got too many of them?"

Shadows crossed her eyes. "No." Her gaze sharpened. "But this is my hotel and my problem. I don't rely on other people."

"No kidding." He softened his words with a smile. "Me, either. But I could use the exercise. Walking on a treadmill at the physical therapist's is boring as hell."

"I'm afraid you'll hurt yourself, and then Jenna will have that skillet out after *me*."

"I can't take new shots for you," he blurted. "This is the only thing I can offer." It was only fair to warn her.

"I didn't ask you to. I would never be so presumptuous," she said stiffly.

Damn it. He'd offended her prickly pride. But he was not going to explain. "I'm sorry. How about we have dinner tonight. I'll drag out my laptop and you can decide on which of the images you want to use." He could stand that, surely. He had to learn to. "I've taken thousands of pictures no one has seen."

"That sounds like it could take a while."

"Then give me the tour, talk to me about what you have in mind and I'll cull through the files on my own, since time is not exactly your ally right now." He hesitated. "Though you do get that artists don't much like their work being chosen because the colors match the room, right?"

"Cade, I told you I don't need your photographs. I don't *want* your photographs. And I don't want you here. You've got to go. Now."

He really should stop for the day, anyway, but she got his back up ordering him around. He wanted to be useful. Needed to. Weird and unusual as the word *need* was for him to use or feel. "Look." He exhaled in a gust. "We both care about Jenna, right?"

She nodded cautiously.

"And Jenna has her heart set on us working together." An idea hit him, and he shook his head. "I don't know why it took me this long to realize that if she's been playing me on your account, telling me this sob story, she's probably also drafted you to help out poor Cade who nearly died. Am I right?"

Sophie looked distinctly uncomfortable but said nothing.

He slapped his cap against his thigh. "That little…"

He couldn't help but laugh. "I should have seen it coming a mile away. I mean, Zane and Jesse and I had a bet going that she was up to something, but I just thought she was..." His voice trailed off as caution reared its head. "Never mind."

"You just thought what?"

"Nope. Not sticking that foot in my mouth."

She studied him for a long minute. Then her face cleared and her mouth curved. "You thought she was setting us up. As a couple, I mean." She shook her head slowly "Oh, Jenna..."

He shouldn't feel so insulted. "Is it so incomprehensible? I mean, you're gorgeous and I...well, I don't clean up so bad."

"You think I'm gorgeous?"

He scanned her head to toe and back up. "I may have been injured, but my eyes weren't."

Her cheeks went red. "I'll have to consider that," she said.

"Consider what? Whether you're interested?"

It was her turn for the slow once-over. But she remained silent.

"You're interested, all right." He nodded in satisfaction. "And so am I."

"It couldn't go anywhere."

"Who says it needs to?" Cade wasn't accustomed to talking women into wanting him. "Or is it that you think I can't pass muster, Queenie?" His grin widened. "I could have you boneless in my bed, so sexually satisfied you might not move for a very long time."

One dark eyebrow arched. "Oh, really? Well, maybe I would have you begging first."

"Oh, babe." He hadn't been with anyone since his fall, and he was just now realizing how long that had been. "You are on." Sex wouldn't fix his problems, but it could sure take his mind off them.

"On for what?"

He stuck out a hand. "How about a bet?"

"Bet?"

"A friendly wager. Let's see who caves first."

She looked intrigued, but then she shook her head. "I don't have time to fool around right now, Cade."

"Honey, everyone has time for great sex. It'll recharge your batteries. You'll sleep better. And you've got an extra set of hands here now. Hell, I'll call in my brothers if need be."

Her eyes went wide. "Your brothers would come work on my hotel for the sake of your sex life?"

He gaped. "I didn't mean... I wasn't saying..." He shut up. Hell, the family was so concerned about him, they actually might do such a thing. But hell would freeze over before he'd get within a mile of that topic.

"Save your bet, Casanova. If we have sex, it will be with full understanding that no emotions are involved, that it's just a fling. And it will be at the time and place of my choosing."

He laughed out loud. "Oh, Queenie..." His grin widened. "Honey, you just keep thinking that." But he hastened to agree. "I mean, yeah, only a fling, definitely. I'll be gone soon and I don't do long-term."

"Neither do I."

"Well, good." He frowned. Somehow the sentiment sounded vaguely insulting coming from her. It was exactly what he wanted, of course, but...the woman gave him a headache.

"I still like a nice, clean bet," he complained.

"Too bad. I don't have one single dime to spare," she said, and started to walk away.

"There are other things to wager besides money," he called after her. Then he noticed a couple of workmen grinning at them.

And Queenie's back going ramrod straight.

"Oh, hell." He was usually smoother than this. Maybe not Zane-smooth, but he could hold his own.

Cade slapped his cap on his head and shoved his hands back in his work gloves. Women were so blasted much trouble. And what man understood them, anyway?

Before he went back to the weeds, though, he turned to watch her walk away. Damned if that woman didn't have a body on her.

Unfortunately a razor-sharp mind and endless supply of stubbornness were part of the package.

He'd finish up, then go check on their dog.

Who'd probably be a lot happier to see him.

As he bent to rip out a root, he realized he'd already won one battle with her—she'd tacitly agreed to let him continue working today. It was only a matter of time before he won the war.

SHE SHOULDN'T BE USING so much water since every penny counted, but oh, how good the hot shower felt on her abused muscles. Sophie let the water beat down on her shoulders, tilting her head this way and that to ease the strain of too much time spent beneath the dining room table applying tung oil.

The area she was calling the gathering room was going to be gorgeous, an open space where a large area of comfy sofas and chairs flowed into the dining area, where the guests would be treated to breakfasts they would never forget. The spread would bear no resemblance to the sad, standardized fare most chains had no choice but to utilize. Hers would continue the theme of home away from home, featuring a full country breakfast prepared to order—not one warming tray in sight—or for those who wanted lighter fare, she'd have seasonal fruits chosen each day for their freshness, hot breads made that very morning, coffee from beans ground as each pot was prepared and special teas made locally by a woman who was even now creating a Hotel Serenity blend.

The dining room had an outside wall with three seven-foot-tall windows that rose from floor level, designed so that a person could walk right through. Those opened onto a section of the deep porch, and guests could dine there, as well. But inside or out, all would have a view of the pergola she'd decided would perfectly complement the cutting garden. Beneath the pergola, as well as scattered along the deep porch, would be willow furniture with thick, sink-into-me cushions.

She was determined to give her guests the full experience of a gracious old home, but with casual comfort and modern conveniences. Though finding space to accommodate everything required for abundant hot water, ample wiring and energy-efficient air-conditioning hadn't been easy to do while maintaining the look of one hundred fifty years of history.

She had to marvel at how on earth people had survived living in Central Texas before air-conditioning. Sophie tried to imagine wearing a long skirt, long sleeves and petticoats in this heat. Or high-collared shirts with cravats.

Luckily, because Cade had accomplished so much outside, she'd been freed up to go indoors to finish oiling the table. *Cade.* She'd accepted his help on the grounds today because he seemed to need the activity and Jenna was so worried about him. It was only for one day, though.

She shut off the water and stepped from the shower, deeply grateful for the ceiling fan whirring overhead.

She glanced at the clock. Did she still have time to make it to the vet's? She could come back and finish oiling the furniture later. Even though sparing the time wasn't in her schedule, he was her dog.

No matter what Cade insisted.

Rusty. How unimaginative for a dog whose hair was a few shades more auburn than her own.

Skeeter was kind of cute, though. Not that she'd ever tell Cade.

But she'd have to get better acquainted with her dog—imagine that, a dog of her own—before choosing a name.

Her phone rang. She glanced at the display. Maura. Her spirits lifted for once—she had something fun to talk about this time. She wouldn't be pretending. "Hi, Maura. Guess what? I have a dog."

Silence. "A...what?"

Sophie laughed. "I know. My, how things have changed, right?" In her past life, travel had been a constant. She'd never tried to take care of so much as a goldfish. Didn't even think herself a pet person.

"I must have the wrong number."

"My life just keeps changing."

"But you sound...good, Sophie. Alive."

"A lot has been happening. I'm not sure what to do about the newest development."

"The dog?"

"No, um... I mean, yes, that's new for me, right?"

"It certainly is. What kind of dog?"

"An Irish setter."

"Oh, they're beautiful. Is it a puppy?"

"No, he's probably five or six, the vet says. I found him on the road. He was hurt, but a...someone else helped me find a vet to treat him."

"Someone else? A male someone?"

Sophie hesitated.

"You said a lot had been happening. Is there a man involved, my Sophie? Come on, spill." Sophie could easily envision Maura slipping off her shoes, settling in for a story.

"He's not—it's not...it's strictly business. Though I don't think it's going to work out, actually."

Cade had certainly seemed insistent about providing photos, however—just not new ones.

"You're going to throw out a teaser like that, then leave me hanging? Talk to me, doll."

"Um…I've met Cade MacAllister—you know, the photographer?"

"Cade MacAllister? My, my. Well, good for you. It's been too long since you and Kurt—"

"That's not what I mean." The only thing Sophie wanted to discuss less than Kurt Barnstone was Cade as a man.

"He's an astonishing talent, no question, but I've seen a photo of him. You're going to tell me he's not one very fine specimen of man?"

"It's not like that, Maura." *I could have you boneless in my bed…*

"Sweetie, you've been working too hard, clearly."

Sophie shook her head, grateful her fiery cheeks couldn't be seen through a phone. "I'm only interested in his work."

"Oh, dear," Maura said. "You're in worse shape than I thought."

"Would you stop it? My focus is entirely on making this hotel a success."

"All right, all right. I'll behave." The smile in her voice came through. "So what's the deal with his work?"

"I shouldn't have brought it up because it's not set in stone, but…well, there's a possibility that I may be able to hang some of his photos in the guest rooms."

"Are you serious? How on earth did you manage that? That would be an absolute coup."

"I know." Sophie resisted the urge to do a happy

dance, reminding herself that a lot of things could go wrong. "His sister has become a very dear friend of mine, and the idea was hers. I didn't see any way I could afford him, but...he's here."

"He's there? Then why on earth are you talking to me?"

"Not here right now, but he's in town and he's...well, he spent the day working on the grounds."

"Excuse me?"

"It's crazy, right? Did you hear about his climbing accident? He was badly injured and he can't go back on the road yet, so Jenna—that's his sister—brought him over and, well, somehow he just started clearing out vines and...it sounds insane, I know." She glanced at the clock. *Crap.* She had to leave now to make it the vet's. "Maura, I'm sorry, but my dog, well, sort of our dog, is recuperating at the vet's and I need to go see how he's doing."

"Our dog?"

"Um...mine and...Cade's. He's mine, really, but Cade is very...hardheaded. But I really do have to go."

"And you think you're just going to waltz off and leave me with a million questions?"

Guilt struck. "I'm sorry, Maura, it's just..."

Maura chuckled. "I'm kidding, Sophie. I mean, my curiosity is definitely killing me, but it is wonderful to hear you sound...flustered."

"I'm not flustered." But she was. And it was all Cade's fault.

"You are. It sounds lovely. You've been too serious in your life, Sophie. I never understood what happened between you and Kurt, but I'm absolutely delighted at this news. I've been worried about you. Cheers to Cade MacAllister if he can discombobulate you like this."

"It's only about his photographs, Maura."

"If you say so." Then Maura relented. "The photographs will be a tremendous draw, kiddo. Congratulations."

"I don't have them yet. And he really can be cranky."

"The privilege of a great artist. Go see your dog, sweetie."

"Thanks for understanding, Maura."

"Oh, I'm not sure I understand…but I think you're a little confused yourself, and that's not all bad."

"Goodbye, Maura." She was not discussing Cade one second longer.

"I told you there would be a much better man than Kurt come along. You deserve it."

"Goodbye, Maura."

"All right, all right. Goodbye, Sophie."

A much better man than Kurt, indeed. Maura had no idea. The older woman thought his involvement in Sophie's life had ended with their brief liaison.

But Kurt had created the scandal that cost Sophie her job and her reputation. He'd turned on her just for having the effrontery to break things off with him and, worse, to surpass him in the race to the top.

He'd gotten even. In spades.

And Maura's beloved nephew, Gary, who had worked under Sophie, had been Kurt's instrument in the scheme to discredit Sophie. He'd doctored the books for various accounts under Sophie's control. But

Kurt was clever and had disguised his tracks well, and Sophie couldn't prove any of it. Even if she found some evidence, she'd be exposing Maura's nephew to prosecution. So Sophie had chosen to perform the acting job of her life and convince Maura that she was eager and ready to open her own place, that she wanted to resign. When Maura had insisted on investing in the hotel, Sophie had been caught in her own deception.

Quickly she dressed and headed out, grateful that the vet was open later on Thursday evenings. She spared a minute to wonder if she should take him something—the dog, not the vet—but then she considered that he was probably on a strict diet and no doubt did not feel like playing, so she was fresh out of ideas on what she could take the animal she so badly hoped would want to be hers.

Less than a half hour later, she was standing in front of his cage. "Poor baby. I'm Sophie. How are you feeling?" She glanced around her to see if any of the staff were still nearby, but she was alone—well, her and about ten other animals. The dog studied her solemnly, brown eyes huge and sad.

"You're going to be okay," she crooned, and ventured a finger through the wires. His hair was so soft. Once, long ago, she remembered asking her parents for a puppy. Her father had made a distracted promise to consider it when she was older. Her mother had talked about shedding hair and who would feed it. Then they'd moved, and their apartment had been too small.... In St. Louis, wasn't it? After that had come Houston.

Then the boating accident. Her parents had been together on a business outing for her dad, and she'd been with a babysitter. After that, no home. No puppy. No living relatives who wanted her.

She'd gone into foster care, where she'd felt as caged as this dog. As forgotten. A burden. After the third home, she'd run away.

"I won't give up on you," she promised. "I don't know where to put you when the hotel is open, but I'll figure something out." She stroked his proud head and bent closer. His tongue swiped her cheek, and she couldn't help giggling. "That tickles," she said, stroking him again. She studied him. "Julian, you think?" She shook her head. "Maybe not. How about Finn? That's a nice Irish name."

The dog remained unmoved. She leaned in closer. "Skeeter?" she whispered.

His head rose. He began to pant, and she wondered if his expression counted as a doggy grin.

"That's a terrible name, you know. You could have something much more dignified."

He nudged at her hand with his nose.

"Let's don't be hasty. We can think about it, okay? I refuse to give Cade the satisfaction," she murmured. But her shoulders shook with her chuckles. "Promise me you'll keep this between us." She bent her head into his nose, feeling both slightly foolish and comforted. *Maybe that's why people like dogs,* she thought. A good dog felt like a good friend.

The noises of the clinic receded, and Sophie experienced a sense of calm for the first time in days. She

laid her head against the cage and the warmth of the
dog's breath huffed softly against her hair.

She closed her eyes and let the peace take her.

CADE STOPPED JUST INSIDE the doorway as soon as he
spotted her. He watched as a different Sophie emerged.
Not the ice queen, not the worn-out laborer wired
tightly enough to snap.

This Sophie was soft. Sweet. Exhausted and vulnerable.

And delighted. The habitual strain left her shoulders
as she whispered to the dog, let her fingers stroke him,
giggled when he licked her face.

She's had a really hard life, Jenna had said.

A many-faceted woman. He found himself wanting to protect her, though he had no idea what from. A
fragile beauty lay beneath that bossy, I-don't-need-you
exterior.

None of that was his concern, however much Jenna
wanted to make it so. And he had his own problems.
But maybe he could focus simply on that body he already wanted to get his hands on. She was attracted, so
was he. He had time to kill and she needed help. They
could keep things simple. He couldn't provide her with
any new shots, but he would wangle a tour from her
first thing in the morning and get a sense of what she
was after. Then he'd mentally put together a selection
of his photos while he was working outside.

He'd even give her a cut-rate price, not because
Jenna had maneuvered him into it but because he could

see that Sophie's back was against the wall and she had something special in mind.

There. He had it all figured out. He'd get stronger from working; she'd get her hotel open. And if a nice little fling came with the package, well…he wouldn't complain.

Even though none of that got him back with a camera in his hand or the itch to shoot it.

Sophie stirred then, a welcome distraction from his dark thoughts. She was gathering herself to say good-bye, he could tell, so he slipped out the way he'd come without her noticing. She looked as peaceful and happy right now as he'd ever seen her in their brief acquaintance, so he'd let her be.

Besides, he was pretty certain he was going to be sore as hell in the morning. A hot soak at Jenna's and early to bed—preferably before he had to discuss Sophie with Jenna.

He was tired, but it was a good tired. Tomorrow he had a purpose, and if it wasn't anything he'd ever imagined himself doing, well…it was still a goal. He was too much a MacAllister to enjoy aimlessness.

He hazarded one backward glance before he closed the door.

"'Night, Skeeter," he said quietly.

Sweet dreams, Sophie.

Before he left, he paid for the surgery and left instructions on where to send the rest of the bill.

CHAPTER SIX

IN THE MORNING, Sophie wandered outside just after dawn with a peanut butter and jelly sandwich and a cup of coffee, stifling a yawn. Her sleep had been broken by worries over the hotel, Maura, the dog…and the man she didn't have time to be thinking about. She yawned again and wished for the leisure to walk over to her favorite coffee shop on South Congress for a real breakfast, but she couldn't spare the hour away from the hotel. She wasn't much of a cook herself. Her guests, however, would be treated to the wizardry of the chef she'd hired. Patty was a native Austinite who'd trained at the Cordon Bleu, then done a stint in San Francisco before getting homesick and returning to Texas. It was Sophie's good fortune to have hired Patty as the chef for the hotel she'd managed for her old company. Stealing her away now from the chain that had chosen to believe Sophie capable of perfidy was icing on the cake.

Patty had mentioned her interest in the slow food movement, using local ingredients as much as possible, which perfectly dovetailed with Sophie's plans for Hotel Serenity. She hoped someday to do Patty one better and put in a sizable garden on the terraced area just down the slope. Patty wasn't due to start for another couple of weeks, though, so Sophie would have to make do with her PB&J for breakfast.

On the back porch, she propped herself on top of the wide railing, leaned her head back against a post and listened to the mockingbird who serenaded her each morning—when, that is, she took the time to listen. Finn—she liked the name Finn, even if the dog hadn't yet given his assent, which she chose to blame on being medicated—would love romping over the grounds when he was well. He couldn't roam free with guests around, of course, unless he turned out to be very well behaved, but the vet had said he was probably five or six, so his pace would be slower than a puppy's. She'd train him, if need be, and she would keep him with her as much as possible. He would have a good life.

"'Morning."

Sophie jolted and nearly spilled her coffee as Cade strolled into view, clad in ancient jeans and a plain white T-shirt, a beat-up straw cowboy hat on his head, which should have looked ridiculous but instead seemed absolutely natural. He wore work boots and had leather gloves stuck in his hip pocket.

He looked strong and male and much too delicious. "What are you doing here?"

His smile did something to her insides. "Glad to know some things never change, Queenie." He tipped his brim back with one thumb as though he'd done it a thousand times before. He was far too cocky for his own good.

Then he frowned. "Sleep badly?"

"That's not your concern. I don't—"

"Don't need my help? Yeah, I got the memo." And was thoroughly unfazed by it.

"Yesterday was a one-time thing, I never said you could come back. So why are you here?"

"Claiming my tour, for one thing. Figured before the workers show up would be better for you."

Of course he was right, blast him. "Then will you leave?"

"Well, now…" He stuck his thumb in his front pockets and rocked on his heels in full-on *aw-shucks-ma'am* mode.

She didn't know where this affable Cade had come from. She liked him better suspicious and surly. He was much easier to dismiss.

"The gazebo needs shoring up, best I can tell," he said. "It'll need painting afterward, of course, but I figure by this time tomorrow it'll be just about done."

She'd been forced to move the gazebo to the *maybe later* list, so to have it ready for the opening… But she couldn't pay him, and she didn't trust favors. No one did anything for free. "Why are you doing this, Cade? Seriously."

His eyes held hers. "Not because you're a charity case." He lifted one shoulder and glanced away. "I've got time on my hands, all right?" He stepped closer. "Let me help you, Sophie. I know how to do a lot of jobs. Growing up on a ranch, you learn everything from nursing cattle to auto mechanics to building barns and repairing roofs." His lips curved. "My dad figured out how to deal with four rowdy boys early on—you work 'em until they drop, then they don't have the energy to get into mischief."

Once again she envied the MacAllister children what they probably took for granted: a close-knit family whose members truly liked as well as loved one another and would battle the world for each other.

"From what Jenna's told me, you somehow managed mischief, anyway."

That grin again, the one that made her stomach flip. "She should talk." He laughed and scuffed his heel on the sidewalk. "But yeah...boys will be boys, I guess."

She considered all he'd already done and how much he really could help her. He was right, she needed it. And there were the photographs.... "Would you let me pay you?"

He scowled. "Hell, no. Friends don't charge friends for helping out."

"Is that what we are, friends?"

He flashed a grin. "For starters, anyway." He waggled his eyebrows. "There's still that hot sex option."

Whatever its origin, his good humor lightened her heart, so she dramatically rolled her eyes at him. "Uh-huh." Though a little thrill zipped through her at the thought.

"I'm pretty good, honey. Bet you are, too, long drink of water like you." His gaze went hot as he scanned her.

"You're not just trying to steal my dog, are you?"

He laughed. "Our dog. I'll agree to joint custody. But to answer your real question, no. I'm not trying to seduce you in order to get the dog. You are plenty of motivation all on your own, Queenie."

Her tummy fluttered. She finished her coffee and slid down from the railing. "The last thing I have time for right now is hot sex. Come on if you want the tour." She walked toward the back door.

"Okay, I changed my mind."

She turned to discover he was right behind her. "About what?"

"If you really believe you don't have time for great sex, then I do feel sorry for you." Before she could react, he halted her with a hand that lay warm on her hip. Everything inside her went still.

With exquisite slowness, Cade lowered his head to hers, hovering just a breath from her lips. "Take it from someone with recent experience… Life is too short to give up on the best parts." Gently he nipped her lower lip then his tongue soothed the faint sting.

Inside Sophie's chest, the beat of her heart skipped, and a sizzle scorched its way up her spine.

Dangerous. This I-want-you man, this amiable, unrelenting character posed a delectable danger that sorely tempted her to forget…everything.

She pressed still-buzzing lips together and slapped a palm to his chest. "I really, really do not have time for you."

He didn't grin, all signs of mischief vanished. "Make time," he said in a gravelly register.

"I have to think." She whirled from his grasp and all but lunged for the back door, wanting nothing so much as to slam it in his face and keep a safe barrier between them.

"I never give up on what I want, Sophie. Just so you know."

Shc gripped the screen door in one hand to anchor herself before she steeled her resolve and continued on.

Even as a very yummy anticipation shimmied through her.

She spoke over her shoulder as she walked. "If you want the nickel tour, get a move on." And told herself that didn't count as running from him.

But the blasted man had the nerve to chuckle knowingly even as he brought that big rangy body once again much too close to hers.

Like a cat, she longed to rub herself all over him.

So she put distance between them again. Quickly.

"We have to start at the front door," she said. "Don't look until we get there."

A few control issues, Queenie? But then he caught a glimpse of her face and saw the nerves there. This was her baby, he reminded himself. "How'd you get into hotel work?"

Surprise skimmed her features. "By accident." A fond smile. "I was… I didn't go to college right after high school, like most people." A lift of one shoulder. "Actually, I didn't go to high school for long." Then her face shuttered as if she regretted telling him so much. "Anyway, a few years later when I had to work to put myself through college, I saw an ad for a night desk clerk at a hotel in Memphis. I had the notion that I could study at night at the desk, since my other job as a waitress was nonstop action."

"I never went to college," he said, to make her feel more comfortable.

"Really?"

"All I cared about was my camera. I was convinced that on-the-ground experience was what was important, not some degree program."

"Did you ever take classes on photography?"

"Nope. I'm not much for formal instruction. Never even read the directions on any camera I've owned. I put more stock in personal experience. Trial by fire, I guess. Eventually you learn what you need to." He grinned. "Digital sure helps, though. Before that, I burned through a lot of film, never positive at the time what was working and what wasn't. I mean, I could always see the shot I wanted, but capturing it the way my mind pictured it? Not the same." A hint of the old adrenaline taunted him, and he yearned to hold on to it with everything in him. But just as quickly, it was gone.

He seized upon the closest topic to distract himself. "So you decided you liked the hotel field?"

"Amazingly enough. I was a business major already, but I went into hotels at first because the industry seemed sensible. Practical."

Did she know how much of a dreamer she was? How her eyes dimmed when she used words like *practical?* "What was it you enjoyed about that work?"

"I was good at a lot of things, I discovered." Her expression made it clear that was a surprise. "I'm very organized, I'm excellent at planning, I have excellent people sense...." Nervously, she tucked a strand of hair behind one ear.

"Jenna said you were way up the corporate ladder." Abruptly he remembered that Jenna had also spoken of something bad happening.

Her mouth tightened. "That's in the past."

And obviously a sore subject. "Okay. So why this place?"

Her frame relaxed. "I first saw it when I worked in Austin before. Jenna and I were out on a walk. The place was so buried in vines and out-of-control shrubbery and trees you could barely see the shape of it, much less its potential."

"But you did." They had that in common.

She nodded. "I couldn't forget this place. I spent lots of off-duty hours climbing around here, taking measurements and pictures, then I'd go back and sketch renovations or get bids. Even when I left Austin and went to work at the Atlantic City property, I'd worry about whether or not someone else would buy this place out from under me. Then when the company—" Her eyes darkened, and she seemed to shrink a little. "When I left the company, I knew it was time to put my dream into action. I've sunk every penny I have into this, along with a dear friend's investment and now..." But she didn't finish.

He wanted to prompt her to continue, but he'd learned enough about Queenie to understand that she'd clam up completely when pressed. At least the shape of her problem was more defined. She had to make this work, not only for herself but for someone she cared about.

Abruptly the vulnerable woman gave way to the executive. "Anyway, doesn't matter. A few years from now, Hotel Serenity will be legendary, and those who didn't believe in me will choke on their..." Abruptly she turned from him. "Never mind that." Faint color stained her cheeks as if she regretted even the smallest of confidences. A bright smile replaced it, the gracious hostess firmly in place. "So you walk in—"

"Let's start at the front gate," he suggested. "The walk up here looks amazing."

The hostess smile was replaced by a real one. "It does, doesn't it? Even when the vines were swallowing up the porch, the possibilities seemed so obvious to me. I knew there was a sanctuary waiting underneath it all." For once, her gaze on him was warm. She led the way to the front gate. "To keep the feeling of refuge for people who treasure privacy, there will be an electric gate off the driveway that leads to the parking lot. So guests will actually enter from here." She led the way to a side gate. "These vines will be allowed to take over the fence to a degree. That way, anyone driving by will catch small glimpses of the roof, but that's all. My guests will have a sense of being tucked away in a secret garden, a place to escape the world. Time out of time is what I'm after... A private universe in which they're comfortable and safe."

He could picture it, and he wondered at the life that had led her to create such a space she would then have to share with others. If it were his, he'd keep everything to himself.

What was it within Sophie that needed peace? She was fierce in her determination to create that haven for others, but Cade sensed she sought her own sanctuary. But from what?

He put a hand on her arm. She started to speak, but he shook his head. Closed his eyes. "Listen." A faint hum that he knew to be traffic was layered over with birdsong and the rustling of squirrels in the trees overhead.

But mostly there was stillness. Peace.

"I was in a monastery in Tibet once," he said before opening his eyes and looking at her. "I stayed there an extra day because there was a cloistered garden... It felt like this. As though your heart beat a little slower. Like each breath went a little deeper."

Her beautiful green eyes were wet. "Exactly. Thank you."

Then the rumble of a pickup at the driveway broke into the moment.

"The crew is here. I really should go."

"Is it okay if I wander through on my own?"

She appeared torn. "I'd like to show you myself, but " Her gaze shifted to the workers spilling out of the truck.

"Go talk to them, then, and I'll wait."

With a grateful smile she hurried away.

SOPHIE WAS STILL PONDERING his remarks as she rushed back from assigning the crew's tasks for the day.

He got it, the spirit she was working to capture here. Perhaps that shouldn't surprise her—his photography clearly demonstrated that Cade MacAllister saw far beneath the surface to what lay beyond the physical beauty of the places he'd been.

But it was the emotions he'd understood that had truly shocked her.... She'd assumed that someone who by his own admission didn't like dealing with people would be tone-deaf to emotional nuances he didn't want to feel.

Want to feel...that was key. Just because he preferred not to spend a lot of time with his fellow human beings was not an automatic sign that he lacked the ability to relate to them.

She'd have to think about that. Not that she could afford to get that involved examining Cade's psyche, but having him understand what she was trying to accomplish mattered if there was the slightest chance they could come to an agreement to allow his art to be displayed here...and oh, how she couldn't help getting her hopes up that they could. At first she'd only thought of the marketing boon, but knowing that he could see, really see into the heart of what she was trying to create here made her want desperately for his photos to complete the ambience she was dead set on realizing.

Cade would be the cherry on the sundae—not *him,* she hastened to correct herself—his photos. The last thing she could afford was to get distracted by him.

Just then she opened the front screen door and caught sight of him standing in her entryway, tall and male and deliciously rugged.

She bit her lip and thought she could still taste him. Not the cherry, no.

Cade MacAllister was the whole yummy sundae.

"Hey," he greeted, spotting her.

"Hey." She nodded back, suddenly self-conscious. *Get a grip, girl.* She gathered her wits to give the most crucial tour of her life.

CADE LOOKED AROUND AS she gestured to a space adjacent to the stairs. "Okay, I'll have a library table here which will serve as a greeting point for guests when they first arrive. There will be a basket waiting for each one, filled with a selection of local delicacies tailored to the individual guest's tastes. Hand-dipped chocolates, local wine, beautiful fruits in summer, home-canned preserves and breads in winter..." Sophie warmed to her task as she led him first to the left of the wide staircase. "In here is the library, cozy chairs, a wide selection of books including local authors, good reading lamps."

"You were right, the woodwork is beautiful. I wish Diego and Jesse could see this." He walked into the center. "If I didn't have work clothes on, I'd try out the chairs."

"Go ahead. This will not be a fussy place."

He sank into one and laid his head on the cushioned back. "This is great." He scanned the shelves for titles. "Some good books, too."

"You like to read?"

"Don't sound so shocked. My folks raised us all to

love books. I always have one in my backpack when I'm on a shoot."

"What are you reading right now?"

He couldn't decide if that was simple interest or a challenge. "*A Confederacy of Dunces,* one of my favorites."

She looked shocked. "Seriously?"

"Why? What do you think I should be reading?"

She flushed. "I don't know, just... I'm sorry. Reading tastes are very personal."

"So what are you reading right now?"

Her shoulders sagged. "Nothing. And it's about to kill me. I adore books and generally am in the process of reading one at all times, but right now..."

"Tell me one favorite, so we can be even." When she hesitated, he cocked an eyebrow. "Only fair, Queenie. I showed you mine, you show me yours."

"Jerk. So do I try to impress you by telling you I love Thomas Hardy or admit that I'm a sucker for a beach read?"

"Which is the truth?"

"Both."

"Good. Makes you more interesting. A well-rounded woman." His gaze scanned her. Lingered.

"O-okay!" she said brightly and swiveled, escaping across the entry. "In here will be groupings of sofas and comfy chairs for conversations or simply watching the fireplace. Plus more lamps for reading." She took him through the dining area and explained the ingenious tall windows that opened onto the porch, talked about the slate pathway she wanted to have to lead to the pergola.

They entered the kitchen. "I like this room best," he said.

"The kitchen? Why? Do you cook?"

"I can—our mom insisted we all learn—but I rarely do, unless you count the occasional fish over a campfire or such." He glanced down at her, his lips curving. "But that's not why this room's my favorite. At least for now. Once I kiss you somewhere else that might change."

She battled a smile and won. "Very funny." She did an about-face, but he would swear that as soon as her back was turned to him, she let the smile free.

"Through here is the pantry."

He whistled in appreciation. "This is as big as my mom's. Except hers is always full of stuff she's canned, along with enough food to feed an army just in case she has guests, which she does half the time."

"I'm hoping to have a garden so that we can do the same one day."

"You a gardener, Queenie?"

"No, not at all. I've lived in hotels or apartments for too long, but I've been studying. I like learning new things, and a garden makes sense, don't you agree?"

"Making sense is important to you, isn't it?"

A line appeared between her brows. "We need to pick up the pace." She all but raced ahead. "Here are the service stairs so the staff can access rooms more quietly and without disturbing anyone in the common areas. They also lead to the attic room I'm using for now."

"How much service? Isn't this more like a bed-and-breakfast?"

"No. I want the homey, comfortable feel of a B and B, but the guests will be treated to five-star service. For at least the first year, I'll live onsite and will have day help, plus I've hired a gifted chef who will prepare individual meals upon request. This will be first-class all the way. Casual doesn't mean sloppy or second-rate. At the prices they'll be paying, they'll expect that." She paused to demonstrate a state-of-the-art communications system plus wiring for routers, modem and satellite dish.

She mounted the stairs then halted. "Sorry, I didn't think to ask if you could climb stairs."

He scowled. "You just worry about yourself, Queenie. I know my limits."

She frowned right back. On the second floor, she guided him through a series of rooms, each one generous and with its own bath. "It wasn't easy to get steam showers in each room and whirlpool tubs in half of them without destroying the beauty of the spaces. It's a good thing historical designation restricts only the outer appearance. I want to honor the heritage of the place without sacrificing comfort."

"You've already got furniture in these," he observed. "Who's your decorator?"

"I am." She trailed a finger over the top of the gleaming Mission bureau she'd discussed with Maura. "Some of these pieces I've been collecting for years."

"You've had this place planned all that time?"

"No. Oh, I knew I wanted my own property one day, but I kept getting promotions, so for the last few years I had assumed it would be in a management capacity, maybe with a piece of ownership or a franchise or something. Nothing like this. But everything changed the second I saw this house. All the furniture refinishing I've done over the years has certainly paid off, even if I've paid a bundle in storage." She frowned. "I'd sure like to have those fees back right now."

"Refinishing?" He glanced around. "You did these?"

"Most of them. I like taking something that seems hopeless and making it shine again."

"Pretty impressive." He'd been raised to respect anyone willing to work with their hands.

"But I'm running out of time, and I have half a dozen more pieces to finish. I'd always planned to complete it all myself, but I hadn't counted on becoming a jack-of-all-trades at the same time."

"So when are you doing the refinishing? At night," he decided without waiting for her answer. "That's why the dark circles. Surely you know that's not smart. Send them out. Let someone else do the rest."

"Absolutely not. They're mine. When this place is finished, it will sparkle, and I'll know, even if no one else does, that I had a hand in every room."

"Not if you wind up in the hospital."

"I won't," she snapped. "And if you insist on badgering me, we're done with the tour."

"Fine," he said curtly.

She sighed. "I'm sorry. It's only that…"

"You're exhausted," he finished for her. "What would you say if one of your employees was working all day and halfway through the night?"

"I'd probably send him home to bed."

He waited.

"Look, I'd knock off early if I could, but I have so much to do and there's no more time. You don't understand." But her posture spoke for her. She was worn-out.

"I thought you wanted to hang my work."

"Are you blackmailing me?"

"If that's what it takes. Sit down while you talk to me. Give me more details about what you're after."

With obvious reluctance, she settled into a chaise. To keep her there, he leaned against the door jamb.

She stared at the ceiling. "Picture windows. That's what I'm after. Abstract images are too easy to ignore, and paintings still make you think you're separate... what I'm after is to heighten the fantasy each suite represents by taking guests that one step further into another universe. I want photographs, but not ordinary ones. I want them to tease the eye, to cause a second look and in the end to resist categorization." Her lids seemed heavy, and she fell silent. For a moment he thought she'd gone to sleep, which would be the best thing for her, but then in a dreamy voice she continued.

"I want to make the viewer feel as though he landed on another planet or into an alternate universe...sort of the way you do when you're traveling and you stumble upon a fabulous spot that's not in your guidebook and is all the more extraordinary for it." Her gaze fastened on his. "You'd know that feeling."

He nodded. He'd been in some amazing locations... a tiny Buddhist temple in the jungles of Thailand, a Mayan altar at the edge of a ravine in the rain forest, places so private only a few outsiders had ever laid eyes on them. And he might never again.

"I want to give people an oasis in the midst of a city, a chance to escape for an hour or a day or weeks from all that's pressing in on them, like reading a good book can take you away or listening to music or meditation…" Her voice slowed. "A rest for the soul and the imagination. A place to be comforted and soothed and pampered but one step more—a place to see possibilities. A place to dream, that's what I'm after…." She grew quiet again, her body relaxing.

"Close your eyes. Describe your dream image." He kept his voice gentle and low.

Another long pause. "The edge of nighttime. The possibility of magic you feel just as day gives way and the sounds shift and slow…."

Cade watched as she slipped into slumber, as her breathing slowed and her body relaxed. He kept watching for longer than she would probably be happy about, uneasily aware that he was cataloguing her features.

And liking too much what he saw.

Slowly, with care for squeaky old wood floors, he made his way downstairs and outside to see what he could about buying her time for a much-needed nap.

CHAPTER SEVEN

CADE AND THE WORKMEN had quickly come to an arrangement, facilitated by his mastery of Spanish—an inevitable consequence of growing up with his Latino half brothers Diego and Jesse Montalvo. His mother, Grace, had been widowed before she met Cade's dad, Hal, and Cade and his siblings had been embraced by the Montalvo family.

Not that Spanish was his only language; he had a passing knowledge of a few more. He didn't like leaving himself in the hands of a translator if at all possible. Talking to people, even if no one in his family believed he knew how, was the best way to find the hidden gems. Sharing meals over campfires or in crude huts…you had to meet people on their home turf, not barge in as though you were superior. Locals knew the magic places they would never share with strangers, especially not Americans who wouldn't try to meet them halfway.

There was so much variety, so much wonder in the world. As Sophie had noted, there was magic in seeing the different.

A tiny prickle at the back of his neck had Cade freezing in place, caught by hope.

He knew that feeling. Oh, God, he missed it. He re-

mained still, praying for the return of the signal, the
fire that had formed his life.

After an endless span, he had to accept that it was
gone, and he mourned it afresh. *Please*. He'd never
begged in his life, but he was begging now. *Please
let me feel it again*. The thought of living the rest of
his days without that inner eye scared him as no risky
climb, no jungle menace ever had. That razor-sharp
awareness of a dimension beyond the ordinary…it had
been his life. If he never felt it again…

What was the point of a life in which he was blind
like most people? Rooted in place?

Cade's fists clenched on the lopping shears he was
using. He wanted out of this dark hole he was in, and
he wanted out now.

SOPHIE STIRRED AND STRETCHED. She'd been having the
most amazing dream. Cade was with her and…

Cade. Her eyes flew open. She sat up so quickly she
got dizzy. She'd fallen asleep in the middle of—where
was he? She glanced at the watch on her wrist and stifled a shriek of horror. Three hours had passed.

Three. In that amount of time, she could have… Oh,
no! The paint store was closed now, and she needed
more stain for the side table she was refinishing.

She peered out the bedroom window and spotted him
almost immediately. He and the foreman of her crew
were earnestly discussing something, and Cade was
clearly listening then nodding as a decision was made.

After costing her both time and progress she could
not afford, he presumed to make the decisions.

On *her* grounds.

With *her* crew.

Undermining her authority and telling the crew God knew what.

Sophie charged down the stairs and outside. At her approach, both men looked up, the foreman seeming far too cheerful while Cade appeared to be without remorse. He said something in Spanish that made the other man laugh.

Sophie hit the red zone. He'd had no right to let her sleep, much less take over her job.

Her job. Not his.

"We're making great progress," Cade said as she approached. "Armando and his guys are good. You're lucky to have them."

Armando's grin was huge.

She tried to get herself under control. *You know better than this. Focus on the crew, the foreman. You can have it out with Cade later.*

She was too smart to be wading in and throwing her weight around, even if she wanted to strangle Cade. As if, she thought wryly, she was strong enough to make the faintest impression on someone that muscular. Instead she glanced around then fastened her gaze squarely on Armando's. "*Gracias*. It looks wonderful." And it did. She had no idea how she'd slept through the hammering necessary to erect the pergola.

It would be churlish to withhold her gratitude not only from the crew but from the man who'd obviously listened carefully to her plans. Except, of course, to the part about her not having time to take a nap.

A three-freaking-hour nap.

"Muy bonita." She let her gaze take in the entire crew. *"Muchas gracias."* All of which was about the extent of her Spanish. Good thing Armando's English was enough for them to get most things squared away.

"We have an idea. I think you'll like it. This way." Cade gestured toward the tool shed. Armando accompanied them. "You didn't mention any plans for this structure."

"Storage building, I guess." She shrugged. "We'll have to have a great deal of that."

"You will, but there's room to add on to the garage if you need more storage." He paused. "Can I make a suggestion?"

"Why not? Since you've apparently decided to take over while you let me sleep."

"Chill, Queenie." Impatience crowded his gaze. "I'm not trying to stage a coup, and you needed the rest."

"You had no right."

"You really want to have this discussion now?" His eyes cut to Armando before returning to her, and in it temper simmered.

The old Cade was back, the cranky, high-handed one. Good. The kinder one she'd gotten glimpses of was too much temptation. She pressed her lips together to stifle the upbraiding she wanted to give and merely shook her head.

He jammed his hands on his hips in irritation, but he hauled in a deep breath and went on. "I stayed in this place in Sumatra where they had a... I don't really know what to call it in English, but it was sort of like a cabana, except made from an old building, as small as this. One side was left mostly open but was screened from view, and inside was a really great chair for lounging. It was a fantastic place to be by yourself. They even had a masseuse available who'd set up a table there if you wanted. You heard the birds and smelled the flowers… It was peaceful. The style's not practical for all weather, but winter doesn't last that long here, and with some wiring for a ceiling fan and—"

She was far too intrigued to hold on to her pique. "We could do that with the storage shed, you think?" Her mind was spinning out scenarios, already sorting through which furnishings could fit. Then she made herself stop. "I don't have any money in the budget for more renovations," she said with more regret than he could imagine.

"It won't take much. I can wire it and install the fan myself." He stepped beside her. "Take out part of this wall then use the same lumber for door facings. The wood, like everything else around the house, is solid. I learned as a kid never to waste materials. Some new nails, a ceiling fan and some wiring is all you'd need to have." He turned to her, and eagerness had replaced his irritation. "Intriguing idea?"

She'd been wanting to offer massage services but assumed they'd have to take place in the guest rooms. If they built this…shelter, there would be some times of the year they still would, but this building could be an amazing space, and if it couldn't be used year-round, so what? That only made it more special.

"Very intriguing." Her mind was racing. "I know exactly the chaise. And there's a ceiling fan we removed from the kitchen that still seems to work."

"There you go."

Her gaze met his. "I'm sorry. And thank you."

"No sweat. Armando has a suggestion for creating a path and relocating a few plants from elsewhere on the property to soften up the look of this structure."

"Really?" She looked at her foreman.

"*Es verdad.* We do this, Señorita Sophie. *Muy bueno.*"

"And there's time?"

"*Esé,*" he indicated Cade. "He is strong. Good help."

She couldn't help grinning at Cade's smug expression. "You heard the man, Queenie. Some people like having me around."

Armando's face split into a smile.

Sophie gave up and laughed. "Thank you," she said to Armando, then lifted her eyes to the blue ones smiling down at her. "And thank you."

The moment shimmered with pleasure.

And hope.

Sophie had forgotten too much about both.

"I, uh, I see to my men," Armando said.

The spell that locked her gaze to Cade's shattered, and she hastily turned away, rubbing her palms on her jeans when her hands itched to touch him, to… "I—I have work to do. And you should go home," she said to Cade, trying to put distance between them. He already had proved himself a distraction she couldn't afford. She could not lose her focus on what was important.

"Scared, Queenie?" His amused voice followed her.

Don't look back. Whatever you do, don't look back at him.

The rich sound of his laughter accompanied her all the way into the house.

CHAPTER EIGHT

ON THE DARKENED PORCH of Jenna's home, Cade drew his laptop from its case with the caution of someone handling a rattlesnake. He'd never been one to submit to the electronic leash so many people accepted. Much of his life had been spent far from cell phone towers or Wi-Fi hotspots, and though he knew it made him seem a Neanderthal to others, he liked the world better that way—observed firsthand, experienced in its raw reality, not on a computer screen. Talking to real people—though, he admitted, no more often than he had to—not via text messages and emoticons.

He was a throwback, and he'd never minded the label. Too many people in the "civilized world" had gotten so far away from the realities of their ancestors that they lived in their heads. Their experiences were made up entirely of the visual, the artificial—the world as seen in the mind, not felt in all its messy, startling, sometimes astonishing truth.

So while he did communicate via email with his editor and agent, he felt not the slightest twinge at being away from communications for long spans of time. His laptop was a tool, a place to store his images, but it was not his lifeline—or shackle.

Since the accident, he'd opened his laptop maybe

three times. Once, he'd gone so far as to enter the directory where his images were stored, even dared to open a folder.

The hardest one, the one containing the picture of Jaime grinning at him only minutes before he would die. Cade closed his eyes, bowed his head. *God, Jaime, I am so sorry.*

Jaime and he had shared amazing experiences that couldn't be explained in words. Jaime was, in many ways, as much a brother to him as his own siblings were.

As soon as he'd been conscious enough to think clearly, he'd asked his dad to ensure the climber's insurance he'd bought for Jaime would pay out, and he'd sent money to the family himself to tide them over in the meantime.

But no amount of money made up for the love of a father and a husband, or the memories his family would miss out on for the rest of their lives, all because Cade had wanted *adventure*.

Every trip Cade had taken, reveling in the risks and the exploration…had stolen Jaime from his family. For short periods at first, and then, permanently….

He hadn't been reckless, no—Jaime wouldn't have let him be—but his definition of reckless was not like others'. He'd told himself that his purpose was important, that he was bringing the world's mysteries and beauty to those who would otherwise be denied them and that was worth the risks.

For the first time in his life, Cade questioned what he'd previously been so certain about. He'd expected to spend his days wandering, searching...and alone. He'd even been prepared for the number of those days to be less than most—only a fool would ignore the dangers inherent in the wild locales he traversed.

He should have been the one to die, not Jaime. His own family would have been devastated to lose him, but if one of the two of them had to be taken, it should have been Cade who would leave behind no children, no mate.

He nearly closed his laptop before it had even powered up. Confronting the one-dimensional nature of his life, considering how few people would miss him if he were gone, was damn near as painful as dealing with the loss of his friend.

And then there was the need to think about what kind of life he could make, robbed of its one essential element. His fingers tightened on the lid. To still them from shutting it took everything he had.

But this time, there was another reason to face his demons. *Sophie.* Admirable, fierce, exhausted Sophie, who touched more than his libido. Who stirred things in him that didn't bear considering. So he wouldn't. He'd focus instead on the crackling heat between them. He had always been a man of action, a physical man more than a cerebral one. She touched him at a very primal level. An intensely physical one.

And she reacted strongly to him, too.

Cade was surprised to find a faint grin spreading across his face even as he watched the program he dreaded begin to load.

He'd be more than happy to lose his non-bet with

Sophie. Getting his hands on her would more than com-
pensate for his damaged ego. It would also distract him
from the ticking clock of his deadline with his publisher.

He and Sophie could have some fun, and Sophie
needed fun more than anyone he'd met in a long time.
She was so serious, so driven....

His chest tightened.

He had been the same, once. His work had been everything to him, too, once upon a time.

His gut twisted as he contemplated a life without
his work. He couldn't look at any more shots, couldn't
stand on the outside looking, a has-been with his nose
pressed to the glass....

But he'd promised her. Grimly, Cade stilled his
hands, closed his eyes, willed the fear away.

Oddly enough, what helped most was picturing
Sophie asleep, the lines of exhaustion easing from her
body.

She needed his help. Cade shoveled everything
else in a mental closet and slammed the door. Then
he began sorting through shots in search of two he'd
known would be perfect when he'd stood in the grand
old house and listened to Sophie lay out her dream.

There. He clicked on a picture he'd taken on a Ti-
betan peak, not from the top, not the expected shot, but
one from a hundred meters or so down the slope where
he'd stopped to gather himself for the final assault on
the summit.

It was more optical illusion than photograph, more
surreal than representational, a pattern of ridged ice

and windswept drifts, with the stark sunlight of high altitudes an unexpected foil for the sprinkling of stars that shouldn't have been possible in daylight.

The last bedroom—the one Sophie had napped in— there was a wall beside the bed, one where you could wake up and see this picture first thing in the morning....

He'd never sent this one for publication. It was too hard to categorize, too mystical to easily peg with a caption, to explain to an audience.

But he'd kept it because it spoke to him. He clicked and saved it to a new folder, then hunted up the Mayan temple series. He focused on one image that exuded a sense of mystery—the jungle's endless shades of color were muted to nearly black but for the hot pink and orange flowers dotting the vines and branches, the focus of the picture leading the viewer's eye to the surprise of one angled stone edge, which revealed that man had been there before. And that man's efforts were nothing in the face of nature.

He saved that one, as well, for Sophie. It was powerful and seductive, but it wasn't pretty. She might hate it.

Cade scowled. Could it be that he was actually nervous? When was the last time he'd felt uncertain about the reception of his work?

Of course he wasn't nervous. If she couldn't handle the image, then that was on her. He shut down his laptop, rose and slipped it into his case, then entered the house.

"I'll be back," he said to Jenna as he strode through to the front door.

"Where are you going?"

"Out." He wasn't used to accounting for his whereabouts. He kept no timetable but his own, answered to others only so they'd know where to find the body if he didn't return.

But Jenna had exerted a great deal of effort not to hover, he chided himself. And being nosy was only her nature. He glanced back over his shoulder. "I have a couple of shots to show Sophie."

"This late? She said she wasn't still working half the night."

"I'm betting she lied. You?"

Jenna sighed. "No bet—you're likely right. Maybe I'll come with you. She might let me do something useful for a change."

Cade observed the stacks of papers scattered around Jenna—the miles of red tape she hacked through on a regular basis to help those she felt responsible for. "Sophie's not the only one who could use more time off, Jen."

"Part of the job."

Cade paused. "I'm proud of you, kiddo."

She looked startled. "For what?"

"For how hard you try to make a difference."

Her smile was tired. "Some days it feels like swimming uphill in molasses."

"Armando told me how you helped his mother straighten out her disability checks. You do make a difference."

Jenna's cheeks stained with color. "Not enough."

He crossed back to her, bent and pressed a kiss on the top of her head. "There are any number of people who would disagree." He laid his hand on her hair. "You could use some sleep, too. You're not getting any younger, you know."

"Yeah, well, at least I'm not almost forty." A saucy grin lit up her tired face.

"I love you, sis. Get some rest, okay? Tomorrow's soon enough to save the world."

"I love you, too. I'll leave a light on. Don't do anything I wouldn't do."

"Sure thing, Mom." He headed out. Turned back and grinned. "Don't wait up."

Jenna made a rude noise and returned to her work.

CADE SPOTTED THE LIGHT on in the garage at Sophie's and made his way over. Of course she wouldn't take the night off.

He was about to knock on the door when he caught sight of her through a window. The space was a jumble of furniture and work surfaces. In one corner he saw a chaise with torn cushions, next to it an end table that seemed already finished. So this was her workspace. He drew closer to the glass.

Golden light pooled around her as she sanded the frame of a chair. She paused periodically to lightly run her long, slender fingers over the curves of the wood.

He could feel the caress of them low in his body.

She was a long way from the tightly controlled hotelier now, no hotshot executive in sight. Her hair was

scraped back in a ponytail as she often kept it when
working outdoors, but in the humid night air, strands
had escaped to curl at her temples and along the graceful line of her neck, lazily disturbed now and then by
the rotating fan.

His fingers itched for his camera.

Cade barely breathed. He closed his eyes and savored
the feeling for an instant before his mind darted away.
He felt almost superstitious about lighting too heavily
on the long-lost sensation and scaring it off.

When he opened his eyes, however, the lines of her
still fascinated him.

Which was odd. He'd never been drawn to photographing people. Viewers brought baggage with them,
and they were too prone to reading that baggage into
depictions of other people. Humans studied other
humans, focused on them more than any other part of
nature, and he didn't normally want that interference
with his vision.

But tonight it was the elements of Sophie that drew
him in. The single line of the tendon at one side of her
throat, the plump flesh at the base of her thumb. The
drift of hair across her cheekbone.

He cursed himself—once, his camera had been
always within reach, and now it was several blocks
away. Damn it, if he didn't grasp the moment, it might
leave and never return....

He must have made a sound because her head
snapped up and she saw that someone was watching
her. Caution crept into her frame, and she gripped a

hammer lying on the workbench as she approached the window.

When she reached the glass, her eyes widened. "Cade?"

He wanted to say, *Wait, I'll be back, don't move,* but he was nearly certain that she would never pose for him. The moment was lost.

Please let it not be gone for good. This impulse was different than what he knew, what he'd built his career on, but one thing was the same, at least: he was eager. Impatient. Alive again.

Then the moment fled, and he feared to his soul it would never return.

"Are you all right?" she asked as she let him in. "What are you doing here?"

He had no choice but to let go and try to believe that the magic would be back. He would never leave his camera behind again, just in case. And he would remember those lines of her. Moments couldn't be repeated, but still...

He brandished his laptop. "I have a couple of shots for you to look at."

"Really?" Delight shone from her eyes.

He sat and patted the sofa beside him. She settled gingerly on the cushions, leaving space between them. Simply to be perverse, he didn't swivel the laptop, thus forcing her to move right next to him.

She smelled good. Wood shavings and an undertone of roses.

He opened the file of the mountain shot for her, and she gasped. She bent closer then looked up at him.

"Cade… Oh, Cade, this is… It's perfect. Exactly perfect. The range of your talent stuns me." She jerked her gaze back to the screen, pressing her lips together. "The bedroom we were in…" Her cheeks took on color, and he smiled, recalling her slumbering beauty.

"That's what I thought, too," he said. Her gaze shifted to him again and the thrill that shone from her eyes took some of the sting from his overwhelming sense of loss. Without thinking, he bent his head to hers, and Sophie went very still.

He brushed his mouth over hers. Her breath hitched then, to his surprise, she met his kiss with one of her own. Heat poured through him like molten steel, and it was all he could do to pull away. Soft air slid between her mouth and his. Eyes still closed, Sophie took in a ragged breath, and he wasn't too far from begging himself.

Her pupils were huge and dark…and worried. "Cade, we shouldn't mix… This isn't wise."

He smiled though he felt more like howling. "Babe, this is going to happen. Count on it." Soon this draw between them would prove too much, and her control would snap—or his would. But for now, he could manage.

He yanked his attention from her to the screen before she could protest his words. "Okay…" He needed a big, deep breath himself. "Pay attention, Sophie. Help a guy out."

"Yeah, right." She snorted, but he heard the grin in her voice.

And liked her more than ever for it.

He clicked on the second image and was rewarded with another gasp of pleasure.

He would seduce many more gasps from her before they were done with each other.

A few of them would even be about photographs.

ONCE SOPHIE FINALLY went to bed, her sleep had been populated by mountains and jungles, by restless dreams and wishes she couldn't hold on to when she awoke.

The next day, she watched Cade come through the gate, but she kept herself back and focused on her own work. After last night, she needed to keep some distance between them. They hadn't discussed him continuing to work here, but waiting for permission clearly wasn't his style. He seemed more at peace, though, when he was active, and Jenna said her family was worried he'd just take off if he got too restless, so she would let things be for now.

Would he really let her hang those stunning photographs he'd shown her last night? Though she'd never been able to spell out exactly what she'd been seeking, somehow he'd come up with something even more remarkable. Those photographs would be amazing in any marketing materials she put together, and she wanted them desperately—but she hadn't discussed price with Cade. And even if she could manage his price, how would she ever pay to have them framed? And after they'd settled on the photos, would he leave—? Oh, he was making her crazy and they'd barely even kissed.

A secret smile played over her lips. They'd barely

kissed, yes, but…wow. What kisses they'd been. *This is going to happen,* he'd vowed.

It couldn't. It shouldn't. She had no time for such foolishness, but…

She wanted it to happen, all of it. Scraps of fevered dreams returned to her then, images of his tough, rangy body entwined with hers—

"Señorita Sophie."

"Hmm?" Oh, good grief. Bad enough her sleep had been spotty, but here she was daydreaming about Cade and hadn't noticed Armando's approach. "I'm sorry, did you say something?"

"We have cleared the path down to the lake. The branches could be chipped to make mulch for your flower beds, if you would like. Renting a chipper would be cheaper than hauling them off."

Renting. Another expense. Did the landscaper have his own? She'd been trying to get in touch with him for days, and had been unable to get through to him. "Do you know how much renting might be, Armando?"

"I will check before I come tomorrow, okay?"

She had to thank Jenna again—Armando worked hard and was so careful with her money. "That would be wonderful, if you wouldn't mind."

"No problem. We will see you tomorrow, then."

With a start, Sophie realized the sun was slipping behind the trees to the west. "Of course. Will you close the gate as you leave?"

"Yes, though Cade is still here, working on the casita."

"Casita?"

"The small house he is making from the little shed. Do you have a name for it?"

"I don't. Maybe casita is best, you think?"

"Perhaps you will know when it is finished. He works hard, that man. It will not be long."

She glanced in the direction of the structure they were discussing, as though she could see it through the walls of the hotel. He did work hard. Aside from a brief, neutral good-morning hours before, they hadn't spoken today.

Though more than once, she'd caught him staring at her, that dark blue gaze unnerving.

Other than those times, she'd only seen Cade in passing as he shouldered lumber she worried was too heavy for his still-recovering body to be carrying. When she'd ventured that opinion, however, his look had said without words that solicitude was not welcome.

I have a mother six hundred miles away, he'd already pointed out.

He came around the side of the house just then and she yanked her eyes away. Was there any sight yummier than a muscular man in a sweat-soaked T-shirt with a tool belt around his lean hips?

No, what Sophie felt for Cade was anything but maternal.

Absently she said goodbye to Armando and returned to her painting, noticing that Cade disappeared behind the house again. When she finished the segment of the border she was painting, she yielded to temptation and decided to go see the path Armando had cleared, the one she'd been eagerly awaiting. She set her brushes to soak and wandered out on the porch, stretching her aching back then bending forward, placing her hands flat on the floor and reversing the stretch. She rocked side to side, easing the kinks from her legs, then went limp, bent over her legs again, letting the day's tension ease from a body that stayed tense too much of the time.

"Pretty impressive, Queenie."

She jolted up to standing. He was staring at her again. "I thought I was alone."

He brandished an insulated bottle. "I was just refilling my water supply."

"Are you all r—" She clamped her lips together.

The corners of his eyes crinkled. "Now I know you weren't going to ask me if I'm okay 'cause you wouldn't want to hover, right?" A slow smile spread. "Yes, Mom, I'm fine. Been staying hydrated. How about you?"

He stood there, hip-shot and cocky, so incredibly male. *This is going to happen.*

She wished he'd hurry up and make it happen.

She wished he'd go away.

She wished...

Sophie tore her attention from Cade. "I'm fine. Are you about finished? I'm going to check out the path Armando cleared." Without waiting for his answer, she moved across the grass toward the trees. She entered the winding path she'd envisioned as a passage to another sort of hideaway, in character with the hotel itself. Branches were still stacked in neat piles, so the view was not yet what it would be, but...

"What is it?"

She hadn't noticed that Cade had followed her until he spoke.

"It's going to be so beautiful. And look, the lake! You can get little glimpses of it through the trees." She turned to him. "Someday I want to have benches at certain spots like this one, and maybe another gazebo and—oh! That little clearing would be perfect for a big swing hanging from that tree." In that moment she knew all the backbreaking work was going to be worth it. This would be the jewel she'd dreamed it would be. For the first time in weeks, she was beginning to truly believe she hadn't made a horrible mistake and dragged Maura down with her.

"Have dinner with me."

"What?" She turned to see Cade watching her. "You're doing it again."

"Doing what?"

"Staring at me. Why?"

"I can't think you're beautiful?" But his gaze slid to the side.

"Looking like this?" She laughed. "I'm a wreck."

He tugged at her ponytail. "You look good to me." That odd stare was gone, replaced by mischief. "But then, I was raised on a ranch."

Her brows snapped together. "What's that supposed to mean?"

"You're so easy to needle, Queenie. Jenna's way tougher to ruffle than you. You must not have any brothers." He relented. "I only meant that I'm not much for painted women. Glamour doesn't impress me. I prefer the authentic." His gaze was warm, and something inside her unfurled. "So I found this great Mexican place on South First…"

"Oh, I couldn't. There's so much—"

"We have to go see Skeeter anyway, and afterward, we can just stop for a quick bite."

"I don't know…" But she wanted to, badly.

"You have to eat, I have to eat. Jenna deserves some time alone. C'mon, Sophie, live a little."

When was the last time she'd done something just for fun? But at the same time, what price would she pay for stealing a couple of hours?

Her stomach twisted. The hours to the opening were dwindling.

He started to turn away.

She took the leap. "All right. But I need a shower."

He glanced back. "Me, too. I'll put up my tools and head over to Jenna's, then swing round to pick you up. Thirty minutes enough?"

"That would be great." And scary. And she was going to do it.

This is going to happen. Count on it.

A fling. With a gorgeous man. Who wouldn't expect more.

Oh, she was indeed counting on everything he'd promised, probably more than she should.

And sooner rather than later.

Cade walked off, and Sophie watched him go, sighing a little, like a teenage girl.

Though the teenage Sophie would never in a million years have had the nerve to imagine herself with someone like Cade MacAllister. But she wasn't that timid girl anymore. The woman she was now made her own dreams come true.

CHAPTER NINE

"I'M TELLING YOU HE wants to be called Skeeter. Surely you can see that—unless you're willfully being blind." Cade glanced over from the driver's seat as he drove them toward the little Tex-Mex café.

"Please. Skeeter is for some coonhound, not a handsome fellow like my Finn."

"Our Finn—I mean, Skeeter." When Sophie laughed at his mistake, Cade felt like the world just might make some sense after all.

When they'd been seated in the restaurant, Cade ordered margaritas for both of them.

"I shouldn't," Sophie protested.

"Can't, won't, shouldn't… You draw up a pretty stiff set of rules for yourself, Queenie." He nodded at the waiter and sent him on. "You don't have to drink it. Shoot, I might have both of them."

"Are you hurting?" She leaned forward in alarm. "I knew you worked too hard today. You expect too much of yourself."

He glowered at her.

"Sorry, sorry. Don't know what I was thinking, caring about you or that thick head on your shoulders."

"Now who's grumpy?"

"I'll have you know most people consider me cool, calm and gracious."

"So it's only me who brings out the worst in you?"

"Apparently."

The margaritas arrived, and they placed their orders. Cade took a sip of his. "Nice." He leaned back. "You should try it, Queenie. How else am I gonna get you naked?"

She glared at him. "When did you turn so jovial? You don't like people, remember?"

"I like you."

"No, you only want me naked." She stuck out her tongue at him then took a sip. "Mmm, that is good." She took another.

"Careful, Queenie. Those are top-shelf, and you haven't eaten since breakfast."

"How do you know that?"

Because I pay altogether too much attention to you. Especially today, when he'd also spent far too much time framing her in a viewfinder—or an imaginary viewfinder, anyway, since he didn't want to draw attention to himself by getting out his camera. To cover, he shrugged. "Seems to be your pattern. Not a good one, I might add. You're too thin already."

"I beg your pardon. It's simply my body type. You don't have to like it."

"Wish I didn't," he muttered.

"What did you say?"

"You don't need me to tell you you're beautiful." But from her uncomfortable expression, apparently she did.

He leaned closer. "Come on, Soph...what kind of men are you dating?"

She glanced away. "I'm too busy to date."

"Now, maybe, but what about before?"

"I've moved around a lot."

"So do I, but—"

"Not all of us have a girl in every port."

"I sure hope not."

She glared. "Stop being charming. It's better when you're overbearing."

He studied her, color high in her cheeks, her eyes anywhere except on him, but he waited to respond until after the waiter had placed their platters before them. He picked up his fork but watched her take the first bite. "Zane's the charming one, not me. The rest of us are more serious." He grinned. "But I'm telling Zane you said I was charming. He won't believe it."

"Is it weird?"

"Is what weird?"

"Having the two-time *Sexiest Man Alive* as your brother. Do people ask you about him all the time?" She shook her head. "Probably not. You're just as famous."

"Not that many people read photo credits. Zane's name and face are splattered all over movie screens and magazines. But to answer your question, I don't even know the guy they write about. Zane's my kid brother who was a skinny little geek we beat up on to toughen him up."

"I can't begin to understand that."

He shrugged. "It's what brothers do. We kicked his tormentors' asses at first, but he had to be able to defend himself. We couldn't always be around. Diego and Jesse are a lot older, so they were gone from home when Zane hit junior high. So it was up to me, mostly."

"Yet you get along, all of you, from what Jenna says."

"Any of us would die for the others. Simple fact."

"And everyone dotes on Jenna."

"She likes to think she bosses us all around." Amusement crossed his features. "Has she made the *I can make my brothers do anything* claim to you yet?"

"Yes, and that worries me. I can't let Jenna run roughshod over you. I mean, I want those photos you showed me almost more than I want to take my next breath, but I won't take them for free, and we have to talk about the cost. Those images are priceless. I have to be fair to you, and I can't possibly afford them if I am."

He laughed. "Are you an only child?"

His laughter wasn't unkind, but still… "Yes. Why?" She tried not to feel insulted.

"Sorry. No offense meant. I'm just saying that Jenna is, shall we say, forceful. Some of that is simply her personality, but part of it is the product of too many people who adore her and who have, I must admit, spoiled her in some ways. We're lucky that she has such a generous heart. She could have been a tyrant, but her nature has always been relentlessly sunny. She was far enough behind the rest of us that it's almost as if she had six indulgent parents. We're happy to make her happy, especially since she doesn't take advantage of that, so yes, we often go along with her schemes, but it's not because

we don't know how to say no. She's just…special to us."
He stopped. "Does that make any sense?"

Not to me, she wanted to say. The concept was completely foreign to Sophie. She'd been loved as a child, but her parents had been so wrapped up in each other that she'd often felt the odd man out. But instead she said, "I think so."

"Your parents—when did you lose them? Must have been early to make you so self-reliant."

She hesitated. She never talked about her early life, but the golden pool of light in which they sat seemed to invite confidences. "I was fifteen when they died in a boating accident."

"Where did you go then? To your grandparents?"

"No. There wasn't anyone."

"No one?" he echoed. "Grandparents? Aunts or uncles?"

She shook her head. "I was put into foster care."

He looked at her more closely than ever before. "Wow. I can't imagine. I mean, I haven't spent much time with my family since I left home, but…" He stared off into the distance. "I always knew they were there. Even if something had happened to my folks—God forbid—Mama Lalita or my dad's family, someone would have stepped in."

"Mama Lalita?" What a great name.

"Has Jenna told you that my two older brothers had a different dad? He was Latino, and his mother was like a grandmother to us, growing up. She's a *curandera.*"

She cocked her head. "A what?"

"A healer. It's a tradition that dates back to the

Aztecs, and it considers the mind and soul to be as integral to healing as the body. Out where my family lives, a lot of people don't seek the care of doctors—at least they didn't until my oldest brother Diego and his cardiac surgeon wife, Caroline, set up a medical practice that incorporates both Latino traditions and Western medicine. Diego succeeded Mama Lalita as *curandero*." He laughed. "As a surgeon who believed the scalpel cures all, Caroline had a hard time of it at first, but…" He shook his head. "Long story. Anyway, I'm sorry. It's wrong that you were deprived of a family…" He paused, then said, "So is foster care why you didn't go to college right after high school?"

"I…" She glanced away.

Then she thought of her beautiful hotel and moved her eyes back to him. She had nothing to be ashamed of. She'd made something of herself. "I ran away from foster care, but I was very naive. The streets…" She shook her head. "Not a good place for kids."

"That's what Caroline said. You'd have a lot in common."

She frowned. "Why?"

"She and her two sisters were separated in foster care. She ran away, too, and she had one hell of a hard climb to make it to the top of her field." His eyes were a soft blue. "You did, too, didn't you?"

Sophie didn't like discussing that period of her life. She hadn't told Jenna anything about Kenny and Sarah. She was all set to gloss over it as usual when she heard herself say, "I met a boy who saved me."

Cade said nothing, only listened.

"He— I'd been sheltered until my parents died. I was too soft for the streets. He was—" She firmed her lips. "He was one of the kids society gave up on, but he was scrappy. He took me under his wing, even though we were only a year apart in age. He had the street wisdom of someone much older. When I got—" She stopped. She'd never told a soul in her current life about her baby, but for some reason—maybe only to warn Cade off from the intimacy that was growing between them—she realized she wanted to tell him. "I got pregnant." She waited for him to recoil, but he only sat there patiently. "He was eighteen and I was seventeen. We couldn't even get married legally until Sarah was a year old." Instead of the ache that usually accompanied any thought of what she'd lost, she was surprised to feel only tenderness for the kids they had been, children having a child.

She shrugged and continued. "We made a life. It was hard, but we were in love the way only teenagers can be. Not that we remained teenagers for long—Sarah changed all that." Her eyes did glisten then as she remembered the warm, precious feel of her baby in her arms. Sophie found herself hugging a phantom child to her breast and quickly clasped her hands together, squeezing them tightly between her knees. "Kenny and our daughter were killed in a car crash when Sarah was three." And she'd been alone again. So alone.

Cade laid his hand on her arm. "I'm sorry."

Only two words, not dripping with pity but quietly supportive. Sophie surprised herself by not jerking away from his comfort. She felt oddly safe confiding in him. She was a strong and determined woman who would have said she was over her losses, that she'd made a life she was proud of, that she never looked back.

All of those were true.

Yet that life didn't afford the luxury of having someone to lean on, and suddenly she was blinking back tears she'd thought she would never shed again.

"So you started all over. Again," he said.

Sophie exhaled and fought for equilibrium. She didn't want his sympathy. She needed no one's pity; she was strong enough on her own. Still, her throat clogged. "I don't really know how I spent the next several months after their death. I…" She bit her lip. "I couldn't stay in that little house. It wasn't much—a tiny place in a bad neighborhood, but we'd…" She sniffed and sat up straight as if a rigid spine would make her insides strong, too. Another deep breath. "I went to work, but I had to move, and after a while, I realized that…"

"That you had to start living again."

Her gaze whipped to his. He understood. "Yes. I didn't want to live, but somehow I had to." She glanced away from him, from those deep blue eyes that would weaken her if she wasn't careful. "I took a good, hard look at my life and realized that I had to get an education if I wasn't going to be waiting tables for the rest of my days. So I got my high school equivalency certificate and enrolled at the local college. I found the hotel night clerk job, and—" she shrugged "—nothing interesting, really. I just worked. Speaking of which, I have to get back."

She tensed, fearing he'd want to probe more into her past, but he didn't push, instead signaling for the check and paying promptly. He rose from the table and drew her with him. "So how did you find those antique pieces you've been refinishing?"

She was so relieved he hadn't asked about the next chapter in her life, she didn't shy away from the arm he slipped around her waist as they walked to the car. He helped her inside then began driving the short distance to the hotel. "I picked them up all over, but my collection began with the library table I showed you. It came from this amazing woman named Maura Halloran, who's now the vice president of operations for the hotel chain. She has this gorgeous house in Connecticut, full of furniture she's collected over the years, and she passed the bug on to me. We met when she was the manager of the hotel in Memphis where I had my first full-time assignment, and she took an interest in me from the first day. She saw something in me I had no idea was there, and when—" Sophie pressed her lips together. "Anyway, she believed in me enough to invest in this hotel."

When he parked the car, she opened the door and turned. "I can't let her down. I won't. And now I have to make up for the lost time, so if you'll excuse me—"

"No."

"What?"

"If you're going to work on furniture, I am, too."

"No. I can–"

"Do it yourself," he finished for her. "I know that, but if this Maura person cares about you, I doubt she'd be pleased that you're stretching yourself to the limit. And if you really don't want to let her down, staying out of the hospital is a good place to start."

"You know, I've been taking care of myself for a long time," she said primly. "Thank you for a lovely dinner. Good night." She spun away from him.

He snagged her arm. "You call this taking care of yourself?"

She glanced back and saw a dark glint in his eyes. "No, I call it foolishness to have yielded to temptation. It won't happen again." She moved toward the workshop.

He stepped in front of her. "Don't you trying freezing me out, Queenie. It won't work." He herded her away from her workshop. "Be as snotty as you want, but you're going to either let me help you, or, better yet, go to bed at a decent hour. Choose one. You're operating on sheer nerves."

She yanked her arm away. "You don't know me. You have no idea what I need." She tried to step around him.

He grabbed her and threw her over his shoulder. "Okay, we'll do it the hard way." Grimly he stalked toward the house.

A hot ball of fury burned in her chest. "Let me go, Cade," she warned. But her voice was shaking.

"Zip it, Queenie, before you really make me mad."

"Let me down, you idiot, you—" She pounded on his back. Kicked.

He made it to the front door then yanked her down in front of him, his own temper simmering.

She smacked his chest, eyes sparking fury. "Don't

you ever— You have no idea— I can't—" Her legs felt weak. Her head pounded, and her vision wavered.

"Sophie, you don't have to do everything alone."

Suddenly, her face crumpled, and she buried it in her hands.

"Hey, now," he said, a little edge of panic in his voice. "Sophie, don't… Oh, hell." Somehow he got them inside, led her to the library and sat down on the sofa, pulling her onto his lap and gathering her into his arms.

And held her while she cried.

CHAPTER TEN

SOPHIE WAS TOO TALL to sit on anyone's lap. Cade was a big man, though, and somehow in his embrace she felt delicate. Cherished. This must be what Jenna had experienced all her life—this sense of safety, of knowing that she always had a home, that someone was there to shelter her if she needed it.

Sophie had not had that luxury in more than half her life. She burrowed into Cade's arms and let his deep voice soothe her with words she couldn't make out, but it didn't matter. All she knew was that she was safe.

She cried it all out—the past, her fears of failing at this dream that meant so much, of disappointing Maura again, her loneliness…all of it.

As her tears eased, mortification swamped her. She tried to rise.

He only tightened his embrace. Tilted her chin up. "No way, Sophie. You don't get to be ashamed. Look at me."

She opened tear-swollen eyes, somehow knowing he'd be kind, tolerant…understanding. Sympathetic, much as she'd hate pity.

What she saw in his eyes were traces of all those but something more.

She saw respect. Tenderness.

"I'm not going anywhere. You're not alone, Sophie."

Then his lips brushed hers in a manner that began as soothing, for him as well as her, she thought.

And a fierce tug of longing made Sophie let go.

She opened her mouth to him, and his tongue swept inside. She drove her fingers into his hair with sudden urgency. Powerful arms banded her waist, locked her against him until breathing was too much to expect.

She didn't care if she never breathed again.

His mouth cruised over her throat, and she barely resisted a moan. Fingers like flame licked down the neckline of her shirt as he bared her to the waist.

Sophie gasped for breath and raked her own fingers down his sides, yanking up his T-shirt and freeing the acres of muscle she'd admired from afar.

"God, Soph," he muttered. "I want you." His mouth branded its way up to her earlobe, and he gathered her closer as his fingers traced tantalizing circles around first one nipple, then the other. His mouth slicked a tor-turous trail across her collarbone then down until he fastened his lips on one breast. Her back bowed, and his strong arm supported her as he feasted.

Abruptly, he swept her up and strode to the chaise in the corner, laying her out like a banquet, his hungry gaze a sharp, sweet stab to her senses.

His blue eyes locked on hers as he flicked open the snap of her jeans and lazily drew down her zipper, lightly brushing the soft skin of her belly, stroking and teasing just out of reach of flesh that was screaming for his touch.

Sophie squirmed, held out her arms. "Come here,"

she said in a rough voice she didn't recognize. She un-buttoned his jeans, slid her hand inside, finding him hot and hard and so very ready.

"Uh-uh, baby," he muttered softly, imprisoning her hand just out of reach. "Not yet. This isn't gonna be fast."

"Cade…" Was that her voice, so low and needy?

For endless seconds, his eyes devoured her body, dark as smoke. Sophie's blood warmed, every nerve ending awakening from a long hibernation.

He bent to her, his warm breath whispering across her belly, his tongue a dangerous, beautiful weapon, his touch taunting her as he licked a lazy trail following her jeans down her legs. Strong hands parted her thighs, and Sophie bit into her lower lip as the anticipation diz-zied her. One long finger caressed the tender creases, skimmed over curls, lingered over plump flesh—then at last, oh God at last, slid inside.

A blue-white flash streaked through her. When his mouth fastened on the curls at her core and began doing devastating things to her insides, Sophie abandoned herself to the searing, stormy pleasure. Craving poured through her like molten gold, and all she could do was cry out and reach for him. "Cade, please…"

He lifted her into his arms again and reversed their positions, wrapping her trembling legs around him.

Abruptly he stopped. "Sophie," he whispered. "Damn it, we can't."

She whimpered, seizing his mouth in a scorching kiss. She wanted to scream. To weep. "I need you."

"I know, sweetheart. But I don't have anything with me."

"I'm okay. And protected. I promise."

"Me, too, but are you sure—"

She wrested herself from his grasp. Slid to her knees and took him in her mouth.

Cade groaned aloud. "Sophie, no...you're killing me."

He yanked her up, kicked off his jeans. She climbed his legs, wrapped hers around his waist. "Now. Please now."

He thrust into her, and Sophie stifled a scream of pure bliss. He felt good, so good. For a very long moment they were still, soaking up the astonishing rightness of how well they fit.

Sophie never let herself go, never truly relaxed with any man, not in years...yet she did so now as every cell in her body drowned in glory. She wanted to freeze time right here, live in this exquisite moment for hours, weeks, centuries.

But Cade's assault on her control wasn't finished. He fastened his mouth on her throat and began a delicious rhythm that dragged greedy sounds from her. With a near growl, Sophie wrapped her arms around his neck and held on for dear life.

Explosive was too mild a word for what flared between them, and in the heat of the flames, Sophie didn't think, didn't reason, didn't ask...she only surrendered to the magic of this proud, scarred, beautiful man.

His arms tightened, his powerful body both refuge

and demand—until one last kiss broke the bonds of her restraint, and the star-drenched night went nova.

No woman had ever made his knees go weak.

Cade needed to sit down. Go somewhere quiet. To figure out what the hell had just happened. Instead he stroked her soft skin, traced the curve of her breast, her waist, her hip as she lay boneless on his lap. He should let her go, walk away now, but he didn't, even though his mind was yelling cautions to him.

Sex this explosive was bound to cause trouble.

But damned if he didn't want to do it again. The sooner the better.

Sophie sighed, and he couldn't help smiling as her fingers began to play with the hair at his nape. He should pull away, separate them....

Her fingers tightened as he tried. "Not yet," she said in a throaty murmur. Her head fell back, and green eyes caught his. She smiled. "Wow."

Cade breathed a silent thanks. She looked playful. Seductive. This didn't have to get serious. Cheered, he grinned back. "Yeah...wow."

Sophie stretched her arms high above her head.

He was already half hard inside her and zoomed straight to ready. Her inner muscles squeezed, and he suspected his eyes bugged out. "Careful now, Queenie. A girl could get more than she bargained for."

Her lids fluttered down for a second, but hers was a wicked cat smile as she glanced up from beneath her lashes. "I already did, but you don't see me running, do you?"

Cade was incredibly relieved that Sophie really wasn't going to make a big deal out of the mind-blowing sex they'd just shared. "You are something, you know that?"

She squeezed him again, teeth coming down on her lush lower lip. "Takes one to know one, cowboy." Then she locked her arms around his neck and laid siege to his mouth. Cade was more than ready to leap right back into the insanely fantastic world of Sophie's body, but first he tore his mouth away and just looked at her.

He'd kill for his camera right now.

Sophie leaned back and propped herself on her hands, a study in what a beautiful woman should look like, hair falling around her face in sweaty curls, beautiful breasts ripe, nipples begging for his mouth. He kept his grasp on those hips that had driven him crazy since his first sight of her, and pulsed inside her as his gaze trailed over her belly and down to the burnished curls. He slid out, then thrust inside again, watching her as she closed her eyes and moaned.

"Sophie," he said. Simply her name.

She opened her eyes. Her pupils had swallowed the irises but for a thin rim of green. "Cade," she answered, low and silky. Sultry.

He yanked her up against him, dared her to keep up the lazy tease. He'd meant to go more slowly this time, but she latched onto him, too, her thighs a vise around his waist, and urged him on, pushing the pace higher, harder.

He fastened his mouth to one breast and gave her the ride of her life.

Though he wasn't at all sure who was actually doing the riding.

Not that it mattered. Sophie not only matched him but egged him on, her voice in his ear setting his mind ablaze, whipping his body to heights he'd never known possible.

She was a sweet fire in his arms, a warm and demanding woman a man would never get tired of—

Whoa. For a second, Cade faltered. Deeply attuned, Sophie relaxed her hold and leaned back. "Cade?" Her eyes were unfocused, glazed with emotion, with the same fear that was licking at the edges of his restraint.

She was so beautiful. So valiant.

And if he wasn't careful, he was going to fall for her.

He crushed her in his embrace to stifle all thought of that impossible notion. Instead he focused on their pleasure, forcing their pace to lessen from the frantic heat, making his strokes long and murderously slow until he thought he'd lose his mind and she was panting. Begging. Urging him on.

After her third climax, he cut the leash he'd tied on his control.

The world went white behind his eyes. Deeper, harder, faster... He couldn't get close enough to her, couldn't quite grasp what he sensed was just out of sight....

Sophie locked her mouth on his, raked her nails down his back.

And Cade forgot everything but the glory of the woman in his arms.

WHEN SOPHIE REVIVED, Cade's head lay heavy on her shoulder. He was still inside her, and she very much wanted to keep him there.

Wanted to place a tender kiss on his temple.

Which was why she would not. The sex had literally blown her mind, but they'd agreed up front—hot sex, that's all this was.

Even though her mind kept threatening to drift off into fantasies.

But she reminded herself that he would leave her. He would go back to wandering as soon as he was well enough.

And she would stay here. Maybe he'd visit Jenna now and again, but he would be a stranger to Sophie. He had a life much larger than her own, his stage the entire planet.

It had been very clear to her in the first moments of their lovemaking—hot sex, she corrected herself brutally—that this was a man who could steal her heart.

And leave it in shreds when he left.

So it would be only a fling, as they'd said. And, she had to smile, that was not a bad thing. She had too much to focus on, making Hotel Serenity a success. She couldn't afford to be distracted by emotion. Hot sex, though…she could spare a few hours here and there. She did, after all, feel like a million bucks right now. More relaxed than she'd been in weeks. Months.

Years, maybe.

"What's got that Cheshire cat smile on your face, Queenie?"

"If I say you…" She raised her eyelids slowly. "Are you going to get all arrogant and conceited on me?"

He grinned, that devastating, killer-sexy smile of his. "Maybe."

His eyes scanned her body and she was surprised by the urge to preen. She lifted her arms and flipped out her hair. "Me, too. I so rocked your world."

His laughter rolled over her like honey. He pulled her up and hugged her. "So you did, Queenie. So you did."

She rested her head on his shoulder and clasped him tightly. Surely simple affection was all right. How could she not feel tender toward someone so generous with his body, so in tune with her own? "Friends with benefits," she murmured. "I never really understood that until now."

"Me, either." He leaned her back so he could look at her. "I like you, Queenie. When you decide not to play the ice queen, or harp on me, anyway." His eyes twinkled.

"You're trying to make me mad, but I'm too satisfied to take the bait."

"What did I tell you? Aren't you glad you caved? Did we ever set an amount?"

"I didn't cave, you did." She tossed her head. "One kiss and you were toast," she said, surprising herself. She'd never flirted like this in her life, always too serious.

She liked it.

"*You* caved," he said smugly. "But hey, I understand. You couldn't help yourself."

Sophie opened her mouth to protest—

But Cade had other plans for her.

CHAPTER ELEVEN

HE LEFT HER SLEEPING.

Because he wanted to stay, to watch her awaken.

A fling, they'd both agreed. It was smart, it was right. Those were his usual terms.

They'd moved to her room sometime during the night, and now he watched her from the chair across from her bed, elbows on his knees, hands clasped beneath his chin. In the moonlight, her skin was nearly translucent, the lines of exhaustion easing when she was relaxed.

He wanted her again.

And he wanted his camera in his hands. To capture the pure beauty of her.

But what if she woke up and saw him photographing her? He could explain the intrusion, he told himself, tell her that photographing her while she slept was only an artistic exercise, that the human body was simply a compilation of planes and curves and angles, that no one would know it was her.

All true.

But still a lie.

He would know, and she would, too. He would be taking advantage of her by displaying her without her defenses, however much he honestly was fascinated by the contours, the tones of skin, the shadows and abstract lines formed by her body and her bed.

With her, he could make art again. He knew that to his marrow.

I need that, Sophie. I need to hope. He could say that, and she might even understand, to a degree.

But she would feel invaded at a moment in her life when she was already so vulnerable. So alone, more than he could imagine being. He spent much of his time by himself, yes, but always secure in the knowledge that people who loved him were only a phone call away, that he was in their thoughts.

Sophie had no one, except Jenna and this friend, Maura, who had put her money into Sophie's dream, money that weighed on Sophie, that kept her working too hard, too late into the night, putting her slender back into work meant for someone his size.

She'd trusted him. Shared herself with him tonight, first with details of her past he sensed no one else knew, then sweetly, generously with her body.

To betray that trust would be the most egregious sin he could commit against her.

But he needed to take those shots so badly that he'd nearly done so, anyway. He'd thrown on his clothes, been halfway down the stairs, already calculating lighting and f-stops and apertures...

To let this moment pass, to open his fingers and let the inspiration fly away, scared him to death. Such a moment might never come again. He was risking everything.

But he would not reclaim his life at Sophie's expense.

By the skin of his teeth and the grace of his upbringing, Cade rose and made his way down the stairs. Locked her door behind him and made himself keep going until he was at Jenna's.

SOPHIE AWOKE WITH A START when she heard Armando and his crew talking outside. She was late, she'd overslept, she—

Oh, sweet mercy, she was naked.

The night flooded in, the fun, the teasing. The astonishing bliss.

She knew he was gone without looking. Cade filled a room with his sheer presence. As she hurriedly dressed, she guessed he was already outside. She brushed her teeth, ran a comb through her hair, then yanked it into a tight ponytail, wincing at the slight headache. She hadn't had alcohol in so long that one margarita had given her a hangover.

She dashed down the stairs. Her head might not be happy, but her body felt terrific. Mamma mia—*terrific* was an understatement.

He'd boasted that he'd leave her so satisfied she'd be boneless in his bed, hadn't he?

Jerk, she thought affectionately. Big, fat, arrogant jerk.

But oh, he had. Sweet heaven, the headache didn't really matter because the rest of her felt so amazing. A week at a pricey spa couldn't have had more effect.

He'd been right about that, too, drat him. She might

not have had that much rest, but the hours she'd managed had been restorative. She couldn't remember the last time she'd slept without worrying.

She wasn't sure she even needed breakfast or coffee or...

Sophie laughed out loud as she crossed the porch. Oh, he'd be unbearable if he knew, wouldn't he? All smug and *I told you so* and Queenie this, Queenie that.

Even that name couldn't aggravate her on this beautiful morning.

Then she spotted the chipper. "Armando, it's beautiful."

"Qué?" He looked confused.

Well, of course a piece of rental machinery couldn't be beautiful, but the morning was just so pretty and she felt great and—and she was acting like a teenager....

Hurriedly she gestured toward the area they'd cleared yesterday. "What you did, it's wonderful."

His face lit with shy pride. *"Gracias."*

She stopped herself before she kissed his cheek or hugged him or— Oh, what the heck. She hugged him anyway. "Armando, what would I do without you?" He *was* a treasure, a kind, strong, responsible man she could trust.

He tugged at the bill of his cap, smiled nervously.

"Thank you so much for everything you've done." She nodded at the other men and realized she was getting misty over all of them. "Thank you. *Gracias.*"

"Nada." In the manner of men everywhere, they clearly couldn't wait to be away from the utterly fright-

ening combination of a female and tears. "We work now," he said cautiously.

She nearly giggled then— Good grief, what had Cade unleashed in her? First she was crying in his lap, nestled in strong arms, then she was limp from astonishing sex, and along the way she'd found a friend who also happened to be an extraordinary lover and— "Where is Cade?" she asked Armando as the other men walked away.

"No sé," answered Armando. "I do not know. He was not here when we came."

"Oh. I, uh, I thought I'd heard him," she said hastily. "No problem." Maybe he'd gone to get breakfast or take a shower before returning or.

Was this where she admitted she'd been thinking about shower sex? Where she revealed that long-dormant appetites had awakened? Sophie couldn't help a grin. She felt a little smug about last night herself.

She'd rocked his world. She'd been an animal. They'd had jungle sex, and it had been fantastic. She all but skipped toward the front yard, barely frowning over the work she hadn't gotten to last night. She felt so energetic that she'd probably be able to accomplish all of it and more today.

She couldn't wait to see Cade again. Not, of course, for any other reason except that, astonishingly enough, Mr. Grumpy had become her friend last night.

Okay, admit it. And you want to get him naked again.

Well, who wouldn't? With a body like that…a man's body, a real man, one who bore the scars of a challenging, very physical life spent mostly outdoors.

Oh, good heavens, if she didn't stop herself she'd be a babbling fool by the time he got here.

Where was he, anyway?

Sophie forced herself to stop gushing over him, this difficult, fascinating, sexy man with whom she was going to have a fling. She reminded herself that she didn't really have time for him.

Honey, everyone has time for great sex.

Point taken, Mr. Rugged and Sexy.

With effort, she wiped the stupid grin off her face and went inside to make coffee, though he might be bringing some when he arrived, but how was a woman to know when her lover left without a note or a word or…

Chill, Queenie, she could just hear him saying.

Right.

Just then the chipper roared into action. Wow. How on earth had she slept through it? But all that lovely mulch… She loved that chipper, just as she loved this day and last night and she loved—

She couldn't breathe as fear struck her. *Oh, no, no, you don't get to do this,* she lectured a heart she couldn't possibly allow to be so foolish.

Yes, he'd held her while she cried. Yes, he'd understood her pain and her fear and her need. Yes, he was charming and fun and he made love like nothing she'd ever experienced before. And that lazy, we-just-had-amazing-sex cocky grin could seduce a saint, but…

She did not, would not come within a country mile of loving any man. Not ever. That was not in her plans, and she had too much to lose not to remain rigidly focused on those plans. No matter how much she'd lost herself in that bed last night, she had not lost her mind.

Abruptly her cell rang. She answered without looking, assuming it was Maura. "Hi, Maura."

"Hello, Sophie." The voice she never wanted to hear again.

"Kurt."

"Don't sound so enthusiastic."

"What do you want?"

"Now is that any way to speak to a friend?"

A friend. His tone insinuated much more. Her skin crawled. The fact that she'd been deluded by him for even a second was humiliating. They'd been together briefly at a point in her life where loneliness had threatened to drown her. But before long, she'd begun to see that his charming exterior was a ruse. He was only using her to get ahead in the company. When she'd broken it off, he'd tried to force himself on her. When she'd managed to escape, he threatened to claim she'd come on to him, to sue her for sexual harassment. In the end, he'd done far worse.

Quickly, she put distance between herself and the workers, grappling for the control that had once been second nature to her. *Blast you, Cade MacAllister, for making me weak.*

But she couldn't think of Cade in the same sentence with the man responsible for destroying her career. She forced her tone to be neutral. "Why are you calling?"

"No time for friendly conversation? Tut-tut. I find it interesting that you and Maura are still so close that you'd assume it was she who was calling. I was also very surprised to learn that you've brought Maura in as an investor. Haven't you let her down enough?"

"My hotel is no business of yours. Nor are my friends."

"Oh, but they are. There is still the little matter of embezzlement charges that could be pressed against you."

Her blood chilled. "You know I did nothing wrong."

"Do I?"

"What do you want, Kurt?"

"To be sure you aren't going to make a mistake."

"What do you want from me? I'm out of the game. The field is all yours. Play to your heart's content." Inside, she bled at her cowardice. Never in her life had she given up without fighting. But if she had, it would have hurt Maura's nephew and Maura herself. What else could she have done? Kurt had been extremely careful to distance himself from any possibility of blame.

"If you meant that, you'd have cut all ties."

"Why on earth would you care about anything I do? You won. I'm gone."

His voice went hard. "Proximity brings...temptations, Sophie." The tone turned oily. "Besides...I miss you."

She shuddered. "Leave me alone, or—"

"Threats are not a good idea, lover."

"I'm not threatening you. I just... Let it be over, Kurt."

"Sophie..."

"I have another call coming in. Goodbye." Stomach burning, she clicked off.

But she knew he wouldn't let it be over. And she was vulnerable in so many ways—he could spread rumors, he could use the grapevine to cost her bookings. He'd figured out how to destroy her once; he could do it again.

CADE DROVE OUT TO JESSE and Delilah's house in the hills west of Austin. He'd managed to slip away from Jenna's before she was up. The few hours' sleep he'd snatched had been troubled by nightmares about the fall, by bittersweet memories of Jaime...by images of Sophie and the visceral impression of her body against his, the taste of her, the textures...that thick, wavy hair, that sleek skin, the contours of her feminine frame with a surprising amount of hard-won muscle.

He touched the camera on the seat beside him and wished yet again that life were simpler.

One day at a time. You'll take other shots.

He'd at least tried shooting this morning while he was waiting for the photo lab to open. He'd walked the downtown streets, seizing on anything that took his fancy—a streetlamp, an ornate door handle, an angle down Congress Avenue toward Lady Bird Lake where his eye could nearly make out Sophie's roof. He'd wondered if she was up yet, if she missed him, if she worried about where he'd gone....

Cade had more advanced instincts for danger than many people due to the hair-raising circumstances he so often found himself in. And every instinct he had was now screaming—he was treading on perilous ground with Sophie. Particularly from the powerful temptation to cross a line and seize the inspiration her sleeping form had presented.

So he would stay away from her today and put some much-needed distance between them. He was doing it for her benefit, not running. At least, that was his story and he was sticking to it.

As he crossed the low-water bridge about a mile from Jesse's place in the Hill Country, Cade forced his thoughts away from Sophie and all the confusion she presented, instead focusing on the one shot he'd gotten this morning that might be worth something—an old man asleep against a building, the runnels time had carved into his face.

Damn it, who was he kidding? It wasn't a good shot at all. Nothing like the one of Sophie would have been—

No, he wouldn't think about the image of Sophie asleep again. He'd won the battle, hadn't he? His conscience had prevailed.

He pulled up in front of Jesse's house, grabbed the bundle that was his purpose today and stalked toward the front door.

"Uncle Cade!" A redheaded tornado charged through the open door and into his arms.

"Hey, there's my girl!" He picked her up and accepted the tight clasp of small arms as Jesse and Delilah's four-year-old daughter, Addie, pressed kisses over his face while talking a mile a minute about her pony and her kitten and how their dog, Major, liked the kitten riding on his back, really.

"Hey, Uncle Cade." Addie's more serious black-haired seven-year-old brother, Jonah, greeted him. "Want to see my horse?"

"You betcha." Cade ruffled the boy's hair and hitched Addie higher on his hip as they walked through the house toward the kitchen where Delilah stood, pouring a cup of coffee and then extending it toward him.

"You are a goddess."

The curvaceous Delilah smiled. "Your brother thinks so." She hugged Cade, scanning his features too carefully.

"Tell Mom I'm fine."

"Was I that obvious?"

Cade rolled his eyes then took a sip. "I came to Austin to escape my medical watchdogs. Mmm, great coffee—thanks."

"You had breakfast?"

"I'm fine."

Fortunately for him, Delilah wasn't one to hover. Instead, she grabbed an apple and tossed it to him. "Well, I'm home today, so you're allowed to change your mind. Jesse's in his studio."

"He working?" His brother's paintings were much in demand.

"No. He just finished a piece. He's gathering what you asked for."

"Uncle Cade, you have to see me ride," Addie demanded.

"Uncle Cade has something else he needs to do right

now." Delilah reached for her daughter, but Addie clung to him like a leech.

"It's okay. I told Jonah I'd see his horse, too."

"You're in for it now. Whistle if you need rescue."

Cade grinned as he left with the kids and glanced around the property.

It never ceased to amaze and amuse him how much Jesse had gone country. His tough FBI brother had not only left law enforcement behind, he'd left the city behind, as well. This place was a return to his roots in West Texas, though certainly with style. Jesse had been a full-time artist for several years now, and given the improvements he'd made around here, the prices for his work had clearly continued to escalate.

The two-story house with the wraparound porch looked fairly traditional from the front, but the back wall was nearly all glass to take advantage of the stunning sunsets that could be witnessed from this perch on top of the hill. Jesse and Delilah had horses and Longhorn cattle, a dog and several cats. It was all terrifyingly domestic.

But that sort of sea change had happened to all his brothers when love had come calling. Cade was the only holdout among his brothers, and he had no plans to change that. All his life he'd been a loner, and there was plenty of family to go around when he wanted a break from solitude.

He spent an hour with the kids, saddling Addie's pony and watching her carefully in the round pen. She chattered endlessly and seemed to pay little attention to her riding yet somehow never bobbled on her mount.

Then it was Jonah's turn, and Cade could see the makings of the man his nephew would become as Jonah did everything but lift the heavy saddle onto his horse's back and, once on, demonstrated that he was a natural. Jesse and Diego had been nine and eleven, respectively, when Cade was born to their mother and his dad. Their deceased father, Roberto, had not been into horses, but Cade's father had put them both on horseback as soon as he'd come into their lives. All the brothers and Jenna were at home in the saddle.

Diego raised horses at his home in La Paloma, and Cade thought Jonah's mount bore the mark of Diego's prized stallion.

"Daddy!" Addie deserted Cade for her father as he walked up. It always tickled Cade to see his silent, serious brother transform when he was with his children.

Watching them, for the first time in his life Cade wondered what he'd be like as a dad.

Forget that. His parents had plenty of grandchildren. That was not his path.

"Hey," Jesse greeted him. And gave him a quick perusal.

"Not you, too."

Jesse shrugged as he let Addie down to play with Major, the dog Delilah had had when she'd met Jesse. "Mom's orders."

Of course. "I'm fine."

Jesse cut him a glance. "Physically, maybe." But to Cade's relief, Jesse didn't pry.

They watched Jonah ride and kept an eye on Addie—though Major, part border collie, was a good babysitter. Addie would get into little trouble with him around.

"Diego's stock?" Cade nodded toward the horse.

"None better."

Silence fell—well, silence if you didn't count Addie's nonstop stream of chatter—and Cade found himself relaxing for the first time all morning.

His brother was good at silence, and this isolated place was one of peace. He'd missed this. One of the things Cade appreciated most about his calling was its solitude. Room to think, to breathe. He was not a city person.

And Sophie very much was. Just one more reason for keeping his heart carefully guarded when he finally returned to her.

But he should have left her a note. Or called.

Damn it.

He stirred beside his brother. "Okay if I get started?"

"You know the way."

Cade knew Jesse could tell something was amiss with him. But he thanked his lucky stars that this brother would never push him to explain. He waved to the kids and retrieved his bundle, then made his way to Jesse's studio to frame the photographs.

A FEW HOURS LATER, CADE stood back, pleased with the moldings he'd chosen.

"They look good." Jesse had been stretching canvases nearby for the past hour, and they'd worked in companionable silence.

Cade was certain Jesse was curious, but he was just

as certain that his brother wouldn't ask. Which was why he would explain. He gestured toward the framed photos. "Jenna's hidden agenda. For her friend."

"The one you borrowed my tool belt to work for?"

"Yeah. She's..." How did he explain Sophie? "I thought at first that she might be taking advantage of Jenna."

"And now?"

Cade rubbed the back of his neck. "No. I'm sure she's not, but..."

Jesse only nodded.

Which made Cade try again. "She's... Her life has been rough, and she's got a lot on her shoulders, trying to get her hotel ready to open. She's got every cent she has invested in it, and she's working herself half to death—"

He halted before he could spill his guts about what he felt for her.

Which he couldn't even explain to himself, really.

"She need another set of hands?" Jesse asked.

This was exactly what Cade had tried to explain to Sophie last night, that his family really was one for all and all for one. He was a lucky man. If Cade thought it was important to help Sophie, Jesse would pitch in without ever having met her.

"Thanks, but I don't think that's a good idea. She's running on pride and nerves right now, and I'm not sure how she would take it."

Jesse only shrugged. "Well, just say the word."

"Thanks. I will." He picked up the two bundles he'd wrapped in brown paper and turned for the door, then stopped in front of Jesse's latest. It was an explosion of color, a garden scene in his grandmother's garden in La Paloma, if he was not mistaken. "Mama Lalita's?"

Jesse nodded.

It would look amazing in Sophie's gathering room, as she called it, the place where dining room and living area met. "What kind of price tag will you put on that?"

"It's yours if you want it." Just that simple, when Cade knew Jesse could command a price in the tens of thousands for it.

"No, I want to buy it."

Jesse slapped the back of Cade's head. "Don't be an idiot. We've got your stuff all over our house and we never paid you for it."

"I know, but…"

"It'll be ready in another day or two. Want to pick the framing or wait until you have a place to put it? I can store it here for you."

"It's for Sophie."

Jesse only lifted an eyebrow.

"And I— She's… I'm probably pushing my luck by not asking her first, except that damned pride of hers would get in the way. But she can't possibly afford it."

Jesse's mouth curved. "Woman trouble, little brother?"

"In spades." Cade sighed.

"Want to talk about it?"

Cade knew Jesse would listen without recrimination or even advice unless he asked for it, but Cade didn't have a clue how to explain what he didn't understand himself. "I appreciate the offer, but I…" His hand rubbed over his heart. He yanked it away when he realized what he was doing. "Hell if I know what to say."

Jesse rose and clapped him on the shoulder in sympathy. "Yep, only a woman can tangle a man up like that." He smiled like someone who understood the predicament, and Cade was reminded of the hell he and Delilah had gone through before Jesse had given up his guilt over their past and accepted how much he wanted her. "I'll store the painting until you decide."

"She'll go nuts over it…once I figure out the right way to talk to her about it, anyway."

"Uh-huh. Good luck with that." They walked outside.

Delilah hailed them from the porch with an invitation to stay for supper, and Cade was happy to change his plans.

The meal was a lively affair filled with much laughter and love. After a bit, Jonah asked Cade a question about his travels and for a second he hesitated, waiting for the pain to strike as it had every time he thought about Jaime and his former life. Delilah gently turned the topic to a story about Zane, but Jonah wouldn't be diverted for long. Cade found himself telling stories of other cultures, of pristine places few men had seen, warming to the topic as he saw how excited Jonah was by it. Even the mention of Jaime didn't hurt as badly as he'd feared. Cade realized that by making Jaime a forbidden topic, he'd remained mired in his guilt and had robbed himself of the joy that had been such an essential part of his friend.

For an instant, the face of Jaime's oldest son over-laid Jonah's, and it dawned on Cade that he had the power to give those children back their father. At least the parts of him that Cade had known. All he had to do was make himself face his photograph collection...and his memories.

An idea stirred. His publishers wanted a book, he could give them one—only not what they'd asked for.

The book would be a tribute to Jaime. And Cade's proceeds would go to a fund for his friend's children.

"Uncle Cade?"

His head snapped up. He realized from their expressions that he'd been asked a question while he'd been woolgathering.

Jesse's expression spoke of concern, as did Delilah's, but neither said anything. Delilah repeated Jonah's question, and soon conversation was flowing again. Somehow he made it through the rest of the dinner and then made a round of goodbyes, promising to come back soon. It was an easy promise to make. Being with family again felt good.

Outside, Cade rounded the hood of his rented SUV and got in, while Jesse leaned on the open passenger window. Cade saw him glance at the camera on the seat, but true to form, Jesse didn't ask.

Gratitude washed over Cade. He might not know what the hell he was doing with his life right now, might never be the gifted photographer he'd been, but he was graced with the blessing of a family that was fierce in its love, that would always be there for him—

and no one more than this brother, who always stepped up when the others needed him but never intruded.

"You know I love you, right?"

Jesse's gaze flew to his. The words were seldom said aloud among the males of the family, and Cade was a little shocked to be saying them now. But Jesse should hear how much he was appreciated.

With a solemn look, Jesse nodded. "I do." Then his lips curved. "You are so gone over this woman."

"Shut up. I am not." Cade's eyes narrowed. "And if you call one single member of this family…"

Jesse slapped his door and stepped back, drawing an imaginary zipper over his lips.

But he was grinning as Cade drove off.

CHAPTER TWELVE

ALL THE WAY BACK TO AUSTIN, Cade's mind was racing about his idea for a tribute book to Jaime. At last, here was something he could sink his teeth into that was meaningful, that wasn't just killing time. When he got into town, he headed for Sophie's, but his mind was on the book and how he would pitch it to his publishers. He would take the prints he'd framed by the hotel first, then go to Jenna's and start culling through his photo files. Looking at the pictures of his friend would be hard as hell, but it felt right, and a bitter piece of the sorrow that had built a dam around his heart had been breached.

When he arrived at Sophie's, he noticed immediately that her pickup was gone and was glad she'd insisted he have a key after one day when a delivery had been expected and she'd had to be away. He'd take the photos to the rooms they were meant for and see how his choices fit while he waited for her to return. She never left the place for long.

As he walked, he spotted the pile of mulch beside the chipper Armando had wanted, and he mentally approved. A great idea from a good man. He wondered if Sophie had thought about hiring Armando permanently to maintain the hotel grounds. The man had a gift for it, and he sure as hell worked hard.

He glanced over at the casita, as Armando called it. He'd meant to finish the wiring today, but he'd do that tomorrow, then start on the drywall. The image he'd had of it in his mind was taking form, and he was already envisioning having Sophie there to christen it. He wasn't half bad at a massage himself, and if having his hands on her led to other things...

He was also beginning to see the hotel finished and with guests on the grounds. It would be Sophie's dream, but he wasn't ready to share her yet with those guests. He thought about what a great home this place could make, kids like Jonah and Addie racing over the grass, Sophie in a porch swing over there—

Oh, man. This wasn't his home, and Sophie didn't belong to him. His life was one day at a time, one minute, one second. Hers ran like clockwork. There was no middle ground for them. Besides, Sophie was intent on a fling, and his thoughts were drifting in a dangerous direction.

You are so gone over this woman, Jesse had said.

No. She was making a home here, not him. He didn't want that.

I so rocked your world, she'd said astride him last night.

Cade laughed aloud now. *You did, Queenie. You absolutely did.*

And with his heart a little lighter about Jaime, Cade was more eager than ever for her to rock his world again.

But an hour later, he was still waiting. He didn't have a phone number for Sophie, but Jenna would. He tried Jenna's cell but only got voice mail. He took the prints to Sophie's room, and laid them against the wall. They looked perfect to him, but he'd wanted to watch Sophie's face when she first saw them, damn it. He'd give her a little while longer, even though he was eager to get to his laptop.

Cade realized suddenly that he was tired. He'd long ago learned to take advantage of spare moments to grab a few winks, and last night had been devoid of much rest. So he stretched out on Sophie's bed.

And promptly fell asleep.

SOPHIE HAD DELIBERATELY kept herself busier than usual all day, but it hadn't helped. Cade was still missing in action, and now she believed it must be a deliberate attempt to put distance between them. What she didn't know was why.

Yes, it had been intense, and yes, she'd caught herself getting more emotional than was wise for a mere fling—but she hadn't revealed even a hint of that to him, nor would she.

Anyway, she didn't have the time or the energy to worry over whatever was going on with Cade, and she wasn't going to dwell on the mistake that last night now seemed.

She had bigger problems.

The landscaper was still AWOL and hadn't returned any of her several calls. He'd insisted on half his money up front to buy materials. That wasn't an unusual request for small contractors, so she'd agreed. Only that had been the last she'd seen of him. She hadn't been worried at first because he hadn't been scheduled to work at that point and the job wasn't ready for him.

Now it was. He should have shown up to work by now, or at least phoned her. Out of desperation, she'd gone looking for him this afternoon. She had no office address, but that, too, wasn't unusual—the smaller contractors often operated from their homes and pickups. She did remember, though, the job he said he would be finishing before he could start on hers. It was an apartment complex on the far north end of Austin, and she'd gotten lost, winding through the hills.

She could blame the hills, but it was really her distraction that was at fault. Cade's unexplained disappearance was part of it, of course, but he was a grown man; they weren't a couple and he wasn't her employee. She had no say in how he spent his time. She'd considered calling Jenna, but she was nowhere near ready for her friend to know Sophie had spent a torrid night tearing up the sheets with Jenna's injured brother whom Sophie was supposed to be helping.

And then there was Kurt Barnstone. She shivered as she recalled their conversation and his threats. He'd won, he held the position she should have occupied. Why couldn't he be satisfied with that? She just wanted him out of her life.

She located the apartment complex at last and drove the entire property looking for the landscaper, but he was nowhere to be found.

And then she spoke with the apartment manager who, in a matter of minutes, sent Sophie's world spinning.

The landscaper had left town.

With Sophie's money.

She wasn't a fool, she tried to tell herself—contractors asked for a draw against materials all the time. But Sophie knew she'd cut corners—most of the bids she'd gotten were out of her budget, so she'd gone with the lowest one, a guy who seemed earnest and honest. He'd had a list of references but she hadn't checked them because she was too busy, too tired.

And now she would pay.

The drive back was a blur as she frantically tried to whittle away her vision of the grounds to what she could do on her own with no more budget and even less time.

Armando could help. He wasn't a landscape designer, but he had a feel for plants and was a hard worker, as were the others on his crew. She wondered if he could help her find more workers…but where would she find the money to pay for extra labor?

I could get my brother Jesse and my brother-in-law Vince to help, Jenna had offered. Cade was also extremely resourceful and good with his hands.

No. She wouldn't ask for a favor. She didn't know Jesse or Vince, and Jenna worked too hard already. Cade had already done so much—even if he hadn't disappeared last night.

Besides, she didn't have the heavy equipment and she didn't know where she could scrape up the extra money to rent it. She could ask Maura, but her friend had already been too generous to Sophie—who didn't deserve it. Not if, she, with all her vaunted skills at assessing and managing people, had made such an elemental and costly mistake.

No, she'd just have to cut back on her ambitious plans. And find someone to replace the landscaper—quick. She still had the other half of the budgeted funds to fund the project. Not that the paltry amount would get her anywhere with a reputable landscaper....

Oh, God, she was so tired.

Then she pulled into the hotel's driveway and spotted Cade's car.

Sophie parked and dropped her head against the steering wheel. She could not deal with him, not now. She was desperate for time to think, to get a firm hold on her shaken control.

She sat there for a long moment, trying to decide what to do.

She could go to her workshop and forge ahead while she reordered her priorities and revised her plans.

Or she could look for Cade, find out why he was here and get one worry off her list. One little clearing in the maelstrom that threatened to overtake her if she didn't hang on tightly to her poise and to the discipline that had gotten her this far.

Then he would return to Jenna's, while she would do the smart thing and go to bed. Wake up tomorrow and pick up the pieces.

There. She had a plan.

Sophie went looking for Cade.

THE LAST PLACE SHE EXPECTED to find him was in her bed, sound asleep.

She paused in the doorway, shaking her head. The sheer gall of the man—he thought it was okay to vanish, not tell her where he was or if he'd be back, then return when she wasn't even there, let himself into her home and crawl into her bed? She'd bared her body to him and all but bared her soul, and this was how he treated her?

You bastard. She took a step forward, ready to yell at him, to tell him exactly what she thought of him, the stupid, insensitive jerk—

Then she spotted them. Sweet heaven. The images she'd seen on his laptop screen, blown up large. They'd been stunning in miniature, but blown up...

They were beyond beautiful. She sank to a crouch before them, fingers covering her mouth in silent wonder. They were even framed, beautifully so. She knew exactly which room each would grace, and would have even if she hadn't been part of the discussion.

Oh, Cade... So this was what he'd spent the day doing.

"Do you like them?" His voice was rough with sleep.

She whirled on her knees. "Cade, they're..." Her voice broke, and she was terribly afraid she was going to cry, so she averted her head.

"Sophie?" Worry shadowed his tone. "Are you okay?"

She reached for one of the prints and rose, struggling for the self-possession that had been second nature until she'd met this man. She'd been doing fine without him, and then he'd taken over the grounds, and the casita, and the decorating, and her bed. He'd invaded every part of her life, and he'd held her while she cried, and, oh God, when he was gone…

She fought hard to steady her voice. If she let herself weaken now… "Of course I like them. Let's see how this one looks hung up." She handled the artwork gently but crossed to the door with swift steps, grappling to hold herself together.

But when she heard his footsteps behind her, that hold began to buckle.

She hit the stairs nearly running.

SOMETHING WAS WRONG, but he'd have to catch her to find out. Charging down the stairs after her, Cade saw her slip into the intended room and shut the door in his face.

What the hell? This wasn't the reaction he'd hoped for. "Sophie, what's going on?"

No response.

He turned the knob and stepped into darkness. "Sophie?"

In the light from the hallway, he spotted her, slumped against the wall, the photograph on her lap, her graceful fingers stroking the frame. "Does that mean you like it?" he finally asked.

She glanced at him, then away—but not before he saw the tears in her eyes. Crying women were scary, that's all there was to it. A smart man stayed away from them because no man on earth ever knew the right thing to say.

But this was Sophie the warrior, and she had her shoulders bowed, her whole posture that of unutterable weariness and defeat.

He must not be that smart because he couldn't bring himself to leave her. He crossed the floor and sank down beside her. *You are so gone,* Jesse had said. *Looks that way, doesn't it, big brother?* Gingerly, Cade wrapped one arm around those slender shoulders that bore too many burdens.

Sophie shuddered at his touch, but when he started to release her, she suddenly buried her face in his shoulder.

"Go ahead," he murmured, stroking her hair with his free hand as he tucked her more firmly against him. "Let it out, Sophie. You don't have to be so damn strong all the time."

"Crying is pointless." She tensed and tried to scramble to her feet.

He tightened his grip. She wasn't going anywhere until he got to the bottom of her troubled state. "Sit still and tell me what's wrong." He frowned. "Is it the photographs?" He didn't think so, but maybe...

"No!" She bolted up straight and faced him at last. "Oh, no, Cade. They're absolutely stunning. They're perfect. And now that I know that's why you left without saying a word...."

He glanced away quickly.

"That's not why." Her voice went flat, and she visibly stiffened, drawing back from him.

"Stop." He held her in place and met her gaze squarely. "It is...and it isn't."

"You had second thoughts. About last night, I mean."

"No— Yes— I mean…didn't you?"

A thousand emotions tripped over her features too swiftly for him to identify. "Of course," she said coolly, staring past his shoulder. "It was…intense. Unexpected."

"Yeah," he responded, relieved that she understood.

"But that doesn't have to be a problem," she continued. "We simply won't make the mistake again."

His relief evaporated. "What mistake?"

Her green eyes flicked over him impersonally. "No more sex."

"Hold your horses, Queenie." That wasn't what he intended at all. "We are definitely making love again." In the next few minutes, if he had anything to say about it.

"Having sex," she corrected.

Oh, man, had he ever screwed up. When a woman got that icy tone in her voice, nothing good ever came of it. "Call it what you want, but you can't tell me you didn't love it. I was in that bed with you, Sophie. I know how it felt. There's something between us."

"There might have been—" she wrenched herself out of his arms and rose "—but that was last night. And we've both had second thoughts, remember?"

He stood to get on equal footing. "That's not what I meant."

"Then what did you mean?"

She was withdrawing from him, and he scrambled to make up ground. "Look, I'm sorry. I should have left a note, I know, but…"

Wrong move. She recoiled as if struck.

"I don't need to be coddled. I don't fall for every guy that I sleep with. I don't get emotionally involved after every roll in the hay. I'm responsible for my own heart and my own body and last night was—"

"Incredible," he said over her outrage. "Unforgettable."

She halted in midsentence and simply stared at him.

"Sophie, I didn't leave because I didn't want to keep making love to you all night and a whole lot longer. I was trying to save you."

"From what? Your deadly charm? Your skill in the sack?"

He ignored the sarcasm. "From me. And the mess in my head."

Her mouth snapped shut. She studied him carefully. "What mess?"

"I was this close—" he gestured with his fingers "—to taking advantage of you."

She snorted. "With sex? Please. What happened was completely mutual."

"No." He shook his head. "With my camera lens. I—" Oh, God. How could he explain? "I... It doesn't matter."

Some of the torment he'd been wrestling with since last night must have shown on his face, because her expression softened and she reached out to him.

"It does matter. Talk to me, Cade. You don't have to be so damn strong all the time."

HE SMILED AT HEARING his own words used against him, but he turned away. For a moment, Sophie thought Cade might leave rather than talk about whatever was troubling him.

But finally he spoke, his voice very quiet, his face averted. "I haven't been able to pick up a camera since the accident." Another long pause. He looked so sad, and that sorrow kept her from pushing him. "It's not like I haven't tried, but when I do, all I can think about is Jaime and how—" He moved to the window and looked out into the darkness, his broad shoulders tensed. "I killed my friend."

"What? Cade, it was an accident."

He whipped around to face her, his eyes hard, his voice fierce. "I took stupid chances, unnecessary risks. All for my precious vision. Jaime was as much a victim of my ambition as of that mountain. A casualty of my arrogance in believing that I was extraordinary, that the rules didn't apply to me."

"Did you force him to go along?"

"Yes."

"How?"

"Because he was my friend!" The cry exploded from deep within him. "He never said no to me. He knew I wanted him along because he was the best, and we worked together seamlessly. The shots were better when he was with me because he instantly got what I was after. He anticipated what I needed, how to set everything up so I could focus solely on what was in front of me because…" His voice grew hoarse. "Because he always had my back."

"You didn't force him. He wanted to be on those expeditions."

"Of course he did—he loved the work. But he had a family—three little kids and a wife who are now alone." Anguish was in his eyes. "It should have been me."

The last traces of her fury at him vanished. She longed to go to him, to soothe, to comfort.

But he wasn't ready for that yet. "So you don't use your camera anymore."

He didn't answer.

"Because that's how you honor him?"

His head snapped back. "Don't you dare mock me. You can't begin to understand."

She gasped but refused to retaliate.

"I'm sorry. That was rude…and wrong. You've lost a lot more than I have."

She took a deep breath. "It's hard to go on without them."

He watched her, eyes shuttered.

"Everyone goes through these recriminations—*I should have been there. It was supposed to be me.* For a long time, I blamed myself because I was supposed to pick up Sarah, but I was running late that day. And I thought my parents wouldn't have drowned if I'd been there."

"You know better," he said.

"So do you," she responded. "Does it make the pain go away?"

He shook his head.

"Will it help if I tell you it will lessen with time?" She met his intense gaze. "It never vanishes completely, but you start remembering the good times more than the loss. And, Cade, you *are* extraordinary. Jaime wouldn't want your gift squandered."

"Doesn't really matter. It's too late."

"What do you mean?"

"I can't see anymore. I used to be able to sense the perfect shot, but now…it's like I've gone blind." His expression was haunted. "Then last night…I could see you. In that way, the special way I've taken for granted all my life. You were asleep and you were so beautiful. The lines of your body, the contours of your face… I sat on the chair and just watched you, and I wanted…" He swallowed hard. "I wanted my camera." He approached her. "I wanted to capture that image of beauty so badly, and I was halfway down the stairs to get my camera, but…" He lifted his hands. "I knew I had no right. That it would be a violation of the worst kind."

She couldn't breathe, imagining Cade focused on her asleep and naked.

"You're too vulnerable, Sophie. You're so damn strong and you're brave and fierce, but…I could hurt you. So all I could think to do was to make myself leave, for your sake."

He was terrified that he'd lost the primary element of his existence, the thing that defined him, and yet he'd sacrificed the chance to get it back. For her. She reached for his hand and clasped it. "Thank you." She squeezed. "And I'm sorry. Maybe…" She should offer to let him photograph her if it would help, but…

He squeezed back. "I won't ask." He found a small smile. "At least not when you're naked."

She gestured toward the framed art. "Cade, your

talent is so immense. And it's not limited to your photography, whatever you think. Just look what you've
done with this place. But I know your gift isn't gone
for good."

"I hope you're right. I owe my publisher a book or
they won't fund my next trip, but I haven't even been
able to go through my files. I see Jaime in every one."

"Would it help if I went through them with you?"

He looked at her oddly. "You would do that, wouldn't
you?" He shook his head. "I don't know. Maybe." Then
his gaze lit. "But today on the way back from Jesse's, I
had an idea. My publishers want me to change the nar-
rative of the book to be about the accident, but damned
if I'll go along with that. Then a solution occurred to
me—I want Jaime to frame the story. I'll use photos
never before published, both of him and from our trips
together, so that his children will get to know the Jaime
I did. And I want my share of the proceeds to go to
them for college or whatever they need."

"That's a beautiful idea."

As he talked about it, his whole bearing became
lighter, his expression no longer dark with sorrow.
"You think so?" He shrugged. "Let's hope my publisher
agrees. I told my agent no way in hell am I spilling my
guts about the accident, but this…this feels right. I'll
do a damn good job of it, too. Jaime deserves no less."

Jenna would be so happy—all his family would—to
see Cade enthusiastic at last. "I know you will."

He grinned, and this was a Cade she'd never seen, a
man from whom a shadow had been stripped, a burden
lifted.

"I couldn't figure out what to do with my life, so I've been hiding out here, working with you. But now...you make me feel like there's hope, Sophie." He drew her close against his hard-muscled body, and a part of her wanted to return to last night's glory. To leap in and take. But...

I've been hiding out here. A reminder that he was only temporary, that he had a career that would take him away sooner rather than later. She was no longer sure she could keep her heart whole if they let whatever this was between them go any further. She had to step back from that cliff. "I'm happy for you." Then she took a physical step back. "Let's go see how the other one looks. They really are beautiful, Cade. I'm not sure how I'm going to pay you for them after what happened today, maybe some installment plan—"

"No freaking way." Before she could slip out the door, he captured her and pulled her into the room again. "I said they were a gift."

Then he frowned. "What do you mean, what happened today?"

"Nothing...never mind."

He cupped her cheek. "You're a lousy liar, Queenie."

She sighed then relented because she knew he wouldn't leave without hearing the full story.

And because it was such a luxury to have someone to confide in. She'd take it while she could...because all too soon, he would be gone.

AS SHE EXPLAINED ABOUT the landscaper who'd taken a powder at the eleventh hour—and taken her money with him—Cade was ready to storm out and hunt the man down.

"I feel like the biggest fool," she said.

He turned his attention where it belonged, on her feelings, not his. "No one can factor in dishonesty."

"But I have excellent people sense—I'm considered practically a prodigy for my instincts. At least I used to be." Her mouth twisted. "So how did I miss that he would do this?"

"Human nature is as changeable as the weather. And people wear masks. There's no way to know what his problems were. Why he needed money he hadn't earned." Nonetheless, Cade itched to get his hands on the guy who'd made Sophie feel so hopeless, to find the bastard and pound the living daylights out of him.

But that wouldn't help Sophie. Solutions would. "Did he draw up plans for the grounds?"

"Not formal blueprints, but I sketched out what I wanted, then he helped me refine the plant selections."

"Where are the drawings?"

"Cade, no. You've done enough. And you have a book to work on."

"It's waited this long. Let me see the plans."

"I can't do all of it now, I only have half the money left and no more coming in. I can't get another cent from the bank, and my savings have already been used."

"What about your friend who went in on the place with you?"

"*No.* I will not ask Maura for anything else."

"Would you let me give you money?" Though he already knew the answer.

"Absolutely not." She looked appalled.

"Sophie, I make good money. I don't spend much of it."

"No, Cade."

"What about a loan?"

"No!"

She was so agitated that he abandoned that line of discussion—for now, at least. "Okay, okay. We'll make it work with what you have. I'll talk to Armando after I've studied the drawings."

"I'll talk to Armando."

"Chill, Queenie. I'm not taking over your job, but it's not like you don't have plenty to do already."

"Cade, I can handle it myself. And you have to let me pay you."

"Oh, sure. You won't accept my money when you need it, and yet now you expect me to put my hand out. Not happening, honey." He decided the mood needed lightening, so he waggled his brows. "Though there are ways other than money to repay someone."

She gasped. "I would never—"

He grinned and picked her up. "You are so easy to rile, Miss Sophie."

"Put me down, you—you idiot." But she relaxed a bit. "Cade, seriously. You can't just swoop in like some white knight."

"Oh, man, if only it weren't the middle of the night, I'd call my family and have you repeat that. They'd never believe it."

"Well, they should. You're a good man, Cade Mac-Allister. They have no right to talk badly about you."

His family did no such thing, and she was getting wound up over nothing, but it was better than the look of defeat she'd worn. "Looks like I got my own defender. Go get 'em, Queenie."

"You mix me up." She turned to head downstairs, but her cheeks were pink.

Ditto, sweetheart. But Cade said nothing as he followed her.

In the downstairs room tucked behind the library—the one she said would be her office—Sophie went unerringly to her perfectly organized, color-coded files and retrieved the one containing her landscaping information. Cade realized he was looking at a hint of the professional who'd risen so high in the hotel chain before she'd decided to leave it.

He'd gotten used to Sophie in jeans and T-shirts, her hair yanked back in a ponytail, and had forgotten that she'd had another life, a very different one, before this. And he wondered suddenly what had prompted the change of direction.

She was exhausted tonight, however, and discouraged. He would focus on fixing both of those instead of asking questions about her past.

"You need sleep, Sophie. This can wait until morning."

"But…"

"I promise I won't talk to Armando without you. We'll go over this first thing tomorrow, then we'll call him in on it."

Resolutely she dragged herself up to stand tall and straight. "We can look over them now."

"Come on, honey. You're dead on your feet. Let me take you to bed." He slipped his arm around her waist and led her from the room.

As they reached the staircase, she stiffened. "Cade, I can't…" Her eyes locked on his.

He mentally completed her sentence. She would go to bed, but he wasn't invited.

"So our fling lasted one night, that it?"

"I don't…" She bit her lip. "I wish…"

He cradled her cheek. "We're not done with each other, not by a long shot, but we can discuss that later. Tonight you just go to bed and rest easy." He leaned in and kissed her gently. When her lips softened and she responded, he smiled inside. *No, we are definitely not through.* But he ruthlessly restrained himself and ended the kiss. "Good night, Sophie. I'll go around and lock up."

Her eyes were huge and luminous and confused. "Good night."

He was nearly out of earshot when he heard her. "Thank you, Cade. The photographs are incredible. And you can take the plans with you if you want to. To save time tomorrow, that is."

"I will. See you in the morning, sweetheart." He smiled to himself. *Nope, not nearly done.*

CHAPTER THIRTEEN

RELUCTANTLY CADE HAD returned to Jenna's for what was left of the night. When dawn broke, however, he was up making coffee and whistling.

"Well, Tweety Bird, what's gotten into you this morning?" Jenna asked. "Here, let me feel if you're feverish."

"Smart aleck." He dodged the hand she'd pressed to his forehead and handed her a cup. "I need your help, Jen."

"Always a catch." Her eyes studied him over the rim. "You okay? Anything wrong?"

"It's not for me. For Sophie."

"Has something happened?"

He explained the situation. "I need more workers, but Sophie can't really afford to pay for more, and she won't let me give her any money. I'm going to call Jesse and Vince to help."

"We'll all pitch in. You know Delilah and Chloe will want to help, too. How soon?"

"Very. The opening is supposed to be in less than three weeks. I also need to figure out how far I can make her money stretch for the materials. I'd buy the rest myself, but her pride is an issue. It's going to be a challenge to have all of us there working without making her feel like a charity case."

"Wow. Who are you and what have you done with my brother? You are being way too sensitive."

"Can it, brat." He ruffled her hair as he had when she was little. "Sophie's never had family like we do. It's not going to be easy to get her to accept the help."

"And you think you're up to the task, Mr. Diplomacy?"

He grinned. "I have my charms. She called me her white knight."

Jenna's jaw dropped comically. "Okay, first of all, she has to be talking about someone else." Her eyes narrowed. "And second, don't you dare break her heart, Cade. Sophie's not a love 'em and leave 'em woman."

"I know that."

"So what are you doing with her?"

"None of your business."

She laid a hand on his arm. "It's not just her I'm worrying about. I don't want either of you to get hurt."

"I'm not going to get hurt, and I'll do my damnedest to protect her, too. But I can't just walk away from her, Jenna. She's lost too much already. I won't stand by when there's something I can do."

Jenna smiled and kissed his cheek. "You *are* a white knight, aren't you?"

He rolled his eyes. "No, but if she wants to think that, I'm not telling her otherwise."

"Okay, so give me details. I'd love to help."

WHEN SOPHIE AWOKE, SHE realized that for the first time in weeks, she felt hopeful.

Because of Cade.

Which was wrong in so many ways she couldn't begin to name them. She was an independent woman who did not need a man to charge in and fix things for her. She wouldn't stand for that, nor would she abdicate control of any aspect of her hotel to another.

He wouldn't let her pay for the artwork. He wanted to give her money. Somehow she had to even things up or—

Jenna's not the only one in the family who cares about lending a helping hand to a friend.

Were they friends, she and this enigmatic man who insisted that he didn't like people but had thrown himself into the middle of her mess? Who gave her exquisite art to make her hotel a showplace? Who worked as hard as any laborer but wouldn't accept a cent?

There are ways other than money to repay someone. She smiled, remembering. Her libido would like that form of repayment just fine, despite her mind being aghast at the very concept. He was only teasing, though—his mischief was an element of him that had surprised her, but it was also one of the most endearing. He wasn't serious about that trade-off because he was at heart a very good man.

As well as an amazing lover. In another set of circumstances, she'd be more than happy to make love with him until they both burned out.

But everything now was complicated. And she'd

learned the hard way about falling into ill-advised affairs.

She had to refocus on the hotel and getting back on track. She was less than three weeks away from opening. By this point in her schedule, she'd planned to be training the staff, but she was still short on housekeeping staff and grounds crew, though she hoped to convince Armando to come on board.

If she was going to make it, she needed Cade's help. But his work called, too. How did she even the scales and not take worse advantage of him than she felt she already had? Free nights at the hotel when he visited town? No, he'd stay with Jenna. She puzzled over what on earth she could do as she went down the stairs.

And found him already in her kitchen.

"Hey," he greeted her. "You look better. Still need to catch up on your rest, though." He moved around the island toward her.

"That's not on the schedule until next year—mmph!" He suddenly pulled her into his arms, his mouth pressed to hers in a kiss so blatantly hungry that the hands she tried to shove against his arms instead curled and dug in.

He lifted his head a few inches. "That's just in case you were still thinking we were done with each other." Navy blue eyes glowed with a heat that roared through her body.

"Cade—" Another kiss, this one even more carnal.

Sophie closed her eyes and savored. Her hands wound up in his hair, and she pressed more closely against him.

He gave a low hum of approval as his arms tightened around her.

She wanted to think she'd have drawn back first, given just a few more seconds, but she wasn't sure.

He broke away and rested his forehead against hers. "Don't want to crowd you, Queenie, but you need to accept that I'm not going anywhere just yet."

But you will.

She didn't say the words, though. She was a big girl, and facts were facts—there was something between them, and all she could do was keep herself ready for the day when it would be over. She'd survived worse than Cade MacAllister storming into her life and leaving just as suddenly. She did better alone, anyway.

"Okay." She didn't look away. Couldn't.

"I don't know where this ride is taking us, and I'm sure if we were both smart, we'd run in the opposite direction—fast." His gaze grew serious. "I don't want to run, Sophie. You?"

She should. Oh, she should. But even knowing the loss that was waiting for her, she couldn't find it in herself to give up this most inconvenient surprise encased in the gorgeous, intriguing man before her. "I'm not running."

"That's my Queenie."

At last Sophie smiled, too. Her life was a mess and she had a host of reasons to worry—but right at this moment, the sun was shining, and a beautiful man wanted to make love to her and to stand by her.

So Sophie tossed caution to the winds and settled into his arms willingly, luxuriating in his embrace.

He was bending to kiss her again when they heard Armando and his men arrive.

"Thanks a lot, man," Cade grumbled, making her smile. He took her hand and led her outside, grabbing the landscaping plans as they left. "Come on, Queenie. Let's get this show on the road."

AN HOUR AND A HALF LATER, Cade disconnected after talking to his, well, sort of brother-in-law. Vince Coronado was married to the sister of Diego's wife, Caroline, so that made them some kind of family. Though he was a cop by trade, Vince had been renovating his Travis Heights house himself when he'd met Chloe, who had redone hers in Rosedale, north of downtown. When they'd married, they'd finished Vince's house together, then bought another one in which they and their children now lived. Vince knew every supplier in Austin and had a contact at a wholesale nursery who'd agreed to sell materials to Sophie at cost because of Vince's long-standing relationship with them.

He walked outside to find her carrying a slate stepping stone that was far too heavy for her slender frame. "Hey—give me that." He took it from her, and she frowned. "Don't bark at me, Queenie. You're strong, but there's no reason to be stupid."

She was firing up to argue, he could see. "Yeah, yeah, yeah. Girl power and all that. Blah blah. I outweigh you probably by a hundred pounds, so deal with it. Anyway, we don't have time to argue. I found you a contact at a wholesale nursery and the guy's waiting for us."

The fire in her eyes morphed to joy. "Really? How?"

"Family. Told you." He grinned as he handed off the stone to one of the workers. "Vince hooked us up. Clock's ticking. Ready?"

"Now?"

"Grab your purse, Queenie. Let's roll."

Sophie was no slacker. She charged inside and emerged within minutes. "We'll take my truck."

"Yes, ma'am." He considered telling her then that he and Jenna had assembled the troops, and tomorrow the entire MacAllister clan would swarm down upon her, along with some of Vince and Delilah's police department friends. Then rejected the idea.

He wasn't a coward, really, to enjoy her excitement for a little bit first, right? "Afterward, let's go see Skee...uh, Finn. Want to? He's about ready to be sprung."

One eyebrow arched. "I wish I could believe you called him Finn because you agree with the name." She smiled. "But I'm beginning to know you. So what do you have up your sleeve?"

"Me?" He put on his most innocent look. "Not a thing. Turn here."

She dragged her gaze back to the road and was distracted when the nursery came into view. "This place has everything!" she said as they walked down the aisles of plants. Her delight warmed him, but he didn't kid himself she'd forgotten her suspicions that he was hiding something.

But hey, that was for later. Right now, they had plants to choose.

"DID YOU SEE THOSE Turk's Caps? Won't they be beautiful just past the pergola?" Sophie couldn't help herself. She was nearly bouncing as she drove away from the nursery. The entire bed of her pickup was full, and a truck would be delivering the rest.

"Gonna look great," Cade agreed. "Let's grab lunch before we go to the vet's. You didn't eat breakfast."

She almost pouted. "I want to plant, not eat."

"You'll plant yourself flat on your face if you don't get some food in you, Mother Nature."

Oh, she was in too fabulous a mood to even argue. Besides, she had turned into an actual handy person, hadn't she? For so many years her life had been conducted in offices and hotels and airplanes. She wore suits and heels, not blue jeans and increasingly ratty running shoes. And now look at her. "You can't insult me." She tossed her ponytail and sniffed.

Cade tugged at her hair. "Wanna bet?"

She laughed then suddenly sobered. "Thank you. Seriously. Without you, I'd never have been able to get all of this. I'd have had to cut way back, and the landscaping would show it."

He shrugged. "I just made some calls."

He'd done more than that, though, starting from the first day when he'd tried to take her wheelbarrow off her hands. "You've been amazing, Cade. I don't know how, but I'll make it up to you...."

He rolled his eyes. "This is not where we go back over old ground, right? You are not still trying to figure out how to pay me back?"

"I will pay you back, count on it."

Cade sighed then cocked his head as if an idea had struck him. "Okay, if you insist, here's how you can do it."

"All right." She turned into a restaurant and parked under some trees so the plants wouldn't suffer while they were inside eating.

He looked straight at her. "You don't complain about what I'm about to tell you next."

"But—"

"You wanted to repay me, Queenie. These are my terms. Take it or leave it."

What was he up to now? Because he was definitely up to something. "Cade, I can't just—"

"Queenie…"

"All right, all right. I won't complain, but that doesn't mean I agree to accept whatever it is."

"Big surprise."

"You can't expect me to give you a blanket acceptance, not when I know only too well how high-handed you are. So tell me, what have you done?"

"Tomorrow my family is showing up to help."

"What? What do you mean, your family?"

"I mean, every last one of them—my dad and mom, my brothers, their wives, their kids, Jenna…and whoever else any of them decide to dig up."

She couldn't breathe. She knew her mouth was gaping, but she couldn't seem to change that. "You— you're kidding." She looked at him, thought about Jenna. "You're not kidding. Oh, my God." She jerked open her door and walked away, head spinning.

He followed her, grabbed her arm. She yanked it away and started running.

He was right behind her. "Sophie…"

She whirled on him. "How could you?"

"You need help. We're less than three weeks from opening. We don't have time to do it all ourselves. And give me credit—I knew better than to pay the workers myself on the sly. Though I thought about it," he muttered. "But I knew you'd be embarrassed."

Her whole chest was on fire. "And this won't embarrass me? To show that I was so incompetent that you had to call in every relative and friend you had just to make up for my bad planning? Your parents live six hundred miles away!"

"I told you, the landscaper wasn't your fault. And my parents like to come and visit. They have grandchildren here."

"Then let them visit their grandchildren and—and… play, not work!" Then something else hit her. "Zane? Your brother the movie star, he's coming, too?"

"He and Roan and the kids are taking his private plane and picking up Mom and Dad, as well as Diego and his family. Linc and Ivy and their three are driving down from Palo Verde. Ivy is Caroline and Chloe's sister."

"Oh—oh, Cade they can't! You *can't!*"

"Sophie." He gripped her shoulders. "It's really okay. I only asked Jesse and Vince. Everyone else offered when they heard about it. My family loves stuff like this. Think of it this way—you've given them a chance to have a family reunion, and it's not even Christmas.

My mom is over the moon to have all her kids in one place."

"But this is not a reunion. This is not fun. This is charity…"

"No, it's what a family does, sweetheart."

"I'm not family."

"You don't have your own, so I want you to borrow mine. You're Jenna's friend, and you're my— Well, I want to help you, too." She wondered what he'd started to say. "It's not a big deal, honest. And the only way they'd think less of you is if you didn't accept."

When she opened her mouth, his eyes warned her. "You promised not to complain."

"I'm not complaining, I'm—I'm horrified. Humiliated."

"Stop that. It's in your head, no one else's." Exasperation was all over his face. "Do you know how long it's been since my folks have had me around this much? Since I wasn't the only one of their chicks missing from a gathering? For that alone, Sophie, my mother would plant every blasted shrub by herself."

"But—"

"It's happening, honey. Now you can be gracious and accept it, or you can make all these good people feel bad because you refuse to take this in the spirit in which it's offered and reject a neighborly gesture out of hand."

Sophie struggled to compose herself. "I just… Cade, I'm not ungrateful, I'm just overwhelmed. I… No one's ever done something like this for me before…"

"Come here." He drew her in and clasped his hands

behind her waist, but remained apart enough to see her. "I come from simple people, Sophie. Some of us might have prospered financially, but at our core we're country people, descended from the pioneers who settled Texas. In that tradition, neighbors help neighbors. You need a barn built? Everybody shows up one Sunday, and a barn that would take weeks for you to build by yourself is erected in one day. The families bring food, and even the little kids pitch in. It was the early version of a block party. That's how they survived, by helping each other out in times of need."

"But what can I possibly do to pay them back?"

"That's not what it's about, sweetheart. There is no ledger—that isn't why they're coming. The shame in all this is that you've had to be alone so long, that you haven't had anyone but yourself to depend on."

"I've done fine." Her chin jutted out.

"You have. I admire the hell out of you for what you've accomplished, but now you do need help. And you're too smart not to realize it. So are we going to keep arguing over this? Do you have the time to waste?"

"No," she said sadly. "I don't." She fell silent, struggling to accept his point of view when it flew in the face of everything she'd ever experienced. "Okay." She blew out a breath and placed a hand on her jittery stomach. "But no one's bringing food. I'm feeding everyone. I have a perfectly good chef who's itching to get started in the kitchen, so we'll use this as her first catering opportunity."

Cade started to say that she couldn't afford to feed so

many people, but he knew her pride was already stung, so he said nothing. "Sounds great."

Her discomfort seemed to ease, and as she made plans all through lunch, he watched her excitement grow. She peppered him with questions about what kind of food his family liked, were there any allergies, what would they do with the kids, how many children were there. Cade was half dizzy watching Sophie swing into action. Before they finished their meal, she'd called her new chef, Patty, and they'd selected the menu with impressive efficiency.

It was fun watching her, and he was surprised to find himself wishing he'd be around when her hotel opened and in the months that would follow as she brought her vision to life. He made a mental note to recommend her hotel to his agent and editor, to others with a taste for the authentic. Austin was becoming a destination for entertainment types and the fashionable crowd, and Sophie's hotel, he was absolutely convinced, would be an extraordinary place to stay.

Even if a part of him balked at sharing it. Sharing her.

But this place was not his and neither was she. God willing, if he ever got past the roadblock in his head, he'd be traveling again more often than not. But oddly, for the first time in his life the thought of wandering didn't excite him.

And that scared him more than anything thus far.

Just then they reached the vet's office, where a surprise waited. The dog was healing beautifully and he was ready to go home. Sophie took it in stride, though, and once again Cade was treated to the sight of the woman who'd juggled huge conventions and angry guests and housekeeping disasters as she calmly compiled a list of what the dog would need.

She didn't fight with him over the bill he'd paid, but he was sure she made a note in her mental ledger.

Cade offered to take the dog to Jenna's until after the opening, but she quickly rejected that suggestion.

"That's only a temporary solution," she chided. "He's been through enough. He needs a home."

Cade thought she might be speaking of herself just as much, but he wisely didn't point that out. More and more, he had begun to understand just how alone Sophie had been for many years. It was a damn shame. She had so much to offer the right man. And Sophie's children? They'd be lucky as hell.

Damn that right man. Cade wasn't ready to think about his replacement. Nor was he keen on picturing Sophie as he'd seen his sisters-in-law, round with their babies.

"What's wrong?"

He realized his hands were clenched into fists over the things he couldn't offer Sophie. Not in the only life he knew.

"Nothing." He tore himself out of the thoughts that would help no one. He was here for her right now, and he wouldn't think beyond that.

He dropped to a crouch as the dog bounded through the half door. "Hey, Skeeter!" He ruffled the dog's fur and grinned up at Sophie, who was sinking to her own heels.

"Don't listen to him, Finn." She glared at Cade, but it was playful. "He's blind to your dignity. Skeeter is all wrong for my handsome boy, isn't that right?" she crooned, then laughed as he slurped her cheek and knocked her backward.

God, she was beautiful, even more so when she laughed.

With a twinge in the direction of his heart, Cade reminded himself that his thoughts were his problem, not hers. She might say she was still open to a casual relationship with him. But that wouldn't be fair to her. She was firmly planted here, more so every day.

She wasn't a part-time woman, not one to let him fly in and out of her life.

And he couldn't stay. Without his career, he was nothing.

The dog turned to him, enthusiastically wagging his tail and slurping at him, too. "She's wrong," he muttered loudly enough for her to hear. "But she's stuck on that name, buddy, so we'll humor the lady, all right?"

A soft woof was his only answer.

"Let's go home, Sophie." Even if it wasn't his to claim. And that shouldn't bother him. Didn't.

He'd hate sharing with a bunch of strangers, anyway.

CHAPTER FOURTEEN

WHEN NIGHT FELL, SOPHIE didn't want to leave Finn downstairs, but the vet had advised that he shouldn't climb steps yet. "I wish I could carry you, but you're just too big," she said softly as she fluffed his bedding one more time.

"I could carry him upstairs for you, but I'd need to be here in the morning to carry him back down." Cade leaned negligently against the door frame, but his gaze was more intense than his posture.

Sophie bit her lip. She wanted him to stay, but it wasn't wise. Her earlier casting of caution to the winds seemed foolish. He would soon leave on another trip and then this idyll would be over. She should protect herself by cutting things off now.

But didn't she deserve this, just one kindness from life? She was sick of keeping herself on the outside looking in, too afraid to take a risk.

Spending more time in Cade's arms before she had to let him go would hurt, possibly more than she could bear. But she was going to do it anyway.

She smiled at Cade. "Thank you. That would be nice."

"You're not expecting me to sleep in a guest room, right, Queenie?"

"The beds aren't set up."

"I'm asking you a question, Sophie. Are you going to let me make love to you? Spend the nights with you until…"

Until. A sharp arrow to her heart, and she nearly backed out.

No. She was still going to do it and damn the consequences. "I was kinda thinking…" She tilted her head. "That I might make love to you instead."

His gaze remained fierce. "Be sure this is what you want, Sophie. Be very sure. Because you know I'll have to—"

"You'll have to leave." She nodded. "I understand."

"I shouldn't stay now. It's not fair."

"Deciding what's fair is up to both of us, isn't it?" She smiled, even if it was bittersweet. "Stay, Cade."

He still seemed conflicted.

She wasn't going to beg. "Suit yourself." She began to turn back to the dog only to find herself spun around and locked into his arms.

"Damn you, Queenie. Why can't I just walk away when it's smart?"

Then he kissed her, an edgy, almost angry kiss.

"Because neither of us is too bright," she murmured. And poured herself into answering his passion.

No, not bright at all, Sophie thought later as she left Finn curled up in his bed in the guest room just below hers where she could hear him if he needed her. But she wanted to be with Cade, even knowing she would feel more alone than ever when he was gone.

She entered the bedroom where Cade waited, shirt

already off, jeans unbuttoned, barefoot with boots scattered on the floor...and so ruggedly male he stole the breath from her body.

To be with him tonight and whatever nights were left to them would be sublime and bittersweet. For a second, Sophie let herself feel a sliver of the sorrow that lay down the road.

But that sorrow wasn't here yet, was it? Besides, she knew better than anyone that happiness was always ephemeral. You only ever got it in brief bursts. So she would live in this moment, the one in which she had a gorgeous, half-naked man in her bedroom.

Who was looking at her with worried eyes.

Stop thinking, Sophie. Don't ruin this.

She sauntered over to him, removing the elastic band from her hair and shaking it out. As she started to comb her hair with her fingers, he picked up her brush from the old-fashioned vanity she loved.

"Let me." Gently he guided her to the bench and began to brush her hair, as the woman who'd owned this vanity a hundred years ago might have experienced with her own lover.

Their eyes locked in the mirror. "That feels amazing."

"Just wait," he promised. He took his time, every stroke loosening the tension that had become her constant companion.

When her bones were all but liquid, he placed his mouth at the point where neck and shoulder met. The scent of him was part sun, part earth. It surrounded her, dizzied her. The simple touch sparked a sizzle beneath her skin. Sophie's eyes closed as his lips cruised back and forth, as soft as a whisper…a murmur…a dark, sweet promise.

The wet heat of his tongue on her skin startled a gasp from her. Her nipples hardened.

Lazily, his fingers trailed into her blouse and down to first one nipple, then the second. "Look at yourself, Sophie. Look at us."

She watched in the mirror, mesmerized by the sight of his big hands on her body, his skin bronzed by the sun. The calluses on his fingers were rough velvet as they traced the edges of her neckline.

"Unbutton it," he urged as he set the brush down and began gently massaging her scalp.

Her lids drifted shut as bliss flooded her, yet she couldn't take her eyes off him, off herself, as she complied to open the blouse with unsteady fingers.

He spread the two halves and slowly bared her, inching the blouse down only enough to trap her arms, then releasing the front clasp of her bra.

"I thought…" She could barely think, let alone speak. "I was going to make love to you."

"Honey, you are," he replied, his eyes a fire barely banked. He slid the bra straps languorously over her shoulders, his lean fingers trailing goose bumps in their wake, until he'd bared her halfway to naked. Who was this woman she saw in the mirror, her eyes gone dark, skin so pale in contrast to his hands?

"You are so beautiful," he said.

She dragged her gaze to his then down to the breadth of his shoulders, the sun-dusted hair on his muscled chest, the corded arms she'd watched work so hard on her behalf, arms that had held her tightly yet never once hurt. "So are you." She was faintly amused by the brush of color over his cheeks.

"I'm not." The golden glow from one lamp didn't hide the marks, old and new, of the dangerous life he led.

"We all have scars, Cade. Yours is a warrior's body, and it's beautiful." She turned a little and traced every mark on his chest, gently kissing each one. "I'm so glad you survived."

"Right now, Queenie, I'm glad as hell myself." But a shadow drifted over his face, and she knew it was the shadow of his friend's passing.

Before she could apologize for making him remember, he shifted her back to face the mirror and stood behind her, cupping one breast in each hand.

The fine hairs on her body rose at the sight of the strong, tall man ranged so protectively, possessively behind the woman in dishabille, so alive with longing…

Cade bent and captured her mouth with his, a kiss so hot and deep and greedy that she melted against him. He kicked the stool out of the way, no longer patient but hungry and demanding.

He held her in place in front of him, one big hand splayed over her midriff as the other roved restlessly over her body. Roughly, he unfastened her jeans and slid his fingers inside her panties with unerring accuracy, arrowing straight to the heart of her.

The climax ripped through her.

"Look at you," he said fiercely. "Just look at you."

She wanted more, needed more. She stripped off her jeans as she faced him, intent on getting him naked, too. They kissed as though the other held the only air in the world, as though life itself were in the balance. When he kicked away his pants and yanked her hard against him, Sophie gasped at the feel of him, so powerful, so tempting. She was ready to whimper, to climb his body to demand what they both wanted.

"Wait," he said, gripping her hips, chest heaving. "Turn around. Look at us, Sophie."

Need raging, she growled her frustration. She didn't want to look, she wanted to touch, to lose herself in sensation and yet… She glanced over her shoulder at the two of them in the mirror, him so strong, so tall that he made her seem delicate. His fingers dug into her hips then slowly he turned her to face the mirror as he stood behind her.

But not before she saw him in all his naked glory.

She drank in the sight of them, her hair streaming over her shoulders, his bronzed arm a slash across her belly. He was a pagan warrior, eyes dark and brooding, claiming his prize.

Slowly she rubbed herself against him, and the mood between them shifted, the storm rising.

"You are unbelievably beautiful," he said hoarsely. She waited, locked in the moment.

But instead of conquering her, he half turned her and sank to his knees, burying his face in the most intimate of kisses.

Sophie grasped for support as her knees went to jelly. "Cade…" Was that her voice, so guttural?

He spared her one glance, his smile a wolf's, a threat as much as a promise. Sophie sucked in her breath, eyes locked on the electrifying sight in the mirror, then dug her fingers into his hair and let Cade take her.

And as the aftershocks rippled through her, he rose to shelter her as she shuddered against him, relishing in the glory of his warm flesh, his strong arms, dizzy from the scent of him, the feel of his flesh straining against her.

Breathing ragged, she kissed his chest and began to lick her way down his body.

Then she sank to her own knees.

"Sophie—" A strangled groan. Soon he joined her, dragged her to the floor. Urged her high again, higher. Sent her spinning, then followed her into the void.

Silence engulfed them, broken only by ragged breathing as they slipped back to earth. Sophie lay splayed over him and smiled into his chest hair. "That was amazing."

He lifted his head, but couldn't hold it up. "You were amazing."

"I will never look at that mirror the same again." Or forget how it felt to lose herself so completely, to let go of every worry, every doubt and simply revel in sensation.

"Honey, we have barely scratched the surface. Just give me a day or two to recover, and I'll show you."

That wasn't what his body was saying, though, as it stirred against her hip. She giggled. "I don't think you're going to need that long."

"Well, how 'bout that?" He grinned as he rolled her

over and surged inside her. "I could tell from the beginning that you were a smart woman."

She was too busy trying to find her breath to respond, except to pull his head down to hers.

IN THE MORNING, CADE turned on the mattress and felt for her, but he encountered only air. "Sophie?"

No answer. He glanced at the clock and groaned. They'd had maybe three hours' sleep. He was too old to be staying up for another night of making love for hours with such a day ahead of him...ahead of both of them.

But he smiled as he stretched. What a night it had been. And the Sophie he'd encountered...she'd met and matched him with her capacity for yielding control—and for taking it back in delightful ways. He seemed to lose about half his brainpower when faced with Sophie naked, warm and willing.

And she'd been all that...oh, yeah.

He wanted her again. Now.

Then he heard her voice below, murmuring to the dog, and a soft woof in answer. Oh, man. He was supposed to carry Finn back down to the ground floor. Cade yanked on his jeans and padded down the stairs to find Sophie rigging some sort of sling. "What are you doing?"

She jolted. "You startled me."

"Good morning. You should have woken me up." He turned to the dog and scooped him into his arms. "Come on, boy." Wishing he had his boots on, Cade treaded gingerly down the wooden steps to the outside and placed the dog on the ground.

"I'll watch him while you get dressed," she offered.

She didn't sound much like his lover from last night. "Mornin', Queenie." He strolled over and kissed her.

She stuck a palm to his belly as if to resist, but then she softened and kissed him back. "Good morning."

"Damn, but you're beautiful."

Again he had the pleasure of seeing Sophie blush. "There's, uh, coffee inside. I can call you when he needs to come back up the stairs."

"Trying to get rid of me?"

A minuscule shrug. "I just thought you might want to, um, get decent before your family…"

Cade grinned. "Honey, I'm pretty sure my family knows I have sex."

Her head rose swiftly.

"I mean, not that we discuss it, but I have been grown up for a long time."

Her gaze darted away. "Well, but they…"

"They might even guess you've had sex, too." He couldn't resist a chuckle.

"Not with you, though."

"Would that be so bad?" When color washed over her again, he knew he should go easier on Sophie, but the devil on his shoulder didn't seem to want to. "Okay, okay. I'll get dressed." He strolled inside, smiling. He grabbed some coffee and stared out over the rolling grounds, watching their dog roam across the grass and lift his leg to mark every possible tree or shrub while

Sophie lectured him. She obviously had never owned a male dog.

Cade shook his head and started to sip, realizing this was the most peaceful he'd felt in months. The place felt like ho— He choked on his coffee and burned his tongue in the bargain.

With haste he set the cup down and retreated upstairs for a quick shower. No. Oh, no. Sophie was not his. This place was not home. In a matter of weeks there would be strangers all over it, and the illusion of peace would be shattered. Cade stuck his head under the shower until all his foolish ideas had been washed out.

When he came back down, a strange woman was in the kitchen unloading groceries. Friendly brown eyes looked out from beneath sassy short black hair. "Hi there," she said with interest. "I'm Patty. The chef."

He shook her offered hand. "I'm Cade." He saw the question in her eyes about why he was coming from upstairs clearly just out of the shower, so he chose to escape. "I'll go help Sophie."

"See you later," she said with a cheery wave.

He waved back and made his way onto the porch, where he discovered that Sophie had hauled over a sheet of plywood and made Finn a ramp that he could walk up instead of climbing the stairs. Currently she was bent over, coaxing him to try it, giving Cade an eyeful of her very pretty behind.

His fingers itched to grab her, but Finn woofed at him and scrambled up to see him. He leaned down and gave the dog a good rub.

"I decided that if I get a baby gate to block off the

stairs and use this ramp, he can live downstairs and outside until he's free to climb steps. I don't know what we're going to do with him today, though."

I decided... She was pushing him away again. He ought to be glad.

But damn it, he wasn't.

"Dogs are pack animals, he'll want to be with everyone. The place is fenced, though people will be coming in and out. I hate to tie him up when he's been stuck in a cage so long, don't you?"

She nodded.

"We'll keep an eye on him, but he'll probably stay with us while we're working. He's pretty laid-back, so he probably won't get in the way. If he does, I'll erect a temporary fence under the trees so he can get out of the sun."

"You don't have to—"

"Queenie, if you spend all day telling people what they don't have to do, not much is going to get accomplished." Why did that piss him off so much when her independence was exactly what he needed so that he wouldn't worry about her when he was gone?

Before the argument could continue, however, he heard his father's booming voice. "Over here, Dad," he called then looked down at Sophie, who was worrying at her lower lip and smoothing her hair. "They don't bite, Soph, I promise."

She glanced up quickly, nerves in her eyes.

He couldn't help it. He had to kiss her.

"Cade!" she muttered. "Stop that."

"Son, don't manhandle the girl." His father walked

up to them, shouldering a bundle of hoes and shovels. "Hi, there. You must be Sophie. I'm Hal MacAllister, father of the reprobate here."

"Hello, Mr. MacAllister." Sophie was putting on her hotel executive face. "You didn't need to…" She glanced at Cade. "It's wonderful to meet you. Would you like me to take those?"

"Of course not." His dad looked scandalized. "Has my son been making you tote things around, a little thing like you? Well, you just come with me. I thought I raised him better, but you know a man can try and try to civilize heathen boys, but they never seem to learn.…"

Cade didn't bother defending himself as his father walked away with her. He just grinned.

"Some things never change, huh?" Zane said as he reached Cade. "Leave it to Dad to hog the pretty girls."

"Hey, bro."

"Hey. This place is amazing."

"Isn't it? But it's actually Sophie who's amazing."

"Really." Zane looked sideways at him. "Hmm."

Cade frowned. "What does that mean?"

Zane's eyebrows rose in an expression of innocence. "Oh, nothing."

"Nothing, hell. I know that tone."

His brother grinned. "Just…how the mighty have fallen. Wait until I tell the family."

Cade stared after Sophie and his father, all too aware of a funny feeling in his chest. "It's not like that. We're just having a good time."

"Uh-huh. Whatever you say, bro. Me, I'm going to go meet her."

Cade grabbed his arm. "Don't tease her, Zane. She's...she's like a frightened doe who's had to survive on her own. Skittish and...vulnerable. Don't play rough."

Zane stopped grinning. "You wouldn't worry if you'd been there to see Roan. Talk about skittish... I finally had to walk away because she was so determined we couldn't be together. Had to give her room, even though it was killing me every day to be without her." All teasing had fled. He glanced over at Sophie. "She's had a bad go of it, huh?"

"She's more alone than anyone I've ever met. Not like me—I may be by myself a lot, but I always know the family has my back. She's lost everyone."

"Never take the easy path, do you?"

"Guess not. Anyway, we both understand this can't last. I couldn't live in a city or stay in one spot, and this is all she wants."

"Sorry, man." Zane clapped a sympathetic hand to his shoulder. "Only cure I know of is hard work. And looks like we have plenty for today. Come on, the family's waiting."

Cade nodded and joined his brother. He couldn't solve the problems between Sophie and himself, but he could get this job done. "I have the plans laid out on the side porch, and the delivery truck should be here anytime."

He couldn't resist one glance backward to where Sophie had disappeared with his dad.

Then he was swallowed up in greeting family.

CHAPTER FIFTEEN

CADE'S FATHER WAS AMAZING. Almost before Sophie could blink, he'd charmed Patty, made Finn his friend for life and cadged a tour from her, all the while making her feel both cosseted and absolutely brilliant.

Did his children have any idea how lucky they were?

She thought they did, as she recalled how Jenna and Cade spoke of him. She couldn't blame them. She wanted to steal him for herself. Bluff, hearty, strong and kind... No wonder Cade and Jenna never doubted they were loved or lacked the confidence that love gave them.

Then Sophie remembered that Cade hadn't told any of his family of his fears that he'd lost the talent that defined him. He'd only told her, and knowing that warmed her.

She didn't have much time to dwell on it, though. Before she knew it, Hal MacAllister had pulled her into the bosom of his family, introducing her to one and all, then insisting that everyone quiet down while she gave them their marching orders.

Sophie felt like a bug on a pin as they stared at her and waited. "Well, really, just whatever you'd like..." Was this the same woman who'd commanded a staff of hundreds?

"Now, Miss Sophie," Hal boomed. "You can take that approach, but I'll warn you that my brood is filled with hard heads. Not my fault, of course. I blame it on Grace."

Sophie was aghast until she saw the fond grins, including the chiding one Cade's mother bestowed on her husband.

"What Dad means," Cade interrupted, "is you can't be shy with this crowd. We'll get everything done, but if you want one shred of control, you'd better speak up now."

Remember who you are. This is your hotel. So Sophie stood straight. "First of all, there is no possible way I can thank you enough for being here. I would never have asked this of you." She cast a glare in Cade's direction.

A tall man with dark hair down to his shoulders and the look of an Aztec chieftain except for his startling silver eyes, spoke up. "You can lay the blame on our little sister here. I'm Diego Montalvo, the eldest. Mom raised me with excellent manners, but it all went downhill from there." His smile was gentle and kind as the others jeered affectionately. But Sophie could see in his eyes that this man knew a great deal about suffering. "In truth, Sophie, we're all here because we want to be. Jenna cares about this place, as does Cade, and that's enough for us. So why don't you begin with me and show me on your drawing what you have in mind?" With one hand on her elbow, he led her to the porch and listened carefully as she described what she had planned.

The Montalvo/MacAllister clan was something to see in action. Within minutes, they had divided up the tasks and scattered to perform them. The children, she'd learned, were all being cared for at Vince and Chloe's place not far away, and they would be joining the family when the work was completed later that afternoon.

Cade's mother was cordial to her, but Sophie wasn't surprised when Grace approached her after everyone had scattered to their various tasks. She expected a mother to be very protective of her son.

Grace's words, however, could not have been more surprising. "Thank you," she said, laying one hand on Sophie's arm. "You've been able to do what I couldn't."

"What?" Sophie couldn't imagine anything this woman couldn't accomplish.

"You've brought him into the sunlight, Sophie, from that dark place he's been in ever since the accident."

"But I..."

Grace shook her head. "He has a purpose, even though I know there are still many questions unanswered for him. You've allowed him to become involved here, and I can see the positive effects of that on him."

Sophie tried to bite back a smile. "I didn't exactly let him."

Grace laughed. "I should probably apologize. I have a flock of extraordinarily hardheaded children. And Hal might even be right about who's at fault."

"I think they're wonderful, Mrs. MacAllister."

"Oh, Grace, please, dear."

"Grace, then. Your children are amazing. You must be so proud."

"I am, but I don't take all the credit. Much of who a child is comes with them from the beginning. Take Cade, for instance. So solitary from his earliest years, though not solemn, as he's been lately." She scanned the area until she spotted him. "This laughing Cade is one I didn't know if we'd ever see again, and we have you to thank for that." Her eyes misted. "Hal told me about the photographs Cade framed for you. I want to thank you for that, too. I was worried when he wouldn't even pick up his camera—before it was always an extension of his arm. Oh, look." Grace bit her lip. "He brought it with him."

Sophie glanced over her shoulder to see Cade with his camera, taking shots of various family members unaware of his scrutiny. Then furtively he tucked it away in his car and returned to work.

Grace's hand gripped her arm. "Has he been doing that all along?"

Sophie thought of the night he'd wanted to shoot her naked and hoped she wasn't blushing. "I don't think so."

"I won't let him know what we saw. He's too vulnerable right now." She brushed at her eyes. "But I will thank you for the part you're playing in resurrecting my son. For that, there is no way for me to repay you, Sophie. You worry about owing us, but the debt is ours." She patted Sophie's arm, donned her gloves again and left a confused Sophie staring after her.

He couldn't sneak around with his family. He didn't really want to—all his life they'd seen him with a camera in his hands, snapping off frame after frame of everything from ant beds to horses grazing. And they didn't know he'd been frozen…or maybe they did.

He was just so damn scared to believe it would come back for good.

But as he watched his family, he felt the stirring of excitement, the prickle beneath his skin, the ache in his belly. The longing that had only ever been eased when he watched the world from behind the viewfinder.

When they broke for lunch, Cade went to his car and retrieved the camera. He thought about everything he'd seen this morning…his father's hands, Diego's back—strong despite the limp he had when he got too tired—Zane joking while stealing a kiss from Roan, her gaze so soft on him. He wanted to capture it all.

And Sophie, too. Bewildered by his family yet so wistful, so eager for what they shared without even thinking, what they took for granted.

He raised the camera and found her, standing off to the side, petting the dog and watching them, the people he loved, the bounty he'd had all his life without understanding how rare it was.

She reminded him of an orphan on the sidewalk, watching Christmas through a window.

He snapped frame after frame of her, the line of her throat, the yearning in her eyes…the tenderness of her hand wound in Finn's hair. The tilt of her head as she leaned into the dog where he stood on the porch above her, his side a shelter for her as she kept herself apart from the rest of them.

Go to them, Sophie. Let them love you. They will.

They did already, he saw, as his father walked up to her, smiling, and wrapped one arm around her shoulders, refusing to let her stay apart.

A kid in a candy store she was, as she sat among them, these people who loved him, who never gave up on him even when he drifted so far.

Cade's chest went tight as he watched them all, recognizing how lucky he was.

How little he deserved the blessings that he walked away from so often.

You could stay, a voice echoed inside him whispered. *You don't have to keep roaming.*

Memories of last night flooded him. Mentally he captured them like photographs, frame by frame, Sophie hesitant yet trusting him as he bared her, as he seduced her. Seduced himself.

God. He wanted her now. Wanted to steal her away, carry her upstairs to that bed, that room that had sheltered them as they loved.

I can't love you, Sophie. I can't stay. Who could he possibly be if he stayed? He'd be a washed-out has-been. And the horizon would always beckon, the unknown would continue to call his name. He would suffocate if he stayed. He could never survive without his wings.

He glanced around at the completed slate walkway to the pergola, the fountain that was nearly plumbed. The billowing skirts that would grow from the plants now nestled in rich soil at the foundation of the grand old house. Soon this place would serve as a refuge for the fortunate few who would be Sophie's guests, who would inhabit Sophie's dream.

His phone rang—it was Karen, his agent. "Cade, I was hoping I would have heard from you by now about the book."

He turned his back on the hotel. "Karen—"

"Before you say anything, listen to this. You got the permission from North Korea. You, my boy, will be allowed to photograph Baekdu from the North Korean side. Isn't that amazing? This is it, the trip you've dreamed of. Are you ready?"

He'd waited years for this. Baekdu was the most sacred site in North Korea, the reputed birthplace of the Korean people, revered by citizens of both North and South. It was a mountain surrounded by a stunning lake, often photographed from the Chinese side in recent years, but the most stunning views were on the other side, and very few Westerners were given access to that view.

But he had to be sure she was clear about the other project first. "Karen, about the book. I won't do the story of the accident," he warned. "If that's the condition, then count me out. But I have another idea."

"Tell me."

He loved that about her. No BS. Just shoot straight. He outlined his idea for the tribute to Jaime.

"I like it. I'll get you a yes, trust me. Now, are you in for Korea, or are you out? You'd have to leave in two weeks."

Two weeks. When Sophie's hotel would be opening. He realized he'd been visualizing himself there, witnessing her triumph.

But expeditions like this were his life, his real life. Now that he could shoot a camera again, what was holding him back? "Yes. I'm ready."

"Great! I'll let them know."

He disconnected and felt his heartbeat speed up.

Baekdu. Unbelievable. He pictured it in his mind and wanted to be there already.

His gaze returned to Sophie. *You have to leave,* she'd said. *I understand that.*

He walked to where his family gathered and tried to decide if it was the right time to share his good news.

Sophie was as aware of him as though he lived inside her skin. He was across the side yard from her, but his gaze was a caress, a constant reminder of last night, of the glory of it, of how he alone was able to woo her out of the prison she'd made for herself, the bars of isolation that had protected her for so very long.

"Hey, there, little girl," boomed Hal MacAllister. "You'll waste away if you don't eat something. Why, you'd blow away in our West Texas wind." He stood beside her, one arm wrapped around her shoulders, hugging her to him as though she were one of his kids. With his other hand, he rubbed Finn's head. "Got yourself a mighty sweet home here, don't you, boy? You're a good fellow, aren't you?" he crooned to Finn, whose tail was a windmill as he woofed his love to this hearty, generous man. "I hear my son wanted to name him Skeeter."

Sophie flushed. "I guess I should have—"

"Now don't you let my boy buffalo you. He's got the devil in him, just like his brothers." Hal shook his head. "Acts more serious, I know, but there's mischief inside him, I promise you. He doesn't have Zane's polish, as I'm sure you've noticed, but the boy's got a good heart. All my children do." He grinned down at her. "Probably should give Grace credit for that, too."

Sophie couldn't help but love him. "Your children are very fortunate, Mr. MacAllister."

"Now, you're making me feel like an old man when you call me mister. I'm Hal to my friends, all right?" His friendly blue eyes studied her. "You've been good for my boy, Sophie, and I want to thank you for that."

"He's been good for me, too, Mr.—Hal." She waved to indicate the grounds. "He just strolled in and made things happen. He told me he learned everything he knows from you."

Hal beamed. "Well, it's true that I tried to teach my children how to be independent and do things for themselves. Looks to me like you're pretty handy yourself, Miss Sophie."

She shrugged. "I've had to learn some things quickly."

"A damn fine place you got here. Gonna be something special." He bent his head in a conspiratorial whisper. "Think I could reserve that honeymoon suite for Grace and me for our anniversary?"

"It's all yours, just name the date. My treat."

"Oh, no, little girl. We can't be having that. Not a bit of it. I'll pay like any guest would."

"But I owe you, you've worked so hard here."

"You think Grace and I aren't happier than pigs in—er, real happy to do it?"

Sophie had to giggle. "But…"

"No buts. I don't let Diego give me free medical care—or at least I insist on donating to his clinics—and I'm not going to take advantage of you. Except to stick myself in the front of the line, that is."

"How about I make you a good deal?" she asked. "And you can tell your friends if you like it?"

"I'd do that anyway." He waggled his eyebrows. "But if you'd throw in a special meal by that chef of yours, I'd pay a premium. Nothing too good for my Gracie."

"You just leave it to me. It will be a romantic paradise."

He nodded in satisfaction. "Now that's my girl. Bet you're real good at what you do, aren't you, Miss Sophie?"

"I am," she said, believing it for the first time in a while.

"Exactly what are you wangling Sophie into?" Cade said as he walked up to the two of them.

"That's between me and her, son."

"Get your own girl, Dad."

Hal glanced over at her, eyes rolling. "You see how my children talk to me?" He shook his head dramatically then clapped Cade on the shoulder. "My advice to you, son, is to snatch this woman up. Only a blind man wouldn't see what a treasure she is." He winked at Sophie. "I'll be in touch, Miss Sophie."

"I'll look forward to it." She watched him go and sighed.

"I swear every one of my brothers' wives would leave them for Dad in a heartbeat."

She had to grin. "Except that it's patently obvious how much he adores your mother." She looked up at him. "They're wonderful, Cade. You have the dream family."

"They like you, too."

The notion warmed her as she glanced around, smiling. "I can't get over how much is finished already."

He was looking at her solemnly and her smile died. "What?"

He seemed conflicted.

"Cade?"

"My agent called." He stopped.

"Good news? Did you tell her about the tribute to Jaime?"

"I did. She likes it."

"But…?"

He glanced away, then back. "There's this place. I've waited a long time to have the chance to photograph it. Westerners aren't allowed in, as a rule."

"How soon do you leave?" Ruthlessly, she ignored the pit that had opened in her stomach, the ache that she was determined to hold at bay.

"Two weeks."

Two weeks. Right before her opening.

"Sophie, I'm sorry. I wanted to be here when—"

She pasted on a smile. "I told you, I understand. I saw you with your camera today. You think you're okay?"

"I don't know. I hope so." He looked over her shoulder. "Jaime would have loved to make this trip. We both waited years, hoping."

"Is it dangerous?"

"No. Not really." His gaze locked on hers. "I want to come back to see you. After. Will I be welcome?"

"Of course," she said automatically, but she couldn't look at him.

"Sophie…" He took her chin, tilted it upward. "I… This is my life. My career is who I am."

"I know." And she did. "It's okay." She took a deep breath, stepping back to put distance between them before the crack inside her became visible. When she was sure her expression was composed, she finally looked at him. "It would be criminal for you to miss this. I'm happy for you." She was. Even as she was screaming inside. But she'd known this day would come. He'd never pretended he'd stay. "If you'll excuse me, I just…" *Have to go. Have to be alone.*

"Sophie…"

She straightened, turned back and faced him. "I'm fine, Cade. We always knew it was temporary. Just a fling, remember?"

"It's not for two weeks. I can still help you until then."

"That's not necessary." *Let me go, Cade. Don't make me break in front of your family.* "Look how much is done already. It'll be fine. Besides, you'll have a lot to do to get ready, I imagine."

She spotted Jenna close by and seized the escape. "Jenna, have I shown you what Armando finished yesterday?" Taking her friend's arm, Sophie walked away from Cade as fast as humanly possible.

So the Queenie he'd first met was back. Cade stemmed his frustration. His help was not necessary? So he'd been useful for a while, worked his butt off for her, but now that he wasn't all hers to command, he was dismissed? Just like that?

Hell if he was. He hadn't even found the rest of the photos for her, and he never reneged on his promises. He all but stomped up the stairs to Sophie's attic abode, muttering to himself every step of the way.

As he strode into the room, he caught sight of the vanity mirror. Got the scent of her in his nostrils again and leaned heavily against the doorjamb.

He didn't want this to be over.

But that wasn't fair. If he were to return to the only life he knew, he would see her far too little for a relationship. She deserved more. He located the wallet he'd left on a chest and shoved it into his pocket. As he began to leave the room, he heard the recently connected hotel phone ring but shrugged. Sophie would get it. Or Patty.

But no one did, and the last thing Sophie needed was to lose a booking. They probably couldn't hear the phone over the racket from outside.

He could take notes, couldn't he? Cade snatched up

the receiver. "Hotel Serenity," he barked, then tried to remember Sophie's customary greeting when she answered a call.

"This is Hilary Swenson from the *Austin American-Statesman*. May I speak to Ms. Carlisle?"

The newspaper. "Can I take a message? She's tied up right now."

"Have her call me." The woman rattled off the number. "I want to discuss doing a spread on the hotel for the paper."

Way to go, Queenie. Sophie would be over the moon. "I'll tell her."

"Thank you." She disconnected, and Cade jammed the piece of paper in his pocket and went in search of Sophie.

This was exactly what he had to keep in mind. Sophie would be too blasted busy for him soon, and that was good. This hotel was the life she wanted. He would do everything he could—whatever protests she might want to make—to set her up as well as possible in the time he had left.

They would part friends. And maybe see each other again. For Jenna's sake, if nothing else, they would be civilized because Jenna treasured Sophie's friendship.

He'd be busy himself with the trip to North Korea, with Jaime's book. He closed the door on her room as he wondered if he'd be back here again. He'd like that—a lot—but what was most fair to her?

He could take a battering ram to the walls she was already erecting between them...or leave her alone as he probably should have from the beginning. Either way, he would hurt her.

This was why he didn't do relationships. Why, unlike all the happy couples here today, he would remain alone. He was solitary, always had been, and he liked it that way.

And the price of stepping out of isolation and feeling too much...was too high to pay.

Queenie would agree, he knew that down to his bones.

Which made his decision for him. So instead of taking the good news about the article to Sophie himself, he sent the note to her via Chloe.

And Cade got back to work.

CHAPTER SIXTEEN

THE NEXT MORNING, SOPHIE raced around the hotel like a madwoman. She blessed the generous MacAllister family who, after hearing her shriek of joy devolving to horror that a reporter and photographer would be there the next morning, had redoubled their efforts outside but also insisted on helping her set up two of the guest rooms, as well as the downstairs public areas.

She'd been too desperate not to take them up on their offer to help.

Her first task after the interview would be to assemble her staff. Armando had agreed to serve as grounds-keeper, and one of his men would assist. He told her he could also do minor repairs like plumbing and some carpentry, so he would be in charge of maintenance, as well.

He had a sister-in-law, he said, who had been widowed and had hotel housekeeping experience. She would be here tomorrow to speak with Sophie, and her chef, Patty, already knew who she wanted to help her in the kitchen.

For the time being, Sophie would be the desk clerk and bookkeeper, then as bookings increased, she'd hire staff to replace her at those duties. She still needed a valet and bellman, but things were taking shape.

The reporter would be here in an hour, and Sophie was down to fine-tuning, wishing she hadn't dithered so much about the artwork that would grace the foyer. The blank spot bothered her, but it wasn't dithering, was it, when you wanted the best? When the wrong choice would be worse than a blank spot? She wasn't open yet, anyway. The reporter would have to understand that this was a work in progress.

Patty was cooking a meal to serve to the reporter, and the scent of bread in the oven drifted through the downstairs. If she liked the food—as Sophie knew she would—that would only help ensure the article was positive.

A delivery truck stopped outside, which puzzled her. She wasn't expecting a delivery. She pushed through the front door to tell whoever it was that she needed them out of the driveway before the reporter showed up—

Cade and Jesse emerged from the cab. Cade waved, and she couldn't stop a stab of longing from going through her. She shouldn't miss him in her bed. He'd only spent two nights there...two unforgettable nights.

Anyway, he'd worked later than anyone else yesterday. He couldn't have had but a few hours of sleep. She certainly hadn't.

It had been hard not to ask him to stay the night, but there was no point in dragging things out. She had to start separating him out of her life...and her heart.

"Mornin', Queenie," he said as he and Jesse shouldered a large wrapped object between them.

"What are you doing here?"

"Good morning, Sophie," said Jesse. "May we come in?"

"Oh—yes, of course, but…" She stepped aside.

"You don't have to like it," Cade said. "But I think you will."

They set it down in the foyer and began to unwrap what turned out to be a painting. A stunning one.

Sophie gasped. Spread one hand over her chest. "It's— Oh, my word—" Her gaze flew to Jesse. "Is it one of yours?"

He nodded. "Cade wanted it for this spot." He glanced around the foyer then shook his head at his brother. "You nailed it, bro." He looked back at her. "But art is a very personal decision. You will not offend me if you don't want it."

"Not want it?" she echoed, still stunned. "It's perfect. Absolutely right, but I—I can't possibly afford your prices." She chewed on her lip. "Is there… Could we work out a payment plan, perhaps?"

"It's a gift."

"Oh, no, I—"

"It's a gift to Cade," he explained. "Where he chooses to hang it is his decision."

She looked at the man who'd already done far too much for her. Who seemed to understand her better than she understood herself, she feared. "Cade, no, you can't…"

"Queenie, I'm pretty damn tired of arguing with you. Anyway, isn't that reporter due soon?"

"How is it you keep maneuvering me into doing things I'm not prepared to do?"

"Then catch up," he snapped. "We'll put the damn thing up for the interview, then you can do whatever the hell you want with it afterward. I'm going to get the ladder and tools." He stomped out.

Sophie watched him go, beset by a stunning, not altogether welcome realization. For whatever unfathomable, insane reason, she was in love with this bad-tempered, overbearing man.

And it was going to kill her to let him go.

But she would.

"Sometimes things seem impossible," Jesse said softly, "when they're not."

Her gaze whipped to his. "I don't know what you mean."

"Yes, you do. He's a good man, my brother. Not smooth and definitely not easy." His lips curved. "But don't give up on him, Sophie. You bring something out in him... He needs you." He studied her. "And I think you need him, too."

"He'll leave soon. He's gotten permission for the trip he's waited his whole career for, did he tell you?"

Jesse shook his head. "But it means something that he did tell you."

"I can't hold him back. He's suffered over Jaime and wondered if his career is over. He thinks his career defines him. He needs to go."

"Sometimes life changes on you and you have to learn to adapt," he said cryptically.

But before she could ask more, Cade returned with a ladder and hammer and hangers.

She stopped him as he shoved past her. "Cade, thank you. I'm sorry…it's just…I'm overwhelmed."

The temper in those beautiful dark blue eyes eased. "I'm only trying to help you, Sophie. Before I go, I just want to be sure you're okay."

She longed to stroke his face, soothe the trouble from his brow, but they weren't alone, and time was their enemy. "I know. I will be okay, I promise. And this…" She looked over at the painting, which absolutely thrilled her. "It's unbelievable. And exactly what I wanted."

She glanced at Jesse, then back to Cade. "There are no words to thank you both for this."

Cade held her eyes with his, searching, worrying.

She found a smile for him, then stepped back to let him work.

ON SUNDAY AS SHE RACED to the newspaper box on the corner, Sophie made a mental note to be certain all her newspaper subscriptions were set for the opening. She wanted to create a place of refuge for her guests, but for some of them the morning newspaper was a welcome and necessary ingredient of the day, however much reading the news was the exact opposite to her.

But this morning, she could hardly wait to see the write-up. The interview had gone splendidly and she knew the article would be terrific. The photographer had scarfed up helpings of everything and the reporter couldn't stop complimenting Patty's gift in the kitchen.

She'd loved the honeymoon suite plan, too, and inspected the progress with great interest, confiding that she might even want to book it for a getaway with her boyfriend.

Cade's little building, which Sophie had begun to call The Haven, wowed the reporter, too, and she'd gone crazy over the artwork. When Patty had let slip that Sophie knew the MacAllisters, the reporter had peppered Sophie with questions about Zane, on whom she admitted having a terrible crush. Sophie had resolved to have a stern word with Patty about confidentiality and had instinctively protected Zane's privacy with the reporter, not admitting that he was still in town and had, in fact, been there the day before working like a common laborer—and demonstrating that the muscles women sighed over hadn't been earned solely in the gym.

Funny—once she might have been one of those sighing women, but Zane had assumed the role of teasing younger brother to her now. He was gorgeous, yes, as all the Montalvo and MacAllister men were.

But Cade filled her mind, and there was room for no one else.

The sharp barb of sorrow lay waiting. The realization that she'd fallen for Cade was not welcome, but she had quit trying to deny it to herself, at least. Jesse might have guessed, but instinctively she trusted his discretion, and she'd be more careful when her paths crossed with Cade's family in the future. Because they were kind, they'd worry over her and be torn because they, too, would see that leaving was the right thing for Cade.

Let it go, she thought as she reached the corner and

spotted the newspaper vending machine. Excitement zipped up her spine as she put in her coins and retrieved her copy, nearly tripping over a crack in the sidewalk as she made her way to the door of her favorite café to order coffee. She flipped through the pages and finally seized upon the photograph of herself standing on the hotel porch and smiled—

Until she read the headline.

SCANDAL BECOMES HER

Sophie scanned the article that both praised and damned her. The reporter had taken the approach that what Sophie had done was impressive, especially in light of rumors about her tainted past and accusations of misappropriated funds at her last job. Sophie supposed she should be grateful that the reporter had noted that no charges had ever been filed against her, but why hadn't she asked for Sophie's side of the story?

You wouldn't have given it, even if she asked. You can't. Both true, but despair crept over her and Sophie stopped reading at the point where the writer lauded Sophie's efforts to begin again, comparing her life to the decaying mansion she was restoring to health.

Her knees wanted to buckle, and she caught herself looking for a place to hide. She would read the rest eventually, but she couldn't do it here. With supreme effort, she pulled herself up straight, forced herself to order her coffee, to smile at the barista, to leave a generous tip and depart smiling as though nothing at all were wrong.

The other shoe had dropped. She had no doubts about who had fed the reporter the details about her past troubles. Kurt had gotten the final word, after all. He'd taken everything away in Atlantic City, but that hadn't been enough for him.

Her cell phone rang, and she glanced at the display. *Jenna*. Oh, God. The entire MacAllister family would read this. They would think she was a failure and a fraud. And Cade... She couldn't bear it. They'd liked her, made her feel a part of something.

She snatched up the paper, suddenly terrified. What if the reporter had dragged the MacAllisters into her mess? Quickly she scanned the rest of the article and sure enough, mentions of Cade's photographs, of Jesse's art, of the connection to the famous movie star... They would think that she had used them.

What did she do now? How did she apologize to such good people?

And...Maura. Oh, dear mercy, if people canceled their bookings because of this and she lost Maura's money...

Blindly Sophie retraced her steps to the hotel. Once inside the front door, Finn greeted her with his usual abandon.

Sophie sank to the stairs beside him and buried her face in his fur.

THE BAD NEWS ROLLED IN with a speed that probably shouldn't have surprised her. She lost an individual booking first, then a travel agency, followed by a festival's hotel liaison—all of them extremely unhappy to have been placed in the position of scrambling for good rooms, and some of them promising lawsuits.

At first, Sophie tried to explain that she was not guilty, that no charges had been filed, but even those whose respect she'd thought she'd earned would not reconsider. She understood. When you had high-roller clients, no one wanted to risk his reputation on someone who'd lost her job due to financial improprieties.

Protesting that she'd resigned, not been fired, didn't help, either. Innocence was a hard case to make when Sophie couldn't explain why she hadn't fought to clear her name.

After the tenth cancellation, she was ready to beg, but she knew it would do no good.

Then came the calls for interviews—television stations, magazines, blogs... The whiff of crime mixed with the magic of Zane MacAllister's name was too delicious a dish to pass up. She began with *No comment* but quickly moved to screening her calls.

And when a concerned Jenna phoned again, Sophie did the same. What, after all, could she say? The truth that could exonerate her would devastate Maura, to whom she owed so much.

When Cade's mother called, Sophie turned off the phones, too miserably conscious of how she'd repaid a whole family's generosity.

Then Cade showed up.

SHE WASN'T ANSWERING her phone, but her pickup was in the driveway.

Finn was barking wildly inside, and Cade's gut clenched. Since Sophie didn't answer the door, he used his key.

"Sophie?"

Finn was upstairs. Cade charged upward, taking the steps two at a time. "Sophie!" he shouted.

Finn greeted him frantically at her door, and as he soothed the dog, he pushed his way inside, his gaze searching the room until he spotted the mound beneath the covers. "Sophie?" His heart was beating too fast as he reached for her.

"Go away," she said in a tiny voice.

Go away. Well, at least some things didn't change. He took his first deep breath in hours.

"Are you all right?"

"I'm fine."

"Are you sick?"

She shook her head without looking at him. "Cade, I'm sorry." Misery swam in her tone.

"For what? Are you talking about that stupid article? I don't believe what it said."

"What?" She peeked out over the edge of her quilt. "You…don't?"

He relaxed a little. She was physically all right, at least. The rest they could handle. "You're not a crook, Queenie. You might have a stick up your behind way too often and have perfected that princess-to-peasant look a little too well, but you learn a lot about a person working beside them, and you're no criminal." He pulled down the covers gently.

She looked like a whipped puppy, and he couldn't stand it. He wanted the snotty woman back. She needed that, too, so he went for shock therapy. "So why the hell are you acting like you're guilty?"

"I can't discuss it."

"Can't? This is me, Sophie." He stabbed a thumb at his chest. "I've been as close to you as breath. We bared more than our bodies in this room. Now talk to me."

Her chin jutted. "You're leaving. Why do you care?"

He recoiled. "But you know why I—" He paced to the doorway then slapped his palm hard against the jamb. He whirled on her and marched right back to the side of the bed. "You are not a coward, so what the hell is going on?"

"Your family must hate me."

"What they are is worried, just like me."

Her defiance broke. "I don't know what to do," she whispered.

"Oh, babe…" He lifted her and settled himself against the headboard and cradled her in his lap.

"This is getting to be a habit," she said softly. "I don't remember ever being held in anyone's lap. I'm too big, really."

"Shh," he murmured into her hair. "Just let me hold you for a minute. Then we'll talk."

To his surprise, she did, nestling her cheek into his chest and resting against him. After a minute, she mumbled. "I am so tired of starting over."

"I know, honey." He stroked her hair and listened to her breathe, unable to think of another way to help her. She touched him in a place no one else ever had. If he could change for her, he would, but he knew better. People didn't change, not when they were nearly forty. He couldn't be what she needed.

But he could be there for her now. "It's going to be all right," he said to her.

Wide green eyes studied him. "You'd slay all my dragons, wouldn't you?"

He smoothed her hair away from her forehead. "Is that so bad, that I wish I could?"

"You are such a good man." She caressed his jaw. "I'm afraid, Cade. This is all I have. If I lose it, I've lost everything. Again."

You have me, he wanted to say, but knew it wasn't fair. So he settled for what he could do. "I have an idea."

"What? There's no fixing this. I mean, I could settle for something less, a bed-and-breakfast, maybe, and cater to tourists who are looking for a bargain until I can prove myself, but not…" She shook her head. "Hotel Serenity is dead."

He lifted her to her feet and stood himself, aiming her toward the bathroom. "Go take a shower and meet me downstairs."

"Why?"

Because if I stay in this bed with you much longer, I'm going to cave and that's not what you need. "Damn it, Sophie, just once can't you agree without an interrogation?"

Hurt warred with indignity. "You can just go to hell, Cade MacAllister." With a huff she stalked inside and slammed the door.

Cade found himself smiling. At last, there she was.

Welcome back, Queenie.

CHAPTER SEVENTEEN

SOPHIE CLASPED HER HANDS together. In the car beside her, Cade drove silently. She dreaded facing his family and the harm she had done them, however inadvertently, but apologizing was the least she could do. She couldn't take back the damage, but she could accept responsibility.

But it killed her, every time she thought about how wonderful that day had been, how it had felt to have Hal boom at her, to be teased by Zane, to meet everyone, including all those beautiful and charming children.

She'd worked very hard that day, and she'd never had more fun. Feeling a part of something so amazing... and now it was gone.

Well, she was familiar enough with that. Had told herself, in fact, that happiness was only ever fleeting. She sighed.

"We're not driving to your execution, Sophie. You can unclench your hands," Cade said as he parked in front of Jenna's.

"Cade, I am truly just so—"

He shook his head as he got out and rounded the hood, then helped her from the vehicle. Before he could say anything else, the front door opened. "Thank heavens you found her," Jenna said to Cade, racing down the steps. She drew Sophie inside.

Not everyone was there, but nearly all of them.

Sophie hauled in a breath to steady herself before she began, but it didn't help. "I know you can't forgive me, and I don't expect that, but I am truly sorry. And I'm not a crook, I promise you."

"Come sit down, dear," said Grace. "How are you?"

"How am I?" she echoed. "I'm— I have to apologize. You shouldn't have been dragged into my mess. I didn't mention you, but the reporter recognized Cade's work and Jesse's, and my chef… I'm sorry. She shouldn't have said anything about Zane. The reporter kept asking questions about him, but I swear I didn't tell her any of you were connected to me."

"What's this?" Hal boomed, entering with a cup of coffee in his hand.

"I am so sorry. After all you…" She gripped Grace's hand. "I did nothing criminal or even wrong, I promise you."

"Of course you didn't. Now come sit down and let's figure out what to do about it."

"I've already got a plan. See what you all think," Cade said.

He looked at her and smiled so gently she wanted to climb into his arms and find shelter against that broad chest once more.

But she was getting too comfortable there. She had to break the chains between them, not add more. "I'll do whatever you ask of me. If there's any way at all for you to disclaim any ties to me, please do so."

"You think this is about us?" He looked disgruntled.

"Stop barking at her, Cade. Have a seat, Sophie," Zane said so kindly it only made her feel worse.

She stood stiffly. "I want to explain."

"You don't have to," Cade growled.

"I do." As though she were reciting in class, she stood before them and told them what she'd never told anyone—the truth. She described what had happened with Kurt, even though she squirmed at having to admit her poor judgment, explained how he'd seethed with her every promotion, especially after she'd ended their relationship. Even though she skimmed over how he'd tried to force himself on her and then threatened to claim she'd come on to him, Cade's face turned thunderous, his expression replicated by the other very protective men in this family. She explained that she'd assured Kurt that she wasn't going to accuse him of sexual harassment because it would compromise both of their chances of advancement, but he hadn't believed her. Instead, with the help of someone Sophie had trusted, he'd doctored the records to make it appear that Sophie had pilfered from multiple accounts under her management.

She didn't even make it to revealing Kurt's recent activities before Cade exploded. "I'm going to kill the bastard. Why isn't he in jail?"

"I resigned to keep the scandal from blowing up and tainting Maura."

"You didn't defend yourself?" Cade was outraged. Then he frowned. "Maura. She's the one…"

Sophie explained to the others about Maura, about

the nephew who would go to jail. "If I'd fought the allegations, I would have had to expose Maura's nephew. I couldn't hurt her like that. So I resigned instead and bought Hotel Serenity."

"Jesse can tap into his resources at the FBI. This Kurt fellow can't get away with it," Hal said.

"No! I can deal with this. I'll find a way to replace the bookings I've lost."

"Are there many?" Grace asked.

"It doesn't matter."

"It does. Just what's been going on?" Cade demanded. "People are canceling?"

She tried for a shrug. "It appears there's no reason to worry about being ready for the opening after all."

"You lost that many?" Cade's wasn't the only voice that exploded with outrage on her behalf.

Sophie was astounded. She'd expected them to be angry, to hate her, not have her back. "I'll figure out something, but—" She turned to Zane. "What do we do about your reputation?" She widened the circle. "About all of yours?"

"Sophie, honey." Zane took her hand. "If I let the gossipmongers bother me, I'd be mad all day, every day. It's no big deal. Compared to some things I've weathered, trust me…this is nothing."

"You're not upset?" She looked around. "None of you?" They all shook their heads. "Well, I am. I'm furious. First of all, I promise an escape, a refuge where people like Zane can get away and take it easy, yet my chef breached that promise too easily and very well may wind up without a job. And secondly, the reporter should have asked me about those rumors. Given me a chance to defend myself."

"Which you refuse to do," Cade said grimly. "I get why you don't want to risk hurting your friend, but you can't let Kurt win again. It's time for a charge, not a retreat."

"I'm only being prudent," she snapped. "This will die down at some point. Maybe I'll have to adjust my expectations, but I can handle it."

"Of course you can," he said bitterly. "You don't need a damn thing from anyone, do you? Well, screw that, Queenie."

"Cade William!" his mother gasped.

"Sorry, Mom, but—" He ground his teeth. "I need coffee."

Eyes stinging, Sophie just watched him leave the room. She'd survived her past by relying only on herself.

"What do you take in your coffee, Sophie?" Grace asked. "After I take a strip out of my son's hide, I'll bring you some." She marched toward the kitchen.

"Oh, please don't…" She rose to intervene.

"Let her." Hal's voice was serious. "He needs to hear it. Then it's my turn."

Sophie sat down, miserable at the trouble she'd caused. Abruptly wishing she were anywhere but here.

CADE BRACED HIMSELF against the sink and stared out the window.

"Honey…" His mother walked up to him and stroked his back. "What hurts?"

How many times had she asked each of them that question when they were growing up? *What hurts?* she would ask with her unerring sense for a child's misery.

"I know I'm a jerk, and that was uncalled-for. I just..."

"Are you in love with her, Cade?"

"No." He gaped in horror. "Hell, no. You know me. I can't—" Could he sound any more like a blithering idiot? "She matters to me, Mom, but this is me we're talking about. I can't even stay on the ranch for a week without going stir-crazy. How could I ever live in a city?" He shook his head. "No, it's not love. I'm not in love with her, but I do care, and I just want..." He ducked his head then looked squarely at his mother. "I have to leave in less than two weeks for a shoot in North Korea, the one I've been talking about for years."

He should have been dancing at the prospect.

"Oh, honey, that's wonderful." She gripped his hand. "Are you sure you're ready?"

"Yes, absolutely." But he had never been able to hold out against her. "I don't know," he admitted. "But I have to try. If I can't be Cade MacAllister, adventure photographer, who am I?"

"Sweetheart..." She wrapped her arms around his waist, and he let her hug him. Relished the stroke of her hands over his head, even if she had to stand on tiptoe to do it.

Then she stepped back. "Then you'll just be Cade MacAllister, wonderful man. Your work is not what defines you, Cade. You're stronger than that."

"I have to go back out there, Mom. Have to stand on

a peak again…as a tribute to Jaime. I can't let his death be meaningless."

"You beat yourself up over his death, but it wasn't your fault. He loved going with you."

"He did. And I have this great idea." He told her about the book.

"Cade, that is fabulous. Oh, wouldn't he love that?"

Her delight warmed him. Then he sobered. "But I can't go until I know Sophie's okay. I wish I could be what she wants, what she deserves, but I can't. I have to leave her in the best shape possible, and I'm running out of time."

"Thus your idea."

He nodded.

"Then let's go back and discuss it, but, Cade…" She restrained him. "You don't know what you can become. You've always been so focused on this path, and in some ways that's fortunate, but most people aren't so blessed. Most of us work our way through various incarnations of ourselves as we search for what really matters to us." She squeezed his arm and cupped his cheek. "You are much more than an adventure photographer. If one day it isn't what you want after all, you're still amazing. You'll figure out what's most important to you, and heaven knows you're single-minded enough to make whatever it is happen."

The words of an adoring mother. She was wrong, but it was comforting to hear. "You're the best, Mom. You know I love you, right?"

She smiled and hugged him. "Always. Now let's go plot."

CADE AND HIS MOTHER returned from the kitchen without her cup of coffee, but Sophie didn't care. His family had been attempting to talk to her, to ease her mind, but she was too frantic. She just wanted to go away, to be by herself and think, as soon as it wouldn't be rude to do so. She didn't know how to fix her situation, but she would figure it out. She always did. However powerless she'd been feeling, it was not in her nature to be weak.

She was a survivor. She would survive this.

Cade stood across the circle, his eyes locked on hers. "First of all, I'm sorry, Sophie. It's just that no one else has the power to make me quite so furious."

"Great apology, dude," said Zane.

Sophie lifted a shoulder. "It's okay. He drives me crazy, too."

Chuckles abounded. "So what's the plan, son?" Hal asked. "We'll be talking about a proper apology from you later."

Cade rolled his eyes at her and winked, and somehow her heart lifted. "Okay, here's the deal," he began. "We have our own photo shoot, all of us, at Sophie's. We get the rest of the house put together, and we photograph—okay, *I* photograph it at its absolute most flattering. And I sell the shots—heavily emphasizing the star power of little brother there and whatever in God's name it is women see in him—for big bucks to selected magazines and websites."

Zane laughed. "Love you, too, bro. Why big bucks?"

"Because you've always been a pain in the butt." Cade grinned. "No, dope, because they'll value it more if I scalp them, and Sophie can use the money to offset lost revenue so she can go ahead and open."

"Cade, no," she begged. "I couldn't."

"I'm not finished. You don't skate out of this without contributing. And maybe a better use of the money is to clear up those allegations." At her protest, he shook his head. "Sophie, if Maura is really your friend, she's not going to want you crucified for a crime you didn't commit. Her nephew was a dupe, but he didn't hatch this scheme, nor did he send the dogs after you."

"But—"

"I'm still not done," he warned her. "Okay, next phase. I call every contact I have in print media. Zane, you contact your film and television buddies—if you actually have any among all the sharks out there." He and Zane grinned at each other. "Jesse does the same with his arty crowd and Linc with his financial cronies. Chloe draws in her society friends. We plug the living daylights out of the hotel, and Sophie throws in some comped nights at the hotel for a door prize. Then we toss an opening bash that's invitation only. An exclusive crowd, and Patty makes up for her loose lips by cooking food that will set their hair on fire. No media allowed. They'll be begging Sophie for mercy." His eyes took on a vicious gleam. "But that *Statesman* woman doesn't get in, no matter what. What do you think so far?"

"How about some of your shots are beefcake of Zane lying across the beds?" Jenna suggested with a wicked grin.

"Jenna Marie!" Hal scolded.

Zane's response was unrepeatable.

Cade looked at Jenna in horror. "If you think I'm taking those, you've got another think coming." He gave a dramatic shudder.

"It would be really popular," Delilah argued, nearly succeeding in keeping her mouth from curving. "So, Sophie, how 'bout it?"

But Sophie couldn't laugh with them. She opened her mouth twice before she thought she could speak without breaking down. "Why would you all do this? I've brought you nothing but trouble."

"Because you're one of ours now, little girl," Hal boomed. "And MacAllisters stick together."

She glanced at Cade, certain her heart was in her eyes. His gaze was warm as he watched her, and she wished...but she couldn't have what she wished for most. "It's an incredible idea. I just don't know why—"

"Queenie..." Cade warned.

She closed her eyes. "It's hard," she said. "I'm not used to...this." She spread her hands wide to include all of them. "I'm accustomed to doing things for myself."

Zane hugged her. "Well, it's too late now. Nothing a MacAllister likes better than a challenge." He glared at his sister. "Except Jenna has no vote in these plans."

Jenna was unrepentant. "The beefcake would work, you know it would."

Grace rose. "Enough, children, or I'll send you to your rooms." She faced Sophie. "Have you had breakfast, dear?"

"I haven't had much of an appetite."

"Well, come on into the kitchen, then. Jenna, grab

some paper and pen. Come along, everyone, time to start planning."

Sophie followed, since it was clear that *no* was not an option. But when she came abreast of Cade, she paused. "Thank you. I don't know how I can ever—"

"If you say the word *repay,* Queenie, I cannot be held responsible for my actions." But he grinned.

She wanted to walk into his arms, but he didn't offer, and his family surrounded them.

So she hoped her expression spoke for her.

IT WAS INCREDIBLE HOW quickly things came together. Words dropped in the right ears, and Cade and his family spent a whole afternoon shooting photographs. Watching Cade in action was fascinating. But agonizing at the same time.

"Hey, bro, you're not half bad at this. You could set up at like, a mall or something," Zane said.

"Bite me." And so it went, but there was laughter along with the hard work. Teasing. Above all, love. Sophie breathed it in like oxygen, let herself enjoy them as though she truly did belong. Maybe she couldn't have Cade except as a friend, perhaps, but she could have his family, it seemed.

How she missed him, though. They were never alone together, and as each day went by, she kept herself apart from him, as he did her, each sensing how much more devastating the inevitable parting would be if they made love again.

But, oh, how she wanted to.

But Cade had been right about other things. She

hadn't given Maura enough credit. She hadn't trusted her friend to stick by her. So that night, as she paced her bedroom floor, she finally picked up the phone and made the hardest call of her life.

"Hi, kiddo," said Maura. "Getting excited about the opening? I can hardly wait myself."

"Maura, I—I have to talk to you."

"Serious tone there. What's up? Are you okay?"

Was she? Heartache over Cade aside, she actually was, she realized. "I am, but...there have been problems. I... Maura, I'm sorry. I haven't been honest with you."

"Oh? Tell me what's bothering you."

Sophie sat on the edge of her bed, hunched over. "I didn't want you hurt, let me say that up front. You've been... Maura, you gave me a chance when no one else would. And then when everything tumbled down, you still believed in me. Invested your money. You won't regret that, I promise."

"Of course I won't. Sophie, stop being cryptic and spit it out." There was the tough executive Sophie admired.

"All right." She took a deep breath and plunged. "It's Gary. And Kurt."

"Gary? My Gary?"

"Yes. I'm so sorry. I didn't want to tell you because he's so important to you."

"What has he done?"

"He— Kurt used him. I really don't believe he'd have done it on his own." When Maura remained silent,

Sophie charged ahead. "The embezzlement. I didn't do it, Maura."

"Of course you didn't. I never understood why you wouldn't fight... Oh, no. Gary? He's the embezzler?"

"I think he just doctored the books to make it look like I was the criminal. Kurt is the one behind all of this. He wanted me out of the way, out of the competition."

"But you had a...relationship."

"It wasn't my smartest move, but I was lonely. And he was handsome and kind, or at least I thought he was. I was wrong. He was trying to slow me down, I think, because I was on track for the promotion he wanted. And when I came to my senses and broke things off with him, he—he wouldn't take no for an answer."

"He forced you?"

"He tried to."

"Sophie, you should have come to me."

"I know that now, but Kurt went a little crazy, and I just wanted to put the whole thing behind me. It would have ruined both of our careers if I'd accused him of something publicly, so I told him I'd forget it if he'd just leave me alone. I thought he had until—"

"Until the accounts under your management started to have discrepancies. And when the company accused you of embezzlement, you wouldn't fight for your job."

"I couldn't. When I confronted Kurt with my suspicions that *he* was the embezzler, he told me I couldn't prove he'd ever been involved and that if I made told anyone my suspicions, he'd throw Gary to the lions, and it would cost not only Gary his job, but you, too."

"Oh, Sophie..."

"I owe you so much, Maura. How could I let that happen to you?"

"But if you left, he'd see that no charges were pressed, is that what he said?"

"Yes."

"He used me to destroy you. Dear God." Maura exhaled. "Gary is a weak man. Yes, he's blood, but don't you know, Sophie, you're the daughter of my heart? I couldn't love you more if you were my own child."

"Maura..."

"So much is clear to me now. That's why you just walked away and started over. You were lying when you said this was what you wanted, weren't you?"

"At first, yes, but I knew I had to convince you that it was. Now, though...this is my dream, Maura. I love this place."

"But you mentioned there are problems. What are they?"

"It's okay now. Don't worry about it."

"You may be like a daughter to me, but that doesn't entitle you to treat me like some helpless old woman."

Despite the seriousness of the moment, the image made Sophie smile. "You're certainly not helpless."

"Then spit it out, and I'll do what I can to help."

So Sophie laid out the long string of events that Cade had put in motion, including her hiring a private detective Vince had recommended.

"You send that detective to me. We'll get to the bottom of this. When I'm done, Kurt Barnstone will

have a tough time finding a job as a pool boy, I promise you that."

It was a satisfying picture, but Sophie was surprised
to realize she didn't need Kurt laid low. Neutralized,
yes, so that he'd leave her alone, but beyond that, she
had so much else in her life now. And the wheels of
Cade's plan were in motion to repair the damage he'd
done.

"I will be making calls, too, Sophie. I still have a
lot of influence in this business, and I assure you that
not only will your name be cleared, but I'll bring some
impressive guests with me to your opening party."

"Maura, you've already done so much."

"I care about you, kiddo. Accept it. Now get off the
phone so I can start making my calls. I'll see you soon."

And with that, she was gone, leaving Sophie be-
mused and grateful. And as though a thousand pounds
had been lifted from her shoulder.

CHAPTER EIGHTEEN

TWO WEEKS PASSED IN A blink. Cade had been busy nearly every second with the paperwork and other details that needed to be settled for the expedition to Korea, as well as hours spent sorting through photos of Jaime and sketching out the story that would accompany them. The book was a go, he'd heard from his agent, only waiting for him to finalize his selections. Meanwhile *National Geographic* had signed on as a sponsor for the Korea trip and was already talking to him about the next one. Any second that could be spared from the book or the trip was devoted to helping out at Sophie's.

His photo spread of the hotel had been a big hit. *People, InStyle* and *Southern Living,* among others, had eagerly bought shots, and *Architectural Digest* was considering including Hotel Serenity in a future issue.

Sophie might not enjoy notoriety, but it was serving her well. The opening party would be a crush of people, and every one of her guest rooms was booked for the next four months, many of them longer than that. Sophie was even busier than he was, and he worried about her. She looked tired, and he wondered how she was sleeping.

He sure wasn't, which was great for getting through his workload but not a great long-term strategy. He'd

258 A TEXAS CHANCE

never cared to *have* a long-term strategy, though, so why start now? He was all about the next adventure, the challenge not yet met.

He was taking tons of photos, but oddly, the shots that lured him most were of people, a lot of them of Sophie.

That would surely change when he was once again standing on a mountainside.

Baekdu. From the Korean side. Unbelievable. He could hardly wait if only he didn't have to leave Sophie.

Of course it was the right thing to do to leave her alone now, to operate as friends to set the tone for the rest of their lives. His family adored her and had taken her into the fold, for which he was glad because she had been alone too much of her life. That meant, however, that he couldn't screw this up, couldn't follow his usual pattern with women where they had a great time, then parted ways and never saw each other again.

He had to be careful, and he was, damn it. So blasted careful he barely contained the howl that wanted to claw its way up his throat. He wanted his hands on her again. He wanted to laugh with her, to tussle over the dog. To argue and let her get all frosty on him. She'd been so nice for days, so blasted careful around him, too.

He hated it, but he didn't know what to do. And he always knew what to do....

Just then Sophie moved out onto the porch and leaned against a column, looking tired and lost and lonely.

He'd chew through broken glass to get to her, if things were different. But they weren't.

Because he loved her, he couldn't keep her.

Cade stared at Sophie across the expanse of lawn and as though she felt his gaze, she looked over and locked eyes with him. The moment spun out, endless loops of *what if* and *I miss you* and *I wish...*

They only had one night left. It wasn't the least bit fair to ask.

But maybe she wanted it, too. And all she had to do was say no.

SOPHIE WAS TWO DAYS away from a dream.

She couldn't be more thrilled at the response to Cade's plan or more grateful for all his family had done to give Hotel Serenity its chance to live, for her vision to become reality. Yet as much as she was excited for the opening, she longed to jam a stick in the wheel that turned inexorably, bringing her ever closer to the day Cade would leave her.

She'd seen little of him in the past weeks since he was so busy getting ready for his trip and preparing for Jaime's book. He had, however, taken time to select more photos for her guest rooms, framing them himself at Jesse's. Each one was more stunning than the last, yet he still refused to even consider payment. The guests would love them, even if she wasn't sure she could bear seeing them every day. They would forever remind her of the time she'd had with him, so they were as precious to her as they were exquisitely painful.

Hotel Serenity was shaping up nicely—her staff had

worked hard, the entire place shone, Patty and her assistant had been cooking for days... Sophie's to-do list was dwindling. She'd done it.

And tomorrow Cade was leaving to pursue his own dream. They'd never kissed again, never held hands, seldom exchanged more than ordinary conversation about the hotel or what else needed to be done before the opening.

She hated it. She missed him like a limb, an eye...a heart. Staying away was the right thing to do, though. He was thrilled about his trip and eager over Jaime's book. He was shooting photos all the time again.

He had his life back. His gift.

She would never forget him, but she couldn't keep him. You didn't cage a wild falcon, clip an eagle's wings, lock a panther in a steel cage. To do so would be a betrayal, and if you loved someone, you didn't betray them or expect them to be something they weren't. Cade was too grand a force to be constricted by an ordinary existence like hers would be in this small hotel.

But, oh, how she ached for him. Longed to rewind time and give them a chance to linger in that golden escape they'd had together. Arguments and all, worries and exhaustion... She'd never been happier than during this time with him. He'd believed in her when she hadn't believed in herself, had seen the lonely person that she'd never let anyone see, and for a while had made her feel like she was not alone.

"Sophie?" Kelly, Patty's assistant, spoke from behind her.

Sophie clenched her fist over her chest and pulled herself back together. "Yes?"

"This is for you." She extended a folded sheet of paper and left.

Sophie opened it to read the bold scrawl.

I shouldn't ask but I'm going to. Meet me at The Haven tonight at 9:00 if you miss me as much as I miss you.

But it's okay to say no. This isn't smart.
Cade

It wasn't smart, no, but could she feel worse than she did now?

Probably. Being with him again and then watching him walk away would hurt her badly, but she was a realist. When he left, she would hurt no matter what.

Not smart, no. But she was going anyway.

For the first time in days, Sophie smiled...and meant it.

THE NIGHT WAS SOFT, the breeze tender on her skin as Sophie emerged from the house and spotted the welcoming glow emitting from the incredible space Cade had created. Peach gauze curtains rustled gently as she neared, and snatches of music drifted on the breeze. Her heart was beating too fast, but calm was impossible. She wanted this night too much. Couldn't stand the thought of it ending.

Then Cade stepped from the shadows, and her pulse bumped up another notch.

"I didn't know if you'd come." He extended a hand.

She took it without hesitation. "You were right. It's not smart." She lifted to her toes and brushed his lips. "But like I said, neither of us is too bright."

One strong arm yanked her to him, and he kissed her back with all the impatience she could have ever wished.

I love you. She almost said it aloud, but thankfully her mouth was busy. Nothing would be served by telling him that. Instead, she poured herself into the kiss, let his taste fill her.

"I've been going crazy without you," he said between kisses.

"Me, too." She coiled one leg around his calf and brought their lower bodies even closer.

He swept her up in his arms and began walking, his kisses a dark fantasy, his touch a starving man's hunger.

Abruptly he drew back from her. "This was supposed to be a seduction. We have to take it slow."

"Uh-uh." She caught his mouth again.

He leaned away. "Sophie." His breath was pumping. Dark blue eyes pinned hers. "Let me love you, Sophie. Let me show you tenderness."

A silent struggle ensued. Tenderness would destroy her. Better the flash of heat, the greedy seduction.

"Please." The one word undid her. Slowly she relented, and he parted the curtains to bring her inside, carrying her like precious cargo.

Inside, candles glowed. The massage table lay ready,

oils lined up in pretty bottles behind it. Champagne was chilling in a bucket. The scent of gardenias twined through the air. "Oh, Cade…"

"I'm no professional masseur, I'll warn you." He grinned, but his eyes held nerves, of all things. "But I have good hands."

"You certainly do."

"Let me take off your clothes, Sophie, and make you feel wonderful."

"Just looking at you does that," she said before she could censor herself.

Pain speared through his beautiful eyes.

She slipped off her blouse and stroked his cheek. "Let's not be sad, Cade. There'll be enough time for that later."

"Sophie…"

"Shh…" Her smile was wry. "We know what you're doing is right. And I'm happy for you, honestly."

"Sophie, I'm—"

She heard the *sorry* and stilled his words with her fingers. "You've done so much for me. Don't be sorry— I'm not. I wouldn't trade anything for these weeks. I'm a big girl." She made herself turn away before he could see her desolation. She slipped off the rest of her clothes and lay down on the massage table.

She tried to relax, but she was afraid of what letting go would allow her to feel. His big warm hands spread over her skin, and a shudder rippled through her. Sophie reminded herself again that she had vowed not to be sad on this, his last night.

CADE STROKED DOWN HER BACK with a long caress, the oil slicking her skin as he painstakingly unknotted the muscles down the length of her spine. Barely, only barely, he resisted clamping his hands on her. Giving in to his greed, his need to bind her to him.

Sophie sighed, and he ruthlessly reminded himself that she deserved this peace, that they would make love tonight, but he couldn't have her forever. That climbing on the table and pressing every inch of him along every inch of her would have to wait because he was going to tell her with his hands what he didn't have the words to express, while preventing himself from uttering what would be wrong and cruel to say.

I love you, but I have to leave you.

I want you, but I can't have you.

I can't be the man you need me to be.

Over and over his hands smoothed her muscles, caressed her hips, slicked over pretty curves, slid between her toes.

Sophie giggled at that, and he smiled, too. He hadn't known she was ticklish.

Some other man would find that out. Cade wanted to beat the faceless man to a pulp.

He yanked his hands away before his own inner turmoil revealed itself to the woman he was trying to care for. When he was calmer, he took one of her hands and used his thumbs to release the tension there, sliding between her fingers and smoothing out across her wrist. He placed a kiss to the bend of her elbow, and Sophie sighed again.

When he reached her feet once more, he tried to remember the points a Balinese masseuse had once told him released the body's yearnings. As Sophie's beautiful behind began to wiggle, and her mound rubbed against the sheet, the atmosphere shifted.

Near-violent greed ripped through him.

He couldn't tell her how she tangled him up, how she made him wish for what he couldn't have.

But he could show her what she meant to him.

He stripped off his shirt and bent over her, sliding his hands over the mystery of her curves, diving beneath her, slicking one finger into her dark, beckoning folds. Sophie cried out, and he laid himself over her, latching his teeth on her tender nape as she rode out her climax.

When she finally sagged to the table, reluctantly he dismounted and gently turned her over.

Then he began again, massaging from her toes upward, pausing for a lick or a nip as he made his way to her thighs. A glide of both thumbs over her curls had her moaning, her fingers flexing, reaching for him.

Gently he replaced her hands by her sides and continued his progress, oiling her belly, caressing her hips, spanning her waist with his hands and running spread fingers up to caress her breasts. Slick circles across tender underarms made her giggle again. He smiled as he stroked across her shoulders and down her arms, devoting a great deal of time to her sensitive palms. He sucked one finger into his mouth, then the next and the next until Sophie was writhing, eyes still closed as little pants escaped between her lips. Then he crushed his mouth to hers.

Her eager kiss nearly broke him, but he wasn't finished yet. Snapping a chain on his urge to devour, he instead painted calming circles over her face, easing the stress from her temples, massaging her scalp until she groaned. As he worked, he tenderly kissed each eyelid and the tip of her nose. His tongue glided over the seam of her lips on his way back down.

Then he kissed her, breasts, belly...his tongue to her core.

She gasped. "Cade, please..."

"Not yet," he said, though he couldn't hold out much longer. He was crazed for her, half mad with need to be inside her, to make them one. He stripped away the last of his clothes, holding on with the barest of control. His pulse hammering, he held on long enough to send her shooting high again. Watched with swiftly unraveling control as the tremors rocked her, as her arms flew wide in surrender.

Then Cade gave them both what they wanted in one powerful thrust.

She came again, grabbing for him, dragging his face to hers. Still he let the exquisite longing spool out until his craving shredded his control.

They let the explosion shatter them, locked in a kiss that said all they did not dare.

And as they fell to earth, Cade knew with a deep and aching grief that he would never find this miracle again.

No matter how much of the world he traveled.

SOMEHOW HE MANAGED TO lift them both off the massage table and got them to the chaise she had been reupholstering back when he still aggravated her.

So few weeks ago, and yet a universe away. Sophie smiled into his throat. If she didn't, she would break down.

"Sophie..." His arms gripped her so hard she could barely breathe.

Tell me. Say you love me, Cade. I feel it. Say you'll stay.

He reversed their positions but kept her close, wrapping her tightly against him. "I don't know what to do," he said.

She forced her suddenly clenched fingers to relax and stroked the side of his face. "You have to be true to yourself, to who you are. You're special, Cade, so special. You give the world a gift with your talent."

"But leaving... I've never had trouble doing that before."

She smiled, determined not to falter. "I'm glad you do. It means you won't forget me. You're welcome back, anytime. You take time off, right?"

"I didn't. But I will."

She could see that it made him feel better to talk about the future as though this wasn't the end. That he had regrets about leaving meant a lot to her, but she was not going to rob him of the gift he'd so newly regained and he thought he needed so much. To love him the way he deserved meant letting him go, not holding him back.

She could already feel the agony of it, but she would handle it. Once he was gone, she'd remember how to be alone again. Get her feet back underneath her. "I'll be happy to see you."

He rested his forehead against hers. "I don't like thinking of you alone. You won't shut everyone out again, will you, Queenie?"

She'd grown to love that name. "You know I'll be fine."

"Will you suffer a little, at least?"

From somewhere she found a smile. "I could probably manage that."

"Sophie." His eyes turned serious again. "Promise you'll let me know if you need anything. *Anything*. Or if you have any trouble."

God. Could he make this any harder? If he'd just walk away whistling, then she could hate him and get over him quickly.

But he was a good man, and that wasn't how he operated. So even though she wouldn't, she nodded. "I will." Then she asked her own favor. "And will you let me know that you're okay, now and again? Tell me how the mountain looks from the forbidden side?"

He wanted to believe that was enough for her, she could see it. Wanted not to hurt her. "I'll email you the first photos. You'll see it before anyone else."

"I'd like that." It would tear out her heart. She couldn't stand this. She scraped up a smile she didn't feel. "So…" She walked her fingers up his chest and circled his earlobe, loving the feel of his body's response. "Are we done talking yet?"

For a moment he looked at her with such sadness she nearly broke down and said *let's not do this, don't pretend I don't love you and you don't love me…*.

But then he kissed her, and she gratefully seized the

respite. Nothing had changed. He was a wanderer, and she'd planted roots here and made a place to stay. And she was a survivor.

"Let's not waste this night," she murmured.

He answered with his body instead of words that would change nothing.

And if Sophie clung to him now and again when she couldn't help herself…he clung to her, too.

Until she slept, then awoke.

To discover that he'd already left her.

CHAPTER NINETEEN

TWO WEEKS AND FOUR ENDLESS days later, Cade stood on a spot where few Westerners had ever been permitted, taking in a sight many would give anything to witness. The journey to Heaven Lake had been interminable— two weeks wasted tied up in bureaucratic wrangling.

He could have attended Sophie's opening, after all.

But at last he'd made it. Baekdu, the sacred White Mountain, the jewel of North Korea. He'd waited years to explore this beautiful and sacred place.

He should have been ecstatic, but instead he was untouched. Frozen. He framed shot after shot, waiting, hoping for that spark...to no avail.

His gift wasn't gone, no. On the ascent, he'd taken some photos he could be proud of. He'd captured more still of the faces of people whose paths he'd crossed— though the shots had angered some and there had been threats of confiscating his cameras, so he'd had to stop taking those.

He'd like to blame his physical condition for the malaise that gripped him as he stood on the summit, but he wasn't in the habit of lying to himself. The fault lay not in his body but his heart. He thought of Sophie every day, whether he wanted to or not. He'd deliberately not called her to find out how the opening went, figuring a clean break was best. All that brave noise they'd made of future visits, of staying in touch?

Screw that. A casual relationship with Sophie? He was light-years from managing that, and it was infuriating. Every mile away from her had stamped a nasty tattoo on his heart, souring his disposition, yanking at his patience, tainting the seminal joy of his life—being free, solitary, unencumbered.

Blast her.

"There is a problem?" his guide asked.

"No." Barely he avoided the impulse to bark and instead summoned basic manners. "Thank you for asking."

"You are ready to depart?"

Cade stared out at the incredible vista. *Buckle down. Get the shot you've waited years to snap. You're a professional.* "No." He strode away from his guide, blanking his mind to anything but what he could see through the viewfinder.

A sick feeling roiled in his gut. If he couldn't capture *this,* nothing mattered. If he had lost the fire, he was done, he would never make it all the way back from the accident and—

There. Oh, God, there it was, the rush, the knowing. He began to snap off frame after frame, adjusting, crouching, scanning… The buzz up his spine was visceral, a greeting, a welcome home from a long-lost friend. "Thank you," Cade murmured while he continued to shoot as the light shifted, and he snapped and snapped.

And then it was done. He knew in his gut he'd

gotten something extraordinary, and it was all he could do not to shout, to punch a fist in the air. Jubilation soared through him, and he reached for his phone so he could—

Share it with Sophie.

Cade rocked back on his heels at the realization that where once the simple knowledge of a spectacular shot had been enough for him, now he needed to share it.

And not with just anyone. With Sophie. The woman he'd walked away from.

You have to be true to yourself, to who you are. You're special, Cade.

Gracious to the end, Sophie was. As he packed his equipment and made his way back down, his mind was a torrent of images, of questions, difficult ones.

Hours later he was still sorting through the tangle. He'd proved he was still Cade MacAllister, adventure photographer, capable of capturing remarkable images. But where that had once made up the sum total of him, now there was a cavern inside him, a dark, looming maw that adventure could not fill. His gift was no longer everything. No longer enough.

Because now there was Sophie. The woman courageous enough, generous enough, to say goodbye because that was what he'd needed. While he'd hurt her. Hurt himself.

Memories of their last night together washed over him. They'd loved, they'd soared… He'd tried to express with his hands what he couldn't find a way to say: *I love you, Sophie.*

Her body had been a feast, and he'd treasured it. But

her eyes…they'd known. They'd grieved, though her lips hadn't said the words.

Don't leave me. No, she hadn't said it, and never would. She'd sent him off with a smile, and he'd accepted it as genuine because he'd wanted it to be. Because he didn't know how not to be solitary. He didn't know how to share his heart.

Had been scared, crazy scared, that he'd lost the only Cade he knew how to be.

You don't know what you can become. You'll figure out what's most important to you, and heaven knows you're single-minded enough to make whatever it is happen, his mom had said.

He'd proved that he was back, as good as ever.

But it was no longer enough. It was no longer everything. And she'd seen that—seen him—all along.

Had Sophie written him off already? Had she moved on, thanked her lucky stars she hadn't yielded that composed core of her that never let anyone all the way in?

You let me come damn close, Sophie. I know you did.

He'd go back, take a battering ram if he had to, break down that wall she'd built out of broken dreams and loss. She needed him as much as he needed her.

Or did she? He went ice-cold with fear. How did he know what she needed? Whether he could make her happy?

He fastened the last zipper on his duffel and rushed to leave for his flight out. She might not want to gamble on him. He had absolutely no experience with sticking around, with being anyone's rock.

But he had teachers all around him, didn't he? His

brothers, his parents—all had formed bonds, had nurtured others. Maybe he'd stumble a lot, maybe he'd screw it all up.

But he *was* single-minded, as his mother had said—and he would kill himself trying to be the man Sophie deserved.

If it wasn't too late. If Queenie hadn't already slapped crossbars on the portal to her heart.

SOPHIE HAD CLOSETED herself in her small office for a few moments of peace. Studying future bookings might not be anyone else's idea of a good time, but for a hotelier, seeing the weeks extending outward at full capacity…the thrill was nearly as great as sex.

No. She couldn't kid herself about that. Cade had ever so vividly demonstrated differently.

Her jubilant mood faltered at the reminder of him, but ruthlessly, she quashed the memories. Thinking about Cade was a losing proposition. He hadn't even emailed her a photo as he'd promised. He'd been gone three weeks to the day—how she hated that she knew it exactly—and not a word.

It hurt, and it shouldn't. She'd prepared herself from the beginning, knowing happiness was only ever fleeting. She'd never truly believed he'd return. He was back in his element, doing exactly what he loved.

And so was she. They'd had fun together, and that was enough. The end. Her story still had to be written, and his would be in a different volume, miles and continents away.

Which only made her wonder again if everything

was working out for him. Was the sacred mountain the thrill he'd hoped? Was he shooting bushels of photos? Was he healing all right?

Did he ever think of her?

She jammed the heels of her hands into her eyes. *Stop that. He's none of your business. It's over and done with. Life goes on.*

It always had.

One of these days she'd feel strong enough to call Jenna, to resume their friendship. Right now, however, anything related to the MacAllisters hurt too much.

Her eyes fell on the names in the list of future reservations. His parents were coming in a couple of weeks. She wished with everything in her that she hadn't agreed to host them for their anniversary…and that was wrong. They were wonderful people who'd been there for her when she'd been at her lowest. They still called to check on her periodically, and it wouldn't be right to hold it against them that they'd raised a son who'd made her fall in love with him when there was no future with him.

All the MacAllisters seemed to find reasons to touch base now and again. Talking to everyone but the Mac-Allister she really wanted was killing her, but that would end now. She would call Jenna and have her over for drinks. She didn't feel comfortable leaving the hotel yet—her staff was too new. She was proud of them, though. Hotel Serenity was getting glowing reviews for hospitality, comfort, food… She couldn't have written them better herself.

And Kurt had been arrested after Sophie's meeting

with one of Jesse's FBI friends. Maura's nephew had been given immunity to testify against him, so Maura didn't have to worry about him going to jail. Maura had also taken it upon herself to ensure the proof of Sophie's innocence circulated through the industry, and she had her reputation back, particularly after the opening. After the roaring success of the opening bash, she'd been besieged by requests for interviews, and the coverage still continued.

Cade had given her a miracle. That was enough. He hadn't lied to her—he was who he was. She understood better than anyone about protecting yourself. He believed he had to be free to roam at a moment's notice, to travel, to take risks. Their careers were incompatible.

Her gaze fell on a present he'd left behind as a parting gift…a shot of her and Finn on the day his family had come to her aid. She'd been tempted to stick it in a closet because looking at it hurt too much, but in the end, she hung it in her office, a piece of Cade she could hold on to. So that she could remember what those heady days had been like.

Queenie. Daredevil blue eyes glinting as he argued, as he teased.

One of these days she would remember without pain.

A knock sounded on her door.

"Yes?"

Trish the desk clerk answered. "Sophie, there's a package for you."

"All right. Bring it in."

A brown-papered rectangle…like certain memorable others. Her heart skipped, but she remained outwardly impassive. "Thank you, Trish." She smiled and waited for the door to close behind the young woman before she looked at the package.

Sophie's fingers trembled as she gripped the edges. *I can't open it.* She didn't actually know it was from Cade, did she? She began carefully with scissors but started tearing at the paper almost instantly, then more greedily as she saw what was inside.

"Oh!" Her heart skipped again. "Oh, Cade..." There it was, his sacred mountain, the lake within the circle of the peaks a glistening gem. It took her a minute to realize there was something out of place. At the corner, so faint others might miss it, was a name traced in the earth in the foreground.

Jaime.

She covered her mouth as her eyes burned. He'd found a way to take his friend there. To make Jaime a part of the place they'd both wanted to go.

"They wouldn't let me leave a photo of him," said a voice from the door she hadn't heard open.

Sophie's gaze whipped toward him. "Cade."

His eyes were so serious as he remained standing in the doorway.

"He would have loved it," she said. She nodded at the photo. "It's stunning. You did it, didn't you? Your gift really is back."

His answering smile was faint. "It seems so."

"Thank you, I—I didn't expect..." she stammered.

He uncoiled from the door frame and shoved the door closed as he prowled toward her. "You never expect much of me, do you, Sophie?" He frowned. "Not that I ever gave you any reason to."

She couldn't figure out his mood. "Not true. You did so much for me, Cade. Much more than I had any right to expect, certainly more than you should have. I don't know how I'll ever repay you…"

He grasped her upper arms. Removed the framed photo and set it aside. "You always have a ledger to balance, don't you? You think that if you keep everything even, then you'll be safe. That if it's all tidy and neat, nothing can hurt you."

She crossed her arms. "I don't know what you mean."

His smile was mirthless. "There she is. Hey, Queenie." His brows snapped together. "We're a pair, aren't we? Neither of us willing to let go an inch for fear we might have to let someone in. I hide behind my career, and you hide behind business."

"That's not true."

"It is. We keep our distance because it's less frightening. Because then we never have to open ourselves up to the messiness of real life. To the hurt. You're afraid of what you could lose, of starting over again—and I've refused to start at all."

"I'm over what I've lost." She stiffened. Took a step back. "I simply realize that balance is important."

"And I've never wanted balance. I haven't let anything or anyone get between me and the life I wanted— but you know what, Queenie?" His voice went soft. "I stood there on that mountain, taking really great shots of a place I've waited most of my career to see…and it meant nothing." He shook her gently. "Nothing. Because you weren't there."

"You can't think—" She gestured around her. "I couldn't have gone."

"I understand that you have to get this place off the ground, that you can't just hop a plane any time you want, not yet. But even if Hotel Serenity *was* established, you wouldn't take a risk on me, would you? Because you might lose me…as you've lost too many others you cared for." She started to object, but he rushed ahead. "And I'm no better. Thinking I was worthless if I wasn't Cade MacAllister, adventure photographer. Who would I be if I couldn't wander, if I wasn't solitary with nothing to tie me down?"

"I don't know what you want from me." She couldn't tear her eyes from him, even as her pulse hammered.

He stared at her intently. "Astonishingly enough, I finally realized I want a home," he said softly. "And so do you."

"But your career…"

"It doesn't have to be all or nothing, Sophie—except in your world, the tidy, orderly one where you don't take risks."

"I don't take risks? What do you think this hotel is? I've put everything I have, everything I am, into it."

"Yeah. Because it's easier than risking your heart on a person. Insurance can replace a house or a business, but not a broken heart. You're determined to stay safe from grief and pain, and no one can promise you that."

Her throat was dry, her palms damp.

"We've both gotten a little too cozy with our careers,

haven't we? Careers don't break your heart. We don't have to worry about drownings or car wrecks or settling down." His eyes were tender. "I realized on that mountaintop that what had always filled me wasn't enough anymore, that there was a gaping hole." His hand caressed her cheek. "And its name was Sophie."

"But, Cade…"

"Look, I don't know how we're going to manage this—I don't have a set of plans for us to follow, but you know what? That doesn't matter. Life doesn't come with guarantees, and it never will. I'll have to travel, and you'll have to stay here a lot—but I've spent my whole life refusing to get tied down, only to realize that that refusal is as much a shackle as any chain."

"But I don't… I can't…"

The warmth in his eyes was dimmed by disappointment, and he turned away, his voice cooler. "I'm going to stay in Austin for a while and work on Jaime's book. I've taken some shots of people that are nothing like what I've done before but they excite me in a new way—and they don't require visas and million-dollar expeditions. There might be more to me than I had dared to believe."

"I believe in you," she said.

He turned back, and she saw the weariness in him. "But do you believe in us? Just because we're not the Bradys, does that mean we can't make our own kind of family?"

"You hate cities. And you don't want to live in a hotel."

"Then I guess I'd better get a little more flexible,

shouldn't I?" His gaze was as open to her as she'd ever seen it. "Forget the details for right now. Are you going to let me into your heart, Sophie?"

Her determination was unraveling. "I really can't travel with you for a while yet, maybe a year."

"I'll wait." He reeled her in, a smile forming. "I'd like to show you the world, but even more, I'd like to be in your world. Is there room for a rolling stone at your inn, Queenie?"

She discovered she'd run out of objections, and that she wanted desperately to meet him halfway. To find a means to mingle their worlds. But… "I'm scared, Cade."

"I know. So am I." He held her close and pressed a kiss to her forehead. "But I don't want to keep my distance anymore. How about you?"

She tilted her head back, studied dark blue eyes that were her window on a whole new world. "Me, either." She swallowed hard, then took the plunge. "I love you, Cade."

He closed his eyes for a second. When they opened, they held everything she could possibly wish for. "I love you, too, Queenie. Can we just start there, or do we need a damn ledger?"

Laughter bubbled up as her eyes blurred with grateful tears. "I'm already so far in debt I wouldn't know where to begin."

"You're crazy to think you're the only one who's been given an incredible gift, but—" he adopted a comical leer "—we did discuss a very attractive form of payment once. It could work well for both parties."

Heart lighter by the second, she rose to her toes, smiling. "Well, then, here's the first installment." She kissed him with all the love she'd been afraid to let herself feel.

Cade picked her up and whirled her until they were both out of breath.

Then he set her down and clasped her so closely to him that she knew exactly what perfect safety felt like. They clung together, each grateful for the miracle of a second chance.

After a bit, Cade leaned back. "There's just one thing we need to work out right up front, Queenie. I'm sorry to tell you it's a deal breaker."

She made herself not stiffen. He'd said he loved her, and though he was trying to look stern, his eyes were dancing, so she went on faith and batted her eyelashes at him. "Oh? Exactly what might that be?"

"Our dog really does want to be called Skeeter."

She laughed. "And what do I get in return?"

Cade merely smiled and waggled his eyebrows. "It's better if I show you."

Sophie smiled right back. "Deal."

They sealed their first negotiation with a kiss.

* * * * *

HEART & HOME

Heartwarming romances where love can
happen right when you least expect it.

Harlequin®
Super Romance

COMING NEXT MONTH
AVAILABLE MARCH 13, 2012

#1764 FROM FATHER TO SON
A Brother's Word
Janice Kay Johnson

#1765 MORE THAN ONE NIGHT
Sarah Mayberry

#1766 THE VINEYARD OF HOPES AND DREAMS
Together Again
Kathleen O'Brien

#1767 OUTSIDE THE LAW
Project Justice
Kara Lennox

#1768 A SAFE PLACE
Margaret Watson

#1769 CASSIE'S GRAND PLAN
Emmie Dark

You can find more information on upcoming Harlequin® titles,
free excerpts and more at www.HarlequinInsideRomance.com.

HSRCNM0212

REQUEST YOUR FREE BOOKS!
2 FREE NOVELS PLUS 2 FREE GIFTS!

Harlequin Super Romance®

Exciting, emotional, unexpected!

Get swept away with author
CATHY GILLEN THACKER

and her new miniseries

Legends of Laramie County

On the Cartwright ranch, it's the women
who endure and run the ranch—and it's time for
lawyer Liz Cartwright to take over. Needing some help
around the ranch, Liz hires Travis Anderson, a fellow
attorney, and Liz's high-school boyfriend. Travis says
he wants to get back to his ranch roots, but Liz knows
Travis is running from something. Old feelings emerge
as they work together, but Liz can't help but wonder
if Travis is home to stay.

Reluctant Texas Rancher

**Available March
wherever books are sold.**

New York Times *and* USA TODAY *bestselling author
Maya Banks presents book three in her miniseries*
PREGNANCY & PASSION.

TEMPTED BY HER INNOCENT KISS

Available March 2012 from Harlequin Desire!

There came a time in a man's life when he knew he was
well and truly caught. Devon Carter stared down at the dia-
mond ring nestled in velvet and acknowledged that this was
one such time. He snapped the lid closed and shoved the
box into the breast pocket of his suit.

He had two choices. He could marry Ashley Copeland
and fulfill his goal of merging his company with Copeland
Hotels, thus creating the largest, most exclusive line of re-
sorts in the world, or he could refuse and lose it all.

Put in that light, there wasn't much he could do except
pop the question.

The doorman to his Manhattan high-rise apartment hurried to open the door as Devon strode toward the street.
He took a deep breath before ducking into his car, and the
driver pulled into traffic.

Tonight was the night. All of his careful wooing, the
countless dinners, kisses that started brief and casual and
became more breathless—all a lead-up to tonight. Tonight
his seduction of Ashley Copeland would be complete, and
then he'd ask her to marry him.

He shook his head as the absurdity of the situation hit
him for the hundredth time. Personally, he thought William
Copeland was crazy for forcing his daughter down Devon's
throat.

Ashley was a sweet enough girl, but Devon had no desire

to marry anyone.

William had other plans. He'd told Devon that Ashley had no head for the family business. She was too softhearted, too naive. So he'd made Ashley part of the deal. The catch? Ashley wasn't to know of it. Which meant Devon was stuck playing stupid games.

Ashley was supposed to think this was a grand love match. She was a starry-eyed woman who preferred her animal-rescue foundation over board meetings, charts and financials for Copeland Hotels.

If she ever found out the truth, she wouldn't take it well.

And hell, he couldn't blame her.

But no matter the reason for his proposal, before the night was over, she'd have no doubts that she belonged to him.

What will happen when Devon marries Ashley?
Find out in Maya Banks's passionate new novel
TEMPTED BY HER INNOCENT KISS
Available March 2012 from Harlequin Desire!